BESTIA
SECRETUM

BESTIA
SECRETUM

Further Explorations into
Classic Cryptozoological Fiction

edited by
Chad Arment

COACHWHIP PUBLICATIONS
GREENVILLE, OHIO

*Bestia Secretum: Further Explorations into Classic Crypto-
zoological Fiction*
© 2025 Coachwhip Publications

CoachwhipBooks.com

ISBN 1-61646-609-X
ISBN-13 978-1-61646-609-1

Contents

The Moa at Last
William Turton (1884)

Jim Ferriss and myself have been prospecting for nine weeks, and at last, on the 22nd of March, we got on it. We worked night and day for five days, and having by that time about 22 ounces we set out for civilization to claim the Government bonus, and the other privileges to which we are entitled. This obliges me to keep the locality dark for the present, though after what has occurred, we will perhaps simply sell out our rights, and take to the easier life of showmen. Well, we struck our tent on the 28th and started. We could not cover much ground in such country. We had to take turns at going first with the tomahawk, and I suppose we did fifteen miles by night. We camped in rather a level spot, where three streams met, and the bush was thin. Jim is a fellow who never gets knocked up. After we had pitched tent and boiled the billy and eaten a little of our scant stock of provisions, he went "bobbing" for eels in a place where the water was deep and slow. About 8 o'clock, as nearly as I could guess, my dog, that I keep for hunting rabbits, began to growl and to look suspicious. After a while I heard a stick crack, and Towser barked. I thought it was Jim. But presently I heard another crack in the wrong direction for him altogether, and as the dog kept growling in spite of me, I began to think about wild cattle, Red Indians, and at last about wild Maoris, until I had to whistle to myself for company. I was sitting on my blankets in the tent, and our last candle was burning in a forked stick stuck in the ground. Towser crawled to me and crouched down, evidently frightened. I lifted my head, intending to go out and call to Jim. My eye fell upon the slit under the ridgepole at the back of the tent. This slit was longer than necessary, as the tent was an old one. At that open slit I saw what at first I took for a star. The error was momentary. It moved, retreated, and approached, and at last *blinked*. It was an eye. I don't know how long I was in making this discovery, as I felt stunned. But I took in the situation and doused the light with my hand, fearing that it might be too sure a mark for a spear or a bullet. I had no sooner done it than something struck the ridgepole violently, nearly knocking the tent down, and then scampered off. I heard great thudding treads. Towser fairly whined again with fear, and crawled between my legs. I went out, and heard something crack and rustle in the bush some distance off. I now tried to laugh at myself, and kicked the dog to show that I wasn't afraid. When Jim came back without any eels, we went in again and I lit the candle. I told him what had happened and he laughed at me, but as I persisted, he began to eye me curiously and I noticed that he took the tomahawk outside and I afterwards found he had hid it. Tired as I was I lay awake a good deal. But I never moved when Jim didn't move too, and that so sharply that I fancied he was raising himself up quickly. He has told me since that he thought I was mad, and was afraid of me. In the morning, I went to the back of the tent, and soon found enough of marks on the ground and bushes to convince my mate. We then looked at the ridgepole just outside of the slit and found there seven short stiff hairs "ravelled out," as Jim said, at the edges—seeming, in fade, to be a cross between a hair and a feather. As we sat boiling the billy I said—"Whatever it was peeping through the hole, it was startled when I put out the light and in drawing back, its head struck the ridgepole. Thinking that that was a blow from me, or from the light, it cleared." "That's it, old man," said Jim, looking at me admiringly; "but what the d—l could it be?" Then he added reflectively—"It ain't seen many light puts out anyway, I guess." After we had tramped for an hour down the gully we came to the edge of the water where there was some sand. Jim, who was leading, stopped suddenly, and exclaimed—"There are thundering big frogs here if there are no eels." He pointed to a large footmark in the sand, seeming quite fresh. It had three great toes and was about nine inches long. We soon dropped our swags, and I said—"Jim, that's a moa, and by all that's blue that was a moa I saw last night." After a moment he was satisfied; and as the direction of the steps was across the stream we left our swags and crossed with a lot of trouble and hunted for an hour without result. We got to our swags again with difficulty, and proceeded, after minutely inspecting and measuring the footsteps. In about ten minutes my dog suddenly fell behind growling. We were at once on the alert and in about two minutes I spotted the game—a real, live moa, by thunder, quietly eating bramble berries about sixty yards away. We gazed for some minutes without a word, and then tried to hit upon a plan to capture the *rara avis*. To the left there was a steep face of rock with a lot of bush at its foot. We agreed to head the bird towards this. But we were too few to surround it, so we stuck up our swags to do duty for one man in a clear place and tied the dog in another. We then approached with fear and trembling. I was armed with the tomahawk and Jim with his sheath knife tied on the end of a five-foot stick. These were for defence, as we did not wish to kill the bird if we could get it alive. The moa was not easily alarmed and let us get so close that we both stopped and looked at each other, as if thinking of the better part of valor. I took a step forward and a stick cracked sharply under my foot. The bird gave a sort of a croak, very quietly, and swayed its long neck round to look as leisurely as it might do to its mate, to whom I believe it attributed the sound. On seeing me it started forward violently, striking its own head under a branch as it got under way. It was a great relief that it was afraid of me. It had hardly gone ten yards or got into running attitude or recovered the blow, when it ran into a network of supplejacks hanging among some young birch trees. Several of them caught it right across its breast. The creature strained, pushed, and slipped in a stupid manner and made no attempt to take another path. When we came up it hissed hoarsely at us, but was evidently terrified, which emboldened us. In its struggles it tossed leaves and soil like a bull scraping; it threshed its head about most recklessly, breaking branches and biting supplejacks, but not the right ones. Jim boldly tried to lash one of its legs to a tree, but did not succeed. At last, when I had almost coupled a loop of rope on a stick to slip over its head, the supplejacks gave away suddenly and the creature fell forward. Quick as thought Jim thrust his five-foot stick over the moa's neck and under an old log. Thus he held on, with ease. The brute gave in at once like a sheep. We first lashed its legs together, then we bound it with supplejacks in all sorts of ways, and then consulted what to do. We agreed to hobble our victim, so that it could take an 18-inch step. We would then fasten a guy, or rein, to each side of its head, and, walking one on each side, steer him to civilization. Jim went for the swags while I kept guard. We had a fair amount of cord and small rope with us on the tent, and for coupling ourselves in crossing rivers and very rough ground. We needed it all to rig the monster out, which as it lay upon the ground must have measured about fourteen feet, though it is only eleven feet three inches standing up. When we were ready the job was to get him to rise. After forty minutes we got him up and he began to struggle again. Then he backed till he came against a tree. Then he went forward with a rush and fell. We then saw the defects of our harness. We took off the hobbles to give him free use of his legs. But we placed a slipnoose lose round his hocks, and Jim tied the other end round his own body, so that in case of a bolt the moa's legs would be drawn together by the noose. We then added to our guys a pole on each side, so that we might be able to keep him from backing. Finding his legs free, we had less trouble to get him up. He tried to start with a run, but we found we could hold him in with our guys, though we made very crooked sailing and found it hard work. After a while we managed better, and before night we must have travelled three or four miles down the valley. We stopped at some fuchsia trees hoping the bird would eat, but he wouldn't. Jim went to seek bramble berries and got a few, but the creature wouldn't eat. We were so anxious to make him safe and yet not to hurt him, that we tore our blankets into strips and twisted them into cables to anchor him. Then we made a good fire and took turns at watching. I have written these notes during my two watches, in pencil and by fire light. The day is now breaking and all is well. I forgot to say that I carefully examined the moa's head, and could not find the slightest trace of a blow on the only place where the thick short hairs grow—the back of the head; they are like a stiff mane or comb. This leads me to infer that there is another yet at large.

WATCHFIRE. MARCH 30. 11 P.M.

This morning, early, Jim suggested an improvement in the harness. Our trouble yesterday was that the bird kept throwing up his head and making us lose command of him. The new plan was to lash a crooked stick along the back of its neck with the turned-up end on the back, so that the head could only be raised a certain distance. We found this answer so well that we shortly dispensed without steering poles altogether. Jim wanted to make the moa carry the swags, or what of them is left. I was afraid of knocking the bird up. It ate a few berries to-day, and also some leaves that I don't know the name of, but some of which I added to my swag. We have had a very hard day. We have hardly done six miles. We had to tether the bird and clear a path several times. The prospect for to-morrow is better. We caught two rabbits, of which we were very glad. But my poor dog got a nasty kick by trotting too close behind. The moa let out and sent him about six yards away. I thought he was dead, but he has come to and limped along all the afternoon. It is middle-watch—10 to 2—and Jim is asleep. The moa has squatted down for the first time. Its back is very bony and strong; It is accustomed to break branches off trees, and does it skilfully. Its legs are hard as horn, and as thick as the hind legs of a horse below the hock. In the tail, which is a short bunch, there are feathers like those of an emu. There are also tufts at the sides where the wings ought to grow. The color is brown. The neck and back have thin, woolly hair, like fine feathers with the fluff clipped off clear. The breast and neck are black, but not glossy. We don't know the sex of our capture. Jim is hoping it will lay an egg for breakfast.

AT A RABBITER'S HUT,
10 A.M., MARCH 31.

We were startled in Jim's morning watch by the violent struggling of the moa. The day was just breaking, and we found the trouble was caused by the mate of our bird having followed up the trail. It was standing close to the captive when Jim saw it first. They both croaked so as to waken me. When we interfered, the intruder strode off sulkily, but upon being hit with a stone ran like a race-horse. He threw his head forward in running, and rolled from side to side very much. I don't think he was bigger than ours. The accident led to an early start. I had to kill Towser, as he was too bad to travel this morning. The bird was very sulky and played up several times, and showed its strength so much that we had to slip the noose about its legs and throw it. It fell violently and on bad ground. We got it up at last and travelled about a mile, when it laid down and seemed done. After vain efforts to start I left Jim with it and went for help. I had not got a mile up out of the valley when I came upon a track that led me to a rabbiter's hut. He is getting breakfast now. He says I can get an out station in about nine miles of passable track.

GORE, IC P.M., MARCH 31.

I sent the rabbiter with breakfast to Jim. I reached the out station by one o'clock. I managed to get two hands with two horses and a dray. One of the hands said he could reach the spot I described in five hours with the dray. I, wishing to make complete train and other arrangements without delay, got a hack and started for Gore, and have just now arrived and offer you these hurried notes. I start at daybreak to meet the train, as I believe they will have got the bird loaded before dark and will easily catch the Waimea train to reach Gore by midday to-morrow. I told the men not to consider the lives of a dozen horses to save the moa. But I also wrote to Jim to nurse the thing all he could, and handle it carefully, and not to hurry if it would eat, and walk in if possible, as carting it might bruise it seriously. Should it not arrive to-morrow I will not be sorry, as that will show that it is eating and doing well.

The visit of the mate caused all this trouble. We could have walked in very well as we were doing.

P.S.—I did not know yesterday was Sunday, till this after-noon. We have been out nine weeks.—W.T.

Editor's Note: This piece of newspaper fiction was published in the Gore, New Zealand, *Mataura Ensign,* on April 1, 1884. Of course, this was an April Fool's story, and 'William Turton' was almost certainly a pseudonym for one of the newspaper staff writers. The story appears to have inspired a minstrel farce that played the following year, using the same title.

The Explorer—What Was It?
J. C. M. (1885)

Probably the West Coast Sounds of New Zealand offer as
large a field as any in the world for a close observance of
the habits of the amphibious monsters of the deep. Seals,
sea-lions, and sea-horses bask themselves on the jutting
rocks of its shores, and not infrequently schools of whales
disport themselves in secluded waters, resting out of danger and buffeting from the ocean outside, angrily roaring
over the bar, awakening echoes that reverberate in boom-
ing diapasons through the sough of the pine, down canyon and gorge, and away into the misty heights, uniting
its sombre harmony with the roar of the avalanche and
the liquid notes of the cataract, is thrown back down the
mountain side across the still waters—a great wave of
Nature's harmony—out again into the arms of the breakers, creating that sound which may be likened to the voice
of God. It is in scenes like these you can observe the
animals I have named in the full play and enjoyment of
their habitat, features now well known to the naturalist. I
am pleased to be able to say that the laws enforcing their
protection are being rigidly carried out by the Government, and I am under the impression that this protection
extends for a further period of twelve months, making in
all five years—a course highly necessary, as the depreda-
tions of traders were seriously affecting their existence,

in fact almost annihilating them. These knowing animals
do not require further notice now, but reference to them
leads up to some very interesting particulars of an exceedingly novel character, so much so that on first experienc-
ing them I almost imagined I was one of the adventurers
of Livingstone or Stanley's party instead of participating
in a stirring scene in the West Coast Sounds.

In a life like this excursions are the rule and not the
exception. Now it is with tucker and swag, away for a
three weeks' jaunt into the bush, with your 10 x 8 rolled
up neatly; then it is exploring down the Sound in your
weatherbeaten canoe, the patches here and there in her
sides betokening the hardships of her life and bush repairs,
but she is a trusty little craft, and we look with loving
gaze on her lines as we reflect on many a pleasant cruise
over hundreds of miles of unknown waters, over bursting
streams and storm-tossed creeks, anon carrying her over
massive torrent-washed boulders out of the rapid into the
smooth amethystine-hued lake, and, rocked by the gentle
rippling wavelets, we rest awhile safe from intrusion, and
away from the busy haunts of men and the mighty boom of
civilisation. When will the day come that these wilds will
be robbed of their soporific tendencies, and these moun-
tains disgorge their hidden treasures? Not long ahead. If
they accomplish practical results out in Colorado 1200
feet above sea-level, why not here? Then indeed my sylvan
retreat and wanderings will be but as a dream.

It was awakening from a recollection similar to this
that my attention was drawn to what I must have often
noticed before without noting anything peculiar about it,
but on this occasion it was so pronounced that I was, as it
were, compelled against myself to look at the peculiarity
of certain marks round about my canoe. I was just about
to shove her off when at my feet and round where she lay,
extending out at regular intervals, were large imprints

about eight inches in diameter. My curiosity was excited, and across the swampy shore at the head of the lake I tracked them—tracked them away inland through the bush some distance up a hill side, across the bed of a creek, where on the dry boulders were to be seen the now dry and muddy marks of my mysterious visitor's feet, until I lost them in the gathering gloom. Puzzled and somewhat baffled at this extraordinary and to me most novel feature of life in these parts, I returned and communed with myself, and came to the conclusion that these tracks had crossed the observation of the last man in this world likely to cry "Hold, enough!" and I determined to see further into this phenomenon. Certainly to me it was a phenomenon, and of no small import either. If I had come here yesterday, and knew nothing of things local, I might perhaps have given it best, but an old hand like I was had no intention of being baffled at the onset. Alas for human egotism! I am as far off an elucidation of the mystery as I ever was, and that's four years ago. However, I determined to have another try on the morrow, and making myself snug for the night, I soon had a break wind and my tent up, and after my billy had been duly drained—we are great followers of Booth, out here—and I had lit my pipe and reflected on those tracks before turning-in time, I had come to the conclusion that there was something bigger than myself knocking about about which no one knew anything of. Moa it certainly was not—I knew their marks too well; and that it was something four-footed I had no doubt. Looking to my rifle more carefully than usual, and placing it within easy grasp, and damping my fire down, I was soon rolled up in my blankets and away into dreamland, where I was accompanied, as a matter of course, by moas, defunct Maoris, and four-footed monsters.

Up with the sun in the morning. We are not laggards out here; every created thing is out and doing at sunrise. The screech of the owl sounding his last note is taken up by all the feathered tribe, and another day is on. I was curious to see if any fresh tracks had been made during the night, being under the impression that my mysterious stranger was a nocturnal wanderer—but no, there they were as I had left them. I examined them more carefully, and concluded they were not old, probably not more than two or three days. Their size was a remarkable feature, certainly not less than I have stated, eight inches in diameter. I again followed the tracks up beyond where I stopped yesterday, and certainly from its size it was a good climber, as the distance I had traversed was through very rough country. I lost the tracks several times from the nature of the rotten undergrowth— the rains here and moisture at certain seasons soon rots the fallen leaves—but with perseverance I picked them up again, and traced them to what has proved my *bête noir*—a water-hole. Emerging from a stiff climb I came out into a little piece of open country, a pretty little glade, in the centre of which, like a diamond in an emerald setting, was this water-hole. Up to this point the same tracks went, and there they ended. There was nothing in the depths of this mountain, pool to prevent the detection of any intruder even of smaller proportions than I opine my mystery to be; but it is a fact, galling as it is to record it, that all signs vanished like an echo. I looked about and examined the locality; certainly there were fissures about and cavernous retreats into which I did not delve on this occasion, but, like one of Fennimore Cooper's heroes, I hid behind this tree and that, and strove as little as possible to make my presence known. It was well on to mid-day, and as I had some distance to go I retraced my steps cautiously nearly as possible the way I came, met nothing untoward, and reached my camp baffled but not beaten, as I thought.

I resolved next morning to try the other shores of the Sound, and see if similar marks could be detected, and with this intent was soon aboard of my craft, and a short sail brought me to a spot I thought I would search in, as it showed features of easy access if my mystery was given to early ablutions. But no, no signs save that of nature.

This sort of thing went on for three weeks, and I must confess to a feeling of despondency at my repeated efforts being futile in the direction of a closer acquaintance with my mystery. A slight change, however, occurred on my returning one day homewards from the last spot I have indicated. I observed out on the lake, about midway, what I at first took to be a snag. Snags are of such frequent occurrence in the near shore waters, that I would have failed to notice it only for a slight incident enough in itself to draw my attention to it. From this apparent snag a small tiny-looking column of water was thrown up—a miniature "blow"—but I knew well enough it was not a whale. In the excitement of the moment I put my rifle up, and blazed. I thought I must have it; but no! there it goes—now it dives, now it ploughs the waters like a paddle-wheel. I ran as well as I could, but slowly, along the shore. If I could only see it land, I could form an idea of what my quarry was. I was sorely impeded in my progress through the rough bush I was in. Now I was in the water, up to my waist; then again I would take to the bush, only getting glimpses of my prey plunging and rolling on in his career ahead; and I was eventually bailed up, being unable to surmount the difficulties I had to contend against in boulders, bush, and swamp. I lost him, whatever it was. Wet and footsore, I was compelled to give up the chase that night. Next day I took up the tracks the same as I have noted, and trending to that water-hole I lost all trace; nothing more—not a vestige beyond what I already knew, of, and apparently as I had left it.

I have been on the trail of this "varmint" for many a day, but I have never seen it again, although repeatedly crossing its tracks. I may see it yet, as I live in hopes, and I long to demonstrate that in my opinion one at least of the species of hippopotami exists in this New Zealand lake.

Editor's Note: This (probable) newspaper fiction was published in the Dunedin, New Zealand, *Otago Witness,* on August 8, 1885. J. C. Meadway authored a series of occasional 'reports' of his travels in New Zealand. Most are typical accounts of geography and personalities. Perhaps he was inspired here, by the previous years' Moa story? The West Coast Sounds are a series of fiords and lakes in south-western South Island.

Spirit of the Woods
T. P. Porter (1893)

It Is Said to Haunt the Dense Forests of Guiana.
The Indians Are as Afraid of Didi as of Death—
An American's Adventure in a Tropical Wilderness—
Escape of an Ugly Monster.

[SPECIAL PANAMA (C. A.) LETTER.]
There is one experience to which, on account of the terrible significance that tradition attaches to it, the Indian of the Guianese forests has never become reconciled. To all else his stolidity, that equanimity of unconscious fatalism which is his most distinguishing characteristic, is invulnerable; but this one exception that "proves the rule" has the power to set his iron nerves a-trembling and make a driveling poltroon of the boldest. It is the voice of the Didi, the Evil Spirit of the Woods, and is the signal that he is visibly abroad seeking whom he may destroy, for, like the rattlesnake, the demon may not approach his human victim without giving this timely warning. Once heard there is no mistaking the sound of the Didi's voice, since it is totally unlike anything else heard in the forest. It is a prolonged melancholy whistle, beginning abruptly as a locomotive's toot in a high key and dwindling down to the merest thread of sound. The sight of this being is supposed to be instant death, for from his eyes shoot forth

flames that blast and reduce to cinders the luckless mortal
on whose vision this hellish apparition looms through the
darkness of the night. Hence, when that piercing cry goes
echoing through the forest, every Indian hurriedly wraps
his blanket about his head and remains thus muffled, preferring the risk of asphyxia to exposing his eyes to the
horrific presence, until the light of dawn drives the Didi
back to the nether world.

Although no one has ever seen and lived to describe
the monster, tradition gives it the form of a gigantic ape,
larger than a man and covered with a matted mass of
fiery red hair. Of course the superstition is absurd beyond serious consideration, but apart from the element
of the supernatural it is thought by many that it has some
foundation in fact; that notwithstanding the pronounced
skepticism of men of science some still unknown species
of simia exists in those forests which avoids the vicinity
of man and roams abroad seeking its prey only by night
and in the farthest and darkest recesses of the woods. And
in the light of a most thrilling adventure that once befell
me I am constrained to share that belief. During frequent
expeditions into the interior of the Guianas I had grown
familiar with the voice of the Didi and had a contract with
myself to trace it to its source, but the opportunity was
never favorable. Time and again had I been roused from
my sleep at the dead hour of midnight during a howling
storm to renew that contract and then quench my irritation in a burst of genuine merriment at the grotesque figures cut by the Indians, as in feverish haste they tumbled
over each other out of their hammocks and wound fold on
fold of suffocating blanket about their heads, grunting in
dolorous concert the while there sounded loud and shrill
above the howl of wind and lash of rain the truly demoniac whistle of the Didi. However, all things come to those
who wait, and my opportunity came at length with an

experience the like of which I should not care to undergo again.

One night, when encamped on the banks of the Caroni river, I awoke with a start to find my Indians bunched in a tangle of legs and arms, convulsively struggling amid fluttering folds of blanket and tumultuous waves of hammock, yelling: "Didi! Didi da, come!" Their terror was unusually acute, and no wonder, for the air was full of the voice of the Didi. It came, not from the far recesses of the woods, but apparently from somewhere in the immediate vicinity of the camp, and the demon might reveal himself at any moment. There was no storm on tonight, and the full moon rode high in a cloudless sky, flooding river and forest with her tropical radiance. Now or never should I identify the Didi, and with contemptuous disregard of the Indians' warnings I was soon on his trail, following the whistle through a darkling glade of the forest down which it receded when I appeared.

Now and then I thought a darker darkness damasked itself on the shadows that filled the spaces beneath the heavy canopied trees, but nothing could be distinctly seen there. The whistle, however, never ceased for more than a few seconds, and I was sure that the chase was not increasing the distance between us. The trail led away into the heart of the forest, but suddenly turned abruptly back toward the river until I could catch the gleam of the water in radiant patches between the foliage. This continued for some time longer, and many miles must have slipped under my eager feet, when a flood of light broke ahead and in another moment I found myself on the edge of an extensive opening on the river shore. Across this, and in full view under the moonlight, raced a gigantic, monstrous creature like a gorilla, which I judged to be at least eight feet in height. He ran, or rather lumbered along, upright on his hind limbs, swinging in his left hand a formidable

looking club. The body was covered with hair, and the face
was the most unutterably hideous I have ever beheld. I had
an excellent view of him as he stood for a moment and
peered apprehensively over his shoulder at me.

Sighting to hit him in the spine, I fired. The incessant
whistle, which he had just begun, instead of dwindling
reversed the process, as it were, and waxed higher and
higher until it attained a frightful compass and volume!
And then— But where was the Didi? Amazed, scarcely
crediting the evidence of my senses, I ran forward to within a few feet of the spot where he had just stood, and halted literally paralyzed by a superstitious dread that took
possession of me and overwhelmed calm reason. The monstrous beast, or rather thing, had *disappeared*—mysteriously vanished. That is, for under the circumstances it was
not possible that he could have regained the cover of the
forest! Was it all a dream? Was I the sport of a nightmare?
No, for there sailed the moon, sloping to the west above
the forest across the river, whilst about me murmured
the restless symphony of the forest, and the firm earth
answered: "Yea, verily!" to the query of my stamping feet.
Then my knees smote together, and the parched tongue
clove to its burning roof. The very loneliness of the wilderness in which I so delighted, and that contributed a
perennial charm to the life that I led face to face with
nature and, as I was wont to hope, with nature's God, now
drove me to the verge of frantic madness. For, lost to the
world and buried amidst that desolation, I had become the
sport of malicious evil spirits!

Pray? I was too distraught to even I think of that! Indeed, after that fierce bout of stamping—stamping on the
earth as if to question her through my sense of feeling as
to the reality of things—all remains a blank until I found
myself back at the camp where the pale flush of dawn
stealing through the trees tinted the cold ashes of the fire,

and roused the Indians who were cautiously unwinding their head wrappings. Then only did reason fully assert herself. But with daylight and companionship courage returned, and feeling heartily ashamed of my scare I determined to thoroughly investigate the mystery; moreover, I had dropped my Winchester, which must be recovered.

After a bath and substantial breakfast I felt ready to face a legion of airy demons, and accompanied by two Indians, who readily detected my trail, I returned to the scene of that terrible adventure. There could be no mistake, for there lay the rifle glistening amid the short grass. And a little farther on lay the solution of the mystery. How absurdly simple it all seemed in the broad light of day! A ragged hole in the ground, about which lay a scattered debris of wicker work, tufts of grass and loose mold, revealed the secret of the disappearing Didi. In my excitement I must have aimed wide and but slightly wounded the gorilla—or whatever else the creature happened to be—and he had fallen into one of those automatic tiger pits that the Indians plant in open spaces near the rivers, where those beasts love to gambol on clear nights after having secured their prey. Thus had the chase escaped me; and after I left, taking advantage of his great height and immense strength, he had reached up and torn away the trap roof, easily freeing himself.

It was truly humiliating to have thus lost an opportunity of capturing a Didi, but at the moment of solving the mystery I was so full of thankfulness at having, as by a miracle, escaped following him into the pit, that I gave but scant heed to the loss. But I have never ceased to regret the ridiculous panic that snatched from me to reserve for another the actual discovery and naming of the South American chimpanzee, of the existence of which I am, of course, convinced.

Editor's Note: This newspaper fiction was published in the *Topeka* (Kansas) *Daily Press,* on August 29, 1893. Thomas P. Porter traveled in and wrote about South America, before becoming the British Consul in Madagascar and Consul-General in Boston.

The Linguin
Lieut.-Col. Andrew Haggard, D.S.O. (1899)

It may probably interest some readers who have never yet heard of the brute, to learn that there is still existing in the Island of Java an animal—or, rather, a reptile—which seems to be the missing link between the ichthyosauri of prehistoric days and the well-known saurians of present times. This animal is, it appears, known to the natives by the name of "linguin"; and at the suggestion of my friend, Baron Alfons Pereira, Consul-General of Austria-Hungary in Tunis, I propose to narrate how he was some years ago fortunate enough to shoot one of these strange monsters.

The Baron is particularly anxious that I should put the circumstances on record, as he has always found when he has recounted the existence of and destruction by him of one of the brutes, that it has been treated as a mere traveller's tale. Moreover, during the years which have elapsed since he shot the linguin, Baron Pereira has never seen any picture or account of the huge reptile in any Natural History book, except a representation of an ichthyosaurus; nor has he seen anything approaching it in appearance in any zoological collection that he has ever visited. Fortunately, however, the Baron has recently received in a letter, written to Count Mailath, one of his friends who made inquiries on the subject in Java, a direct confirmation of his own experiences, and there can therefore be no doubt of the existence of this strange beast in the island.

I shall now try to give the Baron's experiences in his own words, but before doing so must remark that he has painted for me an excellent picture of the linguin being attacked by the Javanese native, after he had himself wounded it with his rifle.

But now to the story.

"I was," says Baron Pereira, "one morning in February, 1869, travelling in a large Javanese canoe with the Assistant-Resident Metman, himself a well-known sportsman. Dawn had only just broken when we found ourselves close to the mouth of the Batavia River. At this point the water was salt, and there was a considerable swell caused by the waves of the sea running up against the tide. As we advanced the rowers had considerable difficulty in making headway against the morning breeze. Suddenly there was enormous excitement among the crew of Malays who manned the boat. 'Linguin! Linguin!' I heard repeated on all sides. 'Linguin! Linguin!' repeated the steersman sitting next to me, seizing me by the arm as he shouted, and pointing excitedly towards the muddy shore, along which we were coasting at a distance of about 150 metres.

"It was, as I have said, barely light, and all that I could make out was the long and dark form of some large creature lying on the mud. I seized my rifle, not knowing in the least what a linguin might be, but at first imagining it to be merely a crocodile. But even with my rifle in hand I hesitated to shoot, for the movement of the boat, which was rolling, made any attempt at a steady aim impossible. However, the natives with me grew impatient.

"'Linguin!' they cried again. 'Shoot! shoot!'

"Standing up, I took a hasty aim and fired. Instantly there was a most tremendous commotion in the mud. I saw a huge creature whirling round and round in the liquid ooze, first on its head and then on its tail—much like the firework called a Catherine-wheel—while liquid mud was being scattered about in all directions. A shout of triumph rose from my crew, and the steersman, seizing a murderous-looking Malay scimitar, instantly plunged overboard to wage mortal combat with the disabled monster. He swam to shore, and boldly entering the mud, which was more than up to his knees, attacked the enormous brute.

"As we advanced quite close to the mud, I was now able to see that the animal appeared to be half crocodile and half snake. It had the body of the former and the neck and head of the latter. Upon the approach of the Malay, it ceased its wheel-like whirlings round and round on its tail, and repeatedly struck out at its new enemy with its head, trying to seize him with its fangs. But every time the linguin darted forward its powerful head and neck, the native struck out with his sword, each time inflicting a wound and saving himself from injury. At length a final blow struck the furious snake-crocodile fairly on the neck, and it fell dead. With great difficulty the brave fellow towed it by the tail through the mud into the water and brought it out to the canoe, when, with a good deal of trouble, we got it aboard. It was so heavy that it nearly bore down under water the gunwale of the boat on the side where we placed it.

"Its length was between 9ft. and 10ft. This I know from the fact that the body alone rested on at least two thwarts of the boat. The long, flexible neck and head fell upon the bottom of the craft. They were much cut about from the blows of the sword: but a peculiarity that I noticed was that, although where cut in deep gashes the flesh exposed was all white, like the flesh of a fish, there was no blood flowing from any of the wounds. In addition to the cuts upon the neck, the Malay had also nearly severed one of the fore-paws of the weird creature. It was in consequence almost too much destroyed for preservation.

"However, I insisted on the men's carrying the carcass along with us until mid-day, after we had disembarked; but at length, chiefly owing to the numerous cuts upon it, it became so decomposed and offensive that we had to leave it behind. Mr. Metman promised me that I should see plenty more; but alas! Never in all the time that I was in Java did I see another linguin."

Editor's Note: This account was published under 'short stories' in the *Wide World Magazine,* for February 1899. Was this a fictional narrative, or did Baron Johann Ludwig Alphons von Pereira-Arnstein (1879-1928) actually run across a strange reptile? From the description, it sounds like a typical large varanid lizard. Adventure stories like this, fact or fiction, were enjoyed and reprinted throughout newspaper networks.

The Something in Black Swamp
Lin Wood (1906)

"Yes, Mr. Bennett, guess you'll find plenty of game round Black Swamp, an' fishin's pretty fair there, too, but I don't believe I care to go with ye."

"Ah, I suppose you are pretty busy at your fall work," said Mr. Bennett, "but if you would go into camp with me and act as guide for a week or ten days, I will make it worth your while."

Mr. Bennett, with rod and gun in hand had arrived that day in Pine Hill, a little settlement near the northern border of Maine, on pleasure bent, and on inquiry had found that a section about five miles north of the settlement, known as Black Swamp, abounded with deer and that also a good string of fish could be pulled from the brooks flowing through it. After hearing such favorable reports of it from different people, he decided that it was just the place for him to put in his vacation, and that without doubt he would bring from it one or more antlered heads to show to his envious friends in the city. The male population of Pine Hill was small, but to his surprise no one seemed at all anxious to act as cook and guide for him in his proposed camp in Black Swamp. No especial reason would be assigned but each one hesitated and finally declined, one or two giving some lame excuse, although Bennett offered very good pay for little labor.

Finally he sought out "Old John Aiken," one of the pioneers of the settlement, tough as a pine knot, who made a fair living by hunting and trapping, and after explaining that he had decided that Black Swamp was the place where he would be most likely to succeed in getting game, he proposed to Aiken that he act as guide for him. Aiken rubbed his chin softly with the tips of his fingers and then hesitatingly made the reply given in the opening of this story. In spite of Bennett's flattering offers he "reely" didn't "bleeve" he could go. Bennett was by this time quite discouraged about getting a guide at all. "What is the matter with you men, here?" he asked. "You seem to have plenty of time to loaf around the village, yet when I offer you $3 a day and board, to guide me around Black Swamp you are all extremely busy; I can't understand it." "Well, Mr. Bennett," said Aiken, gently, "I'll tell ye honest why I hain't got time to go into Black Swamp with ye—it's cause I'm sca't. There, that's all there is to it, there ain't a man here who refused to go with ye that had any other reason. But that's right—I'm sca't to go into Black Swamp."

Bennett looked at the man in amazement. Although called "Old Aiken" he was not over fifty, and strong as the proverbial ox, Bennett could not imagine this man being afraid of anything, and on his own confession, he was "sca't" to go into Black Swamp. "But, Mr. Aiken," said Bennett, "you do not mean that you are afraid of the Swamp or anything in it?" "That's just it—I'm sca't of something in it," said Aiken, doggedly, "an' I'll tell ye just what I mean. I've met bear an' loupcervier, an' all kinds of wild animals, an' I've killed 'em in fair fights an' never was sca't of anything on four legs, yet, but when it comes to something on two legs—something shaped like a man but built like a giant—In fact, a wild man as big as two common men—an' covered with shaggy hair—why, I want's to say that I'm sca't, an' so are all the men here. I seen it once, 'bout two year ago, an' this is how 'twas. I'd heard about queer things being seen an' heard in Black Swamp, but didn't put no stock in 'em—called 'em old women's yarns, an' all that. Well, this day, 'bout two years ago. I went to Black Swamp after deer an' struck hard luck. I hunted all the afternoon an' didn't git a shoot, so 'bout five o'clock I set down on a little hill to rest, an' in hopes that a deer might pass through the gully below. I waited some time an' had about made up my mind to go home, when the most horrid yell I ever heard, came to my ears. I jumped prepared for something, I didn't know what. Just then a handsome doe came tearing down the gully and after her came the awullest thing I ever see. It was, or had been a man, Mr. Bennett, but what it was then, God only knows. Stark naked it was but seemed all shaggy with hair so it kind'er looked as though it had a fur suit on. It must have been over seven feet tall, an' as it came tearing down the gully after that doe, my blood just turned cold, an' I set down an' watched it go out of sight round the hill; then I came home a quick as the Almighty would let me, an' told what I'd seen. I got laughed at, of course, but since that time two or three men have seen him an' now all Pine Hill knows that Black Swamp hides something that men don't want to meet."

To say that Bennett was astonished would be putting it mildly—he was utterly amazed. Coming to Pine Hill after the ordinary game of the forest, he had run up against something like a tale in a "Bogy Bock," and he instantly decided to follow it down and see what there was in it— not doubting, however, but that Aiken had greatly magnified what he had seen. By dint of persistent coaxing und offers of a good sum in cash he succeeded in securing Aiken for the trip and 48 hours afterward they were snugly settled in their tent near a deep, sluggish stream which disappeared somewhere in the middle of the Swamp, just

where, Aiken said no one knew. For two days they hunted
with fair success but Aiken's "wild man" seemed conspicu-
ous by his absence, which fact Bennett was in no wise slow
in pointing out to him, accompanying his remarks with
many a good-natured laugh at Aiken's expense. The old
man made little reply but finally said, "As long as ye hain't
quite sca't out of ye senses, Mr. Bennett, I'd like for ye to
see the thing just once, an' then I bet you'd quit laughin'
fer quite a spell."

On the third night after entering the Swamp the men
retired as usual, both pretty tired, and Aiken was soon
snoring the snore of the righteous. Bennett's eyes, too,
grew heavy, but soon he became wakeful and after tossing
awhile he got up and dressed, and opening the flap of the
tent he stepped out into the bright moonlight. The stream
showed bright and silvery, and finding that sleep had
deserted him he went down to the bank, and untying the
boat moored there, he stepped in and rowed gently down
stream. The boat rowed so easily with the current that on
rousing from the revery into which he had fallen he found
himself in an unfamiliar part of the stream. He was about
to turn and row back, when, lifting his eyes, he saw that
which chilled him to the heart. He knew what it was! Tall
and horrid, it came treading softly along the bank, evidently following him. In the moonlight it appeared twice
the height of an ordinary man; naked and shaggy, with a
great club in its right hand. It was a sight to awe the brav-
est. Cold with fear as Bennett was, he roused himself to
think. This awful creature had evidently followed him, he
knew not how long. To avoid it by rowing back was impossible, for the stream was narrow and the "thing" could
easily reach the boat by wading out and then swimming
a stroke or two. No, the only course open was to row on
down the stream and escape by speed or strategy; so settling himself firmly he began to row steadily and with

increasing power, and as the little boat responded to his strength he shot down the stream like an arrow.

At first, the horrid creature on the bank was left behind, but thinking, evidently, that his quarry was escaping, he uttered a yell, such as might come from the throat of a fiend, and then Bennett heard the bushes and underbrush snap and crackle as he tore along the bank. The stream seemed to flow swifter here, and Bennett inwardly wondered where this dreadful race was leading him. The country on each side of the stream grew wilder and more desolate, and Bennett decided that he was in a part of the Swamp hitherto unexplored. Although the stream grew swifter, and although Bennett rowed with all his strength, yet the pursuer steadily gained on him, uttering at intervals, that awful yell. Bennett now began to distinguish in the stillness, broken only by the noise made by his pursuer, a faint murmur like falling water, which grew louder, moment by moment, yet was subdued as though confined. The race was apparently coming to a crisis. The creature on the bank was nearly abreast the boat and Bennett could appreciate the fact that a little more gain would enable the pursuer to leap into the stream, which was growing narrower, and grab the boat as it came up. Just then, a sudden change in the appearance of the stream took his attention; the banks suddenly grew steep and high as though the bed of the stream slanted suddenly downward, and this seemed to be the fact, for the boat shot ahead at increased speed, and the murmur grew louder. The creature seeing that Bennett was apparently escaping, plunged straight down at the boat, striking the water a few feet astern. Bennett had by this time given himself up as lost, for with the known horror behind and the unknown ahead it seemed that nothing could save him.

Suddenly a great, black opening appeared ahead, into which the stream seemed to drop, and, with a muttered prayer, he grasped the sides of the boat, closed his eyes and waited for the end. There was a roar, an awful falling sensation and then a fearful shock, as the boat, falling through mid-air, struck—somewhere. Water flowed in but did not fill the boat and she again plunged onward in the darkness, with Bennett, nearly dead after fear, still grasping the thwarts. For a few moments the wild ride continued, then, with a shock which nearly broke his hold, he was plunged under water, and a strangling sensation warned him that the end was near. The boat appeared to rise, however, and without warning he was lifted from the water and found himself still sitting in the submerged boat, while about him stretched the calm waters of a little lake. He was about to get out of the boat and empty it by a process well known to boatmen, when, to his horror, the waters parted and the apparition of the swamp came to the surface, blowing like a whale, not ten feet from the boat. Turning his wild eyes about he saw Bennett and with three strokes was beside the boat and one great hand seized Bennett's shoulder. Bennett gave a scream of terror, and—"Well, well, Mr. Bennett, guess ye had the night-mare, didn't ye?" He sprang up, trembling, to find old man Aiken's arm around him, and himself in the tent by the stream. "Where is it—the wild man?" he panted. "Well, I hardly know—guess you've been dreaming 'bout him, hain't ye?" said Aiken, as he guided the trembling man to a seat; and then John Bennett, strong man that he was, broke down and cried, while Aiken stood by in utter amazement. Finally Bennett spoke—"Mr. Aiken," said he, "I've had an awful dream—guess we'll go out tomorrow." On the morrow they went out, and Aiken went down to the stream to make the boat more secure until they could send a team for it, and when he returned to the dismantled tent he forgot to tell Mr. Bennett that the boat was gone and that there were prints of great, bare feet in the mud on the bank.

About a week after Mr. Bennett's departure from Pine Hill some young men discovered Aiken's boat in a small lake a few miles away, which lay about one hundred and fifty feet below the level of Black Swamp, and whose source was a point much discussed by the hunters who sometimes visited it, and the next summer, while old man Aiken was gunning along its shores, he came upon an object, half buried in the mud and grasses, which made him turn white, and he went home, sick.

The wild man of Black Swamp was never seen after Mr. Bennett's hunting trip in that vicinity.

Editor's Note: This story was written for the Lewiston (Maine) *Journal,* and published May 10, 1906. There is a long history of 'Indian devils' and 'wild men' in the northeast woodlands, so plenty of fodder for a story-writer's imagination. The 'it was all a dream' ending was common for many of that period's newspaper speculative fiction, so it is interesting to see the author subvert that trope here.

A Strange Experience
J. C. Du Bois (1908)

My friend, Jack Vandeluer, sat suddenly upright in his astonishment, and surveyed me by the light of the brilliant tropical moon, as if he doubted the evidence of his senses. "I say, old chap," he said, for once forgetting his well-bred drawl, "it can't be possible that you really give credence to such utter rot?"

We had been a week in our camp on one of those natural clearings which occur in the depths of the mighty tropical forest of British Guiana, a district some years ago the subject of controversy between Great Britain and Venezuela, uninhabited except by a few Indian tribes, whose lessening numbers each year proved the efficacy of that bane of all uncivilised races, the rum of the parangheries, or sea people (a native name for the white men of the coast). Vandeluer and I had been for some time warm friends by force of that attraction which obtains in characters the antipodes of each other, I suppose, or through our mutual tastes for scientific research. He was an Englishman, a man of means, whose acquaintance I had made through mutual friends connected with the Smithsonian Institute of Washington, on behalf of which I was then conducting an expedition into this little-known country for the collection of ornithological specimens. Vandeluer, a botanist of no mean order, had joined me on his own account.

He was physically a splendid specimen of his race, standing over six feet, and with a breadth of shoulder and length of limb abnormally great, and possessed of strength far beyond the lot of ordinary mortals. He seemed to be a subject of continual wonder to the native Ackawoise Indians, four of whom constituted our tram of attendants. I have laid much stress, perhaps, on the physical power possessed by my companion, but in the light of future events this will be understood.

It had been our custom during our after-dinner smoke to draw into conversation, if possible, our head man, who, having been blessed with a name most impossible for civilised tongues, had been promptly rechristened Shylock by Vandeluer, on the ground that "he wanted his pound of flesh." He certainly was a queer being and formed on lines, which, taken altogether, presented as grotesque a personality as could be imagined. Thin to emaciation, though of iron endurance, his shock head of coarse, black hair had a perpetual habit of suddenly twisting around at the most unexpected moments, and at the same instant his mouth would distend in the opposite direction, both movements apparently without the slightest volition on his part, a grimace, which, taken with his wild black eyes, produced a startling effect on the unprepared onlooker. His sole garb, an old "lap" or apron of calico displayed his quaint form and skeleton ribs, while his claw-like right hand was minus two fingers. But, despite this unprepossessing exterior, his knowledge of preparing "labba" barbecues, or "abonyah" stews, was as profound as his eye was sharp for a good camping ground, while his control of the men under him (who, indeed, regarded him with no little awe) left nothing to be desired. We had picked him up on a sugar plantation near the coast, where our host, during a brief stay, had recommended him as a native of that part of the wilderness into which we intended venturing, who

knew all that region thoroughly, and was about returning
thither after a short spell of work on the plantation. We
had never regretted the choice of our henchman. Many a
rare bird and orchid had been added to our specimen cases
through his knowledge of the haunts and localities must
favored by them, and on the comparatively few occasions
on which he could be beguiled out of his habitual silence,
we had been able to glean much information regarding
the life, vegetable and animal, of that most wonderful
country.

On the night when my story opens we had been sitting
outside the door of our tent with our cigars, enjoying that
restful content which follows a hard and successful day's
tramp and a good dinner. Shylock was squatting on his
heel, also pulling at a cigar, while at a few yards distant
the three other Indians, sitting about the remains of a
small forest deer, discussed that delicacy with great unc-
tion. Overhead the brilliant moon lighted up every inch
of the little clearing with such a radiance that each blade
grass or gorgeous flower, dew-spangled, was revealed under
the glorious effulgence. Just beyond where the three pack
mules cropped the rich grass, the mighty forest began,
and, across the foot of the clearing, tinkled a clear rivulet,
emerging from the sombre depths on one side to disappear with a farewell splash and gurgle into the unknown
darkness of the other. Altogether, a wonderful, fairy-like
scene, a vision of beauty impossible in northern climes,
with the less profuse vegetation and paler light.

From out those vast, mysterious depths of primeval
forests a perfect diapason of sounds—shrill whistle of
insects and night birds, fierce scream of tiger cats, long
howlings of apes, wailing of sloths, and ever and anon the
deeper bass roar of prowling jaguar, at which danger note
our hands would instinctively reach toward the rifles lying
near by.

My friend's expression of surprise was occasioned by a remark which fell from me, following on the recital of a strange story by our man Shylock. After repeated urging he had told us how the loss of his two digits had occurred, verily a singular episode. He had been in his earlier days a mighty hunter among his tribe, before whose deadly arrow, tipped with poison, almost every variety of the prolific forest life had at some time yielded a specimen. Such was his pluck and skill that he had even longed to meet the dreaded "Didi," a mysterious inhabitant of the forests, half man, yet more than man, with a cunning and strength beyond that of man or animal—a creature firmly believed in and greatly dreaded by the forest tribes. This he had never done until one day when returning to the huts of his people after a hunting excursion, he had suddenly spied, sitting under a bush, what he thought was a baby ape, and possessed with the idea of capturing it. He had stolen quietly up to the thing, which appeared asleep, and seized it. It awoke, screaming loudly, and he had barely time to realise that the sound seemed strangely human, when there was a rush, and the creature was torn from his grasp, while at the same moment he was sent headlong to earth, half stunned, by a blow as from a powerful arm.

Looking up he saw standing over him a creature of the stature of a tall man, but of much greater breadth and proportions, covered with short, reddish hair, and possessing a face most devilish, yet must human-like. One huge arm hugged the smaller creature to her breast, while the other, terminating in a huge hand armed with sharp nails, was raised threateningly over the prostrate hunter, an action rendered more alarming by the red, glaring eyes and huge teeth displayed in a furious snarl. Half dead with fear he recognised the dreaded "Didi" so often described by the older men of his tribe, and then rendered desperate by his terror, he leaped to his feet, and with drawn knife (for his bow and arrows had fallen beyond his reach) struck furiously at the creature.

Quick as he was, his hand was caught in a grasp so paralyzing that he was powerless, and his knife dropped from the crushing force of that grip. With a long-drawn yelling laugh the creature slowly lifted the hand to its mouth, as if exulting in his useless effort to prevent it, and severed his two fingers as if they had been bits of straw. Seizing him then by the shoulders, while he gave himself up for lost, it had drawn him up to the demon-like face, gabbling some unintelligible sounds, for no man understands the language of "Didi," while the young one clung about his neck. Then once more breaking into its harsh, yelling laugh, it dealt him an open-handed slap which laid him insensible on the earth. On recovering he had, though greatly shaken, managed to reach his village, but ever after he carried as tokens of this encounter a mutilated right hand, and the convulsive movement of the neck.

Vandeleur and I listened to this recital with different emotions. His hearty laugh in utter disbelief at its termination was what might have been expected from a man of his matter-of-fact British mind and rugged nature. But I had been once before in that country and was already aware of the deep-seated belief of the natives in the strange legend of the "Didi," or wood demon, and whether this fact, together with a somewhat nervous constitution, and the mysterious impenetrable deafness of the unknown forests around us, coupled with the uncanny appearance of the narrator, acted upon my nerves I cannot say, but as Shylock ceased his yarn, the words broke from me. "Great heavens, I would not care to meet such an antagonist."

"Why," continued Vandeleur, "the 'Didi' and all that sort of thing can only exist in the superstitious mind of the natives. If there were an apelike creature of such dimensions we would surely know of it through the researches of former naturalists in these parts, and beyond the gorilla of the Congo and the orang of Borneo there is no record of anything approaching it. All tommyrot, old chap!"

"It may be so," I replied, "but how do you account for this belief being common to all the tribes of these forests? And considering their vast extent, and in some parts unexplored depths, could not such a creature exist there undiscovered by modern scientists, whose opportunities would naturally be more limited than those of the Indians?"

"Now, look here, old man," said Vandeleur, "you are perfectly aware of the numberless extravagant beliefs of the natives, and it seems more rational to suppose that this is one of them, than to believe there could exist an almost supernatural creature, possessing attributes both human and bestial. For my part I believe that old Shylock was labouring, at the time of his adventure, under the influence of the rum he so much admires, and mistook a row with one of the other tribesmen for his fracas with the 'Didi.' Besides that he is an awful old liar, anyway, and this may be one of his inventions."

But to this latter proposition, Shylock, who understood and spoke the n— English of the coast inhabitants, offered a decided and indignant denial, with such grotesqueness of gesture, accompanied with that involuntary grimace, that we both roared with laughter.

But, as the sound of our mirth died away, there rang out, apparently from just within the impenetrable gloom of the forest, a harsh peal of most diabolical laughter, with the yelp of a beast running through it, a cachinnation so utterly unlike anything ever heard by either of us as to bring us both to our feet, while the natives, terror-stricken, sprang in behind us, crouching in the shadows of the tent, and from Shylock came the single word, "Didi!" as if wrenched from him by sheer amazement and fear.

In an instant Vandeleur had caught up his rifle and sent a bullet in the direction of the sound, but with no apparent result. We waited, staring at each other in wonder, listening for a repetition of the sound, but beyond the usual chorus of nocturnal voices nothing was heard.

"By Jove," at last said Vandeleur, "that was a queer start! What on earth could produce such a noise? I have heard the laughing hyena in India, but this is entirely different."

"Didi," I said with conviction. "So much for your incredulity, I guess you are convinced now."

"What made that noise, Shylock," said my friend, turning to our henchman somewhat impatiently, who from his uneasy glances on all sides, seemed much perturbed.

"Didi," said the Ackawoise, "nebber like you fire gun at it; will tink me do it, and will kill me."

"Nonsense, you old image," said Vandeleur, lighting another cigar, "but you and the other Johnnies turn in now. Call me when your watch is up, Du Bois—and look out for 'Didi,'" he added, with a laugh.

As if in answer to his words, there sounded again, farther away in the forest, the weird laughter with no traces of mirth in it, but as it seemed to my upset nerves, charged with a devilish derision.

The night passed quietly, however, with only the customary changes of watches between my friend and me, and the next day breaking camp, we followed the little stream for about ten miles under the dome-like forest giants, with occasional undergrowth of dense sections of luxuriant tree-ferns scattered along our way. Toward evening we camped on a similar clearing to that of the night before, determined to make this our last march into the interior, being loaded up with as much impedimenta in the shape of botanical and ornithological specimens as our mules could carry. All through the day our man Shylock had seemed depressed, and even more taciturn than usual, and when chaffed by Vandeleur concerning his terror of the night before, made no reply beyond a furtive and apparently uneasy glance through the thick vegetation on each side. We had frequent discussions during the day as to the probable source of the extraordinary occurrence of the night, and could arrive at no satisfactory solution, neither of us having ever heard, in the course of our numerous excursions in various countries, anything at all resembling the sounds. Even my friend's strong nerves and practical turn of mind seemed somewhat nonplussed by the impossibility of a suitable explanation. As for me, I must confess that the dim aisles of the almost unexplored forests through which we were making our way seemed fitting surroundings for almost any mystery, and capable of containing forms of life easily concealed from the investigating curiosity of the explorer.

On reaching our camping ground for the night, our preparations being made, Shylock suddenly announced his intention of going further along the stream, intending to snoot some game, either the small deer of the locality, coming from their evening drink, or some other of the numerous game frequenting the watercourse for the same purpose at the close of day. We thought this a peculiar move, in view of his apparent disquietude of the day, but as no man can ever hope to comprehend the working of the native mind, we gave it up, only cautioning him not to go too far, fearing for his safety should he encounter some prowling jaguar, and also knowing that his absence from the preparations of supper would entail considerable depreciation in its usual excellence. He remained so long away, however, that growing impatient, we were just commenting on his lengthy absence, when we were startled by a loud scream of mortal terror ringing through the forest from evidently a few hundred feet away, instantly followed

by the same demoniacal laughter we had heard the night
before. So appalling was the sound that for an instant we
stared at each other, then Vandeleur sprung toward the
repeated shouts of terror, in his haste empty-handed, our
rifles being inside the tent, while I followed, catching up
from the stump of a tree my shotgun. As we entered the
great arches of the trees we were plunged into a dimness
almost as of night, the twilight of those regions being
short-lived. But we could see sufficiently to keep up our
rapid advance, guided by the infernal medley of yells and
horrible laughter.

Suddenly right ahead of us, where, owing to a less
dense covering overhead the ground was better lighted, we
saw Shylock fleeing for his life, while, close behind him,
bounding along with enormous strides and springs, came
an object which stopped us short in our rush, from sheer
amazement. But even as we hesitated we saw one long arm
uplifted, and a crushing downward blow fell upon the
head of the unfortunate Ackawoise, driving him headlong
to earth.

Instinctively lifting my gun, I sent a charge from each
barrel at the monstrous object, apparently with no injury,
and the next instant I saw my friend, Vandeleur, spring
upon the manlike creature, as I followed in with clubbed
gun. Now, I have before mentioned that my friend was a
man of most extraordinary muscular power, and you may
judge of my astonishment at seeing him the next instant
hurled away with the force of a catapult some 20 feet, and
with an impetus which rolled him over and over on striking the ground. My clubbed gun fell with all my force on
the creature's head, breaking off the grip, and dodging a
sweeping blow from the terrible long arm, I again drove in
a blow with the barrels, this time catching my antagonist
squarely on the side of the demon-like head, staggering it
for an instant. Vandeleur by this time had recovered his

feet and his somewhat shaken senses, and rushing in with his hunting knife, struck furiously at the creature, failing to disable it, but inflicting a severe wound on the shoulder. Again there broke forth the yelling laughter, this time doubly hideous by its close proximity, and with a shambling bound the creature made its escape, disappearing in the darkness of the forest.

We stood panting an instant, for the scuffle had been sharp, and then hurried to the Indian. But he was dead, his skull fractured by that fearful downward blow. Together we conveyed him to camp, where the other terrified camp followers were by this time hiding in our tent, and that night there was no sleep for us, for after forcibly expelling the men, we were compelled to make a grave for our unfortunate henchman in the clearing, where we buried him, retracing our way toward civilization the next morning.

De Profundis

Robert Coutts Armour (1914)

About the junction years of the nineteenth and twentieth centuries, writers of popular fiction were seized by a prophetic fervour of destruction. I think the scientists pointed the way with interesting speculations about such matters as the heat-life of the sun; an eminent French astronomer amused his leisure with a romantic, dithyrambic story of the human race's end; various cheery people of varying authority decreed the speedy exhaustion of the world's coal-fields; and a host of sprightly authors made haste to entertain us with accounts of great cities overwhelmed, and our painful built-up civilisation obliterated by dire and diverse means. Man warred with Terra, Ocean sent forth her devouring monsters, nation hurtled against nation, the Yellow Peril loomed terribly, new diseases devastated the whole world, leaving only a few choice spirits to the task of re-peopling it—and whilst we enjoyed this feast of speculation, the forces prepared for our undoing were already marshalling. Whether any one of those ingenious scribes anticipated what came to pass I am unable to say, though, for irony's sake, I trust it was so, and that he has had ample opportunity to revise his theories in the face of facts.

It may seem strange, but the calamity came without any warning, the few isolated incidents that might have served being misunderstood or disregarded. I myself was witness, after the event, of one such, in this wise.

I had been making holiday in Cornwall, tramping the coastline or occasionally diving inland, in an irresponsible fashion that would have shocked the laborious writer of itineraries. The weather was unusually fine and warm, so, having a large waterproof poncho, a bag of provisions, and a little kettle, I gipsied very happily 'til the eve of the inevitable day when I must return to London. Being by then wise in the selection of a camping ground, I got me at sundown to the sheltered side of a little wood, ate my supper, and, wrapped in my poncho, lay down to enjoy a pipe before going to sleep.

It was my last camp in England, perhaps the last I shall ever make there. At the present time, of course, such a proceeding would be stark lunacy even in the most desolate place. In front of me, looking inland, the ground rose with a gentle swell, dipped and rose again to the horizon quite bare of cover, there being no trees of any growth in that part of the West Country. They were all cut down long ago, I have been told, at the time when every Cornishman turned mole and burrowed after tin, and certainly they must have needed forests to prop the workings with which the country is honeycombed. In the field before me was the shaft of one, ringed by a high stone wall and, with it for text, I speculated drowsily whether, in the far future, the wood underground would have rotted or turned to coal. Then an old horse came and looked over the hedge at me in a friendly way, and the tips of his ears twitching against the sky were my last waking memory.

I awoke once in the dark with a confused sound of hoofs and a long, wailing cry ringing in my cars, but all was quiet. I attributed the noise to a trick of dream, sniffed distastefully a faint, acrid odour drifting on the slow night breeze and, turning over, slept without stir 'til the sunlight crept into my eyes. Within half an hour I had sluiced myself at a runnel, eaten breakfast, and was ready to face the road, the rail, and the Big Smoke.

My direct route lay through the field in front and, climbing on the gate, I stood at gaze, seeing that close beside the walled shaft-mouth lay something which, I was absolutely certain, had not been there overnight—a large skeleton.

I noticed, too, that my friendly horse was nowhere in view, though the boundaries of the field were all in sight and, exceedingly puzzled, approached the bones. They were fresh, raw, though not a particle of meat adhered to them, and unmistakably equine. I went back to the gate, the only exit, examined the ground beyond it, which was soft enough to show a track, and made sure that the beast had not gone out that way.

The conclusion was obvious. Within a few hours a big, strong animal had been done to death, and clean picked! It was incredible, yet there was the skeleton, without a tooth-mark, still held together by its ligaments, and perfect as an anatomist could desire. I began to be a little afraid but, being of a fairly practical turn, set about searching after further facts, and ran against more incomprehensibility.

From the gory patch about the skeleton, to the wall around the shaft, ran two tracks, worn through the turf to bare earth, about four or five inches wide and as much apart, one of which continued in a red stain up the perpendicular face of the stones.

Now, I offer no excuse for my conduct in the face of the mystery. Certainly the wall was high, and had been effectively pointed no great while before, but I could easily have climbed it. Only—I didn't want to climb. Without weighing matters I concluded instantly that the power which could so deal with a horse might very easily treat me in like fashion, left the unhealthy precinct on tiptoe, and ran 'til I came to a cart-road. Decidedly the spirit of research was not in me that morning.

At the time I felt I was doing shamefully, but looking back I see that I acted with common-sense. Had I searched further I should have lost my life as vainly as one who throws himself to a school of sharks; yet my self-esteem barometer went down and down, so I mentioned the phenomenon to no one, but got to town and to work once again, determined to forget an inexplicable incident.

In those days I had just entered on a series of experiments having for object the discovery of some volatile fuel to replace petrol, and my little laboratory contained so many samples of oils, tars, and essences that, despite ventilation, it usually smelt like the interior of a submarine. I suppose, strictly speaking, mine was a dangerous trade, and certainly the top floor of an old-fashioned office building in Fleet Street was scarcely a fitting place in which to distil inflammable liquids. But it happened that the den was my own, the property having belonged to my people for near a century and, with the near prospect of eviction when the ground lease expired, I didn't wish to squander money on other premises.

I had but few visitors and only one intimate friend, Henry Mayence, a short, broad, immensely strong man, devoted to motoring, and consequently keenly interested in my attempts to cheapen his pastime. He used to bring all kinds of absurdly unsuitable material, ranging from camphor to burgundy-pitch and palm oil, though apart from this foible he was entirely level-headed. I returned from Cornwall at the beginning of June; twelve days later—on Friday, the 13th, to be precise—I heard his familiar step on the landing, the heavy thump of something weighty banged on the floor, and opened to find him in the act of upending a large iron oil-drum which smelt vilely of crude petroleum.

"So you're back," he grunted. "That's a good job. Didn't want to lug this thing home again. Out of the way!"

He pushed past unceremoniously with the thing in his arms and, depositing it within with another crash, condescended to explain.

"Right stuff at last," he said. "Wales. They've struck it—regular lake. I've got an option. You try it. It's heavy, but—"

"But, confound you, I don't want a hogshead!" I objected. "It'll stink the place out. Phuff!" I had been at work all night, and so was irritable. "Why on earth couldn't you bring a little? A bottleful would have been enough."

He grinned placidly.

"Because this is going to be a big thing, sonny, and you'll need it all. Besides, what does another flavour matter among so many? Open the windows."

"And kill the sparrows? You'll jolly well have to take it away again! Hang it, man, I'll be run in for causing a nuisance!"

"All right," said he soothingly; "perhaps it is a bit too thick. Didn't notice it on the car. Horrid business, that of the policeman, Kingston way!"

"What business?" I asked. "I haven't been out yet."

"Devilish rummy! Found the poor beggar behind a hedge, uniform on—helmet, too. Beastly! And I may have spoken to him—been held up thereabouts more than once. Poor chap!"

"What are you gibbering about? Was he murdered?" I demanded irritably.

Mayence shivered.

"Ghastly, I tell you! Nothing but his clothes, only bones left inside 'em. Ugh!"

"What?" I shouted. "D'you mean to say— Why, down in Cornwall—"

And forthwith I told him briefly what I had seen.

"Same thing," he said, nodding emphatically. "A horse don't matter, but a man! And a lot of other people are missing, too. Wonder you didn't hear the boys yelling the specials outside."

"I did," said I. "But I'm so used to that, I didn't take notice. Hallo! There's another edition, or—"

We sprang together to the window opening streetwards and craned our necks.

Right opposite, building operations were in progress, and a great hole had been dug in the earth, from which, as we looked, the workmen came crowding and jostling, howling gigantically, in a frenzied hurry to reach the narrow door in the hoarding along the street front.

"Lord!" ejaculated Mayence. "What in thunder's up! Look at that chap!"

A man, who had, I suppose, been in the deepest part of the excavation, came clawing frantically up a ladder, reached the level, put his hands to his head with the gesture of one suddenly smitten to death, reeled, and fell backwards into the pit.

A cloud of dust flew up and hid everything for an instant; then something which looked exactly like a wave of treacle—a brownish-black, shiny, wet-looking, lapping tide—flooded up over the edge of the hole, and flowed out towards the men jammed in the doorway.

They must have felt its coming and redoubled their efforts. A section of the hoarding gave way, falling outwards on the front ranks of the swaying crowd that had collected instantaneously and, as they gave back, the fear-minded workmen charged forth, tripping, stumbling, and striking out fiercely at everything in their path, driven by blind, panic terror. Close on their heels through the gap, over the hoarding's top and through every crevice of the boards, came that amazing fluid mass.

Everybody shouted, abruptly everybody faced about, turning to fly, and I had an impression of the crowd as a heaving, whirling maelstrom, with pinky-red faces for bubbles and a tossing spray of straw hats adrift for foam. I saw a tall man—a Press photographer, I presume—struggle free and present his camera at the oncoming treacly tide, stagger, fall, and lie motionless.

Subconsciously I wondered if he had got his picture, and whether I should see it in the morrow's papers. The treacle swept on and over him—ay, and over many another. Men faltered and fell in rows, even as they fled. A tubby man, with flashing glasses that stayed miraculously firm on his nose, swarmed halfway up a lamp-standard, lost his hold for no apparent reason, and fell, limp and lifeless.

The street within our view cleared, the din retreated a little, and I could hear Mayence.

"Alive!" he shouted "Alive! The stuff's alive, I tell you—alive!" He used language quite unprintable. "And deadly—look at that 'bus!"

It had been at a standstill, unable to move through the swift-gathered throng. Its top was crowded. The driver stretched a hand to put in the clutch, drew it back sharply, lifted it to his mouth, and sagged forward over his wheel.

"What is it? Great heavens, what is—"

Somebody sprang into the room behind us, and banged the door. It was Vidal, a quiet, little, oldish man who, in an office on the floor beneath, practised the nearly extinct art of wood-engraving for such scientific journals as needed clearly detailed pictures, instead of the cheaper dot and smudge variety. Usually he was staid and self-contained, but now, and little wonder, he was livid and shaking with terror.

"They're coming up!" he screamed. "Shut that window! We're done for! I saw 'em once before, but nothing like this!"

Mayence grabbed him by the shoulders and shook him roughly.

"What?" he shouted. "What the blazes is it?"

"Ants!" quavered Vidal. "Millions of trillions! They're stinging everyone to death; keep 'em out!"

It was well for us then that Mayence had piloted racing automobiles; a practice that breeds quick thinking. He didn't stop to question the truth of the statement, but shook his man a trifle harder.

"Will paraffin keep them off?" he demanded.

Vidal nodded.

"Perhaps," he said hoarsely.

"Lucky I brought a big 'un, then!" growled Mayence, and leapt at his oil-drum. "Rags, Tom, a brush, paper—anything! Bathe in it!"

In a twinkling he had the bung out and tipped a pool of thick, yellow, evil smelling, crude petroleum on the floor by the door, spreading it with his handkerchief over every crevice.

"Mother Partington, Atlantic Ocean!" he grunted, snatched a towel, and stuffed a soaked strip beneath the door. "Window, you cripples! Buck up!"

We worked like demons. As a motive-power there is nothing to excel fear; and yet though we wrought swiftly, smearing the sashes and every visible joint in our defences, the ants were already darkening the panes ere we had finished.

"Kill them! Quick!" shrieked Vidal suddenly, pointing. "There!"

From under the skirting-board a score of large ants, near an inch and a half long, came boldly at us, travelling rapidly, halted at the edge of the puddle in which we stood, and sped swiftly back again.

"Don't like it, by jingo!" Mayence shouted exultantly. "Magic circle, spread it out!"

It was done. Panting, soaked with oil and sweat, hardly able to breathe because of the stink, we stood up, saved; perhaps the sole surviving witnesses of that first outburst, since it would appear that parties of the ants invaded every building, slaying relentlessly every human being they encountered. Us they let alone after the first trial; and presently, when the panes cleared, being nearly suffocated, we ventured to open the window.

Speech became possible.

"Don't lean out!" Mayence warned me. "Some of the brutes might drop on you!"

Standing on a chair well withdrawn from the casement, I looked forth. Within my circumscribed view I could see the dead photographer and several of the others on the further side, the top of the 'bus with its lifeless load, and a taxicab wedged into a shop window, its engine still running, the driving wheels slithering and grinding on the pavement. At several open windows men hung or sprawled. The air reverberated with a vast noise; the voices of fearful thousands roaring from every point of the compass beat painfully on the ears; but silently, the cause of it, the river of ants, still flowed from the excavation, each yard of it an army, dividing into streams, which went their way west and east without pause.

"Jumping Jupiter!" exclaimed Mayence, mounting behind me. "It's unbelievable! It's—it's a hallucination."

"It isn't," said Vidal. "I saw something like it in Venezuela once, when I went with a collecting expedition. They kept on for a day and a night, and though they weren't so poisonous as these, everything had to get out of their way or perish. Perhaps they've come out in other places, too."

A duty we had neglected came to my mind, and I jumped from my chair and rushed to the phone.

"Exchange!" I yelled. "Are you there? Are you there?"

There was no answer, though I called again and again. My belated attempt at warning was useless.

"Death everywhere," murmured Vidal.

"Or else the gels have scooted," suggested Mayence. "Don't be too infernally gloomy."

"Perhaps it's the beginning of the end for the human race," persisted the little man.

"Rot!" cried Mayence. "It's horribly bad, of course, but that couldn't happen. A lot of damned insects!"

"And they'll soon be settled," said I. "Squirt acids or poisons on them, or—"

"Or set a dog at them," sneered Vidal. "D'you think they'd stand still and let you do it? Look at the pace they can go. And they've got brains, I'm certain. What if this has all been arranged? Why, I'll bet they're all over the town—other towns, too; perhaps other countries."

We cried out at this monstrous suggestion, yet—though, of course, we didn't know it at the time—he wasn't far out in his estimate of the abominations. He warmed to his dismal theme.

"Even if they're driven back underground for the moment, how are you going to keep them there. Nice job it'll be to make every house ant-proof. And walking about in armoured clothes, or soaked with anticide, will be pleasant, won't it?"

"But they die off or go to sleep in the winter, don't they?" I suggested.

"How d'you know this kind will? Anyhow, they've got lots of time before them. How many of us will live 'til the first frost? How about harvesting, and tending sheep and cattle? We'll all starve if we're not killed. It's a conquest, an arranged business, I tell you. Perhaps some of us will be kept as slaves. There are species who have others to wait on them—"

"Will you shut up?" roared Mayence. "We're in the devil's own pickle, without being driven daft by your maunderings! What d'you reckon we'd better do, Tom? Stay here 'til the siege is raised?"

"How about the river?" I asked hopefully. "The oil keeps the beasts off. If we soaked ourselves, we might get there all right and find a boat."

"Probably a few thousand others have found it already," he chuckled grimly; "and a few billions of our little friends appear to have gone in the same direction. It's risky every way."

We all stared gloomily at that ceaseless torrent of venomous life, pouring, pouring silently, swiftly, with an ordered purpose. Against uncountable myriads so devilishly endowed, what had man to oppose? I could think of no adequate defence.

"Perhaps you're right, Vidal," I said. "One hopes of course. But—"

"Have you got anything to eat or drink?" Mayence interrupted. "We must keep our pecker up."

"Biscuits, whisky, soda—that's all," said I, producing them. And we ate and drank unpleasantly, each mouthful being tainted with the all-pervading petroleum, then stared out of the window again.

"The noise is dying down, I think," said Vidal at length. "But what's that racket overhead?"

Mayence listened.

"Somebody breaking the law. An aeroplane coming—over there, see? By jove! It's the old training 'bus, the biplane at Hendon. What the dickens are they after?"

Moving quite slowly, the 'plane hove in sight, skimming dangerously near the housetops, one of the two men in her apparently searching the ground with field-glasses. Mayence snatched up the linen overall I wore when working,

tied a sleeve to a walking stick, and thrust it outside, waving 'til the airman saw it, and, putting a big megaphone
to his head, shouted something which was drowned by the
rattle of the engine. Slowly the machine swung about over
the pit, a small, dark object fell from it, and—"crash!" a
mighty spout of dust flew up, concrete foundation walls
and scaffold-poles crumbled and rocked, tinkling glass fell
in showers. The man in the plane had dropped a bomb
into the ants' portal.

With the explosion their columns broke, thinned, and
vanished into doorways, the drains and crevices; in twenty
seconds they were all under cover. The 'plane circled out
of sight, returned, and this time we caught something of
what the megaphone bawled to us: ". . . in a dozen places
. . . going to shut 'em down . . . all right soon." We
waved an answer, they shot away, and in a few minutes we
heard the smack of another bomb, followed at intervals by
others, each more distant.

"A dozen places!" exclaimed Vidal. "What did I say? It's
an organised invasion. A fat lot of good those chaps have
done. See!"

The side of the crater made by the explosion began to
heave and crumble, a dark spot appeared and grew larger,
and long before the sound of the last detonation came to
us the ant river was flowing again, steadily as though it
had never been so rudely interrupted.

Mayence mumbled disgustedly, and faced about. "Question is, what are we going to do? Stay and starve, or take
the risk of going out?"

"They won't touch us," said I confidently.

"Don't be too sure. Some of them, maybe, will sacrifice
themselves on the off-chance of getting a bite home. At
all events, I'll go out first and reconnoitre." But at this
Vidal and I protested, and in the end we drew lots. The
short match fell to me, and I confess to feeling horribly

uncomfortable, but I managed to conceal my feelings whilst I was smeared anew with the abominably smelling oil; my boots were soaked 'til they squelched at every step; face, hair, cap, and gloves, all were saturated, and Mayence finished me off by tying a dripping duster around my neck. "In case they drop on you from aloft," he explained. "Now you're all right. We'll get ready while you're gone."

I opened the door gingerly. At the edge of the landing was a group of ants, several score, big fellows, with their heads turned towards me; simultaneously, they darted forward, came almost to my feet—and retreated. Instinctively I squashed the hindmost. "All serene!" I cried. "They won't face it," and slithered down the first flight to find another and larger vidette, which behaved exactly like the others. I had no more fear after that, but went on confidently as a medieval knight in armour of proof hewing his way through a mob of peasants.

On the first floor I peeped into the office of Wardell, an advertising agent, and saw what was left of him lying back in his chair, a half-open sample tin of insect killer on the floor beside him; evidently he had bethought him of this defence at the last moment. The ants were swarming all over him, and I turned away hastily, feeling very sick; it is a shocking thing to see a man you have known and swapped drinks with in process of disintegration. Yet the sight served to diminish the shock I received when I found the entry and the lower stairs completely choked with bodies. I went back and reported, and, since there was no other way, we at last let ourselves down by a rope from the window of Wardell's room, after lowering the precious oil-drum, now half empty, and set foot in a Fleet Street transmogrified to the semblance of a battlefield.

Perhaps a soldier hardened to slaughter could have supported the spectacle, but to us it was near overwhelming. Remember that the view from my office was circumscribed by projecting buildings on either side, and that the portion of street it commanded was abandoned at the first outrush, so that what we had seen before was as nothing compared with what confronted us.

Looking westward, the street was filled from side to side with a horrible barricade, vehicles of all sorts piled and wedged together in inextricable confusion, for a base; and over, under, between, shaken together and trembling to the throb of the engines still working beneath, were piled the dead.

From the accounts since collected it would seem that on this fatal day the ants emerged from the earth, not in a dozen, but in scores of places, from each of which they diverged on either hand, killing as they went, 'til they met the columns of their fellows, and so ringed Central London in a cordon of poison, whilst from other points within the circle other hordes spread devastatingly 'til hardly a nook or corner remained unvisited.

Of the millions of folks so surrounded, comparatively few escaped, and those, curiously enough, mainly by the underground railways, which were let alone for some time; but the majority of the people fled panic-stricken from one army only to encounter another, and most often met their fate struggling amidst maddened crowds.

Horror left us dumb for a little, then Mayence, hugging his oil-drum, turned towards Ludgate Circus, and we followed in silence. With us, on either hand, marched thousands of ants at a respectful distance, and so we came to Bridge Street, and the first survivor, a telephone linesman, slung in a travelling cradle from the cables crossing the road. Intent upon our steps, we were startled by his hoarse cry from aloft: "Hi mates!" he called.

"Can you let yourself down?" answered Mayence. "We've got stuff to keep them off. Come along."

The man became frantically busy with a coil of wire.

"Righto!" he yelled. "Just a minute."

There was a sudden commotion amongst our escort, a thin brown thread shot up the façade of the building directly below the poles supporting the telephone wires.

"They know!" exclaimed Vidal. "They're after him. Quick, man, or they'll get you yet."

Mayence stood ready with his oil, the linesman dropped the end of his cable almost to our feet, unbuckled the strap which held him in the cradle, wound his cap about the wire, gave one unearthly scream, and fell smashing to the pavement. I think he was dead before he reached the ground.

We trudged on towards the river without a word; pity, horror, terror, all capacity for emotion seemed numbed to exhaustion, and we moved mechanically. Blackfriars Bridge was choked by another dreadful barricade, the approaches to the stations were impassable. The river was dotted with people swimming or clinging to lifebuoys or fragments of wood, the barges anchored on the further side were hidden by men clustering like swarming bees, the outermost continually dragged down by others who struggled up from the water; the *President,* the old Naval Volunteer training ship, lay low in the water, weighed down by the numbers aboard her, and dozens clung to her cables fore and aft. I saw one man maintaining possession of a packing-case, which barely supported him, with bloody knife; a dinghy drifted by, laden with women and one man, who threatened any who approached it with a revolver. As they neared the bridge the arch under which they must pass grew black, and though we shouted, the warning was unheard, or unheeded, the insect death rained down, the boat capsized, and we saw no more.

Nearly half an hour we stood there, hypnotised, the petroleum escaping from our saturated clothes and gathering in little pools around our feet, whilst the ants clustered thick in a semicircle behind and darted continually to and fro along the parapet in front, angry perhaps because we had so long escaped them. Then a river steamer without a living soul aboard, though her deck was piled, came in sight, her paddles revolving slowly, swinging uncertainly from side to side of the river, 'til she brought up with a crash on the piles of a wharf and began to settle down.

With the noise we awoke to a realisation of a new peril; London town was on fire. Heavy smoke clouds were drawing across the sun, rolling south-eastward before a rising breeze.

"Nobody to stop it," said I. "But at least some of those infernal things'll get roasted."

"They'll go underground 'til it's over," Vidal said.

"We'll go up with the first spark," said Mayence.

"Can you swim?"

He shook his head.

"Not a stroke."

"And Tom is equal to about a hundred yards. We'll have to make a float of some kind and keep under water going through the bridges; we'll get below these for a start, anyhow. Come on."

With our abominable guard still in attendance we turned our backs on the river, and by great good fortune found the roadway underneath the railway viaduct passable, though we had to climb over many vehicles. The smoke grew even thicker, and we could scarce see our way, but it appeared noxious to the ants, who thinned away and had quite disappeared ere luck brought us to the end of a short street and a little wharf.

"Here we are," said Mayence. "And there are planks and rope. We'll make a raft of sorts. Hurry!"

Somehow, in no very workmanlike fashion to be sure, since we groped in pungent semi-darkness, we got our raft together and launched. It was high time; we were half suffocated, and the flames, spreading unchecked with frightful rapidity, roared near at hand as, sitting awash, we started on our voyage, Mayence, sitting aft, paddling with a short board 'til the mid stream caught us, and we were swept swiftly forward, unable to see more than a yard or two ahead.

Soon a dark mass loomed above us, the raft swerved, we shot through a bridge—Southwark—and never an ant materialised. Either we passed unseen or they had gone before the smother.

"Three more to pass, and we're all right," grunted Mayence.

"Look out! Shove off!" A barge drifting beam-on lay in our path. Vidal howled, thrust out a leg pushing with all his might. We bumped once, and went clear without receiving boarders. I needn't describe what we glimpsed in passing, nor what we presently saw as we circled in the swirl of the Cannon Street railway bridge; suffice it to say that many had sought refuge upon its floating fenders—in vain.

Below was a red flare of flaming warehouses belching showers of sparks, yet none reached us, and we whirled blindly on in the black, smothering smoke blanket, passed beneath London Bridge without seeing it, and narrowly missed running full tilt into an anchored boat, perilously laden with folks, who yelled in chorus as we rasped across their cable; two men with oars out tugged dementedly, another fool struck wildly with a boathook, smote his iron deep into one of our planks and nearly capsized the lot.

"Let go, you idiot!" roared Mayence, whilst the water licked their gunwale, and, fortunately for them, he obeyed, and we parted company, losing sight of them instantly.

Vidal levered the hook clear and crouched ready to fend off from what might come next. With ebb and current together the stream was a race, and we should have fared badly had we encountered anything moored; but our amazing good fortune held, and though we caught sight of many craft, and heard voices all about us, we kept clear of everything 'til, about the neighbourhood of Deptford, the smoke thinned and we could see our fellow-men once more.

Either margin of the river was lined with people standing in the water, knee-deep, waist-deep, up to the neck; beyond these a floating fringe, then boats and rafts, all loaded nearly to sinking; and the voice of their misery was a continuous giant groan, a deep, plaintive note of despair, such as I hope never to hear again. Of the people in boats around, none heeded us, except to curse when we fouled them; but after I had picked up the blade of a broken oar, we kept a better course, and had no more collisions.

"We must get as far down as we can before the tide turns," Mayence explained; and we paddled our best 'til in the broad reach a little below Greenwich, we met a flotilla of torpedo boats. Half dead with fatigue, blistered all over by the oil which had saved our lives at the expense of our skins, we were hauled aboard the first, and stowed in the narrow quarters below, already crowded with refugees, whilst the boats steamed into the smoky pall to rescue all they might, and when they were loaded, dropped down river and decanted us into the cruisers, battleships, and liners anchored about Tilbury.

All night the work went on, and all night and for many days thereafter London blazed unchecked. Of a forlorn hope of bluejackets who went ashore with the intention of blowing up buildings to stop its progress, only two returned, and by the end of a week a great part of the Empire city lay in ruins.

On the night of our rescue, our cruiser set out in company with a fleet of all kinds of vessels, and in the early morning we were landed at Yarmouth, which for the moment was out of the danger zone, and thence we went by train to Glasgow, where I had some friends. The journey took over two days, so you may guess the congestion and confusion that reigned everywhere. I believe that the Norfolk Broads, the Fen country, and many sheltered bays and estuaries grew populous, thousands of people returning to the primitive style of lake dwellings, and building themselves huts upon piles or rafts.

But the most part believed only in flight, and the roads were black with fugitive multitudes who could find no place on the overburdened railroads; if the ants had followed up their first onslaught with the speed of which they were capable, I think it probable that the whole island would have been depopulated.

Perhaps the burning of London disconcerted them, or they had the strategical sense to reduce the country in their rear before going further; at all events, they made no move northward for over a week, but during that time overran the country to the south of a line between the Thames and the Severn estuary, methodically slaughtering flocks, herds, and those unfortunates who had not escaped over the Channel or fortified themselves in some such fashion as we had done.

Then they flooded northward, but by that the country had been cleared before them, and at the Avon-Welland line they were brought to a full stop for a while. Every bridge was defended, and along the banks and in the gap about Naseby, where once a very different battle had been fought, hundreds of fire-engines pumping blazing petroleum went into action, and thousands of men fought right gallantly with hand-pumps and squirts. Surely it was the strangest battle that the world had seen, bloodless but deadly, so potent being the poison, that to be stung meant death before cautery or antidote could be used. For days it continued, the ants tunnelling beneath the rivers' beds at many points, emerging oftentimes amongst thickets or coverts far in the rear of the firing line, and there, ringed about by the reserves, to be driven to earth again.

Across the country from sea to sea was stretched a broad band of fire-scoured earth, miles wide, and by this frontier the invasion is for the moment stayed, at the price of constant, unremitting vigilance, though none knows what the future has in store. Even the most optimistic of our experts, Professor Guy Durham, is gloomy.

"Our real knowledge of the earth's crust is small," he remarks in his report "and a poor mile the limit of our shafts. What fissures, crevices, caverns, lie beneath us we know not at all, but it may very well be that, in the four thousand miles from surface to centre, many such occur. London, it is surmised, lies in part above a great subterranean lake, and it requires but a small effort to imagine such regions inhabited."

He goes on to details of our enemy's anatomy: *F. Horribilis,* as it has been dubbed, is in many respects entirely different from and vastly superior to its sun-loving brother, having a marvellously complex brain, excellent smelling apparatus, and, a somewhat unusual endowment for a subterranean creature, well developed eyes. In fact, the thing is altogether a super-ant, and he comes to a conclusion not hard to credit under the circumstances.

"I have no hesitation in announcing my conviction that *Horribilis* is an intellectual, a rational creature, able to plan, to reason, and, as we have so terribly experienced, to act in combination. I am of opinion that their aggression is a deliberate attack upon human supremacy, intolerable though such a suggestion may be to our self-satisfaction; but, taking into consideration their means of offence, their proved skill as miners, and the immense fecundity of such allied species as we know, I am forced to the forlorn conclusion that mankind may, at no very distant date, be compelled to struggle hard for very existence. And, lest we grow over-confident in our present defences, I am bound to point out that, if analogy holds good, our feeble barriers of fire and water may presently be passed, if not underground, then by the path of the air. Both the male and female of the ant, at one period of their lives, are winged!"

The Horror of Johnson's Flats
Arundel "Andrul" Begbie (1914)
Illustrated by Thomas Somerfield

This is a story of America. Most of the big things come from America, and this is a big thing in the way of horrors. I am well qualified to judge, for I saw it in all its grim nakedness, and in my past years I have seen much that was terrible. It is a story of sixty years ago, and has been forgotten in the rush and hustle of life as lived in America. Even the name "Johnson's Flats" has disappeared, giving place to that of Moving Lake City, and nobody, I expect, besides myself, knows that there was an earlier name. To-day the people there—and there are more than a few, owing to the discovery of silver—see the lake penned in by its steep, precipitous sides, its waters ever swirling from north to south, and recognize it as the obvious sponsor of the place, but not one of them doubts that that lake was always there. I saw it come into being.

The terror of that time is always with me. I have tried to forget it, and, amongst other means to that end, have never talked about it, but I see it always. At times my wife wakes me in the night and tells me that I have been tossing and groaning in my sleep. On such occasions she will say: "Why, John, you're all in a sweat! Something's disagreed with you. You must be more careful what you eat."

She is right. Something *has* disagreed with me, but it is nothing which has passed my lips. It is what has passed my eyes which has disagreed with my mind, and harries my brain even in sleep!

Johnson's Flats was the name given to a plateau some three hundred feet above the rest of the plain, and it was so called because old Steve Johnson was the first to erect a log-hut and start a horse ranch thereon. It was about ten miles long, running east and west, gently sloping at the extremities to the level of the plain below. It was a little under five miles from north to south. On the north side it stood up boldly from above the plain in an almost perpendicular cliff three hundred feet high, save where it sloped to the plain at its eastern and western extremities, as I have already said. Towards its southern limit it also sloped gently to the plain below.

Now, a strange fact connected with that flat was that, on the north, a river one hundred and twenty feet in width ran with a moderate current from the north straight into the cliff which formed the northern boundary of Johnson's Fats, and there it disappeared into that same cliff as a drain disappears under a culvert. Where it goes to Heaven knows, for, as far as man knows, that is the last of it in this world; that is, if one excepts Moving Lake.

There were only eight of us on Johnson's Flats in my day. There was Sam Johnson, son of old Steve—dead some years before my time; there was Mike O'Grady, who bred cattle and worked a stone quarry in a desultory way between whiles. There were two brothers, Angus and Alick Scott—their names witness whence they came—and they worked for Johnson. There was a Frenchman, come from Canada, whose name I never knew. We all called him Jack, because his Christian name was Jacques. He worked for O'Grady. There was Splotch Elin, the biggest man I have ever seen. He could hold a buck-board steady from behind, with his great arms, the while a horse strained to draw it away from him—I have seen him do it. He had a small ranch on the east of the plateau, which he managed by himself. Another of Johnson's men was Abe, who professed to be a half-breed Indian, but whom we considered to be a deal more Indian than anything else. And, last, there was I, just turned twenty, and was from home, having spent four years on Johnson's ranch.

Work filled our days, and there is no need to describe it. That is not what I started to tell of when I took up my pen to write. One day was just like another.

Every now and then we would hear queer noises under the ground, the same as if there were some giant there ill at ease, and these, Abe would say, were due to the river, which, he would have it, flowed underneath the plateau to a certain point, where it fell through a chasm into the bowels of the earth. Lately I have heard that scientific men assert that it eventually finds its way into the Silver Streak River away south, but that is as it may be.

It was the year of the first big drought that the first hint of the horror came to us. It was a parching season; the ground cracked with the heat, and the grass was like so much brown wire, when it should have been soft, juicy green. Many evenings the clouds would come up dark and lowering, and we would rejoice in the thought that at last the long dry spell was ending; but in the morning the sky would be a cloudless, pitiless glare of blue, and only a slight dew on the grass would testify to the grounds for our blighted hopes.

The underground noises grew very loud at times, almost like muffled thunder-claps; and then one day the Frenchman, Jack, comes into the hut in which Johnson, the Scotts, and I lived, and says, as excitedly as if the world had come to an end:—

"My word, boys, there's a hole in the ground over by Lone Tree, for all the world like a well!"

We all went off hot-foot to see this wonder, for such a happening in the monotony of those days was a welcome excitement. Lone Tree was one of the few trees on the flats, and was but a poor tree at that. Now it stood bare of its leaves, which had wilted and dropped dry from its boughs. It was almost three-quarters of a mile from our hut, and close to the track which led to Red Wood, the nearest township.

There, sure enough, was an opening in the ground for all the world like a well—a badly-made well. It was roughly circular, with a diameter of ten feet. None of us measured it, but the eye learns to be accurate to inches in those solitudes of the earth, just as it learns to tell the time without a watch. The edges of the hole were fretted with small fissures running away here and there into the baked surface of the ground.

I was young then, and a greater fool than now—though the Lord knows I do not boast of much wisdom to-day, in spite of my eighty years—and I walked straight up to the hole and looked over the edge into the blackness. The sides of it—till lost in gloom—were raw earth, and there was a noise, far away out of sight, like the lapping of water at the bows of a boat. Yachtsmen know the sound well, and love it.

"Come away, Slam!"—that's what they called me—shouted out Alick Scott. "Some more may fall in at any moment. Keep away from the edge. Don't be a fool."

"I'm all right," I answered, in the foolish pride of my youth.

"Come back, you blamed idiot!" shouted Johnson, and I returned unwillingly, as he was my boss and could give me orders.

We talked much of that hole. Such a happening was a godsend as a topic in a place like that. The horses and the cattle passing near it—attracted, I suspect, by the scent or sound of the water at its bottom—would try to get to it, and we had to keep them away from it. It had been there six weeks or so before the rain fell in sweet, heavy showers which greened the whole country for a time, and, in the rejoicing at this mercy, the hole in the ground lost most of its importance and assumed the matter-of-fact which familiarity brings with it. We still gave it a fairly wide berth, for fear of more ground falling in, but that was all.

It was the succeeding year that the horror came in all its grim reality. It was just such another year as the last had been—if anything, worse, and we were kept hard at it to tend our poor animals. We had to fetch water all the way from Red Wood, for our little spring dried up.

We were very miserable in those days, and there was a gloomy pessimism hanging over us. The only one who succeeded in giving us an occasional cheerful sentiment was Jack, the Frenchman. He was a well-plucked one if ever there was, and I verily believe would have smiled on the rack! So the sadness of the event was emphasized when he disappeared. He had set off walking to the township early one morning, with the intention of returning at night. He would not ride, for we spared our horses what we possibly could, as the bringing of water gave them all the work they could manage. The next morning there was no Jack, and we did not scruple to suggest an explanation for his delay in returning which was not overflattering to his sobriety and morals.

"I don't blame him," said Sam Johnson. "Who the deuce would want to hurry back to this blistered potsherd?"

"Sure you wouldn't be blaming him!" ejaculated O'Grady. "You haven't a sight of foine cattle waiting to be seen to, and it's not for *you* he works!"

"Go easy, man," put in Angus Scott. "He'll be turning up before the day's out."

"Maybe he will, maybe he won't," answered O'Grady; "and a lot of use he'll be when he does! He'll have alcohol over his back-teeth. I know these quiet chaps when they do go on the jamboree!"

We all laughed.

That same morning Splotch Elin, the two Scotts, and I went into Red Wood to get water. We were to bring some for O'Grady, as the absence of Jack kept him to his cattle. Strangely enough, we made no inquiries concerning the absentee in the township. The fact was we had infinitely more serious things to talk about to the few acquaintances we foregathered with. The drought and its effects on individuals was the one topic of conversation; and, besides, we had never regarded Jack's absence as a serious matter. However, when we got back to the flats, and called to leave the water at O'Grady's place, the owner hailed us with:—

"Seen Jack?"

"Hasn't he come back?" we chorused, in astonishment.

"No. Didn't you hear of him over at Red Wood?"

"Never thought of asking for him, Mike," said Alick Scott. "Thought he'd have been back long ago."

"All right, boys. I'll go into the township to-morrow, if he's not back before, and the saints help him when I catch him! I'll teach the little devil to go on the spree when there's work here for half-a-dozen men!"

The Frenchman did not return during that day, and the next morning O'Grady went off to search for him, muttering threats of vengeance.

At sundown we had all foregathered to swop talk—though it was more companionship than talk, for we mostly smoked in silence—and to take a little ease after the work of the day, when we saw O'Grady coming across the flats to us—alone!

We awaited him without greeting, a sense of foreboding keeping us in an unusual silence. O'Grady's face was set.

"He's lit out—the skunk! No wonder he was so blamed cheerful! I guess he could manage to laugh all right when he'd figgered to get out of this drought. If ever I come across Master Jack it will be well for him if there are plenty of witnesses. I'll shoot him like the cur he is if I find him alone!"

He was nearly mad with passion. There was a good reason for his rage. He stood to lose everything if he lost his cattle, and, though one man might have managed to look after his animals for a time in ordinary years, to do so during the drought, with all the extra work entailed, was an impossibility.

"See here, Mike," said Sam Johnson; "one of us will give you a hand with the cattle till Jack turns up. He'll turn up again all right, for sure. He's just having a beano, no more, I guess. Abe can help you, can't you, Abe, till then?"

Abe nodded his head in silence.

"That's good of you, Sam—particularly now when you want all you've got to run your own show. I'll be right glad if Abe will come along," he said, his face brightening as he saw the dawn of a new hope.

"How do you know Jack has gone for good?" Alick Scott asked, in his slow, considering way.

"I asked in the township. He hadn't been on the spree, and had left these at six in the evening, saying he was coming back here. Well, he'd have fetched up here about midnight if he had come. No, old hoss, he meant to go, and he's gone, sure."

"When a man means to go, he takes his best with him," pursued the unconvinced, logical, and argumentative Scott. "I saw Jack that morning on his way to Red Wood, and he had on his oldest clothes, his boots with the rawhide patches, and was carrying nothing. What's he left behind?"

"I dunno. There's his box," said O'Grady, with the air of a man who considered the matter too obvious to dispute.

"Say, you just look in his box when you get back," answered the Scotsman. "You'll likely learn what it all means. If he has taken his hook, he'll have left a letter for you— see? If he has gone, and meant to go, you'll not find any money, or anything like that."

"Yes, I might look in the box," assented O'Grady.

Abe put his outfit together, and accompanied the Irishman to his hut that same evening, which enabled the latter to come over again next morning. Sam Johnson and I were in the corral when he walked up to its bars, and he called us to him with a beckoning nod of his head.

"Say, it's a bit queer, but the little beggar's left all his dollars in his box, beside other things a man don't usually care to part with. And what's more," he went on, after a pause, "I'm durned if he ain't left his gun behind."

That a man travelling far in those days should do so without his revolver was inconceivable.

"Well, what do you make of it?" asked Johnson.

"I don't know," said O'Grady, morosely. "Appears to me he must have meant to go, or else why ain't he here? What was there to stop his coming back if he wanted to? There ain't no Red Injuns, there ain't no robbers around, and it's a straight track. And there again, he's left all his money, his gun, and a bundle of letters which I know he set special store by, for he was for ever reading them over and over again, and when another came it was put in that pile with as much care as if it had been a bank-note."

The next morning to this the first glimpse of the horror came to me. Abe arrived after breakfast, and it so happened that I was the only one in the hut, it being my turn to do the cooking—such as it was. He was looking almost more surly than usual.

"No signs of Jack yet?" I asked him.

"Yes, the *signs* are there," he answered, darkly.

"What signs?" I asked, excitedly.

"Come and see," he replied, and, getting off the table, sauntered out of the door.

I knew hint well enough to know that I should get nothing more out of his taciturnity until he had made his disclosure in his own way and time. He took me past the well—as we called the chasm near Lone Tree—for about a quarter of a mile, then he went on his hands and knees, and tried to make me see a footprint which he asserted was Jack's, and four days old. I could not see it. We retraced our steps a yard or two, and then he drew my attention to another footprint. This time it was plain enough in the dust of the track, and I agreed with him that it was not more than four days old, and might well be Jack's. Thence onward the track could be followed without difficulty, for though an occasional footprint was missing, there was always one within sight to lead one aright, and the nearer we got to the well the plainer the prints became, owing to the nature of the surface soil. Then, when about a hundred paces from the well, the trail suddenly ceased.

To me there was only one inference.

"Abe, he must have fallen into the well! There was no moon that night, and the poor chap must have left the trail, and—"

"Yes, he left the trail all right," said Abe, quietly, and with meaning, *"but not on his feet!"*

"What do you mean, Abe?" I exclaimed.

"Well, he left it in the air. Anyway, his feet were off the ground. You can see for yourself that the tracks stop dead short, *leading to nowhere."*

"When did you find the tracks?"

"This morning as I came along here."

We talked long about it, as may be imagined, I hazarding what seemed to me possible explanations, Abe silent except when he spoke to prove them impossible. He would say nothing in the way of elucidation. I knew his sensitiveness to ridicule, especially about some of his inherited superstitions, and I do not doubt that this kept him from expressing his own beliefs.

The others went with me, later on in the afternoon, to examine the tracks. They were all agreed that it was poor Jack's last trail, and there was a general consensus of opinion that he must have strayed from the track in the dark and stumbled into the well.

When I pointed out what Abe had drawn my attention to they scoffed at any but a natural explanation, and Sam Johnson said:—

"There's no mystery about that. The ground's different, that's all. See here"—and he took two or three steps towards the well to demonstrate the simplicity of it, but his steps left clean-cut tracks. "Well, that's queer!" he ejaculated. "But, all the same, you ain't going to persuade me Jack went there except on his feet."

Some few days after this Abe came across to our hut at dinner-time, and, during the after-smoking, he said, suddenly:—

"Say, you know how we used to have to drive the cattle and horses away from that well when they were grazing or passing round about that way? Well, yesterday I had a couple of O'Grady's steers over the trail, and when they came within a few yards of where Jack's tracks broke off they got that skeered I couldn't force them along nohow."

"How do you mean 'skeered'? What did they do?" asked Johnson.

"Ever see a cow when it is being driven into the slaughter-yard, and gets the scent of what has been done in there? Well, it was like that. The poor beasts were nigh mad with fear."

"Well, what of it?" queried Johnson, with a challenge in his voice. He stood to lose most if the flats got a bad reputation.

"Oh, nothing," said Abe, softly. Then he added, after a pause: "Only at one time you could hardly keep the animals off it."

The well began to exercise a sort of fascination for me after that, and I found myself frequently in its neighbourhood. About a week after Abe's story of his steers I was going to Red Wood, and had made a very early start. When I came near to the well, what was my amazement to see dark marks on the burnt-up ground, radiating from the hole. I approached as near as my fears would allow me, to investigate the phenomenon. I found there were five of the marks, and they were simply caused by moisture on the ground, as if dew had fallen on those five spots alone. But the extraordinary part of it was that there was no dew elsewhere. The marks were five in number and regular in design, being broad near the well and tapering to points at the extremities, which I reckoned to be a hundred paces from the edge of the hole. There was, however, no symmetry in the pattern. One mark stretched out from one side of the hole, the other four from the opposite side.

I puzzled over this experience all my way to the township and back, but could hit on no possible explanation. When I came near the well on my return journey there were no traces of the marks. I said no word of this to the others for fear of ridicule, but the next day I rose early on purpose to go and look at the well, and there, sure enough, were the marks—but only three this time, and one of them, instead of being straight, was very distinctly curved.

Whenever there was nothing particular to do I found my steps turning instinctively to Lone Tree, where I could gaze and gaze at the hole in the ground, as if I expected momentarily to see the solution of the mystery.

The damp marks were very frequently there on the ground in the early dawns when I visited the place, but never at other times of the day. Eventually I took Abe into my confidence. I knew he would not laugh at me. The effect of my story was almost grotesque. He literally shook with fear, and his eyes were eloquent of terror. When I suggested that he and I should sit up the next moonlit night to see how the marks were made he shivered visibly, and vigorously ejaculated:—

"No, no, no! Leave the blamed thing alone. Don't you meddle with it. It ain't the thing to play fool-tricks with anyhow. Leave it alone; leave it alone!"

Two days after my talk with Abe, tragedy befell us. Splotch Elin came over in the evening, after his hard day's work was finished, to Johnson's hut. We had not seen him for some days, as his tired muscles clamoured loudly for bed at each day's end, and it was a fair step from his little ranch; but loneliness out there will, at times, become unbearable, and will drive men to any efforts to see their fellows and hear human voices. It is partly this, and not all mere animalism, which accounts for the jamboree and beano.

We had a little whisky that night—not a great deal, but more than usual, and sufficient to loosen my tongue. As Splotch Elin made to go, with drunken seriousness I impressed on him to be very careful to give the well a wide berth when he neared Lone Tree, telling him that I had seen marks of some uncanny being on the ground there, and that there was certainly some monster dwelling in the hole. There was a certain amount of laughter, and I saw Splotch Elin wink at the others as he took off his coat and bent up his mighty forearm to swell the biceps muscle.

"See that, boy?" he asked me.

I replied that I saw it.

"Well," he went on, "I've never met the man who could not be persuaded by it, nor any devil either, as far as that goes; and if anything comes out of that hole within the reach of my arm—well, its funeral will take place there and then."

The others laughed, but I had all the affronted dignity of the half-drunken man, and warned him again:—

"All right, Splotch, all right. You may laugh, but I've warned you, and it's God's truth I've told you about those marks on the ground. If you don't heed me, you'll be sorry for it."

"That's all right, sonny," he laughed back. "Perhaps you'd better run on ahead and whisper down the hole to say who's coming. If it takes on Splotch Elin unknowing-like, it may find out it has bitten off a bit more than it can chew."

More laughter greeted this sally, and he left us for his dark, lonely tramp.

Two days later Angus Scott and I were out watering some of Johnson's horses, when we saw other animals approaching from the direction of Splotch's ranch. We watched this new portent anxiously. If there is one thing a man learns to do on a horse ranch it is to recognize horses, and we were able to identify these beasts when they were still a good way off. They were Splotch's lot, right enough—the whole of them. They came on with all the boldness of timid animals made brave for a brief space by stress of circumstances, snorting and throwing up their heads, as is the custom of horses under such an experience. When they got quite near, some of them neighed to our lot, and these made answer; then apparently reassured by the noisy welcome, the newcomers hurriedly approached the water-troughs and drank thirstily.

A sickening certainty flashed into my mind.

"Angus," I said, "Splotch has been taken, for sure—just like poor Jack. Oh, why wouldn't he listen to me when I warned him?"

"Was that true about those marks on the ground?" he asked, earnestly. "We all thought it was the whisky talking."

"True?" I retorted, angrily. "Of course it's true. Do you think I am a fool or a liar?"

"Man, I thought you were just drunk; but I know you're sober enough now. Why didn't you tell us about it, though?"

I tried to explain to the best of my ability, but it has never been easy to me to put my feelings into words, and I felt the lameness of my excuses even as I uttered them.

"Well, it doesn't follow that there is anything wrong with Splotch," said Angus, when I had concluded. "It is more than possible that he forgot to quench the poor beasts' thirst before he went off to Red Wood to get his water, and that's why they came here."

But I knew better. I knew as well as if I had witnessed the happening that, when we looked, we should see poor Splotch's tracks end as abruptly as had those of the Frenchman. It was a two-days' drought which had driven his thirst-tortured horses over to us. I felt sure of it, and my conviction impressed Angus Scott sufficiently to induce him to return to the hut and catch the other two before they set out on the daily journey for water. Both Johnson and Alick Scott professed scepticism as to anything having happened to Elin, but as they were about to set out with the water-teams for Red Wood they agreed that we should accompany them as far as Lone Tree in order to see if there were any explanatory tracks there, and afterwards to go to Splotch Elin's ranch to investigate.

Sure enough there were the tracks, just as I knew they would be. They were plainly visible up to a certain point, and then they ceased as suddenly as if poor Elin had flown straight away into space.

Angus and I left the others a little farther on, and made our way to Elin's. Of course, the place was deserted, and his hut contained all the pathos begotten of the common-place belongings of the dead—a dead friend.

Angus and I stood for some moments in silence, realizing what it all meant, then he said, quietly, but with a world of reproach in his voice:—

"Slam, you ought to have told us all about those marks when you first saw them."

I felt the justice of his reproof, and all that it implied, but tried to justify myself by saying:—

"If I had, none of you would have believed me. You would only have laughed at me."

"You ought to have told us, man," he declared, decisively.

We called on O'Grady and told him the news, and he said he and Abe would come that evening to talk over the happening. Talk it over we did; much foolish talk was doubtless uttered before we reached a definite plan of campaign. It was eventually decided that O'Grady and Abe should come over the next morning as soon as they had quitted their early work, bringing some dynamite with them, and that we would all go forth, armed with such weapons as we fancied, to do battle with the monster, which we now all believed to have its dwelling in that hole.

The next morning Johnson and I were visibly excited and anxious to commence operations, but the Scotts showed no feeling even if they were possessed of it. Angus Scott had an old muzzle-loading gun; Alick, Johnson, and I had revolvers. We waited some time for O'Grady and Abe, and then started without them, Johnson being obviously anxious to commence the proceedings.

"They'll come on as soon as they can," he said, "and in the meanwhile there's enough of us, in all conscience."

When we got to Lone Tree I felt much of my courage oozing from me. There was something very eloquent, very daunting, in the cruel silence of that hole. There was no wind, and not even the sigh of a breeze broke the intense stillness.

Johnson gave us our orders. His plan was that we were to separate and slowly approach the hole from four separate points.

"Should anything appear from the hole," he went on, as one who seeks to provide for even the remotest possibility, "well, there are four of us, all armed, and we must show fight. There's nothing to fear."

Never shall I forget that approach to the hole. When we started it we were all about a hundred and fifty yards from our goal, and about a furlong separated each one of us from the next man on either hand. Johnson was on my right, Angus on my left, with his brother Alick between him and Johnson. I own I was perspiring with terror—terror of the unknown, the greatest of all terrors—but naturally I endeavoured to conceal my feelings from the others.

We made our advance in grim silence.

When we were just about a hundred paces from the hole I noticed a strange phenomenon taking place in it—and here I must explain that the events I now record happened, and succeeded each other, with a marvellous rapidity. The description necessarily takes time, and so gives a false impression. The realization was a matter of seconds.

At first it seemed to me as if some sort of commotion was going on at the mouth of the hole, very similar to that seen where a small spring of water wells up from sandy soil, a sort of confused and bubbling turmoil. This turmoil continually grew in volume until there was a seething mass well above the surface of the ground. From this five thin streams shot out with a speed which was awful, and with a silence which was terrifying. One came straight towards me. The mass at the centre was now some feet above the surface-level, and the streams were broad and high at their exit from the mass. They were an unhealthy dull pink, splotched and blurred with purple. When the point of the stream approaching me was some twenty feet away, I realized that it was no stream, but a firm, jelly-like substance, and resembled nothing so much as the magnified tentacles of the cuttle-fish I had found in pools on the tide-deserted shores at home when a boy. I heard the report of Angus Scott's gun, the first sound which had broken that ghastly silence, and the goodly bang seemed to release my being from the paralysis of fascination which had held it. I raised my revolver, but before I could press the trigger the tip of the tentacle, which was now only a pace or two from me, suddenly shot forth with the rapidity of lightning, and curled round me like the lash of a whip. It pinned my arms to my sides with an ever-intensifying grip, and I expected to hear my bones crack at every moment. The pressure was fearful, and I breathed in gasps and with great difficulty. At the same time there was an agonizing contradictory outwards tension, due, I afterwards realized, to the action of suckers on the tentacle.

I was whirled off my feet instantly, and my revolver dropped from my hand. I tried to utter a cry, not from any hope that help would come to me, but from a natural instinct. It was in vain. I could scarcely breathe, much less make a sound.

I looked piteously towards my friends, the others. In a flash I saw them. Poor Angus Scott was almost concealed by the folds of the tentacle which had seized him, and was many yards nearer the hole than any of us. His brother Alick was quivering in the air, held as at arm's length by another tentacle. His face was white as death, and his eyes staring straight into mine with a frozen horror in them. Johnson was gripped round the legs upwards, but his right arm was free. Even as I looked, he fired his revolver apparently into the folds which held him. Then some instinct drew my eyes to the hole, and a wave of sickness came over me as I beheld poor Angus disappear into the earth.

Bang! went Johnson's revolver, and that sent my gaze to
him again. Bang, bang, bang! I watched with eager hope.
Only one more shot was left to him. Bang! I felt myself
flung to the ground, and how I was not stunned by the fall
I do not know. Perhaps my senses would have left me had I
really had them in my control, but I was already mentally
stunned. The tentacle which had been holding me swung
round in a swift curve towards poor Johnson, and in the
twinkling of an eye he was enveloped in its coils.

God forgive me, I got to my feet and ran! It was but
a few yards, and then I turned, with thumping heart, to
look. I saw those ghastly tentacles contract until they disappeared into the hole. How such a mass contrived its exit
from such a space puzzled me. Seeing the tentacles disappear reminded me of thick worsted being drawn through a
piece of cloth by a needle.

I ran, stumbling and staggering in my weakness, all
the way to O'Grady's ranch to tell him and Abe the grue-
some news. My heart thumped until it seemed to me like

a captive animal trying to escape from its prison. How I reached the hut is a marvel to me. When I did get there, it was to find it empty. In my foolishness I had not reckoned on O'Grady and Abe being out at their work. The realization of their absence swept away the remnants of what had been supporting my senses, and I swooned even as my weakness urged me to one of the two beds.

From unconsciousness I must have passed into sleep, for it was getting dusk when I awoke from awful dreams— dreams of the reality which had so recently happened. There were no signs of the two men. I got up and looked about the hut.

Then it came to me. What a fool I had been! There was no O'Grady and no Abe. They had been seized on their homeward way the night before!

I found a little food, and managed with difficulty to force myself to swallow it. More—I found whisky, and drank it very easily and readily. Then I smoked until again I sank into sleep. No power on earth would have induced me to leave the hut and return to my own ranch in the dark. It was early dawn when I rose, a glorious, bright, exhilarating morning, and refreshed by the many hours of sleep, and emboldened, perhaps, by the remaining influence of the whisky, I began to look about me.

Outside the hut was a shed, and I looked in, to discover myself face to face with O'Grady's bull. He was an animal of reputation. He had been imported from the old country, and was a real beauty. He had the greatest strength of any animal I have ever seen, and the spirit of the Light Brigade. He feared nothing on this earth, and was always prepared for the offensive.

We looked at each other, and then I realized that the poor brute, who was tied up, must need water and fodder. I got him both, and he seemed friendly enough, though I took the precaution of keeping at arm's length from the points of his horns. Leaving him, I opened the door of the next erection, a small shed, and found it contained a number of quarrying implements and a large quantity of dynamite. It was the sight of this last which gave me my idea.

It was just an idea, and might prove abortive, but it all depended on O'Grady's bull. I found a pack-saddle, and after slight adjustment and alteration, and with considerable trepidation, I succeeded in inducing the bull to allow me to fasten it on his back. My having fed him after his fast had evidently prepossessed him in my favour, for though he showed plainly that he did not like this new experience, he exhibited no actual resentment towards me. On the pack-saddle I fastened as much dynamite as it would hold, and slung other packages of the murderous explosive at both sides. I connected up the packages, and fixed several long fuses as well, and finally attached a light rope round the poor brute's neck, opened wide the door, and sallied forth holding the rope.

He followed me like a lamb. Doubtless his bovine mind was thinking that this novel experience meant an end to the neglect he had just endured, and good quarters with fair rations. We made straight for Lone Tree, and I got him to within some eighty yards of the hole before he showed any signs of suspicion. A sudden check on my rope caused me to turn my head, and there he was fixed, sniffing the ground with the utmost interest. He gave a short hoarse bellow like a cough, and stamped on the ground with his forefoot. I dropped the rope and stood to one side. He took a pace or two nearer the hole, sniffing the ground as he went, then bellowed several times as if in challenge, pawing up the ground meanwhile so as to send a shower of earth flying into the air.

The time had come. It was not safe to linger near him in his present mood. Rapidly I lit the long fuses, and drew away from the hole with precipitation. A regular salvo of bellows made me turn and look. I saw the arms of the Horror creeping with rapidity towards the bull, who advanced with all his unreasoning bravery to meet them, pawing the ground, alternately lowering and throwing up his grand head.

His bravery and strength were as naught against such a foe. I saw him seized, lifted off the ground, and drawn down the hole, as if he had been an inanimate and resistless bundle. Then I fled farther back until I reckoned I was safe from the explosion, and waited.

It seemed centuries before the huge column of earthy smoke shot up into the air, and then came the noise. Far away as I was, I was hurled to the ground, but with slight hurt. I waited a bit before my courage sufficed to allow me to approach the scene of the explosion. As I went I was conscious of a most nauseating and foul smell, and then I noticed fragments of jelly-like flesh which were at once recognizable as part of the monster whose arm had held me in its embrace. These increased in size and frequency as I advanced, and the smell caused me to retch violently.

My eyes had been directed ground wards as I walked, fascinated by the horrible fragments scattered there, but,

all at once, they were raised, and I beheld a startling realization. The hole was gone!

When I say gone, I mean that it had been converted
into a much larger hole, with steeply-sloping banks descending some two hundred to two hundred and fifty feet,
and there down below was a small lake with the water ever
running and swirling from north to south!

There were no further signs of bull or of the Horror,
and after gazing in stupid wonder at this new feature of
the landscape for over an hour, a sudden fear came over
me, a desire to get away from the spot. I ran most of the
way to poor Johnson's hut, gathered my few possessions
together, loaded them on a horse, got on another myself,
and having freed all such animals as were enclosed, so as
to give them a fighting chance of wandering to Red Wood,
or towards fodder and water, I left the place never to
behold it again.

Later, when the silver was discovered on the flats, a
small colony settled there, and renamed the place Moving
Lake, as I have said, but it knew naught of the Horror, for
events are speedily forgotten in the bustle of life.

The Water Devil
Crittenden Marriott (1916)

PROLOGUE

It must be acknowledged that the public for the most part looked upon Wadsworth's story as a fake. This is not significant, however, for the public regarded practically everything printed in the *Gazette* in the same light. The *Gazette* could discredit the Sermon on the Mount by claiming to have a scoop on it.

It is more significant, though not really conclusive, that Drake, editor of Wadsworth's own paper, who O. K.'d the story for publication, was frankly skeptical about the matter, and—confidentially—explanatory.

"It's a bully good story, anyway," he protested. "Of course Waddy did send a note with it saying it was true, and I guess he thought it was. He'll cool down before he gets back, and laugh at it himself. If he doesn't, I'll advise him to keep still and let it go at that."

But Wadsworth did not come back.

CHAPTER I

Henry Ford was dying. None knew the fact better than he. But Henry Ford had never been one to whine when Fate kicked him. Now, however, the end had come. He knew it and he fought no longer. The bomb that had torn him so desperately that the doctors wondered that he had regained consciousness at all, had utterly destroyed his eyesight, and Henry Ford had no desire to live as a blind man.

What hurt him worst, however, was not that he was dying, but that he was dying by the hands of his enemies. Henry Ford cursed softly to himself as he reflected how Pedro Alvarez must be chuckling over the news.

Not that Henry Ford denied that Alvarez had the right to "get" him if he could. He himself had begun the war ten years before. He himself had tried to kill both Alvarez and his followers, and had failed in the attempt by a hair's breadth only.

And now they had "gotten" him. It was some satisfaction to reflect that at least one of them had paid for the killing,

"The jay that handed it to me?" he questioned eagerly. "—Didn't he get it himself?"

The doctor nodded. "Another man was hurt," he admitted, cautiously. "They say it was the one who threw the bomb! But I'm not sure!"

"Oh! it was him, all right," gasped Ford. "Trust him for that. He always was a mutt! Where'd he get it?"

"In the legs. Both feet were crushed—blown to fragments. But, my man, it is my duty to warn you that you are dying. A notary public is here to take your statement. Better—"

"Statement! I'll make no statement. It was a fair fight. And if it wasn't I'd settle it for myself. You send for Viola, quick's you can get a move on now, bub!"

Viola was his wife. He had sent for her the moment he had regained consciousness. She was a good way off and would be hard to find, but he was confident that she would be found and that she would reach him in time.

So for hours he lay dying. So low was the thread of life in him that it seemed marvelous it did not snap.

Hour after hour wore away. At last the younger doctor came again to his bedside.

"Mr. Ford!" he said, gently.

"Yes!" The dying man's lips barely moved. He did not intend to waste his strength needlessly.

"Your wife has arrived. She will be with you in a moment. Try not to excite yourself. The slightest exertion will be fatal. Keep calm, and you may be able to talk to her for a long time."

Henry Ford did not move. He did not move even when a woman bent over him and pressed her lips to his, and let hot tears splash down upon his brow.

"Viola!" he breathed, so faintly that the words could not be heard a yard away. "Viola! They've got me."

For answer the woman sobbed.

"I wish I could see you, Viola," the man went on. "But I can't. They got my eyes, you know. You'll miss me, old girl, won't you? I know you will, though nobody else will ever find it out. You've been a good pal, Viola, and I wish I could stay with you.

"Don't underestimate them, Viola," he resumed. "They never forget and never forgive. The moment you start for the place they will be after you, if it's twenty years from now. The only way to beat them is to let the secret die with me. Shall I do it, Viola? Shall I do it?"

The woman stared at him strangely. "No! No!" she faltered.

Henry Ford stirred ever so faintly. "You want me to tell you, dear?" he questioned.

"Yes!"

"Say 'yes, old boy! I want you to tell me!'"

So long the woman hesitated that the man grew insistent. "Say it! Quick!" he gasped.

"Yes, old boy! I want you to tell me!" So low, so broken, so muffled were the words that they were well nigh unintelligible.

But the man seemed satisfied. "Then I won't!" he cried, quite loudly. "I won't! I won't! I'll save you in spite of yourself. The secret shall die with me!"

Over the woman's face flickered an expression of passionate anger. "You shall tell!" she cried. "You shall tell." Reaching down she seized him by the shoulder. "I will know!" she screamed. "I will know!"

Under her touch Ford wilted down, just as the doctor came running from across the room and dragged her back. "Are you mad?" he cried. "Do you want to murder your husband? Get out of here." He thrust her toward the door into the hands of the male nurse, who gripped and held her.

Standing between the bed and the woman, the doctor bent over the wounded man and listened for his breathing. To his ear, and to his alone, came the almost inarticulate words: "Tell her I'm dead. Let her go away thinking so. Get my real wife, quick! For God's sake!"

The doctor stood up and drew the sheet gently over the bandaged face. Then he turned to where the woman stood, pallid with rage and fear. "Madam," he said, sternly, "you will leave this room at once and wait in the Visiting hall until I can consult with my colleague as to what is to be done with you. I am more than half inclined to prefer a charge of manslaughter!"

Cowed, the woman slunk through the door. The nurse was about to follow, when the doctor beckoned him back.

"Let her go!" he ordered, swiftly. "She is an imposter— not the patient's wife at all. Go to the front door of the building and keep a sharp look-out. If the real wife comes, bring her here instantly without telling her anything. Go!"

As the nurse went, the doctor spun round and bent over the bed. "Have you anything to say, Mr. Ford," he questioned. "She's gone!"

"Yes!" The words came faintly and brokenly.

The next instant, a taxicab, furiously driven, halted in front of the door, and a woman sprang out.

"Mr. Ford," she gasped. "Mr. Ford? Is he living?"

"This way, ma'am! I don't know, ma'am! This way!" He hurried through the hall, the newcomer at his heels.

As she reached the door of the sickroom the doctor looked up, hypodermic syringe in hand, and saw her.

"Stop!" he ordered, as she sprang forward. "I'll not be fooled by a second imposter. Speak to him and see if he knows your voice. Gently, now!"

The woman brushed his words aside as if they had been unspoken. She dropped on her knees beside the bed. "It's I, Henry." she cried. "Viola!"

The gray lips shaped themselves into a semblance of a smile. "Viola! Good!" he breathed. "This—this is the real one, doctor! Give me some more stimulant. I must speak now! Now!"

The doctor shook his head. "I've done my best," he declared. "I've just given you all I can. More would do more harm than good. Say what you want to say quickly."

"Then—then—Viola! Let everybody think that I died before you came. Don't tell anyone the truth. The doctor will explain. I can't. But I've beaten them after all. Don't go for the treasure till you must. They'll watch you for years to come. Don't think they won't. Alvarez will not forget. And after Alvarez—there's the water devil to be reckoned with! The water devil! You'll have plenty of money. Do without Maynard's gold as long as you can. But if you must have it—if you must have it— Take the blue picture—it holds the secret. Take it and—and—"

The words died away. The lips relaxed. The head rolled weakly to one side. Vainly the woman bent moaning over the still form. Henry Ford's life was done.

But his words followed him.

CHAPTER II

Mrs. Henry J. Ford—Viola Ford—leaned back and contemplated with a frown the pile of bank books, canceled checks, bills and miscellaneous papers piled on the desk before her. She was the sort of a woman whom one looks at twice; forty years before, one would have looked at her many times. Even at sixty-five, she retained traces of an earlier beauty that must have been more than ordinary; and she combined with it very evident marks of strength of character that challenged attention.

The bank books before her bore dates ranging back for nearly ten years. The first one recorded the deposit of fifty thousand dollars; later ones recorded only withdrawals. Steadily and swiftly the fifty thousand dollars had diminished, until the latest entry showed a balance of less than one thousand—a sum that the unpaid bills lying on the desk would reduce to less than five hundred. If, as would appear, Viola Ford had been living on her principal and had practically exhausted it, the situation she faced at her age might well be a serious one.

Her thoughts were far in the past. She was recalling word by word what her husband had said to her when he lay dying.

Ten years had passed since then, and she knew neither more nor less of the "secret" than she had at that moment. The "blue picture" of which he had spoken hung before her on the wall, just as it had hung since Henry Ford had placed it there a year before his death. Viola Ford had not touched it nor attempted to penetrate its secret.

But at last the time had come. "I'll do it," said Viola Ford to herself.

With her, to decide had always been to act. With the utterance of the last word, she pressed an electric button on her desk.

A moment later a maid entered, a woman almost as old as her mistress, with black hair, heavy eyebrows overhanging small, crafty black eyes, and more than a vestige of hair upon her upper lip. As she came in, she glanced swiftly and furtively around the room.

"Matilda," said Mrs. Ford, authoritatively, "get me my hat and coat. Then empty that wastebasket."

Silently the maid brought the outer garments and in a few moments Mrs. Ford was walking down the street. From the window Matilda watched until she was out of sight. Then she sat down and began deliberately to sort over the contents of the wastebasket.

In an hour Mrs. Ford was back. Silently she ate the luncheon that Matilda served, and then sat quietly reading. Matilda did not sleep in the house; she would soon go for the day; and then—

When she heard the house door close behind the maid, Mrs. Ford rose from her chair, walked to the window and stood there till she saw the woman come up to the area steps and start on down the street. Then she walked over to the door and locked it. Next she moved a heavy chair close to the wall, and, climbing carefully upon it, tried to detach from the picture rail the hooks that supported the blue picture.

As she paused, panting a little, and took breath, something moved on the mirror-glass and she turned quickly, just in time to see a man limping towards her across the soft carpet.

At her look he stopped. "Can I help you, ma'am?" he asked humbly.

Mrs. Ford did not hesitate. "Oh! It's you, Carroll, is it?" she exclaimed, not at all in interrogation or confusion. "Yes! I was about to call you. Take this picture down." She climbed from the chair to the floor. "Careful, now! Don't pull the whole rail down."

The man advanced and apparently without an effort reached down the picture.

"Take it downstairs and brush the dirt off it," ordered his mistress sharply. "Then bring it back."

Soon the man reappeared with the picture. "Put it back on the wall," she instructed, over her left shoulder, and went on with her writing.

She did not look up until the man came and stood beside her. "Well?" she queried.

"You want the carriage today?" asked the man, humbly. "I like to get off this evening, yes?"

Mrs. Ford nodded. "Very well! You may go!"

Left alone, the woman waited till she heard the door close, then went swiftly down the steps and made the fastenings secure. From a window she watched until she saw the man depart and vanish far down the street. Then she went back and took down the picture—this time with ease—and began to examine it.

She inspected it in every way and from every point of view. She took it from the frame and studied it minutely, line by line, back and front. She held it against the window, then close to an electric light blazing against a mirror. She heated it over a gas stove, thinking to bring out sympathetic writing. For hours she pored over it with a strong magnifying glass, striving to trace obscure letters in the intricacies of the foliage of the trees and in the ripple of the water over which they hung.

But it was all in vain. Not one indication of writing could she find—not one sign of a message from the dead.

Chapter III

As the elevated slowed down at Thirty-ninth Street, Frank Wadsworth came out of a brown study, slipped his hand into his pocket, drew out a card, glanced at it, and then charged for the platform just in time to get through the closing gates. He ran down the iron steps, crossed the block or two that separated him from Broadway, and entered one of the big hotels that line that thoroughfare. At the desk he nodded to the clerk and pushed over a card. "For Miss Maynard," he explained.

The clerk nodded. "All right, Mr. Wadsworth," he said. "Who is she? Anybody of interest?"

Wadsworth shook his head. "Just a friend," he explained shortly.

Wadsworth was the star mystery man of the *Gazette*. For six years he had spent his life in a constant succession of mysteries, all of which had ceased to be mysteries, sooner or later after he had gotten to work on them.

This time, however, he was not on duty. In fact, he was neglecting a rather urgent duty in order to acknowledge in person the note which he had that morning received from Miss Bessie Maynard, asking him to call. He did not know Miss Maynard himself, but he knew her father.

The girl entered the room and his ideas underwent an instantaneous and radical change.

She was a tall, slim girl with blue eyes and chestnut hair, and a most adorable chin.

"Miss Maynard?" he questioned, idiotically.

"Yes!" She gave her hand. "And you are Mr. Wadsworth? It is good of you to call!"

"Not at all!" Wadsworth meant the disclaimer, too.

"Thank you! Won't you sit down?"

Wadsworth sat down. "You are a stranger in New York?" he ventured, somewhat inanely.

Miss Maynard's eyes twinkled. "No! I'm not a stranger," she returned. "I know New York pretty well and I know how busy newspaper men are. And I'm not going to make any excessive demands on your time. But I've got to consult with somebody in New York, and father has often told me how tremendously clever you are. Last night a letter with a special delivery stamp came to our house in Washington, addressed to father. He—father—is down in Florida looking up some deposits of fuller's earth or something, and so I opened the letter. What it said made me half wild. But to understand it, you must hear the story. Let me tell it to you."

Wadsworth settled back. "Please do." he requested.

"Very well. Father has been a paleontologist—a student of fossils and of prehistoric animals—nearly all his life. Since he joined the Geological Survey twenty years or more ago, he has made many wonderful discoveries.

"Well, about ten years ago, while on a trip to Mexico, he found some very rich gold float. He covered it up and went on with his work. Several months later, he got a year's leave of absence from the Geological Survey, went back to the place and opened up a mine. He took me with him, but I was a child and didn't notice much. Father is the dearest old fellow in the world, you know, but he isn't fitted to run a mine. Down at this mine—the Cruz d'Oro—he waked up one fine morning to find out that his assistant manager, a man named Orde, another American named Pederson, and three Mexicans, had disappeared in the night. With them had gone more than a million dollars' worth of gold bars. Gold is heavy, you know. A million dollars weighs about two tons, so it was evident that the rogues must have fled by water. Father learned that a good-sized sloop had been seen at the landing the night before, and of course he sent out a general alarm at once. But it was more than a year before he heard anything about them, and then he learned only that Orde had been seen going north on the railroad train from Jacksonville, Florida, about a month after the robbery. He never did hear anything about the other American or the Mexicans. The mine was a small one, and the gold that was stolen was pretty nearly all the rich ore that the ledges held. So after a little while, father gave up and came back to the Geological Survey. In fact, I had nearly forgotten it when the letter came. Here it is." She held out an envelope. "Read it, and tell me what you think about it?"

"'Dear Mr. Maynard,'" he read aloud. "'The gold of the Cruz d'Oro mine, which was stolen from you ten years ago, has not been spent. My late husband, Mr. Orde, hid it for reasons of his own, and never went to dig it up. I am by no means certain that I know where it is. He told me something of the place, but not enough. Perhaps I can find it and perhaps I cannot. I know that considerable danger will attend the search—danger from men here in New York and some undefined mysterious danger where the gold is buried. I am willing to join you in the work and to take the risks if you will go halves on all the gold that we regain. You see I am perfectly frank. I know that this gold was stolen from you and that honesty demands that I tell you all I know. But I am not honest. I cannot afford to be. But I am willing to be as honest as I can. The gold does me no good where it is. Getting it is too great a risk for an old woman. Therefore I am willing to divide. Take my offer or leave it.

"'If you think well of my proposition, come to see me or let your daughter come. Please do not write or telegraph. You must bring this letter and surrender it.'"

Wadsworth whistled. "Nice old girl—I don't think!" he observed. "No signature or address, by the way. It's a dandy yarn—a regular thriller—but how does the lady expect you to reach her?"

Miss Maynard unfolded a strip of paper she held in her hand. "She provided for that," she explained. "She didn't sign the letter, probably with the idea of still further protecting herself. But she inclosed a loose slip of a different sort of paper with a name and address written on it by another make of typewriter. Here it is. It reads: 'Mrs. Viola Ford—East 65th Street, New York.'"

"What!" Wadsworth sprang to his feet. "Good Lord! You don't mean it!" Excitedly he extended his hand for the paper.

Miss Maynard handed it over. "Why! Of course I mean it," she answered. "What's the matter? Do you know her?"

"Know her? Know her?" Wadsworth's voice rose almost to a shout. "I've just come from the house."

"And—and—she?"

"Mrs. Viola Ford was murdered and her house ransacked from top to bottom last night."

Chapter IV

For several seconds, which seemed several minutes, Bessie Maynard sat staring breathlessly at Wadsworth.

"Murdered!" she gasped. "Murdered! But she wrote to me yesterday."

Wadsworth nodded. "So it seems," he chimed in, eagerly. "She's been murdered, and I'm guessing that that letter cost her her life. The danger she feared overtook her."

"But how could the murderers guess that she was about to—"

"We don't know yet. But we can guess. Her coachman has disappeared, and there is little doubt that he is the murderer. In the light of your letter it seems to me certain that he was part of the danger that she feared. At all events," he went on, "we will probably know more soon. The police have put out a dragnet for this man—Carroll is his name—and they will undoubtedly catch him soon. Within a few hours his description will be printed all over the United States. He is very peculiar looking—clean-shaven, tall, but of medium weight, with a fearfully scarred and twisted face, and very long, strong arms and knotty fingers. He walks with a very marked limp. Such a man cannot hide himself for long."

Miss Maynard shuddered. "I suppose not," she agreed.

"Meanwhile," Wadsworth resumed, "we've been looking up the woman's history. There seems to be very little to learn. She lived in a brown-stone house on East 65th Street—a house just like hundreds of others. She owned it, but it was mortgaged up to the hilt. She kept two servants, a maid and a coachman. The maid, Matilda Flugel, is either scared out of her wits or hasn't any wits to be scared out of. Neither of the servants slept in the house. The maid came every morning about eight o'clock, got breakfast, straightened up the house, got lunch, and went home about one o'clock. She did not come back; Mrs. Ford got her dinner at a restaurant. The coachman lived over a stable in the rear of the premises. Matilda came this morning as usual, entered with the pass-key, went to the kitchen to prepare breakfast. Later she went to call her mistress and found her stabbed to death. She had been dead some time: just how long the doctors haven't decided yet: there were evidences of a desperate struggle. Evidently, the murderer, whoever he was, was searching for something that he supposed was hidden in the house, and in view of this letter of yours it isn't hard to guess what it was. Whether he found it or not nobody can tell. The maid says that nothing seems to be missing, but of course if the murderer was searching for a paper or something like that he might have gotten it without her knowing anything about it."

Wadsworth went on: "As for the treasure," he said, regretfully, "I'm afraid that the chance of ever finding it is slim. Not that I think the murderer got the clue. I don't think he did."

Miss Maynard clasped her hands. "Then—?"

"No! I don't think he did," interrupted the reporter. "The extraordinary way in which he ransacked the house shows that he had no idea where to look for it."

The reporter had been sitting on the edge of his chair as he spoke. But now he rose. "I must go," he declared, regretfully. "This letter has given me the basis of an extraordinary story, and I must get to work on it. I'll call later with the news, if you'll permit me."

Miss Maynard rose uncertainly. "Please do," she faltered. "But—but—has my name got to be in the papers?"

Wadsworth did not hesitate. "Not if I can help it," he declared positively. "At the same time, this thing is serious. It's murder, you know. Circumstances may come up that will make it necessary for you to tell your story. In that case—"

"In that case, of course. I shall what is right. But until then—"

"Until then, you may rest easy. If Carroll is caught soon, the whole thing may be explained without reference to you or the treasure."

Wadsworth ran down to the public telephone on the lower floor and rang up headquarters. Ten minutes later he was back in the parlor. He was breathing hard. When she saw him, Miss Maynard rose quickly to her feet.

"Have they caught him?" she gasped.

"Caught him? No, they've let him go! But they've proved his innocence. His alibi is perfect. He was arrested at seven o'clock last night, charged with disorderly conduct and was locked up at the eighth precinct until this morning, when he was taken to court, fined, and released. At seven o'clock last night Mrs. Ford was eating her dinner at her regular restaurant. The identifications are perfect and absolutely incontestable. Probably he's on his way to the Ford house now, and I must hustle out there and see him. Good-by! I'll keep you informed!"

The girl gave him her hand. "Good-by, Mr. Wadsworth," she said, "and thank you. It would have been dreadful if I had gone to Mrs. Ford's alone and blundered into this terrible affair. I'm so glad I asked you to call instead."

"Are you?" The reporter looked at her eagerly—so eagerly that a faint tinge of color stained her already rosy cheeks. "Are you? Well! Don't you know, I'm rather glad, too."

Chapter V

Fred Carroll, the missing coachman, did not return to the Ford house. He did not return anywhere. When he paid his fine and walked out of the police court-room, he vanished.

In view of his perfect alibi, no one except Wadsworth was much concerned about him, and he alone endeavored to trace him down.

Wadsworth passed two days in running down clues as to the whereabouts of the coachman; then on the morning of the third day, he went out to the Ford house to make a fresh search of the premises.

The policeman at the door welcomed him with a grin. "Sure, it's just too late you are, Mr. Wadsworth, sor," he said. "The young lady's gone."

"What young lady, Mullan?" he asked.

"A very pretty young lady, indade, sor. Miss Arabella Ford, her name is. She's niece to Mrs. Ford. She was here for half an hour and more."

"Mrs. Ford's niece!" Wadsworth stared. This was the first he had heard about a niece or any other relative at all of Mrs. Ford.

"Who came with her!" he asked.

"Nobody at all. She just drove up by herself."

"Oh!" Wadsworth stared. "Didn't she bring a note from the Chief or anybody?"

Mullan shook his head. "Sure! She'd no time," he pro-tested. "It's just come in from Boston, she had, and taken rooms at the Plaza Hotel, and came around quick in a taxicab."

"Oh!" Wadsworth concealed his dawning suspicion. "And you let her in the house?"

"Sure and I did. And why not?"

"No reason at all. You went with her, of course!"

"Of course."

"Humph! Where did you say she was staying?"

"At the Plaza Hotel on 58th Street, sor. She came in a taxicab from there and went back in it. It's just gone she has. Maybe if you will hurry—"

Wadsworth did not let the officer finish. "What did she look like?" he broke in. "Give me her description quick."

The officer scratched his head. "Sure, she was mighty pretty—" He hesitated. "She has the dark hair and dancing eyes and pretty red cheeks and—"

"How tall was she?"

The officer brightened. "It's a little bit of a colleen she was," he declared.

"All right." Wadsworth did not wait to hear more. Leaving the policeman chuckling to himself he sped away toward the Plaza Hotel, eight or ten blocks distant:

Into the hotel he dashed, nodded to the hotel clerk—Wadsworth knew all the hotel clerks: it was part of his business—and demanded Miss Arabella Ford.

But the clerk shook his head. "Nobody of that name here!" he declared.

"All right." Wadsworth scurried out to the taxicab stand and begin to make inquiries. He soon found the right driver and learned that the girl had come out of the ladies' entrance of the hotel, and gotten into the taxi and been driven to the Ford house; after half an hour there, she had been driven back to the hotel and re-entered. Of course, Wadsworth concluded, she had simply gone through the lobby and out by some other entrance.

But what had she wanted! What could there be about the house that had led her to do what she had done. Wadsworth could not believe that it was mere idle curiosity.

The reporter made these reflections while speeding back to the Ford house in the same taxicab that had carried the girl. Before starting he had checked Mullan's description of the girl by the chauffeur, and had telephoned the result to the *Gazette* office and to police headquarters. It was just possible that she might be caught at one of the ferries or railway stations in attempting to leave the city. Arrived at the house, the reporter hurried from room to room, trying to remember exactly how things had looked when he had been there before, and to decide what change, if any, had been made in them.

The coroner's jury had rendered an open verdict the afternoon before, and a maid was just beginning to straighten the room, untouched until then. Wadsworth watched her as she worked. Suddenly his eyes focused themselves on a torn blue picture, half ripped from a trumpery frame and apparently doubled beneath it.

Wadsworth remembered that picture. He had noticed it on the first visit to the house. But somehow it had looked different then. He bent to pick it up and found instead of being merely loosened from the frame and doubled under itself, as he was sure it had been three days before, it had been torn into two pieces. Three-fourths of it was missing; only one corner still clung to the frame.

Hurriedly Wadsworth searched through the pile. The missing part of the picture was not there, nor could the maid enlighten him as to its whereabouts. Somebody had carried it away since the murder—had done it hurriedly, too! Could it have been the girl—the pretended niece? Carefully Wadsworth loosened the remaining corner of the picture from the frame, folded it up and put it into his pocket. The next moment the maid gathered up the rest of the debris and dumped it into the large basket for removal.

He went downstairs and cross-questioned Mullan, and learned that that officer had accompanied the girl in her trip through the house. At first, Mullan was positive that he had not left her side for a moment but, shrewdly questioned, he at last admitted that he had left her alone for "a minute only" in the sitting-room, while he had gone down to get a handkerchief that she had left in the taxicab.

This settled the thing for Wadsworth. The girl, he decided, was in some way associated with the murderer. At great personal risk she had come to the house and had gone through it. She had gotten rid of Mullan by a pretext and had improved the opportunity to rip loose from its frame a daub worth perhaps fifty cents—intrinsically. She had done it so hurriedly that she left part of the picture behind. To Wadsworth's mind, it followed beyond a doubt that the picture was in some way a clue to the treasure. It was a water-color, painted wholly in shades of blue. The paper on which it was painted was ordinary drawing paper, such as was sold in a hundred shops; the painting, so far as he could distinguish it, was a landscape, carelessly executed, but by a rather clever hand, in great splotches of blue that hid nearly all the original white surface of the paper. A leaf of some sort of palm, probably a palmetto, suggested that the scene was Southern. Beyond that it suggested nothing. And later tests with heat, with chemicals, with magnifying glasses, with everything and anything that ingenuity could suggest, added nothing. So far as any clue to the treasure was concerned, the paper apparently might as well be blank.

CHAPTER VI

The next two weeks were busy ones for Wadsworth. Scarcely taking time to eat and sleep, he raced through the city, running down clue after clue as to the whereabouts of the coachman, the niece and the rest of the picture.

But all in vain. At the end of two weeks he found himself exactly where he had been at the beginning. About the only relaxation he had taken in those two weeks was that which he spent in talking the case over with Miss Maynard, and once he escorted her to a colonial ball. He never forgot the picture she presented in her dainty, old fashioned evening gown, nor the glow on her pretty face as he remarked: "You're beautiful tonight."

Miss Maynard at last informed him that she must leave the city immediately. "I don't want to go," she said, frankly. "But I must. Father has written me to join him in Florida as soon as I can. So far as I can see, the situation is hopeless and I guess the best thing I can do is to forget the treasure as quickly as I can."

Wadsworth nodded gloomily. "I'm afraid you're right," he admitted. "If anything does come up, it probably won't be for a long time. The police have given the case up. Of course, I'll stick to the case and do what I can, you know. I'd do anything to help you."

"Yes! I know it," Bessie Maynard spoke softly.

After the girl had gone, Wadsworth worked alone, but without result, till Drake, news editor of the *Gazette,* called a halt. When Wadsworth explained the situation, he shook his head.

"I'll give you one more week, Wadsworth," he declared, "and then we'll drop the case. In my opinion," went on Drake, "the police are right and the Ford case was just a plain burglary. I believe it all the more because you haven't been able to prove it anything else, and I'm satisfied that you would have done so before this if there had been anything else to prove."

The week passed without developments, and at its close Wadsworth went back to police reporting, pending the appearance of another mystery. But he was not satisfied. Every free moment, including his "day off," he spent on the Ford case—without results. So hard did he work, so persistently did he flog his brain into conjectures in regard to this, the first case that had ever beaten him, that his health began to give way.

Drake noticed his condition before Wadsworth himself did, and called him into his office.

"Read this, Waddy!" he ordered, tossing a typewritten dispatch across the desk.

Wadsworth took it and read:

> PENINSULA CITY, FLA., April 3.—For a week or more, negroes have been coming into town in a panic from the western part of the country. They claim that the water devil, which is said to have been active down here about ten years ago, has again taken up his abode in Lake Okechobee and that he is raiding the nearby region, devouring both stock and men. Nobody seems to have seen the devil, but a good many have seen his tracks, which resemble those of an elephant. They always lead down to the water and disappear. Wire hundred dollars, expenses if you want me to go in and investigate.—Simpson.

Wadsworth nodded slowly as he finished. "I guess that's it," he remarked.

Drake had gone back to his work.

"What did you say?" he demanded.

Wadsworth still was studying the dispatch. "Professor Maynard," he answered. "Working down near Okechobee for six months. I—I've had letters from him—hinting at something curious. Guess he's been investigating this water devil."

Drake's eyes twinkled. "That's the same Maynard who lost the treasure in that dime-novel Ford case, isn't it?" he questioned. "Umph! Seems to me he had a daughter who was up here, hadn't he!"

Wadsworth blushed. "Yes, he had," he admitted.

"Is she with him in the—er—water devil country?"

"Yes!"—fiercely.

"Um! Um!" Drake ran his hand through his hair distractedly. "Sounds better even than I thought. How'd you like to run down there and look the thing up! Take your time. Simpson's our local man there, you know. Get in touch with him. Send up a corking Sunday special if you can. If you can't, why, it doesn't matter."

Wadsworth straightened up. "I'd be delighted," he answered. "But I'm awfully busy just now on some private business and don't want to leave town."

"Yes! I know you are busy," retorted the other grimly. "And I know what you're busy about, too. That's why I'm sending you away before you kill yourself. The *Gazette* can't spare you permanently, but it's got to spare you temporarily. You're half crazy on the Ford case and will be until you get out of New York. Go down to Florida and see Mr. Maynard and—er—Miss Maynard, and play with this water devil thing"—he tapped his dispatch carelessly—"for a couple of weeks. Then come back, and if there isn't anything more pressing on hand, I'll let you take up the Ford case again if you want to. Two weeks' rest will do more to solve the thing than a month's work in your present condition."

Wadsworth thrust out his hand impulsively. "I understand, old man!" he exclaimed. "I'll go."

CHAPTER VII

Laden with umbrella, gun case, suit-case and camera, Wadsworth dashed headlong for the gates that led to the waiting Florida express. As he neared the guide rails that led to the passage-way, he realized that someone else was rushing for it from the opposite direction, and tried to slow down. But his foot slipped and he plunged ahead, to the accompaniment of a feminine shriek.

Quickly Wadsworth recovered himself. "I beg your pardon," he panted. "I hope I didn't hurt you!"

"No!" she gasped. "You didn't hurt me, but—why on earth didn't you watch where you were going!"

"I didn't see you," he was beginning, when someone touched him on the shoulder.

"If you will permit me to pass?" asked a fat, dark little man. "I fear I miss my train."

The girl uttered a scream. "Oh! good gracious!" she cried. "The train! Where is it!" She clutched madly at the articles that strewed the floor.

"Let me!" Wadsworth reached for her suit-case.

But she was before him. Feverishly she caught it up. "Never mind!" she cried. "I'll take this. You may bring the rest."

Wadsworth scurried after her, laden with umbrellas, suit-cases and handbags. and together they raced down the platform between two lines of cars, which to their excited imagination, seemed already quivering into motion.

Behind them the dark little fat man puffed along. The girl ran swiftly and well.

Half way down, the girl turned. "Hurry!" she panted. "It—it's moving."

Wadsworth spurted. He came abreast of an open vestibule in the train on the right and tossed the suit-case into it, into the hands of a dusty porter. "Florida express?" he gasped.

The porter swung the suit-case back. "Train on the left for Jacksonville, suh!" he grinned. "Jus' behind you, suh. Plenty of time, suh. It don't start for five minutes yet."

Wadsworth turned and met the grinning face of another son of Dahomey. Meekly he passed the valises over and fished out his sleeper ticket. "Car J!" he said, humbly.

The girl, who had kept her ticket in her hand throughout the race, passed it over. The porter glanced at the two, caught up Wadsworth's suit-case and reached for the girl's.

But she held it back. "Never mind!" she declared. "I'll bring it." Carefully she followed the porter up the steps and into the car, Wadsworth meekly following.

The porter came to a stop beside a vacant section and put down the valises he carried. "Berths three and four, suh," he said, passing both tickets back to Wadsworth.

Wadsworth looked at the girl and the girl looked at Wadsworth.

Wadsworth, however, did not quail. Laughingly he held out the tickets. "Which will you have?" he asked.

The girl hesitated. But Wadsworth had a very taking way. The look of anger faded from her face. "Well!" she cried: "if this ain't the limit. Say! Honest now! Did you put him up to doing this!"

Wadsworth grinned. "No, I didn't!" he confessed regretfully.

The girl's eyes flashed appreciatively. "You're all right, I guess," she declared. "My ticket is for Peninsula City."

Wadsworth smiled. "So is mine," he announced.

The girl gave a little shriek. "Say! That is sure a coincidence."

Wadsworth sat down. Evidently his trip South wasn't to lack amusement. "Where's the rest of the company?" he asked.

The girl did not pretend to misunderstand. "You win," she granted. "I quit 'em three months ago."

Wadsworth smiled. "How strange!"

"Dad's got a place in Florida that's going to make our everlasting fortune some day. I been staying with him. I just run up to New York the other day to keep tab on the Great White Way. Say! What's your name!"

"Wadsworth!"

"Wadsworth, eh?" the girl repeated. "Mine's Lillian St. Clair. Dad's name is Peterson. It used to be Pederson, but I made him change it. He ain't my real father. He's a low-brow, you know, but I'm good to him because he was ma's husband. What you going to Florida for?"

"Pleasure! Hunting! Exploring! Health!"

"Health." Miss St. Clair stared at him. "Florida'll set you up all right if you don't go too far with your hunting and exploring and get fever when you're far from home and mother—an' if the water devil don't get you."

"The water devil!" he echoed, in a tone as idle as he could muster. "What is a water devil?"

"Search me!" responded Miss St. Clair, promptly and emphatically. "I've never seen it, thank the Lord. Nobody ever seen it and come back to tell. Say! Did you ever hear of the Snark?"

"Of course!" Wadsworth did not add that he wondered that Miss St. Clair should ever have heard of it.

"All right! You know in the Snark it says: 'But beware! If the snark be a boojum, you'll silently vanish away.' Well, the water devil is a 'boojum' all right. Everybody that sees it vanishes."

"Then how—?"

"By its tracks. I've seen them myself. They're as big as a dinner plate and they're a foot deep in the sand and mud. They're round, with just a trace of something that might be real short toes. They lead up out of the water and back into it again."

"Where do they go between!" Wadsworth was getting interested.

"Nobody's traced them far. I know I didn't."

Wadsworth leaned back in his seat and listened interestedly. There was evidently something in Simpson's story, wild as it had seemed. "How long has it been hanging around?" he asked, curiously.

"Two or three months this time," returned the girl promptly. "This ain't the first time it's showed up, you know. Once in so often—once in five or ten years—it seems to come out and make trouble. The rest of the time it stays hid."

"Where?"

"In Lake Okechobee, I reckon. Lake Okechobee ain't exactly a real lake, you know. It's more of a swamp. He's got the whole Everglades to browse around in. Dad's place is at the edge of the Everglades. He raises truck for the North. At least he's getting ready to raise it when we get a railroad in. You know they're doing big work down there?"

"I'm afraid I don't."

"Well! They are! They're draining the Everglades. Say! It's a wonderful country. There's a layer of soil ten feet deep that'll raise anything in the world. Dad got in there early and owns a great big place. What paper'd you say you was on?"

Wadsworth started. "Stung!" he remarked lightly, when he had caught his breath. "How did you guess?"

"'Twasn't any guess. It was a cinch. You're going to Florida to look up that water devil, aren't you! How'd you hear about it?"

Miss St. Clair's voice ceased for almost the first time since the train had started, and she lay back and stared triumphantly at her vis-a-vis.

"You've guessed it," he admitted. "We heard of the water devil through our local man, Simpson—"

"Simpson! Oh, you're on the *Gazette,* then."

"Evidently Simpson is known!"

"Known! I reckon he is. He's from up North somewhere, but he's been living down in Florida for a long while now. So Simpson told you about the water devil, did he?"

"He did, and I needed a rest. I'll show you Simpson's dispatch." Wadsworth thrust his hand into breast pocket and pulled out a sheaf of loose papers and letters.

An exclamation from the girl made him look up. Her eyes were distended and she was staring at the last paper he had laid down. "What's that?" she asked, in a high, cracked key, with a nervous laugh which she was clearly trying to make natural. "What's that?"

Wadsworth's eyes followed hers. "That?" he questioned, picking up the ragged piece of blue paper to which she was pointing. "This! Oh, this is a clue! Did you ever hear of the Ford case?"

The look in her face told clearly that she had.

"The Ford case? Seems to me I have. Wasn't she—?"

"Yes! She was!" Wadsworth completed the sentence, as the girl faltered. "And this is the clue." He was watching the girl narrowly. Could she be the pretended niece?

"Yes," he went on cautiously, but with assumed frankness. "Yes, it's a clue. I picked it up in the room where Mrs. Ford was murdered. The rest of it was missing. In fact, the rest of it seemed to be the only thing that was missing. So it's a clue. I'm keeping it in hopes that it will lead to the murderer." Without offering to show the paper, he gathered it up with the rest and put the lot back in his pocket.

Wadsworth could see very plainly that she was dying to look at the blue painting, but hesitated to ask directly. "Say," she went on, "—about the Ford case: Do you know I'm just crazy about mysteries and gore and—and all that. Tell me about the Ford case and how you're going to catch the murderer with that piece of blue paper."

"Delighted!" Wadsworth leaned forward. "Mrs. Ford," he began, "was a widow of uncertain age and uncertain everything else. She—" He went on telling the story of the murder as he knew it, but omitting all reference to Bessie Maynard's story of the gold and to the appearance of the pretended niece.

"Somebody killed her to get some particular thing she had," he finished. "I'm guessing that it was the rest of this blue water-color picture I've got here. I'm no Sherlock Holmes. But when I get rested up and get back to New York I'll bait a trap with this piece of paper and see what I'll catch."

The reporter rose. "Last call for dinner's gone," he observed. "May I have the pleasure of your company?"

But the girl shook her head. "Not tonight, thank you," she said. "It's you and me for the lonesome feed for tonight, anyway. The rubbernecks in this car are watching us to beat the band; especially that globular little Dago that tried to get past us at the gate. Back off, Willie! Back off, and let me establish myself as a maiden lady. After that I'll be charmed."

Wadsworth backed off, raising his hat and departing in a manner so polite that he felt sure the most suspicious observer must conclude that Miss St. Clair could not be his wife. Moreover, he kept away from her during the entire evening.

Before he went to sleep, however, he took one precaution; ensconced in the privacy of his berth, he took the fragment of blue painting from his pocket and placed it beneath his pillow. In its place in the sheaf of letters, he substituted another piece of paper of practically the same size, shape and color. Then he hung his coat close to the edge of his berth and went to sleep, confident that Miss St. Clair would get the wrong paper if she were daring enough to steal it.

The next morning the paper in his pocket was gone. Wadsworth smiled grimly. Beyond a doubt Miss St. Clair was the pretended niece. He had her at last. Exultantly he drew the other paper from beneath his pillow and restored it to his pocket. Then, moved by a sudden impulse, he took it out and looked at it. Then he swore. It was the substitute that he held in his hand. The real picture was gone!

For a moment Wadsworth believed that he himself had erred in placing the two papers. Thinking over the matter, however, he became convinced that he had made no mistake.

Not for an instant did he doubt that the girl had taken it. It was too preposterous to imagine that the one train could carry a third person who was interested in that blue drawing. The only question was what she wanted with it and what connection she had with the Ford case—and this he determined to find out.

He remembered that the robber Orde had been seen going north from Jacksonville years before, just after the robbery. He remembered the danger that Mrs. Ford had declared to exist at the place where the treasure was buried. He remembered the water devil, that, according to Simpson, had disappeared in the Everglades ten years before. All the cords seemed to be centered in Florida. So much the better. It would go hard if he could not follow them to their point of union.

Chapter VIII

Two days later, Wadsworth was afloat in a motor boat on a strip of water that wound backward and between high and low hummocks and patches of reedy marsh. With him in the boat were Simpson and Miss St. Clair—and a miscellaneous pile of luggage, including suit-cases, umbrellas, cameras and gun-cases. Simpson was there because Wadsworth had requisitioned his services; and Miss St. Clair was there because she wanted to be—though, it must be confessed that she was there with Wadsworth's full consent.

He had wired to Simpson to meet him at Peninsula City with some means of transportation to Lake Okechobee; and on his arrival at the place, he was on the lookout. He saw no one, however, that answered his idea of what Simpson should be, and was about to turn away to seek a hotel when a tall, thin personage, of uncertain age, with a weary mustache and a short imperial, and a rumpled shirt bosom that bulged above a half-open vest, slouched forward. To Wadsworth he much resembled the imitation Southern colonel so often portrayed upon the stage.

"I reckon you're Mr. Wadsworth, suh!" he remarked, removing his prehistoric straw hat. "I'm Colonel Simpson. I sho'ly am glad to meet you, suh."

Wadsworth ran his eye over the amazing figure. "Yes! I'm Wadsworth," he admitted. "I suppose you got my telegram."

"Of cou'se, suh. I've got a motorboat waiting back in the creek; an' we can start at once, suh—after you have done me the honah to join me in a little prime Bourbon, suh!"

Wadsworth accepted the proffered hospitality with an enthusiasm he was far from feeling. "By the way. Colonel, is Mr. Peterson in town? His daughter—"

A frown seemed to hesitate on Simpson's brow, but before it could decide whether or not to stay, Miss St. Clair appeared, suit-case in hand.

"Hello, Colonel!" she called. "Where's dad!"

Simpson's sallow face brightened and his dull eyes flashed. He swept off his hat in a low bow. "Miss St. Clair, yo' most obedient, ma'am. I regret to say, ma'am, that yo' pa got tired of waitin' foh you an' depahted foh home yesterday, ma'am."

Miss St. Clair sat down on a baggage truck suddenly. "Well! What d'ye think of that?" she inquired, of no one in particular. "Ain't he the loving parent?"

Wadsworth was about to offer his boat, when Simpson regained his voice. "I took the liberty, ma'am," he declared, "to tell him that Mr. Wadsworth would be here today and assured him that though Mr. Wadsworth had the misfortune to be a Northern gentleman, he would certainly take pleasure in placing his boat at yo' disposal, ma'am."

"Surest ever!" Miss St. Clair sprang up. "When do we start!"

"Right now. That is as soon as—"

"As soon as we have lickered up, suh. Allow me!"

Miss St. Clair sat down again. "Right-o," she agreed. "I will wait here in the shade."

An hour later the motor boat coughed, spat, and snorted away up the tortuous channel that ran from the landing.

Scarcely had the little town dropped out of sight when Miss St. Clair turned on Simpson.

"What's doing, Mr. Simpson?" she demanded. "What's the water devil been up to now?"

"Well, Miss St. Clair, ma'am," he answered, uncertainly, "the water devil is not regarded as exactly humorous any more, ma'am! I reckon he got Tom Waters the other day."

"Tom Waters! You don't mean it. Well. I ain't as sorry as I might be! Tom treated dad pretty badly not three weeks ago. How'd the water devil get him, Mr. Simpson?"

"Nobody knows how, ma'am. Tom went out in a boat fishing, and he didn't come back. His boat drifted in to Willis Kent's place, but Tom wasn't in it. The very next night the water devil broke down Tom's hawg pen and carried off a big hawg. He left his tracks all around over everything. Professor Maynard's been a-studyin' them ever since. Professor Maynard's from Washington, suh, an' he's bo'ding at Will Kent's."

Wadsworth nodded. "I know Professor Maynard and his daughter," he said. "Does this Kent live far from where we're going? I'd like to get in touch with Professor Maynard as soon as I can."

"Kent lives about a mile from town, suh. I have no accommodation, suh, and so I intended to lodge you with Mr. Smith Lee, justice of the peace and a gentleman of the highest character. But if you would prefer, we can easily stop by Kent's and ask him if he can accommodate you, suh."

"All right," Wadsworth agreed. "Suppose we do."

Miss St. Clair had listened without speaking. Now, however, she threw herself back in her seat and wrinkled her pretty nose. "Oh, sugar!" she cried. "That lets me out all right. Willis Kent hates pa, and that stuck-up Maynard girl just naturally despises me. So I reckon I won't see much of you boys once we get back to the lake."

Wadsworth answered quickly. "I'll be charmed to call on you and your father, Miss St. Clair," he asserted.

As a matter of fact, he had no intention of being cut off from association with either the girl or with her stepfather, whom he had now begun to suspect would turn out to be their missing coachman. "I think, too," he added, "that I can bring Miss Maynard to call. I know her to be a very pleasant lady, and I think any stiffness she may have shown must have come from her not knowing you."

Miss St. Clair stared. "Maybe," she answered slowly. "Maybe! But I don't reckon we'll chum much."

Wadsworth felt perfectly safe in promising that Bessie Maynard would be willing to call on Miss St. Clair, when he had explained his suspicions in regard to her connection with the lost treasure.

Suddenly Miss St. Clair leaned forward. "Oh, say, Mr. Wadsworth," she cried. "See that island over to the right there—the one with the big white rock on it?"

Wadsworth looked and noted with surprise a great limestone pile rising out of the dense jungle on a small islet. "Of course," he answered. "Where in the world did a rock like that come from in this flat country!"

Miss St. Clair shook her head. "Search me!" she answered cheerfully. "It's the only one down here, so far as I know. But that ain't what I wanted to say. That island's where I saw some of those water devil tracks when I came here last. S'pose we run over and see if they're still here?"

"Sure thing!" Wadsworth's assent was willing. "Run over, if you can, Simpson," he directed, "it won't take but a moment. Maybe they'll be distinct enough for a picture!" He picked up the camera that lay on the seat.

Simpson gave the wheel a twist and the motor boat shot off toward the little island. As they neared, Miss St. Clair pointed. "Right by that palmetto," she directed, standing up and shading her eyes with her hand. "Say, I believe they are there yet. I can see them."

Wadsworth rose skeptically, camera in hand and moved to her side. The beach was very close now, and he could make out an undeniable double line of holes leading up to it. To him, however, they did not greatly resemble footprints.

"They're just holes someone's been digging," he scoffed.

"Holes!" Miss St. Clair's scorn was intense. "Where'd somebody stand to dig holes in that soft mud and not leave any tracks of his own?"

Wadsworth was silent. The girl's words were unanswerable. Doubtfully he stared at the double line of prints, each as large as a dinner plate and more than a foot deep. Clearly they were old, for despite the stiffness of the mud.

the sides had partly fallen in. Nevertheless, they were something, and he raised his camera and snapped them.

As he did so, he felt Miss St. Clair's grip on his arm with a frantic pressure that actually hurt. "Look there!" she babbled, shaking finger extended. "Look there! At that other line of prints. They weren't there before. They're fresh! Oh, for God's sake, let's get out of this." The girl's whole body was shaking like a leaf.

Wadsworth's eyes followed her quivering finger, and mechanically he raised his camera.

Across the beach, leading from the water's edge to a jungle of trees leaves, and hanging moss, ran a line of prints, sunk deep in the soft muck. They ran up to the jungle and did not come back. They were fresh.

Wadsworth fell a faint tingling along his scalp as he stared at them. Swiftly he snapped his camera twice at them and at the background of bushes, then dropped it on the seat and caught up his rifle, hearing Miss St. Clair's terror-stricken babbling behind him the while.

The boat moved beneath his feet. Simpson had wasted no time in starting. Before Wadsworth could formulate a course of action, the boat was a hundred yards away, going like mad. In another moment a turn in the channel hid the inland.

CHAPTER IX

Swiftly the motor boat sped on. Simpson talked almost volubly, for him, and Miss St. Clair filled in the intervals with a chatter too vivacious to be altogether genuine.

As Wadsworth meditated, the miles dropped behind until the channel widened out into a broad lagoon. The motor boat slid into it, and then, turning, followed the shore toward a short wooden landing that projected into the lake. Simpson indicated it with a gesture. "That's Willis Kent's yonder," he explained.

Two minutes later Wadsworth leaped ashore, and turned to help Miss St. Clair.

But that young lady shook her head. "No, thank you," she demurred. "I'll stay here and let Colonel Simpson run me down home. Dad's place is only about two hoots farther down."

A sudden explosion of voices, raised high in wrath, broke in. Wadsworth turned to listen. As he did so, Miss St. Clair leaped from the boat to the pier beside him.

"That's dad and Willis Kent!" she cried angrily. "I won't have dad imposed upon."

With the last word she was gone, flying up the pier and along the path that led to a house, dimly visible behind a screen of trees.

Wadsworth followed.

As he came out of the bushes, he saw a man, misshapen and shaggy, standing at the foot of a short flight of steps that led to a porch. His strong, heavy, barrel-like frame was tense with rage, and his long fingers moved convulsively, clasping and unclasping. Wadsworth did not need to be told that this was Peterson, nor any further confirmation of the belief that he was the missing coachman. He fitted the description like a glove.

"I'll get even with you for this, Willis Kent," the man snarled, shaking his fist.

Another man, big and blonde, stood at the top of the steps and stared contemptuously down. "Perhaps," he agreed. "You're just the sort that sneaks around when a man's back is turned and plays him some dirty trick. Now, be off!"

For a moment the man hesitated. Then, before he could utter the words that plainly trembled on his tongue, Miss St. Clair sprang to his side, a small fury in petticoats. "You keep a civil tongue in your head, Willis Kent," she shrieked. "Come, dad!"

Willis Kent grew apoplectic with rage. "Oh, it's you, is it?" he choked. "You get off my place, too, and stay off."

So suddenly the storm had arisen that Wadsworth was bewildered. As he instinctively stepped forward to champion the girl, Simpson sprang past him and shook his fist in Kent's face. "By Ged, suh! You'll answer to me for that, suh!" he hissed.

Kent snapped his fingers. "Tush! Tush!" he gibed. "What you wasting yo'self for on a little baggage like that, Tom Simpson?"

He got no further, for Simpson, quite frantic, sprang up the steps, and launched a blow at him. It fell short, and the big man swung his arm around with an open-handed blow that sent the other reeling backward into Wadsworth's arms.

By this time a score of faces, black and white, had appeared. A little woman, white and anxious looking, caught Kent's arm and hung there: behind her, Wadsworth could see Professor Maynard and his daughter looking on with wondering faces. He caught Bessie's eyes and nodded to her; at the moment, more was not possible.

Kent had grown quite beside himself. "Off my place, the pack of you," he yelled. "Off my place!" He started down the steps, raging, towing the little woman behind him.

Wadsworth threw up his hands. "That will do, Mr. Kent," he commanded, authoritatively. "We will all go gladly. Kindly spare us further vituperation."

The reporter's tone was commanding, and Kent hesitated, checked in spite of himself. The next instant Wadsworth and the three others were moving down the path.

Bessie Maynard ran after them. "Mr. Wadsworth!" she called, softly. "Don't go. He doesn't mean it! I've heard about that girl and her alleged step-father. They're people of no character at all. Don't go with them."

"I must. Don't you see I must. I can't leave them under fire. I'll be back as quick as I can. I have great news for you. I'll come—"

"Don't trouble!" Miss Maynard drew herself up stiffly. "Don't trouble. Go with your—friends." With a last glance at Miss St. Clair's retreating back, she turned on her heel and started back to the house, leaving Wadsworth to follow the others, slowly, sadly, and more or less angrily.

Angry and troubled as he was, however, he retained enough self-possession to note the peculiar wabbling gait with which Peterson moved, and to wonder what sort of an affliction could make a man walk like that.

Without a single word the four plodded down the path, out on the little pier, and climbed into the boat. Wadsworth was last and as he prepared to join the others, Miss St. Clair looked up and saw him.

"Whoa!" she cried. "Back up, Johnny!"

Wadsworth stared. "What's the matter?" he demanded, laughing.

"Everything! Say, you've been dead nice to me all this trip and I ain't going to get you in bad with your friends. You ain't got anything to do with this row. Dad and Willis Kent have been making faces at each other for months— ever since dad came down here. It was mighty good of you to say you'd try to get Miss Maynard to call, but I guess it was a pipe dream all the time. Guess she told you that I was no good when she spoke to you, didn't she?"

"Not exactly." Wadsworth hesitated. "I'm bound to admit that she seemed prejudiced, but—"

"Prejudiced! She hates me like poison: and"—enigmatically—"she'll hate me all the worse now. No, Mr. Wadsworth, I'm obliged to you, but I ain't going to let you get mixed up with us. You go back and make your peace and—"

"My dear young lady!" Wadsworth interrupted the girl emphatically. "You really must let me be the judge as to all this." He stepped by her into the boat and dropped on the seat beside Peterson. "Let her go, Simpson," he ordered.

Simpson obeyed. He had said not a word: his lips seemed frozen, as if they could never again soften to utterance; and his eyes were chill as steel. Simpson meant murder. The fact could not be doubted.

Miss St. Clair also looked at Simpson, wonderingly, as if she really saw him for the first time. Then she turned upon her step-father, who sat silent, stunned by the rapidity of the events.

"Say," she cried, "ain't you the frisky dad to go fooling round Willis Kent's? What'd ye go there for?"

Pederson scowled. "I went to give him Colonel Simpson's message," he mumbled. "Simpson sent word that Mr. Wadsworth would be along today and I went to tell him. But the scoundrel didn't give me the chance to say nothing."

"You see," Wadsworth broke in. "You see, it's my quarrel, after all, Miss St. Clair," he asserted.

The pulsation of the engine ceased; and Wadsworth, looking up, saw a second boat was just coming alongside a second landing. Back among the trees he caught a glimpse of a rough shack.

The girl stood up. "Come, dad," she called. "Here's home."

Once on the pier, she turned and gave the newspaper man her hand. "Good-by, Mr. Wadsworth," she said. "Mr. Simpson will take you to the settlement, half a mile farther down. You'll find the accommodation there as good as Willis Kent's—and you can go to see Miss Maynard real easy! Good-by."

Wadsworth colored slightly. "Not good-by," he demurred. "Au revoir!"

"No! Good-by! You'll have to drop me, you know. Dad and I have an awful bad name down hereabouts. Keep watch over Mr. Simpson till he has time to cool down," she added.

Wadsworth nodded. "I'll watch!" he promised. "Au revoir," he repeated significantly, as the boat moved away.

CHAPTER X

During the run to the village Wadsworth tried to engage Simpson in talk, but the latter refused his overtures.

"Mr. Wadsworth, suh," he said, at last, "you will oblige me, by desisting, suh."

To this last appeal Wadsworth could answer only by acceding. Fortunately the settlement was close at hand and arrival thereat proved a relief.

After supper, however, he got his host aside and explained matters. "I don't like butting into your affairs down here," he began, diplomatically. "Of course, you wouldn't like a stranger interfering, especially one not familiar with your ways. But murder is murder everywhere, and I'd hate to think that Simpson had killed if anything I could do would stop him. So I'll tell you the whole thing, knowing that you will do what is best."

When he had finished the tale, Mr. Lee combed his beard reflectively with his fingers. "I appreciate your words, suh," he drawled. "They do you honor, suh; they would do a Southern gentleman honor. Of cou'se, Simpson'll have to fight him, but I'm mighty afraid Simp'll get laid out. But I'll see what I can do, suh!"

With this assurance, Wadsworth had to be content.

He did not wake till late the next morning—late, that is, according to country standards. The sun was about an hour high when a hammering at his door aroused him.

"Breakfast is ready, suh!" came the tones of Mr. Smith Lee. "I regret to disturb you, suh, but it is unavoidable."

It was ten minutes, however, before Wadsworth joined the Lees at breakfast. So far as he could count, everybody was there except Simpson, and for him he inquired with some uneasiness.

Lee shrugged his shoulders. "Simp took the boat and went off to his place last night, suh," he explained.

Wadsworth's brows contracted. "Where is his place?" he inquired. "Isn't it up towards Kent's?"

"It is, suh."

"And you let him go after what I told you?"

"I sho'ly did. suh." Mr. Lee's response was positive and unhesitating. "I proffered my services, suh, as one gentleman to another, but he declined them in such a way I could not interfere further, suh."

Wadsworth gulped the remainder of his coffee and rose. "How can I get to his place?" he asked. "Are there any boats here?"

"Certainly, suh, but I reckon they're all in use just now. But you can get to Simp's place on foot, easy, suh. It's only a quarter of a mile through the woods."

"I'll go on foot, then, if you'll start me on the road. Er—does the trail go by Peterson's place, too?"

"Most assuredly, suh! Peterson's place's half a mile off, and Kent's is about a mile." Lee rose and walked to the door, followed by Wadsworth. "Yonder's the trail, suh," he directed.

The day was rapidly becoming warmer and his pace soon insensibly slackened, especially as he had to pick his way along the trail. For the most part it ran very close to the beach, but in others, where it cut across the necks of points, it led far back among the trees.

Coming out into the open from one such crossing, he caught sight of a motor boat, far out, racing back toward the village from where he had just come. Quickly focusing his field glasses he made out that the lone figure in the boat was that of Simpson. Evidently for the moment the local correspondent was not seeking Kent.

Beyond, the road ran deeper in the woods, and as Wadsworth went on, he caught glimpses from time to time of the backs of houses that faced the lake. After going what he guessed to be about a quarter of a mile, he turned in by a footpath that led to one of these, intending to inquire his way to Peterson's.

The path was less than two hundred yards long and very much like the one he had glimpsed from Peterson's landing the day before. No one was visible about the house, and he went to the door and knocked. No answer! He knocked again, more heavily this time, and the door swung silently back before him, leaving him staring into an interior, well lighted by two windows, and by numerous cracks, both in the roof and in walls.

His ranging eyes instantly lighted on something blue stretched out on the table before him, and almost involuntarily he strode across the floor and looked down at it.

It was the blue picture—not a fragment of it, but the whole picture.

Not for an instant could he doubt it. The fragment stolen from him on the train was there, with its characteristic tear, and close against it, fitting the tear, jag by jag, was the remainder of the picture—a tropical landscape of water, trees, Spanish moss and palms.

Silently he stared at it. He was not exactly surprised, for he had been confident that the two parts of the picture had been rejoined somewhere close at hand. He was, however, a little saddened. Almost without knowing it, he had begun to hope that Miss St. Clair might prove innocent. But here was the proof. Doubt was no longer possible.

He began to wonder why the picture had been left exposed so openly as it was. He looked about him for an explanation—and found it instantly. The room showed every sign of hurried departure. A chair had been turned over: papers had been thrown to the floor; a breakfast ready prepared had been left uneaten: these, with the unlatched door, bore eloquent evidence that Miss St. Clair and her father had left in great haste. On the other hand, a locked trunk and some clothing left hanging against the walls, and the blue picture itself, made it improbable that they had left permanently. Certainly, Wadsworth concluded, they had not left in consequence of any clue to the treasure that had come from the blue picture. In that case, they could scarcely have forgotten it.

An idea occurred to him. He would leave the picture, but he would take away a photograph of it!

Swiftly he pinned the picture to the wall in a strong light. Three times he pressed the button, each time with a different exposure, and a different stop and a different distance, to allow for any unconsidered variation in the quality of the light. Then, confident that he would carry away an accurate picture, he hurriedly put up the camera, caught up his gun, and left the place.

CHAPTER XI

Fairly bursting with eagerness to see Bessie Maynard and tell her of his discoveries in regard to the Ford case and the brightening prospects of regaining the million dollars, Wadsworth hurried along the road toward Willis Kent's.

As Wadsworth went up the steps of the porch, someone called his name. He turned and saw Bessie Maynard coming toward him from the grounds. Close behind came her father, with a book in his hand. She was smiling, with no trace of her irritation of the day before, and the reporter felt his heart lighten wonderfully at the sight.

"I wondered how long it would take you to get here," she observed demurely. "Father—you know Mr. Wadsworth?"

"He certainly does," exclaimed the reporter, stepping forward and gripping the hand that the other extended. "Professor, I'm mighty glad to see you again."

"And I you, sir. I have wanted for some time to have the chance to thank you for your kindness to my little girl up in New York last spring."

Wadsworth laughed the thanks aside. "It was the other way around, professor," he declared. "I was awfully obliged to Miss Maynard for letting me talk my theories into her ears, but now I have great news for you. Can we go somewhere and talk?"

"Of course. Come this way." He started towards a bench that stood beneath a magnificent, moss-draped oak, and waved his guest to a seat. "Sit down, Mr. Wadsworth," he invited, "and tell us of your news."

Wadsworth obeyed. With his eyes fixed on Bessie's face, he poured out his tale, delighting the while to see the color come and go in the girl's cheeks, and to watch the vivid sparkle in her eyes. "It all sums up to this," he finished. "It's apples to ashes that Peterson was the Ford coachman, and that his stepdaughter, Miss St. Clair, was the pretended niece. Between them, they stole the blue picture, which somehow contains a clue to the hiding-place of the treasure. The nub of the clue must be the fragment I had, else Miss St. Clair wouldn't have risked stealing it from me. But there's nothing on that piece that any test I can think of will show—that is, there's nothing except the whole picture, and I've got a photograph of that right here in my camera. Perhaps it is a picture of the place where the treasure is buried, and perhaps someone about here may recognize it. In fact, someone is likely to if we are really anywhere near the treasure's hiding place, and we would seem to be. I'll show it to you just as soon as I can get it home and develop it."

"Why wait?" Miss Maynard rose eagerly. "Why can't we see it now? I've got everything necessary in my room and if you'll give me the film I'll develop it and dry it in alcohol and have it ready for you in ten minutes or so. Meanwhile, you and father can sit here and talk about the water devil," she laughed.

Wadsworth handed over the camera meekly. "We will," he acceded. "After all, it was the water devil that brought me down here and I ought to give it some attention. By the way, Miss Maynard, you will find some photographs of the water devil's hoof-marks among the exposed pictures on the film.

"What do you think of the water devil, anyway, Professor?" he asked gaily. "I've got an idea he walks on two legs. I mean that I suspect that there is human agency behind the thing—perhaps Peterson."

But Professor Maynard shook his head. "How is it possible?" he asked. "How can a man make tracks like that? And how can a man carry off a hundred-pound hog in his arms, as this water devil undoubtedly did on at least one occasion?"

If Wadsworth were staggered he did not admit it. "Oh, well, of course there's a lot to explain," he admitted. "But we'll try to explain."

"I hope you may, sir. As a matter of fact, however, there is no actual real reason why some large and powerful animal should not exist in the Everglades here. So far as I have been able to ascertain by inquiries, the Indians have traditions of some dangerous animal that was secreted here. Their tales are very vague but seem to be based on something real—perhaps on some huge amphibious animal of unknown species. Such animals might have lived here for centuries and their existence would account pretty well for everything. For my part, I believe there are such animals."

"Really?"

"Why not? America had many huge animals in pre-historic days. They used to range over the swamps and savannas that now form the Western prairies. Hundreds of their fossil bones have been found; you can see restorations of many of them at the National Museum at Washington."

The reporter's head was swimming. "But," he protested, "you surely don't mean to suggest that any of these beasts could be surviving here!"

"Of course not! Of course not!" The professor's response was prompt. "Of course they all perished hundreds of years ago. But it is just possible that some species, weak and degenerate in comparison with its mighty ancestors, but still great and formidable compared to the beasts we know, has survived unknown and unsuspected in these swamps. Here, for instance, are views of triceratops and stegosaurus, both of which almost certainly once inhabited this country. I was just looking at them when you came."

Wadsworth whistled. "Heavens! What a nightmare!" he exclaimed. "He looks like an armored train. I'd hate to meet that fellow after dark."

The professor nodded. "It wouldn't be pleasant," he admitted, "though the chances are that you could get away. Stegosaurus, like all his race, was a fool. He had only a spoonful of brains to a ton of flesh. That was what enabled the later and cleverer mammals to exterminate him. Oh, yes! You could outwit him."

"Thank you. I'd rather not try. Er—what sort of a track does he make? Anything like that of our friend the water devil?"

The professor looked a little serious. "Standing on his hind legs, as he usually did," he answered, "stegosaurus must have left a track much like that of a hippopotamus. But here comes Bessie."

The girl was running toward them, waving a long strip of darkened film. Her face, however, showed no elation.

"I'm sorry," she panted, glancing regretfully at Wadsworth, as she came to a halt beside the two men. "I'm sorry, but the picture isn't at all good. The background is all right, but the picture itself is all black in every film. Nothing shows."

Wadsworth caught the film from the girl's hand. On the film in all the exposures, the blue picture appeared only as an oblong of black, which in the print would show as an oblong of white.

"I ought to be fired," he groaned, with instant realization of the cause of the fiasco. "Of all the fool tricks, that's the limit. Of course it didn't copy! No blue picture can copy. Blue takes white in a photograph. Every fool amateur knows that. And I never thought of it. Oh! Darn it!"

Professor Maynard took the film from the reporter's yielding hands and examined it carefully. "Perhaps it's not hopeless," he suggested. "I can certainly see some faint marks on it. Suppose we try intensifying it. It may come out clearly enough to show what it is."

But Wadsworth shook his head. "It's just as well to try," he responded, "but it won't do any good. I'm the prize idiot! And I've lost you your million dollars. I don't know," he went on, with a ghastly attempt at jocularity. "I don't know how I'm going to pay them back to you. If the devotion of a lifetime will be of some small reparation,—"

Bessie laughed. "Nonsense," she exclaimed, happily. "I don't believe the blue picture was any use, anyway. But I'll intensify that part of the film and make prints of the other photographs you took and then we can see what's what." With a last look at Wadsworth, she flitted away.

The two men said little while she was gone. Wadsworth was utterly subdued and the professor found little consolation to offer him. Glumly they sat until Bessie came back with her hands full of prints.

"You can see something," she called. "But not much. Look!" She distributed the prints.

It took no second glance, however, to show that the thing was hopeless.

Suddenly the professor started.

"Good Heavens!" he cried. "What's this?" With shaking fingers he held out one of the prints. "Where—where did you take this picture?" he demanded.

Wadsworth glanced at it. "That? Oh! That was taken on an island near here. Miss St. Clair had seen some tracks there once, and we stopped by to look at them. We found some others quite fresh, and I snapped them. Here they are. See!" He pointed to the lower part of the print. "I took the picture just as we were going away. The marks were pretty fresh and I wanted to go ashore and trace them, but Simpson and Miss St. Clair wouldn't let me."

"Thank God they didn't!" the professor's tones were shaking. "It is possible that you didn't see? Look here! Here in the bushes! Look closely! Good God! Man! Can't you see it?"

"See what?" In spite of himself, the reporter's tones were awed. The professor seemed terribly in earnest. "See what?" He took the print and held it so that Miss Maynard could see.

"Here! Here!" the professor's forefinger rattled on the paper.

"I don't—yes, by heavens, I do. Good Lord. Professor, that—that isn't anything alive. It's just the bushes." He felt Bessie clutching his arm in terror. "It can't be any-thing real," he repeated. "It's a nightmare."

"A nightmare! A nightmare! Not unless this book is a nightmare, too!" The professor's voice rose to a shriek. "It's a stegosaurus or the next thing to one. It's a beast that was thought to have perished, root and branch, a hundred thousand years ago. If you had landed, you would have gone the way of all the poor fellows who have vanished."

Chapter XII

For a few minutes the three stood silent, staring at the print. Then Wadsworth laughed. "Gee!" he exclaimed. "Gee, Professor, you had me going for a minute. Of course we all know it's all nonsense. There isn't any such beast in the picture—not really. It's only a queer combination of stumps and branches and lights and shadows—that's all!"

"Is it?" Professor Maynard stared at the reporter for a moment. Then he shrugged his shoulders. "Very well," he said. "If you're satisfied, I have nothing more to say—at present."

None of them had any chance to say anything more, for at that moment a shriek rang out and Mrs. Kent flew out of the front door and down the walk to the landing.

With a sudden premonition of evil Wadsworth craned his neck to toward what she was hastening. As he did so, he heard the explosion of a motor and caught sight of a boat sliding swiftly shoreward from the direction of the town. Beyond a doubt it was the one that had brought him from Peninsula City the day before. Two men were in it: one of them he could not see distinctly, but the other was certainly Simpson.

What, he wondered, had the fellow been doing?

"Shall we go?" he asked, turning to Bessie.

"Of course!" Bessie was off, running with a free Atalanta-like gait that the reporter found some difficulty in matching.

Just as he reached the landing the boat shot alongside, and Simpson stood up. Behind him was Smith Lee. Wadsworth could see now that both men's faces were white.

"Mrs. Kent, ma'am," he faltered. "Mrs. Kent, ma'am, I—I—"

A little, slight woman—she who had clung to Willis Kent's arm the day before—broke in. "Oh! Oh!" she cried. "Tom Simpson! Have—have you killed my husband?"

"No! No! Good Lord! No! ma'am! No!" Horror, real or counterfeit, spoke in Simpson's voice. "No, ma'am. It wasn't me. It—it—Lee and I were in the boat looking for him. I don't deny I was looking for him. He hit me and he said—said—but we never found him till after he was dead. We saw something dark lying on the beach and went closer and saw it was Willis Kent. We went in real close and we see—we see he was dead for sure, and we come away quick."

"Went in close! Didn't you go ashore at all? How do you know he was dead?" It was Wadsworth who asked the question, and his voice was stern.

"He was dead, all right," Smith Lee broke in for the first time. "You wouldn't have gone ashore either, if you'd see what we see!"

"What you saw! Good Lord, man! What did you see?" Wadsworth's excitement was growing.

Smith Lee glanced at Mrs. Kent, who was sobbing in Bessie's arms, and he gesticulated toward the house. Bessie nodded and began to lead the little woman away.

Wadsworth waited till she was out of ear-shot. Then he bent forward again. "Well, well," he cried, "what killed him? Couldn't you see what killed him?"

"Know! Of cou'se I know. The tracks was there, plain as print. There was Willis' coming down from the water and there was the devil's going up to meet him and then coming down again. The water devil got him! The water devil got him!"

"Oh, ho!" Wadsworth's tone was singular. "The water devil happened along very conveniently. Where were you—?"

The reporter paused. He had been about to question Simpson about his trip toward the village an hour before, but he decided that it was better to wait.

"I'll go with you to the body," he declared. "Professor!" He turned Maynard, who had stood by, pale and worried. "Professor, will you go with us?" Maynard nodded. "Surely!" he replied.

Willis Kent's body was lying about thirty feet from the edge of the water. His footprints, leading from the edge of the jungle, were plainly visible. Close around his body, the beach was trampled into an indistinguishable mire, but between the trampled spot and the water's edge extended two lines of the well-known holes commonly ascribed to the water devil.

Quite naturally Wadsworth took command. Under his direction Simpson drove the boat ashore, bow on, at some distance from the point where the tracks ended.

Cautioning the others to stay where they were, Wadsworth leaped out and made a circuit that brought him to the body without disturbing the mysterious tracks. A moment's investigation showed that Lee and Simpson had made no mistake. Willis Kent was dead. His throat had been literally torn out.

With a gesture that needed no explanation, Wadsworth went back to the boat, carefully following his own tracks. "He's dead," he said briefly, as he climbed in. "We must let him lie for a moment and get what light we can on this thing before the evidence is destroyed. Now, Simpson, I want you to bring the boat very gently in between the two places where those tracks touch the water. We'll see how far out they go."

Simpson nodded and obeyed. When the ripples caused by the movement had died away, the clear water made it easy to distinguish the tracks on the sloping bottom for about six feet out. There they ended abruptly. Wadsworth plumbed the depth with his arm. "It is not more than eighteen inches deep," he said, reflectively. "That means, if it means anything, that the beast could swim in water a foot and a half deep. It must be a darn queer beast to have legs as big around as an elephant, and only eighteen inches long. Could your stegosaurus swim here, Professor?"

Professor Maynard shook his head. "Neither the stegosaurus nor other beast, ancient or modern, with feet like that could do it," he answered. "An enormous alligator might swim in eighteen inches of water, but no alligator and no existing saurian could make tracks like that. All saurians have claws."

But Wadsworth interrupted. "It's a very rare beast that Professor Maynard thinks might have made these tracks," he explained hurriedly. "It's only a guess, however; and we haven't time to discuss it now. We must take Kent's body home."

He paused for an instant; then he went on. "In getting ashore," he cautioned, "please be very careful not to trample or confuse any of the tracks. They may be important later on."

In some mysterious fashion, the news had spread, and curious spectators came flocking to the spot. Long before Wadsworth and his party could complete their preparations for conveying home the body, at least a dozen had collected. Neither Peterson nor his step-daughter were among them, however, a point that the reporter noted with some surprise, as he had understood that their home was very near the spot where they body had been found.

"Is Peterson's place near here?" he asked of Smith Lee.

Lee glanced around him. "Right yonder, suh," he answered, panting. "There comes Peterson now, durn him!"

Following with his eyes the other's outstretched finger, Wadsworth saw the Swede hurrying down the beach towards the throng. He moved with his customary wobbly gait.

Frowning, the reporter watched him, wondering, as he had wondered the day before, what cause could make a man walk like that. Then all at once the revelation came.

Swiftly he stepped forward to meet the Swede. "We are trying a little experiment, Peterson," he said, chillingly. "Willis Kent has been murdered,"—Peterson started and cast a swift sideways glance at the body—"Willis Kent has been murdered by someone or something who made these tracks here. We want to know who it is."

"Yes? Yes?"

"We want to see whose feet fit the tracks. Sit down on the sand, Peterson, and take off your shoes."

The blood surged crimson to the Swede's face, then fled away, leaving his cheeks as colorless as those of the corpse on the sand. Twice he opened his mouth to speak, but no words came. Pitilessly the reporter drove on. "You killed Willis Kent, Peterson," he declared. "You made these tracks—you, and no one but you. Take off your shoes."

The crowd of spectators were hushed as death. Scarcely did they breathe. Uncomprehendingly they watched.

Peterson tore at his collar. "It's one lie," he shouted. "You want to put it on me. But it's one lie. He was dead before I come to him."

Wadsworth swung round to the crowd. "Grab that man," he ordered, "and roll up his trousers and unbuckle his legs at the knees. Then we'll see the stumps he walked with when he played water devil."

Chapter XIII

Peterson turned to run, but before he had taken two steps the crowd was upon him, sweeping him off his legs and suspending his feet in the air. Another instant and a yell went up, telling that Wadsworth's guess had proved correct.

The Swede's legs had been amputated at the knees. Fast to the stumps were two artificial limbs, terminating with shoes, but easily removable. The stumps with their harness formed an elephant-like pad, well fitted to make the holes that characterized the tracks of the supposed water devil.

For a moment the crowd stood spellbound, unable to take in the full bearing of the revelation. Wadsworth's voice rang out:

"Bring him here!" he ordered.

Instinctively the crowd obeyed.

Wadsworth looked him up and down. "How did you do it, Peterson?" he questioned, sternly, with a sweep of his hand toward the dead man. "How did you tear Kent's throat out?"

The Swede cowered. "I not do it," he moaned. "I not do it. He was dead when I come."

"Nonsense! Don't lie."

"I not lie," panted the man. "I come out of the creek yonder," he pointed—"in my boat. I see something on the sand. I come near and look. I see it is Kent. I think he is dead. I want to help him—"

Wadsworth laughed. "Bosh!" he exclaimed. "You killed him and tried to make us think it was the water devil. You've played water devil before."

The Swede turned pale. "Water devil!" he echoed. "No! no! What you mean?"

"What do I mean?" Wadsworth's tones were chill. "Oh, come, Peterson, don't lie. It's no use. Look at those tracks." He waved his hand and the throng divided, letting the Swede look through at the two lines of holes. "Those are your tracks, aren't they?"

The man glanced at the holes with distended eyes. "Yes! Yes! I make 'em!" he gasped.

"Well! They're water devil tracks, all right. Now, own up. You played water devil so that you could steal hogs and fruit and scare people and—"

But Peterson shook his head desperately. "No! No!" he cried. "I never play water devil! No! No!"

Wadsworth jeered at him. "Nonsense!" he repeated. "Next, I suppose, you'll deny that you are Carroll, the New York coachman who murdered Mrs. Ford."

Slowly the Swede's eyes widened. "Gott!" he cried, "How you know?"

"How shouldn't I know! Own up. Why did you kill the old lady!"

"I not kill her!" The Swede found his tongue at last. "I was lock up when she was kill. Alvarez, he kill her."

"And you escaped by taking off your legs. People were looking for a tall, lame man and not for a short one without legs. Oh, that part's plain enough. But I think I can guess why you played water devil!"

"Own up, you scoundrel," resounded from every side.

Under the assault the Swede cowered. But he stuck to his denial. "I never do it," he protested. "I never do it."

"Oh, come," Wadsworth remarked, banteringly. "That won't do! You'll have to tell us all about it later. Boys, take him down to the town and lock him up and let him think over things till after we have cared for Mr. Kent. Don't let him get away. He's wanted in New York to explain a murder there."

Unstable as water, the crowd shifted its position instantly. "That's right, Lee, you're justice of the peace. Lock him up and don't let him get away!"

Smith Lee shouldered his way forward. "I sho'ly won't," he asseverated, clapping the man on the shoulder. "Come along now, Peterson," he ordered.

A moment more and the crowd had split. Most of it accompanied Smith Lee and his prisoner toward the village. The rest, after lifting Kent's body into the motor boat, set out along the shore for the Kent place, to see it lifted out and borne into the house. Professor Maynard went with Simpson in the boat.

Before the boat started, Wadsworth spoke to Simpson, who had sat silently in the motor boat throughout the entire scene. "Tell Miss Maynard that I will be along as soon as possible, Simpson," he ordered. "Perhaps you had better wait at Kent's till I come."

The boat chugged away from the shore. When it was well out from the land, Wadsworth, who had stood watching it, turned and saw with intense satisfaction that he was alone. The moment he was sure of this, he started toward the house dimly visible through the bushes, that Lee had pointed out to him as Peterson's.

As he broke through the fringe of trees, however, he saw that he must have misunderstood Lee's words, for the house was assuredly not the one he had entered earlier in the day. Nevertheless, he went toward it, after a moment's hesitation, intending to ask the way to Peterson's.

As he rounded the corner, some one on the little porch rose hurriedly to meet him and he found himself face to face with Lillian St. Clair.

Certainly she showed no signs of knowing of Kent's death. After the first look of surprise, her pretty lips wreathed themselves into a smile and she greeted the reporter gaily.

"Hello!" she called. "So you really have come to see me after all. I didn't believe she'd let you do it."

Wadsworth frowned. He did not like the allusion to Miss Maynard. But he answered serenely: "I was just trying to find my way to your place," he explained. "It's lucky I met you here."

"Met me here! Where else should you meet me!" Clearly the girl was puzzled. "But never mind. You look as sober as a judge. Has anything happened?"

Wadsworth nodded. Evidently the girl had not heard of Peterson's crime—unless, indeed, she was really a far better actress than he had supposed her to be. "Yes. Something has happened," he answered. "May I sit down!"

"Of course." Miss St. Clair pushed forward a seat. "Sit down and disclose the secrets of your life. Simpson and Kent ain't been fighting, have they!"

Wadsworth did not answer directly. He mounted the stoop and sat down. Then he turned to the girl. "Miss St. Clair," he began, "something very serious has happened, which you may or may not know. Anyway, you and I have got to have an explanation, for your own sake, if for nobody else's."

The girl caught at her heart. "Simpson has killed Kent!" she declared, with utmost conviction.

"No! Simpson has killed nobody!" Wadsworth looked her in the eye. "We have caught the water devil!" he declared.

"What!" The girl's voice showed amazement, but Wadsworth noted with real satisfaction that it showed no guilty knowledge. "When! Where! What sort of a beast is it!"

"It is not a beast at all. It's a man masquerading!"

Miss St. Clair stared; then she laughed with frank incredulity.

"It's true. The water devil was a man—a man who had lost the lower part of his legs and who walked on pads—when he wanted to disguise his steps."

The shot went home. The girl grew pallid to the lips. "Dad!" she breathed.

"Yes! Peterson! The proof is ample. You asked whether Simpson had killed Kent. I told you no. Simpson did not kill Kent. But—"

"But dad did! Dad did!"

Wadsworth nodded. "He was caught almost red-handed," he explained. "There can be no doubt about it. I am sorry to say that it became my duty to cause his arrest."

Miss St. Clair buried her face in her hands. "He did it on my account," she sobbed. "He was always too good to me. And these old cats down here—

"Where is dad! Have—have they caught him!"

"Yes. He's under arrest at Okechobee City."

The girl sprang up. "I must go to him," she gasped. "I must—"

"Wait!" Wadsworth put out a restraining hand. "He is all right and perfectly safe for the moment. If he killed Willis Kent on your account in the heat of anger, as I guess he did, no Southern jury will punish him for it. But he isn't popular down here and if he is to get the lightest possible punishment, all the facts must be known—particularly what he was hunting for when he wandered around the islands hereabouts on his pad feet. What were you hunting for, for years! What did you go to Mrs. Ford's house in New York to hunt for!"

The girl paled, but did not falter. "I don't know what you mean," she declared stoutly.

"For your own sake, you had better be frank. But I'll go on. Why did your step-father hire there as a coachman?"

"My step-father! As coachman?"

"Yes. Oh, there's no use in evasion. I know pretty nearly everything—even how he escaped on his stumps after being released by the police. But I'll ask you one more question. Why did you steal the blue picture from me on the train?"

The girl flashed into sudden movement. "I didn't! I swear to God I didn't," she panted.

"Who did, then? Who else in all the world could have been on that train and have wanted that picture enough to steal it? Oh! There's no use in dodging. I know all but a few details. I know about the Ford treasure—"

The last words stung the girl to sudden anger. "The Ford treasure! If you know so much, you know that that treasure wasn't Ford's at all. It was dad's—dad's and Senor Alvarez's. Ford stole it from them, and we had a right to get it back."

"Oh!" Wadsworth drew a long breath. "How did the treasure come to belong to Peterson?"

"He got it out of a mine in Mexico, and hired Ford and three others to help him to take it to the city by boat. They were blown over to Florida by a gale and came up the Caloosahatchie to the lake here. They got out to make a camp and Ford sneaked into the boat and ran away and left them. They wandered around a long time and got separated. At last Senor Alvarez and dad got to the coast. The others never did get there. They must have died of fever or something. Do you wonder that daddy and Alvarez, hated Ford?"

Wadsworth shrugged his shoulders. "No. I don't wonder," he admitted. "They had good cause, both according to that story and according to the true one. That gold did not belong to Alvarez and Peterson. It belonged to Professor Maynard. Peterson and the others stole it from him. Then Ford seems to have thrown down his pals. Perhaps you understand now, why they made no complaint against Ford, but relied upon themselves to run him down."

"I didn't know," she faltered. "I didn't know. They told me—"

"They would, of course. But you see how the truth straightens out everything. Go on—they found Ford?"

"Yes. They found him!" The girl drew a long breath. "They found him, and they found out in some way that he had buried the gold down in Florida in the Everglades here somewhere and had never dug it up again. Dad had a fight with Ford. There was an explosion and dad lost both his feet. Ford died. Alvarez's wife tried to find out from him at the last just where he put the gold, but he wouldn't tell. But dad knew he had told his wife. So we watched her. She had a good deal of money and didn't need to go after the gold for a long time. Alvarez's wife got a place as maid in the house to watch her."

"Matilda Vogel."

"Yes! That was her name. At last Mrs. Ford's money began to run low. Matilda told me and I wrote to dad. He had gotten a place down here and was spending his time hunting for the gold. When I wrote he came to New York and got a place as coachman to Mrs. Ford, so he could watch her better. One day he saw her examining a blue picture. He made up his mind that it contained a clue to the hiding place of the treasure. He told Alvarez and they got into a quarrel, and the police came. Alvarez ran away, but dad was locked up. That night Mrs. Ford was murdered. Dad knew that Alvarez must have done it. He was afraid Alvarez had got the secret and that he wouldn't play fair. So he came down here to watch and make sure that Alvarez didn't get the gold without his knowing it. I told you he already had a place down here. Alvarez didn't show up and dad sent me back to New York to see what I could find out. I went to Mrs. Ford's house, but I didn't find out anything."

"You did. You carried away the biggest part of the blue picture."

"I didn't. Honest to God I didn't. I saw it there and wanted it, but I didn't get any chance to take it. That policeman stuck to me like a brother."

"You sent him down to get your handkerchief from your car."

"Yes, I did. But a strange maid—not Matilda—came in just as he went out and I didn't get any chance to take it. Besides, the picture was torn in two and most all gone. Matilda may have taken it."

"Then why did you steal the fragment from me on the train?"

"I didn't! I told you I didn't! I'm telling you everything true. Why should I lie about the picture?"

Wadsworth shrugged his shoulders. "I don't know," he replied. "And I don't want to be insulting! But you must have taken it, because I saw the whole picture in your own house on your own table not two hours ago!"

Miss St. Clair's eyes grew bigger than ever. "You saw that picture here!" she exclaimed. "In this house?"

Wadsworth laughed shortly. "No, not in this house," he answered. "Of course not! I saw it in your own house. In fact, I took a photograph of it. Here it is." He drew a bunch of prints from his pocket and held them out. "See," he went on, "this square of white is the picture, pinned against the wall. It took white in the photo, because blue always does take white. I was an ass to forget that. But the surroundings are enough. You can't deny your own house. Now please own up!"

For a moment Miss St. Clair did not speak. She bent over the photo and studied it intensely. When she looked up a curious expression was on her face. "You are a mighty clever young man, Mr. Wadsworth," she said at last, deliberately. "But you're just a mite previous sometimes. This house where we're sitting is dad's. The house in the picture ain't. Whose it is, I don't know. What is more, you ain't quite so thorough as you might be, Mr. Wadsworth. If I were you, I'd take a magnifying glass and look at that photo real close. If I ain't mistook, there's writing across that blue picture."

"Writing?"

"Yes! Writing! Something funny's come out in the picture. I'll make you a present of the information."

"You're right!" he ejaculated. "You're right! Good Lord! I wish I had a magnifying glass!"

"Professor Maynard's got one, ain't he?"

"Of course he has." Wadsworth sprang to his feet. "I'll go to him at once and—" He paused. "And you?" he finished.

"Me! Oh, I'll go and see dad!"

Chapter XIV

If Wadsworth did not run all the way to Kent's it was only because, in that climate, he was not physically capable of it.

When he reached Kent's, he found the place steeped in the curious hush that death usually brings. Simpson was sitting in his motor boat at the foot of the lawn, but nobody else was visible about the place. Wadsworth found considerable difficulty in getting someone to go and tell Miss Maynard of his arrival.

He succeeded at last, however, and in a few minutes the girl was with him. "Mrs. Kent is quiet at last," she said, gravely, "and I was just about to ask Mr. Simpson to go to town in the boat for you."

"I came as soon as I could. You know that!" Wadsworth's tones were expressive. "You know I wouldn't have left you without grave reason."

The girl nodded. "Yes, I know!" she acceded happily. "You've been the same always. I don't know why you've been so good to me!"

"You don't? You don't? Don't you? Don't you know, really?"

"Oh, I guess you took pity on my greenness. But"—hastily—"tell me what you have been doing. I understand you caught the murderer."

"Yes. We caught him. At least I suppose so. I'm not feeling quite as sure as I did at first. But that isn't what I came to talk about. Has your father a magnifying glass—anything that magnifies?"

Miss Maynard wrinkled her brows. "Why, yes," she answered. "Of course he has. But I don't know just where it is. Father has gone to town, you know—"

Wadsworth uttered an exclamation of disappointment.

"Yes," reiterated the girl. "He went half an hour ago. Did you want to see him very much?"

Wadsworth hesitated. "That depends," he admitted. "Can't you find that magnifier. It's important."

"I'll try." Turning, the girl vanished into the house.

In a few minutes she was back with a reading glass in her hand. "Will this do?" she asked.

Without answering, Wadsworth took the glass and with trembling fingers held it over the photo. An instant later he uttered a cry. "It's true! It's true!" he shouted. "Here's the clue to the treasure! The clue to the treasure! You're rich, Bessie! You're rich." The given name slipped out unawares.

Eyes alight, the girl leaned forward. "What do you mean?" she demanded hoarsely.

"What I say. Quick! Come over under the tree here. Sit down! Write what I read to you."

For perhaps five minutes Wadsworth read slowly, often hesitating over some almost indistinguishable word. At last, however, he finished, and he and Bessie, side by side, pored with wondering eyes over the message from the grave.

It read as follows:

Dear Viola—I am writing this so that you can find the gold in case anything happens to me. Few people know enough to suspect a record like this. Certainly Alvarez and his friends do not. No mortal eye can read it. Only the actinic gaze of the camera can ever decipher it.

I am writing in ordinary ink on a piece of drawing paper. When I finish, I will take any one of the dozen of ink eradicators on the market and remove every sign of the ink, leaving the paper apparently clear and un-blotted. It is not a question of sympathetic ink that can be restored by heat and anything like that. Nothing will restore it. But if you make a photograph of it, the original writing, apparently blotted out of existence, will show up in the negative as clear and distinct as it ever was.

If I were sure that the paper would not be thrown aside as valueless, I would simply leave it as it is. But to make sure that it shall be preserved, I will paint a water-color sketch on top of it. Blue does not photograph, and will simply vanish under the camera's eye and the original writing will show through.

Half a mile east from the cast shore of Lake Okechobee, on a small island, amid the swamps of the Everglades, stands a high lime-stone rock—the only rock, so far as I know, in all that region. The gold is buried at its eastern base. It seemed best to bury it there. Alvarez shot me through the leg as I escaped, leaving him and the others behind, and I dared not risk going back to civilization shot through the leg with a boat-load of gold. Of course, I never expected Alvarez and the others to escape, and I did not think I should have any difficulty in getting the gold any time I want-ed it after things had quieted down. But, as you know, Alvarez and some of the others did escape and they have run me down. However, I can afford to wait. After a while they will get tired, and then—

But they may get me first. So, I leave this
for your benefit. Remember: dig at the east
base of the tall, white rock.   Henry.

The two readers looked up. Then, impulsively, they
flung out their hands and their palms met in a long and
hearty grip. Miss Maynard was the first to speak.

"Do you know the place?" she gasped.

Wadsworth nodded. "Sure I do!" he declared. "It's the
place where Miss St. Clair showed me the water devil
tracks—Great Scott! What was Peterson doing on that
island?"

"Peterson?"

"Yes! He's the water devil, you know. Good Lord! He
couldn't have found the treasure, could he?"

Miss Maynard's lips were pale. "Oh, I hope not! I hope
not," she breathed. "It would be too cruel. You don't think
he did, do you?"

Wadsworth shook his head. "No, I don't think so!" he
decided. "And yet—it was his step-daughter that called my
attention to the writing. If she's fooled me— Oh, I've got
to find out. Yonder's Simpson and the motor boat. Shall
we go and find out. Or shall we wait for your father?"

The girl hesitated. "I don't know," she said. "Father
may be a long time coming. Suppose we go and see."

"All right. Come ahead."

Side by side the two hurried toward the landing. Half
way down, Bessie stopped suddenly. "Mr. Wadsworth," she
gasped, "I want you to know—whether we get the gold or
not—that we're just as grateful to you. I think you just
splendid and if we do get it, father and I are going to
divide up with you."

Wadsworth laughed. "If you think I'm going to take
your money, you're badly mistaken," he answered frankly.
"There's just one thing your father's got that I want and

I'm afraid he won't give me that!" The reporter's words came thickly. Something seemed to be the matter with his tongue.

Bessie, however, did not seem afflicted. "Why not?" she inquired, innocently. "You never can tell till you ask, you know."

Wadsworth stopped short. "Will you—Bessie?" he asked, tremulously.

"Goose! Why else have I been throwing myself at your head for the past six months?" The girl was half laughing and half crying. "Oh, no! Not here! Not—not—oh, some one will see. Oh! Oh! Besides we must hurry or we'll lose the gold."

"Confound the gold!" But Wadsworth hurried, nevertheless, and a moment later the two were beside the boat.

"Simpson!" Wadsworth was speaking. "We want to go to the island with the white rock—the one where we saw the water devil tracks, you know. You've got gasoline enough, haven't you?"

Simpson tugged at his goatee. "I reckon so, suh!" he answered. "Maybe, though, I'd better see if I can get some more up at the house."

"All right, if you think best. It's up to you to have enough. We don't want to run out. And, Simpson,"—as the local man started up the landing—"Simpson! Get some of the men to bring two or three picks and shovels down. We may want to dig."

Simpson slouched off, the two in the boat following his progress with their eyes until he passed out of sight behind the house. Soon he reappeared with an attendant train of negroes laden with picks and spades and with cans that evidently held gasoline. One negro, who carried nothing, separated from the bunch and trotted off toward the town.

Rapidly the implements were stowed away in the boat, and the little craft chugged away.

CHAPTER XV

The boat sped swiftly over the clear waters of the lake. Soon it reached the mouth of the little creek that gave access to the lake and started up it, its rapid-fire reports waking the solitudes and startling the birds from their perches on the trees. As it went, Wadsworth explained the situation to Simpson.

There was nothing else to do. Now that the hiding place of the gold was known, there was no longer need of secrecy. Besides, Simpson's aid would be needed to dig it up. "Or course," he finished, "we know that Peterson has been out there, and it's possible that he's got the gold."

"I sho'ly do hope not, suh. But if he has we'll wring it away from him, suh."

The beach of the island was still screened by the jungly growth, above which the high, white rock could be seen. Soon, however, the boat slipped through a narrow channel, darted across the broad stretch of water, and ran gently toward the sloping stretch of sand.

Wadsworth pointed. "Yonder are the tracks we saw here yesterday," he commented, "and yonder's the place where we saw the water devil—in the picture. Say, the joke certainly is on the professor, isn't it?" He ran his eye over the massed foliage. "I can't see what it was that could have looked so queer, though," he finished.

The boat grated on the beach and Wadsworth, picking up a spade, jumped out. Once on the sand, he turned and helped Bessie to follow him. "Can I help you to get the boat into position, Simpson?" he asked.

"No, suh, I'll fix that, suh. You go 'long with yo' digging."

Side by side they scurried up the beach, tramping the supposed water devil tracks. "Peterson came right here, didn't he?" remarked Wadsworth. "But I don't see any traces of digging!"

The white rock, though perhaps twenty feet high, was not large and its east side was not more than five feet long. Wadsworth promptly sunk his spade into the soft sand a foot or two from the rock and flung the first spadeful far down toward the water's edge.

Bessie insisted on helping, but her skirts so hampered her that when Simpson came to help them, she was glad to surrender her spade to him.

Steadily the two men worked, flinging the sand wide, and soon a trench a foot or more deep yawned across the foot of the rock.

"Ford was alone and crippled. He couldn't have dug very deep," panted Wadsworth. "He—ah!"

His spade grated on something hard; and stooping, he plunged his hand into the yielding sand. His fingers closed on something. He gave a mighty yank, and fell back, holding in his hand a bar, dull indeed, but still conspicuously yellow. Its weight alone would have showed it to be gold.

For an hour the three worked furiously. As they dug out the bars and tossed them to the sand, Bessie picked them up and carried them to the boat.

At last it was done. The motor boat was very low in the water, but not low enough to be at all unsafe. Wadsworth climbed out of the hole and stretched himself. "Gee," he called happily. "I haven't worked so hard since I was a boy. But it's worth it."

Simpson looked up. "'Yes, it is," he agreed. "You're right. It is worth it. Miss Maynard, please step up yonder beside Mr. Wadsworth. Quick, now!"

Bessie did not understand, but Simpson's tone was so insistent that she obeyed. She stumbled on the sand pile and Wadsworth caught her hand to keep her from falling. When they looked up, Simpson was facing them, rifle in hand.

"Hands up!" he ordered, sharply.

Simpson raised his rifle with a warning click. "Hands up!" he cried again. "Can't you hear! Quick now!"

Slowly Wadsworth raised his hands. "Better obey!" he counseled, in a swift aside to Bessie. "What does this mean, Simpson?" he questioned.

"It means that you've got just five minutes to say your prayers." The man's drawl had disappeared, and a chill, implacability sounded in his tones. "You've got to die, both of you, here and now, but I'm not going to kill you without giving you a chance to make your peace."

The words were plain enough, but neither Wadsworth nor Bessie could take them in fully. They were too preposterous. Bessie uttered a faint cry, and Wadsworth muttered something that sounded like an imprecation.

"Have you lost your senses, Simpson?" he demanded. "What do you want to murder us for?"

"I don't want to kill you people, but I've got to."

"For the gold, of course!"—grimly. "I don't want to kill you people, but I've got to. I've been after this gold for ten years—"

"Ten years!"

"Yes! Ten years. When you were telling me that yarn, you didn't know that I was one of the men that Ford marooned, did you? Well, I was. Peterson and Alvarez and I got out. And we've been chasin' after that gold ever since. I've got it! Why, you fool, that wasn't Peterson's house where you saw that picture. That was my house. I left the picture there when I went out to kill that dog, Kent."

"Kent! You killed Kent!"

"Yes, I killed him. I blew his damn throat out with a bullet. I don't mind telling you, because I'm not afraid you'll pass it on. I killed him just as I am going to kill you. Now you say your prayers and be quick about it."

Wadsworth looked around him desperately. Simpson's words had carried conviction at last. The man's very confession of one murder made another almost imperative. Still, Wadsworth knew that it took extraordinary resolution to kill a man, and especially a woman, in cold blood.

"By Jove!" he cried. "You fooled me, all right. But how in thunder did you get the blue picture?"

Simpson hesitated: then. "Alvarez got most of it when he croaked the old woman," he explained. "He got the rest from you on the train. I reckon you saw him there. He was watching Miss St. Clair to see that she and Peterson didn't cheat us. He passed you at the gate and sat near you in the sleeper."

"Whew! You're thorough-going, all right, Simpson!—I suppose you and Peterson fixed up the water devil stunt between you?"

Simpson shook his head. He looked slightly crestfallen. "No!" he answered. "He never told me anything about his making water devil tracks. Peterson and me ain't been on any too good terms. I guess he's been using them to hunt for this here gold without letting on to me and Alvarez."

The man paused and cocked his ear. Distinct, but distant, there floated through the air the rapid-fire explosions of a motor boat. Wadsworth heard it, and hope dawned in his heart.

But Simpson showed no fear. "That's Alvarez coming," he explained. "I sent him word from Kent's place to follow. He thinks he's coming to get his share in this gold. But he's fooled. I ain't sharing with anyone—and I ain't leaving anyone to tell tales."

"Talk sense, Simpson," he demanded. "You don't dare to kill us!"

"I don't dare do anything else!" answered the man, ferociously. "I ain't taking no chances of being caught and jailed, or lynched or hung. Not me! I'm going to kill you and bury you in that hole you've dug."

The chug-chug of the motor boat was louder now. Obviously it was very near at hand. But death was nearer. Despairingly Wadsworth glanced around, seeking some pretext, any pretext, that might hold off Fate a little longer. As he did, Bessie, with a little sigh, sank unconscious to the ground.

Before the reporter could stoop to pick her up, defiant of death, his eyes caught something in the bushes. His form stiffened and a curious look—a look almost of triumph—came over his face.

In the jungle behind Simpson, something was moving —a huge Something that yet moved silently as a cat—a nightmare Something with a small head set with ravening jaws sunk deep between two short but terrifically powerful forearms. Above its back towered a ridge of huge, armoured spines. Slowly it crept into the open, its wicked, deep-set, eyes fixed on the unconscious form of the would-be murderer. Slowly it rose upon gigantic hind legs that sank deep into the sand and mud of the beach as it moved.

Wadsworth's dry tongue rattled between his teeth. "Simpson!" he quavered, and his voice seemed very faint and far away. "Simpson! Did it ever occur to you that perhaps Peterson was not the only water devil—that there might be a real one somewhere?"

Simpson shrugged his shoulders. "Naw!" he growled, and raised his rifle.

"There is!" Wadsworth voice broke into a sudden shriek. "There is! Look behind you!"

Derisively Simpson laughed. "You can't fool me by any old trick like that," he rumbled.

"I'm not trying to fool you. Look!"

TANGLED WITH THE CRASH OF THE RIFLE CAME THE ROAR OF THE GREAT BEAST AS IT SPRANG.

Simpson looked. Then, with a strangled shriek, he sprang round and flung up his rifle. Mingled with its crash came the roar of the great beast as it sprang.

Cowering back against the great white rock, Wadsworth watched the brief encounter. He saw the spitting flame from the repeater, saw the black blood spurt from the monster's chest as the bullets went home, saw the huge form tower above the victim and the short forearms close about him in a hug that could mean naught but death— saw the great beast totter and sway upon its elephantine feet. Its arms relaxed, letting slip its crushed prey. Then, with a last desperate struggle, it splashed its way out into the water and disappeared beneath the crashing waters.

A moment later came a yell! Wadsworth, looking up from Bessie's fainting form, saw a second motor boat, crowded with armed men, come into view around the point of the island. In it stood Lillian St. Clair. Behind her, obviously a prisoner, was a short, dark man, whom he did not know, but whom he guessed to be Alvarez.

Rescue had come—rescue none the less welcome because it was no longer necessary, and because it had come too late to see the disappearance of the water devil.

Afterwards, Wadsworth learned that Lillian, hearing that he and Bessie had gone away with Simpson, and suspecting many things, had gone to Smith Lee with the whole story just in time to stop Alvarez from following, and to commandeer his boat to go to the rescue.

Later still, Peterson, released and acquitted, departed for parts unknown, after selling all of his Everglades holdings to Wadsworth and Bessie for a home. Lillian went back to her beloved New York, where she is making a really substantial reputation as an actress.

Professor Maynard is still excavating in the prehistoric boneyard that he discovered. More particularly, however, he is searching for the skeleton of the monster that ended the Ford case forever. That it survived the encounter he does not believe, for no further trace of its existence has ever been found. He is convinced that it crept away and died somewhere near, but so far he has never been able to discover the exact spot. From Wadsworth's description. he is satisfied that it was a last survivor of some species of stegosaurus that had somehow managed to endure in the solitudes of the fast-disappearing Everglades.

Nightmare!

Francis Stevens (1917)

(Pseudonym of Gertrude Barrows Bennett)

CHAPTER I

"Philip, did you notice that tall, thin man in the gray ulster, who was walking up and down the boat-deck just before dinner?"

"Yes, sir. I observed the gentleman. Very haristocratic appearance, if I may say so, Mr. Jones."

"Exactly. He never bought that ulster in New York. When we reach London I want you to look around and see if you can find a tailor who will make me one of the same cut."

"Very well, sir. Very good taste, if I may say so, Mr. Jones."

"You may. And—let's see—I need a few new golf sticks, and—a dozen new shirts. Why did you pack this automatic in this trunk, Philip? Put it in that suitcase."

"Yes, sir. I 'ardly thought you'd require it while on board the *Lusitania,* Sir, if I may say so, Mr. Jones."

"Certainly you may. No, events requiring a pistol as stage-property are not frequent on a liner. By the way, you never showed me how to work the thing, Philip."

"No, Sir. The shopman from whom I purchased it declared it simple of hoperation, but I 'ave not found it so sir."

"Well, find out in London and show me. I never met a burglar, but if I ever should it would be embarrassing to point a pistol at him and not be able to fire it off. I admire the heroes of burglar stories. They're always such efficient people."

"Hunder exciting circumstances, sir, one becomes much more efficient. They bring it out of a man, if I may say so, Mr. Jones."

"By all means. Well, golf is exciting enough for me. Merridale and I are going to run over to the St. Andrews links. It's been the dream of my life to play the St. Andrews, but something has always come up to prevent."

"Nothing is likely to hoccur, I am sure, sir. Shall I repack the steamer trunk now, Mr. Jones?"

"Yes. And call me a little earlier, in the morning, Philip. I have an idea it's going to be fine weather, and since it's the last of the voyage I want to make the most of it. What time is it? Eleven, eh? Well, I'll go to bed early for once and get a good night's rest. Thank Heaven for a quiet life, Philip. Cribbage and the *Times* for you, golf and—"

"Beg pardon for hinterrupting, sir, but do you want this book packed in the trunk?"

"*Paradise Island?* Yes, pack the thing away. Did you ever read it, Philip?"

"No, sir. I don't care for them himpossible stories, if I may say so, sir."

"And welcome. Now, I'm thirty-two years old, I've yachted, ridden, motored and been about the world a good bit, and I've never had a real adventure in my life. People don't have adventures unless they're gentlemen in the filibustering line, or polar explorers, or something like that. This modern world of ours is as safe as a church, barring accidents, and they are never romantic. End in a hospital or a beastly morgue. Anybody I suppose, can find trouble by looking for it, but that's not exactly in my line."

"No, sir. Very bad form, sir, if I may say so, Mr. Jones."

"You may indeed. Here, I'll help you with that strap, and then—bed."

Ragged fragments of cloud raced across a sky where great, brilliant stars beamed fitfully. The wind hurled the wave crests through space, so that the air was almost as watery as the wide waste of billows and creaming surges in the midst of which Mr. Roland C. Jones, of New York City, found himself most unexpectedly struggling.

How it could be that he was here battling for his life, with the stars, the wind and raging, tumbling seas for his sole companions, did not immediately trouble him. He was too thoroughly engaged in trying to get a breath that was not half or all salt water to concern himself about either past or future. The mere physical present was a little bit more than he could comfortably handle.

But the fight between man and sea was too unequal. Mr. Jones was a fair swimmer, but not being provided with gills he found it impossible to get a living modicum of oxygen out of the saturated air, even when the waves did not go clean over his head. Thoroughly exhausted, more than half drowned, he had just decided that he might as well throw up his arms and let the sea have its will of him, when he found himself rising upon the shoulder of a particularly mighty billow.

For an instant he caught a glimpse of something dark and huge looming above him. Then he was in the trough again, but only for a moment. Up, up he was borne in a long, swift, surging motion. The water seemed to fall away from under him. He was on his knees in sand and the receding breaker was trying to drag him back with it. The next wave, however, carried him much farther up the beach, dropping him with a vicious thud when it was done with him.

Barely conscious of his own efforts, Jones dragged himself along on hands and knees until he was actually out of
reach of the ocean which had been so unappreciative as to
spew him up.

For a time he lay still, gasping the water out of lungs
and stomach, then rolled over and sat up. He felt like a man
in a dream, yet the pain he suffered informed Mr. Jones
that this was no dream, but a grim, incredible reality.

It was not alone the question, where was he, although
that seemed pressing enough. But how had he gotten into
the water at all? The last thing he remembered was a little, pleasant, white-finished room—a state room—ah, that
was it. He was in his state room on board the liner. He
was on board the *Lusitania,* and he was going to London to
visit his cousin, the Hon. Percy Merridale. And he had—
let's see, he had been going over the things in his steamer
trunk with his man, Philip. And then—then he was going
to bed. He must have gone to bed, and then—

He cudgeled his memory, but failed to beat out one
single further recollection back of that dazed, strangling
moment when he had found himself struggling with the
waves.

Where was the liner? While in the water he could not
recall having seen any lights, receding or otherwise. Stare
earnestly as he might now across the sea, there were certainly no lights visible other than the stars, which storm-
clouds now obscured at ever-increasing intervals.

Where was the *Lusitania?* And how had he come to part
company with her so inexplicably? If the huge ship had
melted away from about his slumbering form like a dream
thing, instead of the vast solid steel hulk she was, she
could not have vanished more thoroughly or mysteriously.

Only one explanation occurred to Mr. Jones, and even
that was inadequate to explain the liner's total disappearance. When a boy he had been given to the habit of

sleep-walking. He had usually slept locked in, in those days, but had thought the habit long since dead and gone. Nevertheless, he must have risen in a dream, gone on deck, and in some way fallen over the rail without being seen by any one.

What an extremely awkward predicament! Where could he be? What land lay near enough for him to have reached it undrowned? In view of the approximate position of the liner, so far as he knew it, Ireland seemed the only possible answer to that question. Had he been cast upon some portion of the Irish coast? Certainly the only thing for him to do was to get up and walk along this lonely, God- and man-forsaken beach until he came to some place where he could get dry clothes and cable his friends in London.

His clothes! He was fully dressed, and he examined the garments as well as he was able by starlight. They seemed wrong, some way. They were not his clothes, at all, but the clothes of a stranger. Had he, in his sleep, wandered into a neighboring stateroom and robbed some innocent stranger? He recalled that he had been talking to Philip about burglars and pistols—lightly it is true, but perhaps the suggestion of that conversation had led him into such an astounding exploit.

Mr. Jones searched this hypothetical other person's pockets, but all he brought to light were some wet, useless matches, a small penknife, an unmarked handkerchief, and a little loose change. There were no letters or anything by which the rightful owner could be identified.

By a mighty effort Jones forced the problem of the clothes out of his mind and fixed it upon the greater one of finding shelter and means of communication with London.

While he sat there the sky had completely cleared, and even by starlight he could make out that he was on a long, bare stretch of sand, which curved smoothly away on either side. From the inner edge of this strip a black wall of rock rose sharply, looming to the stars above Jones's head. This enormous cliff also curved away on either hand, following the line of the beach.

Selecting a quarter from the small coins he had found, Mr. Jones flipped it into the air. "Heads to the right, tails to the left," said he. The coin fell with the eagle uppermost and the castaway obediently started off in the direction indicated by Fate.

Walking was easy on the smooth, wet sand. The night air was so warm that even in his wet clothes Jones was not uncomfortably cold, and although the interminable breakers still roared in almost to his feet, the storm had evidently blown itself out. These rushing seas were only the aftermath.

Presently the beach dwindled away to nothing, and the cliff extended itself into the sea in a sort of long, sloping foot of jagged rocks. Mr. Jones managed to feel his way around this point, drenched again with spray, and wading through shallow pools of water. He tore his clothes and scraped his hands raw, but at last achieved the place where the beach began again.

"Halt!" commanded a stern, uncompromising voice.

Before him loomed the dark bulk of a figure which seemed to be pointing something at him. The figure came closer and the "something" developed into an unpleasant-looking rifle, along whose leveled barrel the starlight glimmered. Behind the figure, a hundred yards or so, Jones, saw a yellow gleam of lights, and not far out to sea, on the comparatively quiet waters of a little bay, some sort of vessel lay at anchor.

"Halt!" the man of the rifle again exclaimed in yet harsher tones.

"I have halted," replied Mr. Jones mildly. "May I ask—"

"None of your lip!" said the stranger ferociously. "Who are youse, and what do youse want around here?"

"Nothing—nothing at all. I was just walking along the beach—"

"Ho! Takin' y'r evenin' stroll up Fift' Avenoo, was youse? Well, just stroll along ahead of me now, and no more of your lip. I'll turn youse over to the captain, see? Now, march!"

Perforce Jones marched. He was unarmed, but even if he had carried the automatic pistol (and known how to use it) he could not see what would be gained by opposing this determined and ruffianly person. He stumbled along ahead of his captor, who occasionally hastened his footsteps by prodding him in the back most uncomfortably with his rifle-muzzle.

Luckily it was not far to the lights, where Jones presently discovered that three small tents were erected on the sand.

Another man came forward to meet them. He was a tall, well set-up figure. Even by the dim light of three ship's lanterns, set about in the sand, Jones could see that he was handsome, after a dark, foreign manner, and generally rather aristocratic in appearance. Neatly attired in white-ducks and of a fairly amiable expression, he seemed to Jones far preferable to his first acquaintance.

"What is this, Doherty?" inquired the gentleman in white.

"Youse c'n search me, y'r excellency." replied the man with the rifle. "I found it up there by the point, and I brung it into camp for youse fellers to cut up or keep, just as you please. I don't—"

"That will do, Doherty," broke in the other, a shade of annoyance in his even, cultivated voice. "You may return to your post. And now," turning to the castaway, "who are

you, sir, and how did you come here?" He spoke courteously and with the slightest trace of foreign accent in his
otherwise faultless English.

Several other men had now gathered about them. They
were rough-looking fellows, unshaven, and with dull, un-
educated faces. Their costumes were not elaborate, consisting mostly of a shirt and a pair of more or less ragged
trousers, the only exceptions being the man in white and
a tall, powerful-looking brute of a fellow who was dressed
in a blue serge uniform, like a ship's officer.

The moment had come for Mr. Jones to relate the tale
of his strange misadventure and receive the aid and sympa-
thy to which he knew himself entitled and which he fully
expected to get, since rough clothes are by no means the
natural insignia of unkind hearts.

"My name is Roland C. Jones," he began. "I am an
American, and during the storm I was cast up on the
beach—over beyond that point. By the way, is this the
coast of Ireland?"

"Is this—what?" exclaimed the man in white with a
look of intense astonishment.

"Oh, isn't it?" stammered Mr. Jones, rather taken aback
by the stranger's amazement. "Well, you see I couldn't very
well know what place it was. As I said, I was cast here
by the storm, and of course I am very glad indeed to run
across you fellows. That's a yacht you've got out there, isn't
it? I thought by the look of her. I'm a yachtsman myself.
My craft's the little *Bandersnatch*, New York Yacht Club."

These words should have been an open sesame to
instant solicitude and hospitality, for to own a yacht is to
belong to a sort of freemasonry, extending over the whole
wide seas; but this stranger. only stared at Jones with
increasing coldness and suspicion.

"Exactly," he commented briefly, his lips curling in a
curious little smile. "And how did you come to be cast

away? Has your yacht been wrecked? Did no one else come ashore? Where are your companions?"

In the teeth of this fusillade of questions Mr. Jones launched once more into his explanation.

"My yacht was not wrecked. I was not on my yacht. I was on board the *Lusitania,* and Heaven knows where she is now."

"Heaven probably does," interrupted the stranger, smiling coldly. "The *Lusitania* was torpedoed by a German submarine early this morning. We have but just received the information by wireless. If you were one of the victims you are indeed to be pitied. You have been forced to swim a very long way—several thousand miles, I think. Did you come around the Horn, or through the canal, my friend?"

Jones stared at him blankly. Was the man insane? Torpedoed—by Germans—thousands of miles! He clasped his head in his hands and groaned. It must be he himself who was mad. Then raising a very white face he spread out his arms in a gesture of despair.

"I'll have to admit that I don't know what you are talking about. I—I am afraid something has happened to my head—or I don't hear you correctly. No one could possibly torpedo the *Lusitania*—unless it were an anarchist, and I can't imagine what you mean by several thousand miles."

"That is sad. Yes, your brain must be affected, sir. You recollect that you are an American, and that is much, but I think you are mistaken about your name. Well, we will keep you with us. I do not really think it would be safe for you to stray about any longer alone in your pitiful condition. Captain Ivanovitch," he turned to the tall man in blue serge, "I will turn this young man over to you. You have heard him and will agree with me that it is wise to guard him carefully—against himself, of course. Do you understand?"

He still spoke in English, and it was in broken English that the captain replied. He spoke with a grin.

"Excellency, I und'stand. He have forgot his name. He have forgot even that there ees war. Have you suggest a name which he know perhaps better than that one he say?"

"Not yet. My friend, if I should address you as Richard Holloway, would it arouse no recollections in your mind?" The words were pleasant enough, but the voice was keen and cold as a winter wind.

Jones looked at the man in increased bewilderment. For the sake of peace and until he could escape from these madmen, had he better accept this now cognomen? Before he could make up his mind, "his excellency" turned aside with a short laugh. "Take good care of Mr. Holloway, Ivanovitch," he flung back over his shoulder. "It is just possible that we may arouse his memory and make him useful."

"Eester way," said the captain, with deceitful politeness, "eet is great pleasure to entertain you. So leetle we theenk Reechard Hol'way come to us so, free of weel. Weel you accept shelter from one of our leetle tents? Yes?"

Some inner instinct informed Mr. Jones that this Holloway personality was a dangerous one to assume. Playing himself off as another man did not appeal to him, anyway.

"I am not the person you seem to think I am," he said rather doggedly. "But I'd go anywhere to get something to eat. I'm nearly starved."

The captain grinned again, mockingly, hatefully. "At once, Meester Hol'way. We are all humbly servants. Dmitri—" Here he turned to one of the seamen who stood by staring stupidly and launched a command in some language which was unfamiliar to Jones, although, judging by the captain's own name and that of the man addressed, he assumed it to be Russian.

The sailor sprang to obey, and Captain Ivanovitch led Mr. Jones to one of the small tents. "Here," said he, "weel

Meester Hol'way, permit to lodge himself. The tent, he is leetle, but you not mind that. Eet is more better than the ocean, no?"

"Humph! Perhaps," grunted Mr. Jones. He had taken an immediate dislike to the amiable captain. "By the way, you people seem to be very chary of introductions. Who is that gentleman I was just now speaking to? Your owner, I presume?"

"You not know? But of course. I forget you have jus' been sheepwreck. That ees his highness, Preence Sergius Petrofsky. The name also—it call nothing to your mind?"

"Nothing but Siberia and—er—Russian cigarettes. So, he's a connection of the royal family, is he? Now, tell me, what is all this fuss about, this man Holloway? There's no particle of use in calling me Holloway any longer, you know. I never even knew one of that name."

"So sad, Meester Hol'way. Perhaps you receive the blow upon the head—from wreckage, you ur.d'stand? Eef you will show the place, we try to play the good part. We weel put upon eet the bandage."

"My head is all right, I tell you. My stomach is the only part of me that is in need of attention."

"Ver' good. Here come my man now weeth the good food. We shall not starve you, my friend. Also comes once more hees excellency."

The prince indeed came up at that moment. His features were set in a haughty frown, and he addressed himself immediately to Mr. Jones in a domineering tone.

"See here, Holloway, I have been considering this matter carefully, and can see no reason for your continuing the farce. How you came to fall into our hands is your own affair. But you must not rely upon the fact that your face is unfamiliar to us. There can be no question of your identity. You are the only man on the island—at least on the outside of it, for you yourself are the only person who knows what is inside—who did not come here in the *Monterey*. Which places you beyond the shadow of a doubt as Richard Holloway. Now, answer me, yes or no. Will you tell me where lies the entrance to the caverns? If you help us we will make it well worth your while."

"What caverns?" queried Jones impatiently and with rising anger. These Russians were intolerable.

"Your feigned ignorance will not help you in the least, my friend," replied Petrofsky sternly. "I mean, of course, the caverns that lead beneath the cliffs. Out of all the caverns, the one which leads to that inner valley of yours. It was your story and yours alone which brought my brother across half a world to seek it.

"Come, sir, it is true that all of us here belong to the Brotherhood, and Paul has poisoned your mind against us. Also, by American eyes, I know that the great cause of nihilism is regarded askance.

"That is because you have experienced nothing of the evils which we plan to correct. But at least you know that I am a gentleman. If I give my word, I keep it. My brother has your trust."

"I am glad to hear it," murmured Jones wearily.

"What is that? I say that I, too, am a Petrofsky, and I swear to you that neither Paul nor those with him shall suffer the very least harm if you will help me. Nay, I will go further and promise that he shall receive his full share of the gains. The cause will not begrudge him that, although he has done his utmost to thwart our participation in this venture. But he and his little party can do nothing now. They have scarcely any provisions, hardly any arms or ammunition. We could sweep down and annihilate them at this moment if I did not always remember that Paul is indeed my brother. Come, Mr. Holloway save him against himself and for the time at least cast in your lot with us. Will you give me your hand on it?"

Jones hesitated. To him this long rigmarole of nihilists and caverns failed to carry any meaning whatsoever.

"How can I convince you, Sir," he said at last, "that I know nothing whatever of these matters? That all I desire is to get away from this place and continue my quiet, respectable journey to London. And last and most emphatically that my name is certainly not Holloway, but Roland C. Jones, of New York City. You are making a serious mistake, Prince Petrofsky, and a most absurd one, if you will pardon me."

The Russian's eyes flashed angrily.

"Ho! You are yet stubborn? We will see if we cannot loosen your tongue a bit. Now, listen to me, and remember that I pledge my word as a Petrofsky that this promise will be kept. If you persist in your present attitude you will be taken on board that yacht and triced up to the signal-mast. Then you will be beaten—they beat criminals in Russia. With the knout. Do you know what the knout means? I can see by your expression that you do. Well, make up your mind which it is to be. You may expect either our gratitude or—the other! You have until morning to decide. While making up your mind you may remain in that tent. Ivanovitch, set a guard over this man and see that he does not escape. Mr. Holloway, I give you a very good evening!"

Sergius Petrofsky turned his straight white back upon the dismayed American and stalked off down to the shore. There he got into a waiting dingey and was rowed out to the yacht.

Jones started, shivering slightly, as the captain touched his elbow and said in a soft voice, "You are foolish man, Meester Hol'way. But do not be so foolish as try leave us to-night. You und'stand?"

And Mr. Jones was left with his guard of two bearded sailors.

"Good Lord!" he muttered to himself. "What a crazy mess! Is knouting any worse than drowning, I wonder? I'll bet it is!"

CHAPTER II

Midnight found Mr. Jones sitting in his prison tent disconsolate.

There was a neat cot and blankets, but he had never felt less like sleeping in his life. He clung to his wakefulness and the few hours intervening between him and the morrow, like a sick man anticipating an extremely painful but inevitable operation. For something told him that Sergius Petrofsky was not the man to make empty threats.

Mr. Jones could see no way out of his predicament— unless he might anger the Russian into shooting instead of torturing him. The man certainly possessed a violent temper behind those haughty eyes of his.

While the captive was still revolving in his mind this desperate expedient, he suddenly felt something poke him sharply in the back. At the same instant some one said "Sh!" in a sharp, sibilant whisper.

The pain of the unexpected jab made Jones spring to his feet, crashing into the tent-pole and shaking the whole tent so violently that one of his guards appeared in the entrance. He thrust a large, hirsute countenance into the aperture and said something that sounded like the name of a Russian province.

"Get out, get out!" exclaimed Mr. Jones, gesturing violently to make his meaning clear. "It is nothing at all. Nothing. I bumped into the pole. Go away!"

The guard stared at him suspiciously for a moment longer, glanced about the little tent, which was dimly lighted by a lantern, and at last withdrew himself.

Once more the prisoner sat down, close to the canvas wall, and cautiously whispered, "It's all right. He has gone. Who are you and what do you want? What did you poke me like that for?"

There was a moment's silence, followed by a slight ripping sound. Through the canvas close by his shoulder Jones saw the point of a knife appear. It deftly cut two sides of a small triangle, then the flap so made was lifted and a face appeared. The face looked familiar. Then Mr. Jones recognized Doherty, the man who had captured him.

"Say, where are youse from?" The question was barely breathed in a voice which could not possibly have carried beyond the walls of the tent. Jones replied in the same bated tone:

"New York. Why?"

"That settles it, bo. Wait a jif."

The face was withdrawn, and the knife came into use once more. This time, however, it sawed out an aperture about three feet square near the bottom of the canvas wall. "Come on out, bo," whispered the rescuer.

Mr. Jones obeyed, moving as stealthily as he could, and having first made sure that the lantern would not cast the shadow of his escaping form upon the side of the tent. The situation required caution if ever a situation did.

Once outside he straightened himself, and felt a powerful hand grasp his arm. "This way, bo," came the whisper, and rescuer and rescued crept softly across the sands, behind the tents, and away, keeping close to the cliff. Glancing seaward, Jones saw the riding lights of the yacht, otherwise a dim, black bulk upon the quiet waters of the bay.

His guide led him away from the camp, not in the direction of the point where the two had first met, but onward along the beach. As soon as they were out of earshot of his Russian companions Doherty halted and said:

"I don't go no furder wid youse, see? G'wan on along until youse comes to a ravine. Go up there, and pretty soon youse comes to where dis other prince guy is, see? I don't know whether youse and this Holloway feller are the same guy or not. If you are, then youse don't need no more help from me. If youse ain't, then take a tip and hold your jawr about comin' straight from this camp, see? Now, beat it!"

"But see here!" exclaimed Jones, laying his hand on the other's shoulder to stay him. "Why have you helped me out this way? I'm everlastingly obliged to you, and—"

"Aw, ferget it!" snapped the other, shaking off the detaining hand roughly. "I ain't no friend of youse, neither, see? But no Russian dook ain't my boss when it comes to beatin' up another N'York feller with that knout thing. See? Now, will youse beat it, or d'youse want t'go back there and get what's comin' to youse?"

"I'll go. But, thank you, just the same. Say, can't you tell me something about all this business—"

But already Doherty had disappeared in the darkness, and with a slight sigh Roland C. Jones turned his face in the direction he had been instructed to follow. At any rate, the knouting was indefinitely postponed, and he could think of nothing much worse which could befall.

A short distance beyond the place where Doherty had left him the beach again ended in rocks. The man had spoken of a "ravine," so Mr. Jones again climbed and scrambled, coming at last to where the cliff seemed to be split in two parts. How far this split penetrated into the rocky wall, he had no means of knowing, for it was all as dark as a pocket.

He discovered by stumbling into it that a little rill of water flowed down the middle of the split and into the sea. His best chance of exploring the ravine was to walk up the bed of this stream, which was no more than ankle deep. The water, he found, had the bitter chill of a glacier stream, and his feet were soon numb with cold. He had been offered no opportunity to dry his clothing, and it was still very damp and uncomfortable. He hoped that the extreme warmth of the night might prevent him from getting pneumonia.

Mr. Jones was not accustomed to such privations and hardships, and he found them extremely annoying.

Having no means of making a light, he stumbled along in the darkness, alternately cursing himself for having fallen overboard and the Hon. Percy Merridale as the (however remote) cause of all his misfortunes.

At length, however, the watercourse made a sharp bend, and rounding it, he beheld, a short distance ahead of him, a reddish glow upon the rocks. Then a black figure appeared in silhouette against the glow. He was considering how he could best make his presence known, for this he correctly surmised to be the place of that mysterious other encampment, when a voice exclaimed, "Hands up, there, or I'll fire!"

"Twice in one night!" muttered Jones rebelliously.

"What's that? Stranger, you've strayed onto the wrong range. Come into the light, and don't make no false moves, or you'll sure get perforated."

The voice had now come close to his side, and Mr. Jones felt the hard muzzle of some sort of weapon pressing against his ribs.

"I assure you that I am not armed," he said.

"I'll assure myself in a minute," responded the unsympathetic voice. "March, now!"

And again Jones marched. The light which Jones had seen reflected upon the cliff was cast by a fire built between two huge boulders in such a manner as to obscure its radiance so far as was possible. Emerging into the full glare, the unfortunate halted again, obedient to the pressure on his arm.

About the fire, which they were probably maintaining for the sake of illumination, since they were cooking nothing, and the temperature of the night was so high, several figures were gathered. All save one of these persons were men, the exception being a slender young girl, who at that moment turned her face and stared straight into the eyes of Mr. Jones.

"By Jupiter!" he murmured. "What's a girl like that doing with this crowd?"

The young lady was attired in a somewhat dilapidated white yachting costume, which looked as if it had been soaked more than once and not pressed in a long time. But she was not of the type whose social standing or personal attraction would ever be judged by her clothes, however she might be dressed. Her crisply curling hair gleamed almost red in the firelight, though in daytime it would probably be no more than auburn. Her skin was of that clear, transparent whiteness which sometimes accompanies such hair; her features clean-cut and firm to a point which would have been almost masculine had they not been relieved by, a pair of blue eyes so pure, childish, and innocent that looking at them one could only be reminded of the eyes of a suddenly awakened baby.

For the rest, she was slight of figure, with small, tapering hands and feet, giving an impression of physical weakness which Mr. Jones later discovered to be deceptive.

He did not, of course, absorb all these details of appearance in that first brief meeting. At the moment he saw only that here was a beautiful, well-bred girl in the midst of surroundings entirely unsuitable—unless she happened to be a movie actress, which seemed improbable.

Of her companions, one was a tall, rather good-looking man with a sensitive mouth and slightly receding chin, also in yachting costume. Another was a rangy, lanky sort of fellow, attired in nothing more formal than a shirt and shabby trousers. The two remaining men were plainly of a lower class, probably seamen from their general appearance.

With a look of astonishment the girl glanced from Jones to his captor, who stood slightly behind him, and said:

"James, who is this person? How did he come here?"

Yes, she said it exactly as if she were standing in her own drawing-room, inquiring of the butler how some unknown vagabond had penetrated into her domain. Something humorous in the whole situation smote Jones abruptly, so that he laughed aloud, and she stared at him more haughtily than ever.

"I beg your pardon," said Mr. Jones, hastening to correct his involuntary rudeness, "I have had a rather trying evening, and—er—I did not expect to see a young lady in this place."

"And why not, pray? You are one of Prince Sergius' friends, are you not? Paul, this must be one of your brother's men, although I for one have never seen him before. Do you know him?"

She addressed the handsome man with the weak chin, and Jones knew this must be the brother of the Russian who had imprisoned him.

"No," he replied, rising lazily. "I have never seen the fellow before. Do you know him? Dick Holloway?"

"Not yet, but I've no objection. What is your name, anyway?"

So the man in the shirt and trousers was Holloway. Jones looked at him with considerable interest, since it was in his name that he had nearly suffered so much, and saw that he was a young man with a keen, rather strong face. Dressed differently, he might have been either a reporter or an automobile salesman—or a member of Jones's own club.

"My name is Roland C. Jones," stated the castaway, somewhat weary of reiterating that fact. "Some hours ago, early in the evening, I was cast up on the beach by the storm. I—think I had fallen overboard in my sleep. I was

on my way to London. Then I—" He suddenly remembered Doherty's warning. He decided that he owed it to
his benefactor to keep faith. "I came on up the beach and
stumbled into this ravine and walked up it and—and here
I am, you know."

This simple statement was met by dead silence for a moment. Then the Russian asked: "You were going to London,
you say? That sounds a little peculiar. And you say you were
wrecked, some hours ago? Where were you, pray, in the
interval? Do you mean you have met no one since that
time?"

"Yes," admitted Mr. Jones, realizing that his story
lacked strength. "I met one man—or, rather, I saw a man;
but as soon as he caught sight of me he made off. I chased
him, but he was too quick. Then I wandered around a
while, until I found my way here."

"H—m. What ship were you on?"

Jones started to reply, "The *Lusitania,*" but checked himself. He was actually afraid that these people, too, would
insist on that nightmare tangle of German torpedoes and
impossible distances. Then he would know that something
had crone wrong in his brain. He did not want to know it
just then. There was too much to attend to without that. "I
was on my own yacht, the *Bandersnatch.* We were just cruising around, you know. We had thought of running over to
the Azores." (Jones was not at all sure by this time where
in the Atlantic he might be, but the Azores, as occupying a
fairly central position, seemed safe.) "I must have walked in
my sleep, for first thing I knew I was in the water, and the
only wonder is that I was not drowned. I am a New Yorker,
but we sailed from Savannah." He was rather proud of
this touch of realism, but Holloway burst out laughing.

"First London, and now the Azores," the latter remarked
in a tone of good-natured amusement. "You seem to have
put out on a remarkable voyage."

"For my part," interposed the young lady, who, despite her infantile eye, seemed of very determined and decisive character, "I don't believe a word of your story. If you were on a yacht, which I don't doubt, it was the *Monterey,* and she lies in the bay now. I believe you were on board at the same time we were, although we didn't see you. That about London and Savannah and the Azores is merely ridiculous. I can't imagine your object in making such absurd statements. Paul, this man has been sent here by your brother to spy upon us and find out the secret of the caverns."

Paul nodded his head, saying: "Holloway, do you not think that Miss Weston is right?"

"It's a one best bet she is, prince. All that gas about his yacht and the rest of it was probably planned to make us think he's a bit light in his upper story."

"What?"

"Bats in his belfry—nobody home—you know."

"Oh, you mean insane. But why should he wish us to think that?"

"So we won't take too much pains to keep our cards face down. If you'll take a tip from me, prince, you'll keep this angel-faced little castaway tied right to mama's apron-strings till time's called."

The prince laughed amiably, but the amiability was for Holloway, not Mr. Jones.

"Your expressions—your idioms—they are so very charming, Dick Holloway. But you are right. We cannot afford to be betrayed. James Haskins, you will kindly remain close to this gentleman's side. Take him with you and return to your post. And now, my friends, we have already sat too long talking. Let us sleep for the two hours that remain of night. Remember, we start at dawn."

Chapter III

As if stricken dumb, Mr. Jones obeyed the guiding hand of James Haskins, as it steered him back to the point whence he had first sighted the camp-fire. It seemed as though something even stronger than Fate were against him. Whatever he said was turned back upon him; whatever he did, it merely led him into fresh disaster. There was no use in fighting the tide. Henceforth he would keep still and permit events to shape themselves, unhelped or hindered by his efforts.

Perhaps, presently, he would wake up. Yes, this must be some unusually vivid nightmare which had him in its clutches.

"Squat right down on that rock, stranger, and make yourself at home." Of course, it was Haskins who broke in on his reverie. "If any more mavericks stray off your range up this way, I'll be right here to throw, tie, and brand 'em. Have a cigarette?"

"No—Yes, thank you, I believe I will."

For a few moments the two smoked without speaking. The night was silent, save for the low, distant murmur of the sea and the occasional squeak of a bat. Overhead the great, brilliant stars, which hung so strangely low and near, seemed to wink at Jones, as if they were sharers in some huge joke of whose nature he was not yet informed, but of which he was unquestionably the butt.

"Strange," he reflected. "I can't remember ever having smoked in a dream before. I can taste the tobacco, too. And my hands hurt like the dickens, where I scraped 'em on the rocks. I wonder if I ever will wake up. That girl is a winner for looks, all right; but, oh, mama, I don't like her disposition one little bit! Seems to have it in for me, all right. I wonder—"

"Pleasant dreams!" It was James Haskins again. "Say, did you really get washed ashore like you told the bunch?"

"I certainly did," said Jones with convincing vigor and promptitude. "Look here; if I should tell you the whole story about what has happened since I reached this place, would you believe me?"

"Fire away!" the other replied noncommittally.

Jones obeyed, and his jailer listened patiently and in silence to the full tale of his misadventures. Barring the fact that it was a liner and not his own yacht from which he had fallen, he adhered closely to facts; for, in the light of his reception, it seemed it was only for his own good that Doherty had warned him not to speak of the other camp. And in this opinion his listener presently confirmed him.

"So this man Doherty told you not to tell you'd been in his camp, did he?" was Haskins's comment at the end of the recital. "Well, he was dead right, friend castaway. Prince Paul has got just the same love for Prince Sergius that a grizzly has for a rattlesnake.

"But me, I think you're straight. For one thing, you haven't got the map of a bunco-steerer; and for another, I think you are because she thinks you ain't. Do you get me? I never saw anything in skirts yet that you couldn't copper her guess and be on the right trail. Only your swim seems to have twisted your geography some. It isn't the Azores you mean—it's the Philippines, or Hawaii. Now, if you and me should swap yarns, will you give me away to my outfit, or will you keep it under your hair?"

"Prince Sergius' knout wouldn't extract it from me," sighed Mr. Jones, with the happy sense that here again, where least expected, he had found a friend.

"Well, to commence with, me, I'm riding a long way off my own range, which is Colorado, by rights, though I was born in Arizona. Arizona Jim, that's me. Well, this prince fellow come along when I was on my uppers in Frisco, having gone up against a few large doses of redeye and an outfit of card-sharks some simultaneous. But, say, you fellows started from Savannah, you said. Did you get into the Pacific through the canal?"

The Pacific? Jones's brain reeled again, but he managed to keep his voice steady and reply: "Yes, of course we went through the canal."

"I asked because I know a fellow that runs a café in Colon. Did you stop there?"

"I didn't go ashore there. But how did you meet the prince?"

"Oh, yes. Well, as I was saying, he met up with me, and he offers me a job. Says he's goin' on a big trip and wants a guy with a good gun-eye. That's me, all right; so I joins the outfit immediate. Then's when I meet this brother of his, they bein' on good terms then, just like an owl and a prairie-dog.

"So brother Sergius, it seems, he's gone right ahead and chartered a yacht without waiting for brother Paul to approve the deal. This annoys us some, but not half so much as when we get away out on the broad, be-yutiful, lonesome Pacific Ocean and finds that the captain and the crew are all 'brothers' of his, too. Yes, little Annie, Sergius is in with the anarchists, saddle, bridle, and spurs, and the great and noble cause has got to get its share in the profits, even if brother Sergius has to knife brother Paul to do it. Oh, yes, it was some rotten deal, take it from me."

"But where does this Miss . . . Miss—"

"Weston come in? Not yet but soon. We picks Miss Weston up out of an open boat, along with a couple of half-dead sailors. She's a Boston young lady that's been taking lessons in nursing. She aims to join the Red Cross, but she's some foxy, so she comes clear across to Frisco and takes a boat for Japan, figurin' to get into the festivities by the back gate, so to speak. No German torpedoes in hers."

(Jones gave a mental groan. Again!)

"And right then, was when the lid blew off the kettle for keeps. I never did see two brothers take a shine to the same girl quite so simultaneous and sudden. Gee, they ought to have been twins, their tastes are so similar. Was she going to be Princess Sergius or Princess Paul? I suggests to Paul, casual-like, that they cut her in two and divide her up, it being my idea that there ain't any female woman born that's any real good in a round-up like this one. But he didn't seem to take to it.

"So brother Paul, he reveals to her the perfidy of brother Sergius, and right away that swings her. No nihil-anarchists for hers. In which she shows more sense than I'd expected.

"Right about then we sights this here Joker Island. Some name, Joker; but she's some Island, too, believe me. There being considerable hard feeling, what with one thing and another, me and Prince Paul and this Weston girl and her two sailors, we thinks it wise and becoming to withdraw ourselves from evil associations, and we drops off the yacht the first dark night. Then Prince Paul he says there's a guy on the island expecting him, which is the first I heard of Holloway. As near as I can make out, this is Holloway's island, by right of being wrecked here and finding out some darn thing about the inside of it. These cliffs go all the way around, you know, but there's a cave runs under 'em, and Mr. Holloway, he's the only one that knows where it is."

"I shouldn't think it would be very difficult to find a cave in a wall of rock like this, if one hunted for it," suggested Jones, deeply interested in the narrative.

"Oh, no, it's dead easy—like three guesses at which is the right hole in a colander. There's about fifteen hundred other caves, and they all run back under the cliffs, and there's only one that goes clear through. And if you get lost in a blind lead—good night!"

"But what is there inside, anyway?"

"Me not being Prince Paul's confidential secretary, I don't know, nor I don't know how Sergius thinks he's going to get there without dear brother Paul and friend Holloway. But it's plain he knows something about Holloway, or he wouldn't have made that nice, kind offer to persuade you when he thought you was Holloway. One thing, it's clear he don't know him by sight. The way I figure it is that when Holloway was wrecked here, after he comes out of the inside again, he was taken off by some ship, and then he hikes right after Prince Paul, who, it seems, is his dear old college chum. It must be some secret, all right; for Paul, he gets leave immediate from his regiment by the Czar's special permit.

"But brother Sergius, who's some unpopular at home, he don't need no permit, because he's in America already. I don't think Paul was lookin' to run across him; but when he does, he takes him in on the deal for the sake of them old days back on the farm. Well, while Paul is rustling this outfit together, friend Richard gets himself put on the island alone again, with provisions, and stays right on the claim to wait for Paul. Paul comes along with a brother and a aggregation of nihilanarchists and a Boston schoolmarm girl, and now the only way out is in."

"What?"

"Just like I says—in. We're going through the caves at daybreak. Holloway says even he might get the wrong one at night."

"Good Lord!" murmured Mr. Jones softly. From boyhood he had suffered from a dread of dark, shut-in places, running parallel, perhaps, with his habit of sleep-walking. Even now be never slept without a light in his room, and he would not have explored the Mammoth Caves with a guard of fifty guides for all the money in the world. "Are you—are they going to take me along?"

"What's the matter? Don't you want to sit in? Take it from me, you're better off with Paul than you would be with Sergius, and you've only got Paul and Sergius to choose between."

"What sort of lights are you going to use?" queried Mr. Jones anxiously.

"Oh, we have some electric torches. Stranger, I've talked myself into the finest thirst outside of Arizona. But it's wasted—absolutely wasted. Ain't that a sad thought? By gracious, I'd almost go over and take up with this naughty Sergius party, if I thought he had anything stronger than water to give me. But, alas! The *Monterey* is like Russia—she's gone prohibition. Don't you notice a different feeling in the air? What time's it getting to be?" He glanced at his watch.

"'What time were you intending to start?" inquired Jones.

"Half an hour. It's three now. Here comes Holloway."

CHAPTER IV

"Did you catch any more bugs, Jim?" called Richard Holloway cheerfully as he approached. "No? Too bad. Hoped we could start a collection. Say, Mr.—er, what did you say your name was? Something unusual, wasn't it?"

"Jones," replied the castaway rather stiffly. He was a trifle tired of the disdainful attitude which every one except the cowboy had so far assumed toward him. "Roland C. Jones."

"Mr. Roland C. Jones, I salute you." Holloway bowed very low and straightened with a laugh. "Did you leave any last will and testament with his serene and nihilistic highness when he sent you over here? Because, you know, it's just possible that something might happen to you inside. You've no idea how wonderfully exciting 'inside' is, Mr. Jones. Don't let me alarm you, though."

Jones laughed almost hysterically. "It can't be much more exciting than—than everything else," he said. "And as for getting killed, I'm beginning to have a suspicion that that's the best thing which could happen to me."

He was thinking of his own mental condition, but Holloway understood him differently.

"So bad as that?" he asked with mock commiseration. "No home? No friends? Somebody cooked your chestnuts for you? Never mind, sweet child. We'll buy you some more—if we ever get off Joker Island. Coming, Prince?" he called back, as a voice hailed him from the little camp. "Come on, Jimmy; and you, too, Rolly! You don't mind if I call you Rolly? I feel in my heart that we're going to be friends, Rolly, and what's a name between pals?"

"I don't care what you call me," replied Mr. Jones, smiling in spite of himself. After all, there was something very likeable about this impertinent, good-natured fellow. He felt that he could get along very nicely if he had nobody but the cowboy and Richard Holloway to deal with.

They found the rest of the party eating a very informal breakfast, consisting of hardtack, a few rashers of bacon, and some really excellent coffee. Jones received his share thankfully. He could not remember a time when he had been so hungry, or hungry so often, as in the few hours since he had come to Joker Island.

Then the fire was extinguished; what provisions were left and some simple impedimenta were divided equally among the men, and the expedition started with only Miss Weston unburdened. She tripped lightly along beside her Russian admirer, apparently as merry and light-hearted as if they were bound on a picnic.

Dawn had come upon them with extraordinary suddenness as they ate, it seemed to Mr. Jones. There had been a few moments of ghostly twilight. Then the sun leaped into the sky, like a tiger springing from its lair, and flung at them his first rays with an ardor which promised insufferable heat later on.

Now that it was light, Jones perceived that the ravine, or split in the cliff wall, ended abruptly just beyond the camp. There the precipice towered as forbidding and unscalable as it hung above the outer beach. The little stream sprang from a mere crevice in the otherwise solid wall. There were certainly no caverns in that direction, and he was not surprised when Holloway, in his capacity of guide, led the way back down the ravine toward the sea; but he did wonder how they could emerge upon the beach without being seen by the nihilists.

They had followed the watercourse only a short distance, however, when Holloway turned aside and led them into a yet narrower crack in the rocks which branched off from the main ravine. The going became more and more difficult, and Paul Petrofsky was obliged to almost carry the girl over some places, while the rest of the party scrambled and sweated and swore *sotto voce*.

At last the crack widened; they caught a glimpse of blue beyond, and in another moment they came out upon a part of the beach which was cut off by a jutting promontory of rock from the small bay where the *Monterey* lay anchored. Jones thought that a bird's-eye view of that island must show the cliff to be fairly scalloped with little bays and promontories.

And here the black rock was honeycombed with dark holes, bored out either by the sea or by volcanic agency; some of them no more than a foot or so across, a few large enough so that a motor-truck could have been safely driven in.

"This is only the beginning of 'em," declared Holloway, addressing Petrofsky, but in loud enough tones to be heard by all. "Half way 'round the island the rock is fairly-perforated. Some place for a tribe of cave men, no?"

Then, suddenly assuming the manner of a tourist guide: "Just step this way, lady and gentlemen. Here you may behold the finest—oldest—most dog-gonedest aggregation of black holes—"

His voice died away and became indistinguishable, for he had dropped to hands and knees and crawled into one of the smaller caverns.

Petrofsky, pausing only to draw an electric torch from his pocket, immediately followed, and close upon his heels crept Miss Margaret Weston. To Jones's amazement, the girl was laughing just before she disappeared. He could not have laughed himself to win a medal. However, Jim Haskins and the two sailors were looking at him expectantly.

There was nothing else for it, so he, too, dropped to his knees and crawled into the hole, pushing ahead of him the small bundle which had been assigned him to carry. He wondered bitterly if they were to crawl all the way through the cliff.

Ahead of him he could see a moving black mass against a dim glow of light, which he knew to be the intrepid Miss Weston, of Boston, Massachusetts. Jones had no light himself, and was too far behind the leaders to get any benefit from theirs. The rock was wet and a trifle slimy. He thought of snakes, but remembered gratefully that if there were any they would have a good chance to bite three people before they got to him.

Behind, he could hear a grunting and scraping, and knew the other three were following.

Then the glow ahead abruptly disappeared, and there was a scrambling, thumping sound. Had Holloway and the Russian fallen into some abyss? He halted, but immediately after heard a voice calling, "Come ahead! It's all right! Oh, what a perfectly lovely, splendid place!"

It was the voice of Margaret Weston, and a moment later Mr. Jones scrambled out of the narrow hole into an enormous, scintillating cavern. The lights of two electric torches were reflected dazzlingly from a million fiery points.

"What perfectly gorgeous stalactites!" exclaimed the girl rapturously. "Oh, Mr. Holloway, I'm so glad you found this place! It's worth anything just to have seen it. Why, if it were not so hard to reach, this would be one of the show places of the world, would it not?"

"It would," admitted the flattered Mr. Holloway. "But I only wish I could let some sunlight into the hole for you. I've taken some pieces of this stuff out, and in daylight they are all colors of the rainbow. Look like stuff out of a jeweller's window. The colors don't show up in this light."

"Thank you, but it's quite beautiful enough as it is."

Even Jones had to admit to himself that Miss Weston was, in a measure, right. Above their heads was a black void. The roof was too high and probably too dark in color for their lights to show it, but all about them, depending almost to the floor, hung a thousand icicle-points, which reflected the electric rays as if they had been encrusted with diamonds. From the floor, also, rose points and mounds of brilliant crystals. This lower forest of stalagmites seemed to extend itself indefinitely, certainly beyond range of the torches.

"Dick Holloway," said the prince, "this is fairyland to which you have brought us. The air, too, which I had thought would be almost poisonous, it is fresh. It smells of the sea. There must be many more openings into this place than that by which we entered."

"There probably are," agreed Holloway, "but I'd hate to hunt for them. I was lost in these caves once—that was the way I happened to locate the way through—but I'd hate to risk it twice."

"But tell me," continued the prince, gazing upward curiously, "is there no danger from the falling of some of these huge masses from the roof?"

"Sure thing there is. But— Jimmy, there goes a beauty right this minute!"

There was an ominous crackling sound, the mild fore-runner of a thunderous, deafening crash. The air was filled with a cloud of choking white dust, through which the torches gleamed faintly as through a fog. The noise was followed by a series of lesser crashes. Then came again the calm, unagitated voice of Holloway.

"Did that hit anybody? If it did, farewell to the dear departed. Is every one here?"

One by one the little party answered with their names, Jones last, and in a voice which he rendered steady with some effort. He had always known that caverns would be just like this. For a moment he had been deceived by the treacherous beauty of this one, but no more. Surely they would turn back now. Nobody could expect to pass through this place where at any moment a thousand pounds of glittering stalactite was liable to drop on him—

It was the voice of Miss Weston which answered his unspoken thought.

"Well, there is no need of our standing here, is there? How in the world can you find your way, Mr. Holloway?"

"Been here before," replied that gentleman cheerfully. "Know it like the streets of my hometown. Come along."

By this time the white dust had somewhat settled, and Jones could see his companions clearly. They were starting off single file between the innumerable stalagmites, apparently careless of disaster. On an impulse he crouched down behind a white mound.

Jim Haskins passed within hand's reach, but did not see him in the shadow. The two sailors were a little behind, and on a sudden thought Jones cautiously pushed his bundle of miscellaneous camp articles out from behind his mound.

An instant later one of the sailors stumbled over it, and as Jones had craftily foreseen, imagined that it had been dropped by one of the men ahead. Grumbling, the man picked it up and added it to his own load, and with no thought for a possible escaping prisoner, passed on.

In fact, nobody gave Mr. Jones a thought. He was alone, neglected and forsaken, and the fact gave him supreme relief. He had looked carefully, while there was still sufficient light, and a seen a black hole yawning, the hole by which they had entered this place of terror. Having honestly restored to his captors the goods with which he had been entrusted, Mr. Jones felt no scruples about deserting them.

Just before the last gleam of light from the electric torches faded and disappeared, Mr. Jones plunged back into the small tunnel and began rapidly wriggling his way toward open air and the blessed light of day.

Somehow or other the passage seemed much longer than when he had come that way at the heels of the Boston girl. Jones crawled and crawled, until his knees and elbows were sore, but still he could see no gleam of light ahead. It seemed to him that he had been crawling for hours. What could be the matter?

Suddenly the horrifying explanation dawned upon him. This was not the tunnel by which they had entered, but another of the labyrinthine system of caves to which Holloway had referred!

Mr. Jones stopped crawling and tried to turn himself about. There was not room enough, however, and he only hurt himself still more upon the slimy rock. There was no use in trying to wriggle backward, for he knew that he would become exhausted before he could ever regain the cave of stalactites by such a laborious process. Besides, he reflected, even if he did get back there he would be no better off. Surrounded by impenetrable midnight darkness, how could he hope to rediscover the passage he had been unable to identify while there was light?

With a sinking heart he contemplated the many hours of mental and physical suffering which lay before him if he should fail to extricate himself. He must go on. What a fool he had been to desert the party of adventurers! After all, they were kindly, honest folk and it would have been far better to have died suddenly by the fall of a stalactite, or in some merciful abyss, than here alone in the darkness of the damned.

He must get out! And when "must" drives, a man will do a great deal more than appears possible. Roland C. Jones did. He crawled literally for hours, turning, winding with the tunnel, like an unhappy and desolate angle-worm in the black bosom of Earth.

Once, exhausted, he let himself subside, and despite all the terrors of darkness went to sleep. He had not slept for a long time, and when he awoke, though he ached in every limb, he felt refreshed and took new courage to crawl on.

Crawling is a slow process—at least, for a human being—but if a man crawl far enough, and encounters no obstruction, he is bound to get somewhere sometime, and that is what happened to Mr. Jones. He had long since given up all hope, and become a mere, dogged crawling-machine, when it happened. It was a tremendous thing and an experience which in all his after-life he never forgot. He saw the rock beneath him!

Then he raised his head, hopefully, prayerfully, and there, far ahead, beamed a glorious star of light!

Then did Mr. Jones perform prodigies of crawling. As if he had just started, he wriggled and scrambled along, and at last actually emerged from the black womb of death into the adorable, intolerable brilliance of day. Also into the very arms of Doherty, his former rescuer!

Behind Doherty stood Captain Ivanovitch, and beside him was Sergius Petrofsky. Mr. Jones had crawled windingly through the rock, all the way from behind the promontory, around the end of the ravine, and back to the little bay whereon the *Monterey* still lay at anchor.

He had expected anything—but not this. In the eternity which had elapsed since entering that black rat-hole he had forgotten that such a person as Sergius Petrofsky existed. His clothing was ripped to slimy rags. In a dozen places his body and limbs were scraped raw, he was faint and sick for lack of food and drink—and before him stood the man who had promised to torture him that day. The villainies of Fate were too prodigious.

Mr. Jones slipped suddenly from the sustaining grip of Doherty, and dropped in a wretched heap upon the sand.

CHAPTER V

When sense at last returned to the castaway, he opened his eyes and stared blankly about for a moment. He had dreamed that he was in his own bedroom in his own New York bachelor apartment, and these walls of brown canvas, that strange face bent above his, seemed incredible, far more visionary than the dream itself. Then the whiff of an agreeable odor reached his nostrils. Food! Mr. Jones sat up, and reached out his hands in one single motion. Doherty placed the bowl which he carried with them.

"I've brought youse your scoffin's," he said. "Gee! Youse was a sight when youse fell out of dat hole. His nibs is waitin' to see youse."

"Let him wait," commanded Jones in a determined voice. "Keep him out, can't you, till I finish this? This is the first thing I've had to eat for—for week's judging by the way my appetite feels."

Doherty laughed and seated himself on the side of the cot. "I'll tell him youse was pounding your ear so hard I couldn't wake youse up."

"Thanks, old man." There was an interval of silence, then Jones handed back the polished bowl with a great sigh, swung his legs to the floor and sat up. "Where are my clothes?" he asked.

"Your clothes? Gee, youse ain't got no clothes. There was a couple of old rags hangin' to youse, but if dat Anthony Comstock guy ever seen youse he'd t'row a fit, sure. Them things youse has on now belongs to the captain."

"But what am I to do? I can't walk around in these pajamas."

Doherty grinned. He seemed in an uncommonly good humor.

"Dat's all right. His nibs has came across wit' dese here glad rags. Climb, into 'em and look sharp, or I'll get the hide tore off me for keepin' him waitin'. There's a basin over there if youse wants to wash some more, but gee! They sure had to give you one bath before they could put youse to bed even."

"Well, I guess a little more water won't hurt me."

Jones also found a safety razor and a mug of luke-warm water beside the basin, and was glad enough to shave, although his beard was by this time a very stiff one to get rid of.

Then he dressed in the "glad rags" indicated by Mr. Doherty, which he found consisted of a suit of thin silk underwear, breeches and tunic coat of khaki, socks, puttees, and a pair of heavy, but well-made shoes. In fact, as good an outfit for a tramping or hunting expedition as Jones could have bought anywhere in New York.

Very gratefully he donned the garments, which to his joy fitted him quite passably. The shoes were a little loose, but that was much more satisfactory than if they had been too tight.

He thought, as he dressed, that if they intended to abuse him—they had made a peculiar beginning. Sleep and food had done a great deal to bring him back to a normal outlook on life. His limbs still ached, but that was hardly strange in view of the strenuous character of recent experiences. Mr. Jones presently announced his readiness to go to or receive the waiting Sergius.

"Youse can wait here. I'll get him," said Doherty, who all the time preserved the same astonishing amiability. He did not even question Mr. Jones in regard to how he had come to return there, and not only return, but return in such a singular manner and condition. Some species of relief or joy fairly radiated from the man's every glance and word.

Mr. Jones did not have to wait long after Doherty's departure. He had gone to the entrance and stood looking out. The sun beat down from almost directly overhead, and he correctly surmised that this was the day following that on which he had emerged from the cave. He must have slept the clock fairly around.

Some distance up the beach a number of men were gathered about a large object which was partly obscured by an intervening tent, so that he could not quite make out its nature. In a moment he saw Sergius Petrofsky coming toward him alone.

"My friend," said the nihilist, glancing him up and down with a smile, "you have a much improved appearance."

"Thanks to you, Prince Sergius," asserted Jones, wondering yet more at the apparent friendliness of every one.

"You are entirely welcome, Mr. Holloway. But come inside, please. We must talk together."

They seated themselves, Jones on the cot, Sergius on the camp-chair.

"And now, Mr. Holloway, perhaps you will explain what has become of my brother and—and the young lady, Miss Weston."

So that was it. They had discovered that the other party had vanished into thin air and looked to him to recover the trail. Jones determined in his own honest mind that he would never discover to them the location of those caves. Besides, they might try to make him enter them again! But he could not feel that any loyalty to a party which had, after all, treated him only as a spy and a liar, demanded further sacrifice than this.

"In the first place, Prince Sergius, I am not Richard Holloway. When you found me I had never seen or heard of such a person, but since that time I have met the man himself."

Without reserve, save as regarded any implication of Doherty, Jones proceeded to tell his story, to which the Russian listened with an impassive face. At the end, however, he rose and extended his hand to his involuntary guest.

"I was mistaken, Mr. Jones, and I have to ask your forgiveness. We must have seemed to you not only inhospitable, but boorish in the last degree to so threaten you who deserved only our help and kindness. But your story of the *Lusitania* you yourself will admit was—well, let us speak no more of that. Perhaps some day you will entrust me with your full confidence. Now, however, you are in a position to extend to me a very great service.

"No—" he raised a protesting hand as Jones started to speak, "I do not longer ask that you reveal the cavern entrance. Your own experience shows what is the most likely fate of those attempting it without good guidance. We have done all in our power to make you forget our past unjust treatment, even while we still deemed you Richard Holloway. May I expect your favor in return?"

"Why, of course," replied Jones in some surprise. "But I don't exactly see what I could do—"

"You will see," said the prince, with a rather peculiar smile. "Will you be pleased to follow me?"

Together they left the tent and walked across the sands toward the object of which Jones had earlier caught a glimpse. Now he saw what it was. It was an aeroplane. The nihilist was again speaking:

"I had planned to take with me the man, Doherty, but he is an ignorant fellow, entirely unsuited to such an undertaking. Also, he was afraid to go. None other of the men are suitable. Ivanovitch, he must remain to look after our crew. My mechanic is ill on board the *Monterey*. The others are too stupid. They are fellow Russians and brothers in the cause, but you see I speak frankly. You, on the other hand, are young, intelligent, and—"

"You want me to go up in that thing with you?" gasped Mr. Jones.

"Of course. I am a good airman. You need feel no alarm, for in the air you will be in no danger. It is when we descend to what is within that I desire with me a reliable companion. Are we to be comrades?"

"You give me a choice?"

"But yes. Unless you come willingly, I would better make my flight alone."

"All right. I'll go."

Yes, it was really Roland Chesterton Jones, the coward of the caverns, who said these words! As a matter of fact, Jones was not a coward at all, but a victim of subconscious terror of the dark. Given a fair chance and the open air, he had always felt perfectly willing to face danger, although his life before coming to Joker Island had not been an adventurous one and he was by choice a young man of quiet life and manners.

The prince gave him an approving nod.

"I am not a bad reader of features. We will meet everything like comrades, eh? And you will not be tempted, if we should come upon them, to return to my brother and his people?"

"I will not," said Jones firmly. He had nothing against any of them, but he possessed a natural predilection toward any one who treated him courteously, nihilist or not.

BESTIA SECRETUM

Moreover, there was something about Sergius Petrofsky which had attracted him from the first, in spite of his brutal threat that first night. Fanatical, cruel even, when thwarted, there was yet about him that invisible aura which we term personality, for lack of a better name. If he had been an actor he would undoubtedly have been an idol of the matinee girls. Jones wondered, when he thought of it, that Miss Weston had turned from him to his less attractive brother.

They had now reached the group of sailors gathered about the monoplane. Captain Ivanovitch was nowhere in sight, and they were lounging about in the sand, but all sprang to their feet at sight of Sergius. He said something sharply to them in Russian and all save two went off toward the tents. Then he turned again to his guest.

"I have been obliged to do almost all the work of assembling the plane with my own hands, because of this unfortunate illness of Thoreau, my mechanic. Are you in the least familiar with this sort of engine? It would be too much to hope that you know anything of the science of flight."

Mr. Jones hastened to disclaim any knowledge on either subject. He had always left even the mysteries of his own motor-cars, and his big power-boat, the *Bandersnatch,* to the expert attentions of their respective chauffeurs and captain. The most he knew about gasoline was that it sometimes exploded, and was used to drive automobiles, powerboats, and aeroplanes. Of the dark secrets of spark, ignition, carburetor, and so forth he was as innocent as a child.

"Then it is of no use for me to try to instruct you in the brief space which lies between us and departure. Your part will be to sit quiet in that seat which you see behind the pilot's place, and if we come to any grief I will endeavor to play the part of driver and mechanic also. We are taking with us no provisions, save a slight luncheon in that hamper, but these rifles may prove convenient. It is my purpose to make, as it were, a reconnaissance, and we may not even descend into the inner valley or crater until a later flight."

At this moment Captain Ivanovitch came up, accompanied by Doherty. The captain entered into conversation with Sergius in Russian, and as Mr. Jones waited for the next move, Doherty said in a low voice, "Gee, ain't I glad youse showed up? I ain't got no use for them flyin' things. If ever I gets to be a angel I suppose I'll have to flutter me wings—but till I gets 'em I sticks right to the ground floor."

"You may be right," Jones admitted.

"I thought we'd butt into the valley by the subway after all when I seen youse come out. But, gee, this lets little Willie out complete. Youse is welcome to the job."

"Mr. Jones," interrupted Sergius, "will you put these things on? It is not so warm up above there, you know."

He was holding out a heavy coat and a sort of hood, which Jones donned, while the nihilist put on a similar outfit. To the hood was attached a pair of large goggles which could be pulled down over the eyes. It was not a regular aviator's costume, but near enough for the short flight contemplated.

Then the two strangely assorted companions climbed to their places. Needless to say, it was the first time Mr. Jones had ever been in an aeroplane. He had attended meets, watched the daring evolutions of the dragonflylike things against the sky, and had one or two opportunities to go up himself, but he had never experienced any desire to rise higher above solid earth than the top floor of a skyscraper.

Yet now he found himself strangely cool and unperturbed. Sergius Petrofsky inspired him with a great deal of confidence in his ability as a man of action.

Now Ivanovitch and a seaman had grasped the mono-plane, one on each side at the rear, and were standing with feet braced as if expecting some great strain upon their muscles. Sergius did something with a lever and the engine burst forth into a roar which startled Mr. Jones extremely. He had forgotten what a racket the things make.

Then he felt a slight jerk and the plane was rolling swiftly along the sand. He was thrown back in his seat, as the machine tilted upward, and a moment later shut his eyes; for he had seen the beach dropping away from un-der them, and it seemed as if a violent wind had suddenly arisen. Remembering the goggles he reached up and pulled them down over his eyes before opening them again.

Glancing downward he saw the sea, rocking and sway-ing beneath them, had a moment of nausea, and realized that it was the plane which was rocking. They were up, they were actually flying through the air. The wind of their flight was beating upon his fate. The experience was different from anything which he had ever imagined, and yet it was strangely exhilarating too. For the first time since he had found himself adrift in the sea, he was glad that he had fallen off the liner.

No matter what might befall, nothing could ever rob him of the memory of this moment when he learned the real meaning of man's victory over the air.

Sergius turned slightly and shouted something over his shoulder, but the roar of engine and propeller drowned his voice. Jones shook his head and shouted back something equally indistinguishable. He had meant to say "Grand! Glorious! Splendid!" but the wind seemed to hurl the words back down his throat.

He looked down again and saw to his amazement how high they had already climbed. The island lay beneath them, with that maplike appearance which one notices in bird's-eye views. The black cliff which had appeared so awesome and forbidding was now no more than a huge, irregular oval line of black. And this line surrounded— what? A sea of green, it seemed, probably the tops of trees, although the foliage was indistinguishable from that height. Moreover it all appeared to be swinging in vast circles, for they were ascending in a steep spiral.

Jones began to wonder how high they were to mount. He had imagined, in the brief time given him for thought, that they would simply rise above the cliff and immediately descend upon the other side.

Then, abruptly, the steady roar of the engine slackened and died. The nose of the plane dipped earthward and they were sliding down the air, swiftly, but so smoothly that the sensation was one of pure delight. The circles of their descent were so wide that, as they came nearer, Jones had plenty of time to study the strange valley which lay shut off from and unsuspected of the outer world.

That the island had been one huge volcanic crater at one time in its history, there could be no doubt. Now, however, there was nothing to suggest a volcano save the wall itself, and within was a wide expanse of the greenest verdure. The great oval was about ten or twelve miles long. Its floor was of a slightly undulating, parklike appearance, the upper, darker green being broken here and there by lighter patches which. Jones presumed to be little lawns and open glades in the forest.

The engine roared out again, but this time Sergius did not ascend. He turned so sharply that the plane "banked" at what seemed to his passenger an alarming angle, and shot straight across the valley. Then he once more cut out the engine and shot downward swiftly and steeply.

Suddenly Jones perceived what they were aiming at, a broad, smooth space of green, about a quarter of a mile in length, which the prince in his circlings had picked out for a landing place. An instant later dark masses shot upward on both sides, the pilot deftly straightened out the plane, and with a stiff jolt they had struck the earth.

The lawn, which had looked so smooth and even from above, proved to be an expanse of villainous hummocks over which they bounded and sprang for fifty yards or so, and at last came to a creaking, swaying halt.

CHAPTER VI

"That, my friend," cried Sergius, turning a beaming face, "that was a good landing, no? Coming down in such unknown country something is always liable to break, but we have better fortune."

"What funny-looking trees!" exclaimed Mr. Jones, paying no heed to the Russian's self-congratulations. "Why, they look like—like cabbages! And what a horrible smell!"

The word "horrible" was none too strong to describe the intolerable odor which permeated the air. Descending as they had done from the clear, clean, fresh upper atmosphere, it seemed at first almost impossible to breathe at all. It was a sort of concentrated, well-nigh visible stench, suggesting nothing less than decayed slaughter-houses or open graveyards. Even the prince lost his smile after the first moment of delight over his successful landing.

The "trees" to which Mr. Jones had referred, were indeed not trees at all, but some sort of vegetable growth entirely unfamiliar to either of the men. If they had really been the cabbages they resembled, they would have made the everlasting fortune of the market-gardener who grew them, for the smallest was as large as a fair-sized hen-house, and some of the larger ones must have measured at least a hundred feet from root to crest, with a diameter at least one fourth as great. They were a dark purple in color, shading upward into a sickly green. None of them grew very close together, and the spaces between were filled with an astonishing variety of mushroomlike things, whose vivid coloring, red, yellow, violet, and orange, jarred upon the eye in a disharmony of which nature is very seldom guilty.

Like a giant's vegetable garden, these monstrous growths entirely surrounded the glade where they had alighted. But even though they towered so high over the heads of the aeronauts, they caught glimpses between and above them of other and different growths, yet higher.

There was no wind in the glade. The sun beat down and the stench rose up. Mr. Jones had a strong feeling that if they did not get out of the place in a short time he was going to be very ill indeed.

"This is awful," he said appealingly. "Can't we go up again?"

The Russian, who had been looking about with much interest, shook his head. "Of what use to rise now when we have just made such a very nice landing? Another time we might not be so lucky. The odor is certainly unpleasant, but after all it is only a smell. It is only the vegetation. I knew that here in the crater valley we would find some very peculiar things. We must not be too easily deterred. Let us penetrate past these vegetables and find what lies beyond."

Sergius undoubtedly had the final say so in regard to their leaving or remaining, so his companion followed his example, unstrapped himself from his seat in the monoplane, and descended to earth. The prince handed him a rifle and cartridge belt and took one himself. They discarded their coats and hoods and advanced toward the nearest passage between the "cabbages."

As they approached the dreadful charnel odor became more intense, if that were possible. Shoulders thrown forward, eyes half-shut and smarting, they pushed through it as through some tangible obstruction.

Then the first of the many-hued mushrooms were crunching beneath their feet. They crushed and squelched, with a semiliquid sound, sending up a sort of acid gas into the faces of the two adventurers, somewhat like the fumes of hydrochloric acid. The prince took out his handkerchief and bound it over his mouth and nose, signaling to Jones to do likewise, for both of them were past speaking. With these improvised and inadequate gas-masks, they waded doggedly on through the fungi.

They were within fifteen feet of one of the smaller cabbages, when with a sort of swishing sound it began to move. Its outer sheath of purple and green leaves, twenty-five feet long and five broad, began to open out and descend.

Jones caught a glimpse between them of a huge, scarlet, writhing mass, and tried to turn and run. The crushed mushroom things held his feet. It was like trying to leap or run in a quicksand.

Then the rough, thick, sawlike edge of the nearest leaf struck him a glancing blow on the shoulder, and he was down in the mess of fungi. A long, writhing, bright-red thing, like a nightmare fishing-worm, lashed out above him, curled back and encircled his neck in a strangling grip.

"Help!" he tried to shout. "Sergius—help!"

Then his shoulder was seized and he was being pulled away from the giant cabbage. The tentacle which held him straightened out and actually stretched as if it had been made of India-rubber. A knife flashed over him, severing the tentacle, and a moment later he was out of reach of a dozen more which were shooting after him. That was the last thing he remembered until he came to under the shadow of the plane, to look up into the anxious face of Sergius Petrofsky, who was fanning him with a handkerchief.

Mr. Jones sat up and felt of his neck gingerly. Luckily his collar had somewhat protected it, but it felt very stiff and sore.

"I thought you were gone, my friend," said Sergius, standing up and wiping his perspiring face with the handkerchief.

"So did I. What I can't understand is why the thing didn't get you, too. Look at it now—ugh, the horrible, nasty, writhing beast!"

The "death cabbage" (as they afterward named the interesting vegetables) had not closed its outer sheath, and its inner hideousness stood fully exposed to the sun. Straight up from the center sprang a sort of slimy, blue-black stalk, terminating some twenty-five feet above the ground in a wide plume of green fronds. Surrounding this stalk was a dense, intertwined mass of the long, scarlet tentacles which had nearly dragged Mr. Jones to his doom. To be eaten by a vegetable—and such a vegetable! Jones shuddered and looked away, feeling very sick and disgusted.

"Look!" cried the nihilist. "It is twisting itself about like a thing in agony. I wonder if the brute has eyes and sees us here and still hungers after its prey? But that is curious. See, it is becoming of a bright orange color!"

Jones looked again, rather unwittingly, but what the Russian said was quite true. The wriggling scarlet mass was rapidly changing to orange, and from orange it faded to a sickly yellow. Moreover it was wriggling more and more feebly. The outstretched sheath-leaves lifted themselves spasmodically two or three times, then wilted limply among the fungi at its base. The central stalk began to droop over to one side, and the green fronds hung dispiritedly down. At the end of five minutes all motion had ceased. Even the now pale tentacles writhed no more. The death cabbage was itself dead.

"Do you suppose it perished of a broken heart?" asked Sergius whimsically. "You resisted its ardent caresses, and it died of disappointment. But rather, I think, it possible that another than either of us has killed this monster, my friend."

"What do you mean? Have you seen anybody else?"

Sergius pointed upward solemnly.

"I mean him," he said, and he was pointing at the sun. "There is but one explanation. These are creatures of the night, and they get their—their food in the night, whatever it may be. They are not accustomed to grasp their prey by daylight. This one was tempted, and he opened his protecting sheath, and he was slain by the sun! But he would have killed us first, if I had not been able to spring back more quickly than you, my friend, and escape his first gropings."

"I owe you my life," said Jones earnestly. "I never knew anybody before who would have had the courage to throw himself within reach of that—that thing, and drag another man away from it."

"It is nothing," Sergius demurred, looking very much pleased nevertheless. "Now we will be comrades, indeed—no? I think, however, that we have done and seen enough for one day. Mount again to your seat and we will leave this valley of death. But we will return to-morrow and alight in some more favorable spot."

"I'm with you," Mr. Jones assented joyfully.

But first they cleaned themselves as well as they could of the pulpy fungoids with which they were both plastered; Jones from head-to foot. Then they started to put on their heavy coats. Mr. Jones was buttoning his and Sergius had just slipped his arms into the sleeves, when a voice behind them said sharply: "Stand perfectly still, please! If either one of you moves a finger I'll kill you first, Prince Sergius Petrofsky!"

Chapter VII

Startled and amazed, Jones and the nihilist yet obeyed, for there was a certain sincerity back of the command which was not to be denied. Their rifles lay on the ground a few feet distant and Sergius himself, with his arms half into his coat, was peculiarly helpless.

Both looked over their shoulders, however, and there behind them, rifle pointed at the middle of the Russian's back, stood Richard Holloway! He was still attired in his simple costume of shirt and trousers, now very ragged and dirty, and his face wore a grim smile.

"Who are you?" asked Sergius, although he may have guessed.

"It's Holloway," supplied Jones in a whisper.

"You don't need to murmur it in his ear, sweet child," interrupted the newcomer. "I'm so glad to meet you again, Rolly. You know I said I was sure we should be friends. But we thought after all a stalactite must have dropped and crushed out your innocent young life."

Mr. Jones could think of no reply. Of course, now, the other party would never believe that he had not been lying when he said that he had nothing to do with Sergius Petrofsky. Even Jim Haskins would no longer believe him. Then he forgot his own troubles in wondering how this unexpected meeting would affect his newer friend, Sergius.

"Move farther back from those rifles," commanded Holloway. "That's right. And just remember that I don't love either of you one little bit. The only pity is that my dear little vegetable garden didn't succeed in getting both of you for its luncheon. It's a lucky thing for you that you didn't try conclusions with one of the really big fellows. That one was a mere child—poor innocent thing!" He shifted his rifle to the hollow of his arm and came toward them.

Sergius, his face white and strained with anger, still stood with his arms half way in the coat. "May I—have I your very kind permission, Mr. Holloway, to finish putting on my coat? I give you my word that we are neither of us armed, except for the rifles."

"In just a minute, prince. Sorry about your word, but if you did happen to get careless about it, where would

I be? Rolly, I've got you covered. Just go over and turn your friend's pockets inside out for me, will you? And now your own? That's right. No, I wronged your serene highness. You can put your coat on, though you must be a cold-blooded fish to want it in this sun."

"We were just about to ascend," said the Russian stiffly.

"Oh, I see. Well, you're just about not to ascend now, so you won't need it. We saw you fluttering gaily about over the valley, and saw you drop into this place. Paul (he really seems to retain a regard for you, for some reason), your brother, asked me to come out and pick up the remains, if there were any, which I doubted myself, knowing what sort of place you had landed in. He asked me to extend to you his apologies for not coming himself. He sprained his ankle in the caves, but Miss Weston is looking after him so well that really it can't be much hardship."

Sergius' eyes narrowed, and Jones remembered that Jim Haskins had told him both brothers were seeking the girl's favor.

Holloway picked up the two rifles from the ground and tucked them under his other arm. "So nice of you," he murmured. "We're rather short on arms and ammunition. But I know you're anxious to be welcomed in camp. Turn to the right, please, and straight ahead. Don't be frightened of the little cabbages. I won't feed you to them this time."

Jones was beginning to detest the young American as much as he had formerly been inclined to like him. His mocking banter in this place that smelt like the tomb and was the home of detestable death, seemed as out of place as the tinkle of a pianola in Purgatory.

However, the man must know a safe way out, or he could not have appeared there himself, so the two prisoners turned their faces in the direction indicated and started off, with Holloway close behind.

They crossed the glade obliquely and came into view of a broad road, or trail, which had apparently been trampled over and through the fungi and several of the young and comparatively small death plants which lay crushed and broken. Two of them, each well above ten feet from root to crest, had been actually torn up by the roots and tossed to some distance from the place where they had been growing.

What power or agency had been strong enough to perform such a feat with such victims?

As they involuntarily paused, staring, Holloway's mocking voice answered the unspoken question:

"That's the work of another of my lovely island's children. Don't get scared. He doesn't prowl around much by daylight, but when he does take a walk, and things get in his way or annoy him, he just pushes them gently to one side—as you see. He's a foul brute, but not foul enough to feed upon such carrion plants as these. He was probably hunting something."

The nihilist was too proud, and Jones too overcome, to question Holloway in regard to the mysterious "brute" to which he referred, and after a moment of hesitation they marched on through the sickening mess of broken fungi and wilted, blood-sucking tentacles. But first, at Holloway's own suggestion, they all three again bound handkerchiefs over mouth and nose as a partial protection against the thrice-vile fumes rising from beneath their feet.

At last, however, a breath of purer air reached their nostrils, and raising his head, Jones's watering eyes beheld a scene of weird and unearthly beauty. Behind them lay the field of death cabbages, in all its foul ugliness. Before them was a forest—but such a forest! The trees were mere slender, graceful stems, shooting up to an unbelievable height, where they branched out into a feathery tuft of graceful leaves, resembling palms.

But these slender stems were all wound and garlanded with gorgeous blossoms, like glorious floral butterflies swaying and fluttering to every breath of air.

Here and there huge balloonlike growths had forced their way upward between the palms, bending them aside and so making their own path to the sunlight. These, however, unlike the cabbages, had nothing horrible or loathsome in their appearance, but were of the most delicate shades of pink, shading into lemon yellow at the summits. They, too, were overgrown in the riotous embrace of a thousand blossoming vines.

Underfoot the ground was thickly carpeted with moss in wide patches, like rich rugs of velvet green, starred all over with little points of brilliant blue and scarlet, which were also flowers. Between the butterflylike blossoms of the vines innumerable real butterflies were flitting. Their colors were so similar to the flowers that it was impossible to tell if a blossom one's eyes rested upon were really such or a butterfly, unless it suddenly spread its wings and flickered away through the slanting sunlight.

Moving forward slowly, like men in a dream of fairyland, they came at last entirely out of the zone of vile odors; and the more delightful by contrast, their nostrils were filled by the divine fragrance of this unlegended Garden of the Hesperides.

Again Holloway had his comment to make.

"You like this all right, now—but I just invite you to take the trip by moonlight!"

"By moonlight," said the Russian softly, forgetting for the moment his animosity toward the speaker. "I should think by moonlight this place would be—ah, celestial!

"H—m! Well, I've been here, and take it from me it was more like the other place."

"Impossible!

"In the bright lexicon of Joker Island, there ain't no such word, dear child. Your imagination needs exercise— or you wouldn't have come here, so I'll just permit you to exercise it on this. But I'll give you one tip: You've seen the flora, but you haven't seen the fauna—yet. Straight ahead, now, through that little lane between the vegetable balloons. No, not that way. Halt! Good Lord, man, if you'd gone down there you'd have wished you was safe inside one of those mild-tempered little cabbages back yonder!"

Sergius, absorbed in gazing at the wonders about them, had started to go to the left of the balloon in question instead of the right. The ground sloped sharply downward there, and as he drew back his foot in surprise at Holloway's evident agitation, there was a sudden rattle and slide of falling gravel.

Both he and his fellow-captive looked keenly down the incline, but could see nothing out of the way. A tangle of gray, leafless vines formed a veil across the bottom of the slope, through which they could see nothing.

Then, the perspiration sprang out on Sergius' forehead, and for the first time since Jones had met him the prince looked really frightened. For over that tangle of vines something was moving. It was a leg, and it had come out from between the vines. It was jointed in two places, the space between the upper joints being about three feet long, and at the end of it was a single, great, curved claw, black and gleaming like polished ebony.

Another similar leg followed it into visibility. Then two eyes came into view, round, black, and fastened upon the ends of stalks like those of a lobster.

"Good God!" breathed the Russian.

"What is the thing, Holloway?"

"Just a little spider," responded their captor cheerfully. "But plenty big enough to make three mouthfuls of you.

That's its web it's sitting in, wondering why you don't come on down to dinner. I'd shoot the old devil, but what's the use? He's only one. Shall we go on now?"

With cold shivers running up and down their spinal columns, Mr. Jones and his companion stepped carefully back from the entrance to the giant spider's den, and entered a little path or trail which led windingly away through the lovely, treacherous forest. Jones, for one, heartily wished that their guardian would march in front instead of the rear. The death cabbages had been bad enough, but they had seemed such vast, unnatural prodigies that already his memory reproduced them dreamily.

That spider was another matter. He had heard of spiders as large as dinner plates, and shuddered at the thought of them. This spider had been as large as—well, judging from its forelegs it could better be compared with an extra-large dining-table.

And Holloway had spoken of it as "only one." How many more such fiends lay hidden, waiting for the false tread of a foot, or the careless speed of some hunted jungle thing? He began to be careful indeed to look where he trod, and suspicious of even the supposedly harmless flowers and butterflies. Beauty becomes more horrible than frank ugliness when one has learned that death lurks behind it.

Fortunately, however, for their peace of mind they saw no more of the "fauna" of which Holloway had hinted, although once in skirting a dark morass they heard distant crashing sounds, as if some large beast were threshing about somewhere in the depths.

"This place is like a Broadway café," Holloway informed them. "Nothing much doing in the daytime—but—oh you midnight suppers. Eat and be eaten, that's our motto after sunset."

"You seem to know a whole lot about the place," Jones ventured.

"Yes, indeed. Regular old homestead to little Willy. You see, I lived here for two years, and got real well acquainted with the inhabitants. Maybe we'll let you and your dear friend Prince Sergius try it, when it comes time for us to leave. You'd learn a whole lot you never knew before, believe me. That is, if you survived the first week or two."

Mr. Jones looked at him hopelessly. Was the man in earnest?

But Sergius laughed scornfully. "I should not particularly mind," he said, "so long as we were relieved of your company, Mr. Holloway."

"You don't say! How very rude and unkind you are, prince. But never mind. I'd be sore, too, if I were in your place, so I forgive you like a true Christian. And here we are—home at last all safe and sound."

For the path, turning sharply, passed out of the jungle and into the full light of day. Half a mile away, across a broad expanse of green meadow, the rim of the crater raised its black height, hidden from them until now by the forest. To the right, in the distance, some unidentifiable animals were grazing, and ahead, close to the wall, a pillar of smoke was rising, almost white against its dead blackness.

"There's our camp. Keep right on going. Don't worry, they're expecting us."

That they were expected was presently evidenced, for the figure of a man appeared coming toward them across the meadow. In a few minutes Jones was able to identify him, for it was Jim, Paul's cowboy retainer. He met then, with a grin, which suddenly faded as he recognized Mr. Jones. He looked from him to Sergius and then back again.

"Well, of all the—snakes!" he exclaimed, and his hand dropped suggestively to his hip-pocket. "So that yarn of yours was just a string of whoppers, was it? By jiminy, I've a notion to drill you right now, you—you low-down horse-thief! Lettin' me get the notion that you was layin' smashed back there in the cave, and me mad as thunder because they wouldn't let me hike back to look for you. An' all the time you pikin' around with this here nihilan-archist bunch. Say, what kind of a low-down, lyin' cattle-rustler are you, anyhow?"

"Shut up, Jimmy," interrupted Holloway at last, al-though he had listened to the arraignment with a grin of pure enjoyment. "Rolly's nerves are all upset as it is. How is Prince Petrofsky?"

Jim's face relaxed again into a grin.

"Doin' fine," he answered. "I know now why he brought that female woman along. Gee! I wouldn't mind sprainin' a leg or so to get nursed that luxurious."

"He'll get well for pure joy when he sees who's here. Forward the army. We'll be right behind you, gentlemen. Sorry the hotel bus wasn't running, so as to save your walking all this way, but you know what these summer resorts are."

His cheerful nonsense bored Jones wretchedly, as they went on toward the camp. What sort of a greeting were he and Sergius likely to get? Not a very pleasant one, judging from the sample offered by Haskins. He heartily wised that Sergius had stuck to his original intention of "a mere re-connaissance." They would have been back with the nihil-ists by this time, and at that moment the nihilist camp actually seemed like home to Mr. Jones.

What could there possibly be in the crater valley of sufficient value to make all these people so very anxious to reach it? Unless they were seeking the rather morbid pleasure of being killed and eaten, he could conceive of nothing liable to be there which would repay the extreme trouble and risk attendant upon obtaining it.

A gold mine? How could anybody work a gold mine in a place like this? Diamonds, perhaps? He himself would have cheerfully forfeited a full ownership in Tiffany's just to escape from the place.

He had never had any opportunity to question Sergius Petrofsky, and as that gentleman stalked along moodily by his side now he did not look in a good humor to answer such interrogations. Both men had long since removed their heavy coats and were carrying them, but even so their clothing was saturated with perspiration.

Hot, weary, and disgusted, they neither of them looked as they came into camp, as if they had been upon any pleasurable expedition.

A fire was snapping and crackling cheerfully in the cliff shadow, and about it lay scattered various paraphernalia, but no one was in sight.

"All in the cave," said Jim, in an explanatory tone. "Some cliff-dwellers, our bunch, ain't we, Holloway?"

"First-class apartments," corrected the other. "Dry, airy, cool, but dogs and children barred. Hey, there! Anybody home?"

At Holloway's hail a woman appeared in the entrance to one of a large number of the dark openings which perforated the crater wall. It was of course Margaret Weston.

"Oh, did you find them, Mr. Holloway? Who is that with the prince? Isn't that the man we lost in the caverns?"

"It sure is, ma'am," grinned the cowboy, not giving Holloway a chance to reply. "He ain't crushed none, not so you could notice it. I take off my hat to you, ma'am. You was dead right about the snake, but I was too plumb pigheaded to know it."

"That is all right, James," said the girl, smiling sweetly. "A woman's intuition is sometimes correct after all, is it not? Prince Sergius," with a sudden severe formality, "your brother would like to see you as soon as it is convenient."

The nihilist bowed with a dignity equal to her own. His face was sternly set, but Jones, watching curiously, saw a look flash up into his eyes as they rested on the girl which confirmed the cowboy's statement in regard to his feeling toward her. He could hardly be blamed, either. Miss Weston looked a good deal more than attractive, standing there with one white, shapely arm extended to support herself on the precarious foothold of rocks at the cavern door. She looked very young, girlish and utterly out of place in that nightmare valley. Her smooth cheeks were slightly flushed, her scarlet lips were set just sufficiently to bring out their exquisite lines, and her big blue eyes were shining with some emotion, but one hardly favorable to Sergius, if Mr. Jones were any judge.

In fact, Miss Weston was angry, and Jones felt vaguely sorry for Sergius Petrofsky. He wondered again at the girl's ardent dislike for his friend.

"I am grateful to my brother," said Sergius slowly, "for sending such a charming messenger!"

"Thank you. But kindly reserve your compliments for some one who will better deserve and—appreciate them. Mr. Holloway, will you kindly accompany these gentlemen? The sailors are in the other cave, and I hardly think it safe for Prince Paul to receive them alone—"

Sergius flushed deeply. The thrust evidently went home.

"Certainly, Miss Weston," assented Holloway, with a smile of amusement. "But I was just going to start cooking supper."

"I am not myself such a bad cook as you seem to think," laughed the girl. "What use is a woman in camp if she can't do the nursing and cooking?"

"You're dead right, ma'am," commented Jim, but in a most respectful voice. Jones reflected sadly that even this woman-hater appeared to have been converted to admiration for the girl. Probably he regarded her diagnosis of his, Jones's, character as a symptom of most unusual wisdom.

"Go right in, gentlemen," commanded Holloway. "Here, Jim, will you take these rifles? And lend me your little popgun? Thanks. A rifle is no good at close quarters."

With a disdainful shrug Sergius turned his back on the voluble American and entered the cave, Mr. Jones close at his heels.

Chapter VIII

On one of the dark but cool chambers in the rock a rude couch of blankets had been laid. Beside it, upon a flat-topped stone, stood an electric lantern of the type which, using large batteries, will burn for eighty or ninety hours, and which illuminated the place quite brightly. Beside it a bottle of arnica and some carefully folded bandages were arranged.

Upon the couch lay Paul Petrofsky, the lower part of one leg swathed in more and beautifully adjusted bandages. As the two captives entered, however, he sat up and gave utterance to an exclamation of joy as he recognized his brother.

For the first time, seeing them together, Jones realized the strong resemblance between the two men. There were the same broad, intelligent brow, the same high-bridged, symmetrical nose, the same thin-lipped, sensitive mouth, and pleasant, dark eyes. The only real difference between the two faces lay in the expression and in that slight inclination of Paul's chin to recede.

Sergius' eyes were keen as well as pleasant, his mouth was set in firmer lines, and his chin was of a squarish and very determined shape. Also, at time, his face wore a haughty and somewhat domineering look—a look which Paul's countenance never assumed.

If, knowing neither of them, Jones had been asked to choose, he would have unhesitatingly named Sergius as the supporter of aristocratic government, and Paul as the man to be easily led, particularly into any scheme, however wild, for the betterment of his fellow Russians.

"Sergius!" exclaimed the man on the couch. There was pure relief in his voice. "Then you are safe. I was afraid—"

"That some of your friend Holloway's pets had made a meal of your dear brother? I should not have thought that would have appeared to you as a great trouble, Paul."

His brother shook his head impatiently, with a slight frown.

"That is absurd, as you very well know. Because you have been misled by these murderous, bomb-throwing companions of yours is no reason for me to forget that you are my brother."

Sergius flushed and straightened himself.

"My companions are not bomb-throwers, and you very well know the difference between nihilism and the madness of anarchy, although you choose to pretend that there is none. You are in a position to say what you please to me, Paul, but you know my feelings on that subject and it seems hardly generous—"

"It is not a question of generosity, but of common sense," the other broke out. "Someday you will thank me for standing out against your fanatical views. Russia will never be saved by such mad dreamers as your so-called friends. It is I who truly serve Russia in her hour of need. How long, think you, will the war which is slaughtering our people continue after I turn over to the government the—that which we have come to seek?"

"Long enough, I hope, to destroy every member of the cruel bureaucracy which holds her in its bloody grip. Yes, it is your friends who are bloody, Paul, not mine."

"There is tyranny in every fixed government. Moreover, it is not the rulers of Russia who suffer most. It is the very peasantry which you profess to love so much. Turn your face from the mirage you are pursuing, my brother, and cast in your lot with us!"

"I will not desert my brothers," replied Sergius briefly, but with evident sincerity.

"Then," said Prince Paul with some firmness, "you will not be allowed to return to them either. Dick Holloway, I had hoped that after all I might persuade my brother—I have no brothers—to ally himself with us. Since he is not yet ready to do so, I must ask that you and James Haskins see to it that he remains in this camp. As for his companion, the spy, it would be no more than right if we should shoot him outright."

Jones started slightly. This amiable-looking Russian seemed to be even more arbitrary than his nihilist brother.

"Oh, I wouldn't go that far," counseled Holloway, with an amused grin. "I'll be responsible for it that—he doesn't leave us so easily as he did before. By the way, prince, I left the aeroplane where they landed. Do you want the thing brought into camp?"

"No, I think not," said Paul, after a moment's hesitation. "I fail to see how it could be of any use to us. If you or Jim chance to go that way again you might see to it that it is rendered useless for any one, however." He gave a significant glance in the direction of the plane's rightful owner.

Then he dropped back upon his couch with a little grimace of pain. "Sergius, will you remain here with me? I should very much like to hear of what befell when you descended into the valley. That is, if you don't mind telling me. Dick Holloway, please take this man Jones out with you and set him to work about the camp. We may as well make him useful since you are set on keeping him."

Holloway looked doubtfully at the two brothers. Sergius saw the look and laughed bitterly.

"You had better assure your friend, Paul, that I am unlikely to murder you in his absence. Also you are mistaken

in regard to Mr. Jones's relations with me. I never met
the gentleman until night before last, and we parted then
because he managed to cut a hole in the side of his prison
tent and escape. I will admit that I do now regard him as
a friend, but that is because of his very excellent qualities.
We are friends, however, and any treatment which you
accord him I must beg you to offer me also."

He looked very haughty and dignified as he uttered
these sentiments, and Mr. Jones's heart went out to him
more than ever. The man had not only saved his life, but
now he was defending him from undeserved oppression.
Somehow, he determined, he would endeavor to repay
Prince Sergius.

Paul shrugged his shoulders and smiled rather dubious-
ly at his brother. "Of course, if you say he did not come to
our camp as a spy I shall have to take your word. You are
in a position to know if any one is. Holloway, we will have
to treat the gentleman courteously, since my brother is
determined to share his fate." He laughed. "I really don't
care to make you wash dishes, Sergius."

Holloway and Mr. Jones went back to the camp fire,
leaving the two brothers alone together. There was no exit
to the cavern chamber, save that by which they had entered, and even Holloway did not really believe that the nihilist would harm his brother for mere revenge.

Jones longed to ask some questions in regard to this
mysterious war which had been again hinted at, but he
still suffered from a deep-seated dread of what the answer
might reveal, and also of being regarded by these strangers
as hopelessly feeble-minded.

"Let it wait. If I'm really crazy I'm bound to find it out
soon enough," he thought bitterly.

In a short time supper was prepared, consisting of
canned goods and the fresh meat of some animal, probably one of those creatures which still grazed quietly in the

distant meadow. Jones, for one, was ravenously hungry. He had eaten nothing save the bowl of stew brought him by Doherty for thirty-six hours or more, and did full justice to Miss Weston's cooking, which was excellent. She explained this by saying that she had taken a course in domestic science to supplement a brief hospital training, preparatory to her work as a Red Cross nurse in the European battlefields.

The European battlefields! How much of Europe then was involved in this mad, chimerical war of theirs? Whoever the fighters might be, he felt that they had missed a very beautiful and determined young nurse when Miss Weston was sidetracked into this equally mad island affair. Mr. Jones was feeling more and more as if, having slept a single night, he had awakened into a new and entirely unfamiliar world.

Paul had managed to hobble out of his cavern retreat, supporting himself on the shoulder of his brother, and the whole party, including the two sailors, ate together without regard to caste or rank. Paul was glad to sit down at once, but Sergius first wandered about for a few moments, apparently inspecting the arrangements. Jones wondered if his reckless companion had designs on the rifles, three of which lay together close by; but if this were so he resigned them as impracticable, for presently he came and seated himself between Holloway and his brother.

As he did so he leaned across, behind Holloway's back, and whispered something to Jones, who had taken his place just beyond. Jones, however, did not catch the words, and he thought best not to attract the attention of the company by asking for a repetition.

The upper rim of the sun was just disappearing below the western wall as they finished, and only a few minutes later the sudden tropic night was upon them, with its wonderful stars and refreshing, fragrant breath of coolness.

It brought something more than coolness in its wake, it brought a rising wave of sound from the jungle beyond the open meadow. The valley of the day was no more, and the valley of night had swung wide its doors for all the creatures which crouched, awaiting the liberating touch of darkness.

The first intimation of this other valley, which none of the party save Holloway really knew, was a deep-throated roar from the jungle immediately opposite. This was followed by a sort of wild, bubbling shriek, as of a creature slivering from nightmare. The sound ended so abruptly that one could only judge the shrieker to have been swallowed by the roarer. Next there was a great snarling and yowling and crashing of branches, as if two enormous tom-cats were engaged in a combat to the death. The noise of battle was soon drowned out, however, by the full rising chorus of night life, the separate notes of which, all blended as into one mighty, discordant cry, rising harshly toward the white, indifferent stars.

Only Holloway remained entirely unaffected by the uproar. Miss Weston, the intrepid, actually trembled and shrank toward the protecting of her Russian lover—that is, of the Russian lover she favored.

The two sailors sprang to their feet and looked longingly in the direction of the caverns. Arizona Jim reached casually over and drew his rifle up beside him. Sergius also gazed desirefully in the direction of the rifles, forbidden to him and Jones, while the latter, shuddering inwardly, remembered that they had actually walked through the midst of all that only a couple of hours ago.

"Some opera, isn't it?" remarked Holloway, with an amused glance about the little circle of white faces. "When I first came here I used to lie all night and shiver and shake and try to make up sleep in the daytime. I had a gun, but only a little ammunition, you know. I found that a good-sized fire would keep all but the really big fellows away, though, so I got in the habit of building one in front of a small cave and sleeping behind it. If a little fellow came along, he was afraid of the fire. A big one couldn't get in the cave. Great Scott! For a while after I got taken off the island I couldn't sleep at all. Missed the noise, you see."

"Great Heaven! What was that?"

The whole party, except Holloway, sprang to their feet and stared wildly into the air. Something huge, black, monstrous had flapped out of the darkness and into it again, passing so close that the wind of its flight scattered burning brands right and left from the fire.

"Guess we'd better be going to bed," said Holloway, rising but with no undue haste. "I don't know exactly what those things are, because I've never caught a glimpse of the brutes by daylight, but the fire really seems to attract them instead of keeping them away. Once one of 'em made a grab at me in passing. Made a nasty gash on my cheek. I just dodged into my little boudoir in time."

"It looked like a—like a great, impossible bat," cried Margaret Weston, and there was a hysterical note in her voice. "Oh, why was I brought to this frightful place? Why did we not retire into the caverns before sunset, as we did last night?"

"Poor little girl," said Paul Petrofsky gently. "I never would have brought you here, if there had been any other way. Come. You shall sleep to-night on that nice, soft couch you prepared for me, Miss Margaret, and Dick Holloway and I will sleep in the cave entrance. Nothing shall come near you that can harm."

"There's really no need for you to be frightened," interrupted Holloway in a more serious and considerate tone than one usually heard from his lips. "There are five men of us, at least, who are well-armed, and any one of us would die before we would let harm come to the only girl in Joker Island."

Sergius bit his lip, but said nothing. By his "five men" the American had carefully left him and Mr. Jones out of the number of Miss Weston's protectors.

"You and Rolly," continued Holloway, addressing the nihilist, "can sleep in Room 5, Suite A. Here it is, and here's a torch. Be sparing with it, for we haven't many more batteries."

He pointed out the cave which he humorously dignified with the title of Room 5. "Jimmy boy will be right at your door in case you want anything in the night," he added significantly.

The prisoners entered, Sergius leading the way with the torch. They found it to be a small but dry cavern, and as they spread down their heavy coats to sleep on, it seemed as decent a bedroom as could be expected. It also formed a very efficient jail, since, like the other where Paul had lain, it had but the one exit, and that way led past the presumably wakeful Jim Haskins.

At least he had enough to keep him awake in listening to the wild night chorus of Joker Island and keeping his little fire going at the entrance.

For a time the two companions in misfortune lay silent, listening to the uproar which was somewhat muffled by the rocky walls about them. It was Jones who spoke first, voicing a question which had been all along in his mind.

"Prince Sergius," he said, "what on earth are you and the rest of them after in this place? I mean, why did Holloway want to come back, and why did he persuade your brother to fit out a yacht and come after him, and why did you—" He paused suddenly, wondering just how sensitive the prince was on that subject.

But his companion laughed softly in the darkness.

"That American—that Jim—he did not tell you every-thing, eh?"

"I think he told me all he knew. But of course, if you don't want to trust me, just say so. I'm only curious, that's all."

"But I do trust you." Sergius reached over, caught Jones's hand, gripped it hard, and then dropped it as sud-denly. "Really—do not laugh—you are the only friend I have within two thousand miles at least. Those men of mine? They are of the rough peasant type whom I pity but cannot love. My Captain Ivanovitch? He is—well, to be frank, I do not like him. He has not the least refinement. My brother? Ah, yes, I love him, but we are not friends—not now. He is my elder, the head of my house since our father died.

"Paul was educated in America, and our father sent me to Oxford, for he was a man of broad, splendid ideas. He thought thus we two should share the education of two continents, but instead it was so we grew apart. At Oxford I met other Russians, thinking men, one of whom—alas, he is now in Siberia—changed the whole course of my life. But I cannot now tell you of all that. Paul, in your free America, clung still to the old, I call them the cruel and tyrannous, ideals.

"But you I liked, even when I thought you were that beast, Richard Holloway. It is true that I threatened you, but then I was angry, because I wished you to do some-thing reasonable and you would not. But when we met again and I asked you to come with me into this place of hell, you did not even hesitate. You came like an old friend—a comrade."

"But you saved my life afterward, prince," said Jones, amazed at this tribute and the evidently sincere feeling which lay behind it. "I am in your debt for that and for standing up for me to your brother."

"And why not? Comrades must not desert one another. And I do not like to be named prince. Such titles stand for all I most abhor. Call me Sergius and I will call you Roland, as friends should. Tell me, would you go yet further and accompany me upon a greater adventure than any of these dogs that hold us dare attempt?"

"What do you mean?" asked Mr. Jones, somewhat startled.

"I mean," the other replied, lowering his voice to a whisper, "that to-morrow they will destroy our only means of escape—the aeroplane. To-night it still stands there, safe unless some night-devil has trampled it. In half an hour we could be on board the *Monterey*. Is it not worth some risk to attain that? And we could return, but next time we would not be trapped so easily. We would be upon our guard."

"Good Lord," groaned Mr. Jones. "What you propose is impossible, prince—I mean, Sergius. We should be killed before we had gone fifty yards into that nightmare out there."

"You hesitate? But I have not yet answered your question. Listen. In this island—this island which contains so many strange and unaccountable surprises—in its soil is a substance more valuable a thousand times than gold."

"Radium?" hazarded Mr. Jones.

"Radium—bah! No, it is a strange, secret substance, which for ages has been sought by science until it has been termed a vision of fools and madmen." He lowered his voice yet more. "It is that which was once named the Philosopher's Stone—and it will change the nature of what have been called the elements. My friend, this substance will transmute common lead to gold!"

"Oh, is that all?" sighed Mr. Jones. "I thought it was probably something about gold, but believe me, it isn't worth it, prince—it really isn't."

Sergius sat up, and Jones knew that he was staring at him in amazement.

"You are a very strange man, my friend. Has gold no temptation for you?"

"Not a bit—not that sort of gold, anyway. Do you realize that if this mythical stuff of Holloway's proves what he has claimed to you people, it will upset the financial systems of the entire world, and become itself of no more value than—than mud?"

"Not at all. Do you think we would be so mad as to flood the world with gold? No, we will give out that we have discovered a very valuable mine and we will only release it in such quantities as may prove judicious. For myself, I desire it only for the cause. Russia shall be freed from herself and become a blazing lamp of liberty to enlighten the whole world. Paul, he desires only to help the government in overcoming the Germans. I desire to make the Germans my brothers."

So, it was really Germany that Russia was fighting! It all seemed very strange. If it had been England, now—

"As for this Holloway," continued Sergius, "who discovered it, he thinks only of himself. He says he wants to be a captain of industry."

"But why didn't he bring some of the stuff away with him in the first place?"

"He could carry only a little, and that was used up in demonstrating to us its value. But there is a great deal more here—the whole soil is impregnated with it, and he discovered it by the chance of a leaden bullet falling into the fire. The heat melted the bullet and it sank to the earth beneath. And in the morning, when he swept away the ashes from before his cave, there lay a splash of gold upon the ground. He is a bright man, this Richard Holloway, and after thought he experimented with another bullet."

"Yes, he would," sighed Mr. Jones. In spite of Sergius' assurance, the effect on himself and all his friends, if this improbable tale proved true, was staggering to contemplate. "Now I know why I dislike the man so much. Isn't the air in here frightfully stuffy? I can hardly keep my eyes open."

"A little smoke from the fire at the entrance, perhaps. Or—my friend, do not tell me that you ignored the warning I gave you!"

"Warning? What warning?" Jones felt himself growing drowsier and drowsier. He wished Sergius would shut up and let him sleep.

He realized that some one was shaking him vigorously. "The soup—the tomato soup! Tell me, surely you did not eat of it?"

"Yes—sure. Good soup. Mighty nice soup—nice girl—too—"

His voice dwindled away. He was drifting comfortably off upon a sea of the softest down. Then something hard, unpleasant, was thrusting itself against his teeth. His mouth filled with fire-liquid fire. Coughing, strangling, he sat up and recovered sufficiently to push his companion's hand away from his mouth.

"Wha'—wha' you tryin' to do?" he asked hoarsely. His throat and lips felt stiff and numb.

"Trying to revive you, my friend. Here, drink some more of this."

"No. 'S horrid stuff. Take—away."

"Drink. You must."

Again something was forced against his teeth in the dark, and his mouth was flooded with the fiery liquid.

It was "horrid stuff," but it was effective. Jones felt the numbness going out of his vocal organs, and his brain cleared.

"What's the matter with me?" he gasped. "Have I been poisoned?"

"No, no, just a harmless drug, but it would have been disastrous had you succumbed to it, though I pray Heaven the rest have done so. I warned you not to touch that soup. Why did you do it?"

"Was that what you whispered to me? I didn't understand. But do you mean to tell me that you have—that you have—"

"I've put them all to sleep, that's all. The stuff is a perfectly harmless soporific, but it tastes a little, and that is why I put it in the highly seasoned soup, which all would be most likely to eat. But it is fortunate I had with me also the antidote, or my plan would have surely reacted upon myself, for I would not leave you here to meet their anger."

Jones staggered to his feet.

"I can't say I like the idea, my friend, but I suppose from your point of view you were justified. What are we to do now?"

"Get back to the aeroplane. It is useless for us to attempt the cavern without a guide, and even if I could awaken Holloway, I doubt if he could be induced to help us."

"You would leave them here—in a drugged sleep—defenceless? Why man, what are you thinking of? It would be worse than murder! And the girl, too. Why, the idea is criminal!"

"For what sort of devil do you mistake me, Roland Jones? No, I have thought of everything. We will place them all in the cavern chamber where Miss Weston now lies. Then we will block up the entrance with large stones, build before it a great fire, and they will certainly be as safe until morning as anyone can be in this perilous place."

"I see. Well, perhaps it could be done. But first, hadn't we better find out if every one is really asleep?"

CHAPTER IX

Having first lighted the electric torch, the two men crept stealthily through the narrow passage. In the doorway the fire had burned low, and beside it lay sprawled the figure of Jim Haskins. The nihilist stooped over him and felt cautiously of his heart. Then he straightened himself. "All right," he murmured, and they passed on out. At each of the two other inhabited caves they made a similar examination, and in every case Sergius' little dose had done its work. Every one of their captors lay helpless.

"Let us begin with Paul," said Sergius, in his natural voice, since no need of caution seemed to now exist. But he received an unexpected reply. There was a sudden rustling, a sound of footsteps, and there behind Paul's outstretched form appeared a slender figure.

"You here!" exclaimed Miss Weston. "What have you done to Paul? Have you killed him? Oh, you—you anarchist!"

She dropped on her knees and felt anxiously for Paul's heart.

"My dear Miss Weston, certainly I have not killed my brother." Sergius' voice showed not the slightest agitation at this discovery by the girl he so much admired. "He is only asleep. They are all asleep. We grew tired of seeing so many people asleep, and we are therefore about to leave."

She sprang up and faced him with flushed cheeks and blazing eyes. "You have drugged them all! How did you accomplish this dastardly thing?"

"The tomato soup, Miss Weston. You did not eat of it?"

"Of course not. I detest canned tomato soup. Well, I—I hope you are proud of yourself. I hope—I hope something will eat you! So, you were going away, leaving your brother and all of us to be killed, were you?"

"By no means. We were just about to provide against that little contingency. But your being awake alters matters."

"Oh, does it? Perhaps you are ashamed of your work, now that a woman has seen you at it?"

"Not at all. But on the other hand, I cannot leave you here, awake, to be terrorized all night. Asleep, it would not have mattered. When you awoke it would have been daylight and the others would have also awakened with you. Mr. Jones, the aeroplane will easily carry three passengers. We will have to take Miss Weston with us."

"Oh, I say," protested Jones, "do you think that is really necessary?"

"But yes. She will be far safer on the *Monterey* than here, under any circumstances. You need not fear me, Miss Weston. I am a gentleman and Paul's brother, when we have settled our brotherly differences, you may return to his side, if that is your choice."

He looked at her a trifle appealingly, but she flung back her head defiantly.

"You dare!" she stormed. "I will not go a step and leave my friends to be devoured."

Sergius took one stride across the body of his brother and seized the young lady in his arms, holding her firmly, but as gently as he could. She did not scream, but she fought desperately, and with an amazing strength.

Jones's gorge rose at the sight. This was going much too far. He sprang forward and seized his companion by the shoulder.

"Here, this won't do," he exclaimed. "You can't force the young lady in that way, Sergius."

The Russian turned a disgusted face to him and said over his shoulder, "Do you prefer to leave her here to be frightened into insanity? Is that your idea of chivalry?"

"Let me go—let me go!" cried Miss Weston, beating fiercely at him with her hands.

And just at that moment something black, monstrous, hideous shot down upon them out of the blackness

beyond the fires. There was a harsh, grating scream, and
the shoulder of a giant wing struck Jones, knocking him
down, and grazed the rock wall. He was involved in a
swirl of beating, struggling pinions, there were two more
screams, one human, the other quite the opposite, and the
thing, whatever it was, was gone.

Jones picked himself up, bruised and trembling from
head to foot. The girl lay limp in Sergius' arms, her face
white, arms and head hanging. Sergius himself was pale as
a ghost, but he had not moved from his position.

"I don't know what it was, Roland Jones," he said with a
rather stiff-lipped smile, "but do you still think we ought
to leave her here?"

"Great Heavens, how can we take her? How can we go
ourselves? Sergius Petrofsky, I believe that you have gone
mad!"

"Not quite," said the prince patiently. "We have the rifles
and the electric torches, and I really believe we can make
the trip safely. I have myself passed through an African
jungle in the same way, and never received a scratch. We
will carry Miss Weston as far as the outer edge of the meadow, then we will revive her and go on. Later we will open
negotiations with my brother—he will not then have so
much advantage—and Miss Weston, for whom I have great
reverence and respect, will be far safer on the *Monterey*.
Come! In the midst of so many perils, the boldest course is
best. You say that I saved your life. It was a very ordinary
deed, but for this one night let me claim your gratitude!"

Jones was in a quandary. His innate chivalry revolted at
the idea of forcing a woman into accompanying them, yet
the arguments of Sergius seemed very plausible. And he
loved this daring, fanatical, imperious new friend of his as
he had never loved any man in his life before.

"All right. I'll do it. But afterward Miss Weston is to be
free to return here if she chooses."

"Very well, if you wish it. I give my word."

With no more talk they hastily dragged the insensible members of the party into the selected cavern, and with considerable labor blocked up the entrance. In the morning the imprisoned ones could easily pull it down from within. Then they gathered all the fuel together and made one enormous bonfire, that blazed and roared skyward. Some of the logs were of very satisfactory size, and they felt sure the fire would burn for some hours. It was then nearly midnight and dawn would break shortly after three.

While they worked Jones found himself casting many apprehensive glances upward, but the flying monster did not return and they completed their task unmolested. Miss Weston, fortunately or otherwise, had not awakened from her swoon.

Their own two rifles and ammunition belts, together with an automatic pistol and cartridge clips belonging to Prince Paul, and a heavy, old-fashioned revolver looted from Jim Haskins, they had kept outside the cavern, together with two of the most powerful electric torches.

With one last anxious glance skyward, Mr. Jones picked up the two rifles, both torches and their heavy coats, which he was to carry until they reached the place where Sergius' remarkable scheme involved reviving the fainting lady. Sergius himself carefully raised his scornful idol in two muscular arms, and so burdened they started out across the meadow.

How they were to find their way along that thread-like trail, between the hidden dens of impossibly large spiders and past the other roaring, screaming, bellowing natives of Joker Island, remained to be shown.

Chapter X

They had reached the first of the scattered outer sentinels of the forest of slender palms. Dimly beyond it, by grace of the tropic star brilliance, they could see the looming mass which they must penetrate to reach the aeroplane.

So far they had met with nothing alarming. Everywhere, in and out, giant fireflies danced in a mystic saraband, very beautiful to behold, but also quite confusing to the eye. They had not yet used their torches, fearing to attract more of the terrible flying monsters, of which they had already seen quite enough to satisfy any morbid curiosity they might have felt.

"Here," whispered the prince, although he could almost have shouted without fear of being overheard above the general uproar, "we must awaken Miss Weston."

Jones saw his dark form bending over at the foot of the slender tree, and knew that he had laid his burden down.

"Shall I light up?" inquired Jones in an equally low tone, and speaking close to his companion's ear.

"On no account. Not yet, that is. Will you hold up her head, please? That is right. Now—this liquor would well-nigh rouse life in the dusty veins of an Egyptian mummy."

"If it's the same you gave me, you're right. Look out—there's something behind you—look out, I say!"

Over Sergius' shoulder he had caught a glimpse of two green eyes glaring, balls of fire set in the black velvet of night. Sergius, with the swiftness of a prestidigitator, replaced the stopper in the small flask he had been holding to Miss Weston's lips, reached with unerring grasp for one of the rifles laid across Jones' lap, rose from knees to feet in the same motion and laughed softly and lowered the weapon. Stooping, he picked up a small stone and flung it straight at the glaring eyes. There was a startled snarl, a fiendish yell, and the eyes vanished, accompanied by a scuffling and crashing in the underbrush.

"A hyena," commented Sergius, resuming his interrupted task with unruffled composure. "No use wasting a shot on that sort of vermin."

"Good Heavens, man, have you the eyes of a cat? How could you tell what it was?"

"Oh, I can see better than most in the dark, I will admit. I should never have suggested this venture if it were not so. Now—ah, she is awakening."

There was a cough, a little, strangled gasp, and Miss Weston sat up very suddenly. Unlike more ordinary people, she did not exclaim "Where am I?" although the query would certainly have been excusable, but seemed to spring instantly to full consciousness and knowledge of the situation.

Without a moment's hesitation she reached up in the darkness and delivered a slap in Sergius' general direction which would have been splendidly effective had he not sprung back with the same speed he had shown in dealing with the hyena. A second later she was on her feet, panting and sobbing, but not, Jones feared, with panic.

"Oh, you did it—you did it! You cowards! You left them there and carried me away when I was helpless. Oh—if I live till morning you shall be punished for this. You shall, I say!"

Gently, but with irresistible strength, Sergius took her small hands in one of his, and placed the other over her mouth.

"Be silent," he said softly and sternly. "You must not endanger your own life because of your anger against me. Paul and the rest are a thousand times more secure at this moment than we, unless you control yourself and use your splendid vigor and determination to a better purpose than recrimination. If I release my hold, will you come with us quietly and softly?"

A miracle occurred, for Miss Weston yielded—on that one point, at least. She must have nodded her head, although Jones could not see the motion in the darkness, for Sergius released her and stepped back.

BESTIA SECRETUM

"Do not imagine that you have greater concern for my brother than I, Miss Weston. We placed them all in safety, barricaded the entrance, and built a fire which will burn until morning. And now, you will please keep between Mr. Jones and myself. If we run, you must run also; and if we should crouch suddenly down, you must do likewise. Do you understand?"

"I understand," came the answer in a tone of suppressed rebellion.

"Very well. Will you give me one of those torches, Roland? You have your rifle ready and cocked?"

"Yes—but I'm a darned bad shot."

The nihilist sighed. "One cannot expect everything," he said. "If I tell you to shoot, aim between the eyes—you are likely to see them, at any rate. And now, forward!"

Two long, white beams sprang into being, and by the shifting rays Mr. Jones saw the narrow, trodden trail from which they had emerged in the afternoon. More than ever he marveled at Sergius' almost supernatural abilities. How had he managed to strike that one single place where they had a bare chance of entering the jungle successfully?

The Russian led the way, followed by Miss Weston, and Jones brought up the rear. And now they had entered the very center of pandemonium itself. Roars, shrieks, grunts, bellows rent the air upon every side.

"Don't be frightened!" Sergius called back over his shoulder. "These torches will keep most of the brutes off—but, good God, not this one!"

Jones caught, a glimpse of a mighty bulk rearing itself high over the head of their leader; there were three sharp, rapid reports; then the thing, whatever it was, with a terrific snarl of rage, had lurched forward and downward upon the unfortunate nihilist. Miss Weston, with remark-able presence of mind, had turned, run back to Jones's side, and then turned again to face this midnight terror, without a scream or act which could have impeded her sole remaining guardian.

He, staring with horror down his little, wavering beam of light, saw only a monstrous black head with snarling, savage jaws and two red eyes that glared like coals of fire.

"Shoot him—shoot him!" It was Miss Weston's voice, and she was shaking his arm viciously. "Shoot him—or give me that rifle!"

"Between the eyes!" gasped Jones. "You're likely to see them!"

He had no idea of what he was saying, or that he had spoken. Then, as he stood there, shaking in every limb, he suddenly reached the extremity of terror, and passed beyond it into that unnatural coolness and calm which is so efficient and, sometimes, so hard to reach. The trembling palsy passed, and every nerve and muscle tautened to abnormal firmness. From numbed quiescence his brain leaped to lightning action.

He knew what he, "a darned bad shot," must do if he would save the friend who lay invisible somewhere under that dreadful head.

With a sure swiftness of which none of his acquaintances would have deemed Jones capable, he handed the electric torch to the girl, darted forward to within ten feet of the monster, raised his rifle and fired, aiming at the center of the forehead, and pumping one cartridge after another into place as fast as he could work the lever.

Undoubtedly the fact that the brute had paused at all in its attack was due to the dazzling effect of the electric torch, and if it had not been for an unusual piece of luck Jones would probably never have lived to marvel at his own feat. For at the first report the light-blinded brute snarled again, started to lift itself, failed, drooped, and sank slowly down upon the path. Jones, however, emptied his magazine before he realized that he had actually killed the creature with that first fortunate bullet.

Then he called back to the girl: "Come quick, Miss Weston; we've got to pull it off from Sergius!"

She ran up, still bearing the light, and the two looked down in consternation at the mighty bulk which lay like a monstrous black tombstone over the body of Sergius Petrofsky. It was a great, hairless mountain of flesh, The dropped head looked like the face of some gargoyle carven in unpolished ebony. Its fore legs were invisible, doubled under the body. Move it? They might as well have tried to move an elephant.

Nevertheless, catching hold of the upstanding, rounded ears, they tugged and heaved with all their might, but could only succeed in shifting the head a little to one side.

"Sergius! Sergius!" cried Miss Weston, dropping suddenly in a little heap of pathos beside that mountain of brute flesh.

She was answered by a moan. To their amazement, it did not come from beneath the monster, but from some little distance to one side of the path. Yet it was certainly a human moan, for it was followed by a voice: "Over here. I'm—I'm coming."

Miss Weston sprang to her feet and accompanied Jones in a wild rush toward the voice. There, sprawled out among the flowering, tangled vines, they found the nihilist himself; and as the circle of light struck his face, he sat and stared back at them with an amazement equal to their own.

"What—what hit me?" he gasped.

Jones laughed aloud in his relief. "*It* did. How in the name of all the saints did you get here?"

Sergius passed a bewildered hand over his head. "I—I begin to remember. Something seemed to come right up out of the ground. I—I fired at it—and then—and then—"

"It must have struck you with its paw and knocked you clear away from the path," interrupted Miss Weston in a calm, indifferent voice. Jones glanced at her in astonishment. Was this the girl who had been sobbing out the name of Sergius a few minutes before? "If you are hurt, you had better get up and go on with us—although I would suggest that you let Mr. Jones take the lead, as he seems much the better shot."

Jones helped his friend to rise, and as he did so Sergius laughed without a trace of annoyance. "If you actually killed that brute, my friend, Miss Weston is right. Did you kill it?"

"I must have, because it's certainly dead, although I can hardly believe it myself. What on earth is the thing, Sergius?"

They had recovered the narrow path and stood beside the black hulk which blocked it entirely, overlapping on both sides into the underbrush.

Sergius examined the huge head with interest. "I never saw anything exactly like it before. Where did you hit it?"

"Between the eyes. You remember you told me to fire between the eyes, so I did. I fired about ten cartridges into it, but I think it died at the first shot."

The nihilist looked up at him with a curious expression. "It did? That's rather odd. The beast has a frontal bone as thick as a rhinoceros', if I am any judge. No; here are three bullets embedded in the bone, but not a sign of a hole. Ah, that was it, eh? My friend, by very well-deserved good luck your first bullet did not strike the forehead at all, but penetrated this left eye and went straight into the brain."

"Great Scot!" exclaimed the American. "And I was about ten feet away! It's a good thing the brute has a head as big as a barn-door, or I'd have missed it entirely."

Sergius smiled. "Nevertheless, you deserve great congratulations. If your first bullet had not gone a few inches astray, we should perhaps none of us be alive at this moment. But what a strange brute it is! I should say it was a monstrous bear, from the shape of the head, if it were not so hairless. I wonder, now, if this is the creature that pulled up the death cabbages there by the plane?"

"Prince Sergius," again interrupted Miss Weston, with a slightly impatient note in her voice, "would it not be better to come back in daylight to continue your zoological researches? If this creature has a mate, and it should come this way, Mr. Jones might not be able to kill the second one."

"And you are quite sure, after what has happened, that as a protector I am an entire failure, eh? Well, perhaps you are justified, but still I had better continue to lead the way. What do you think, Roland Jones?"

"Don't be absurd. I'm a rank, bungling amateur, and you both know it. Shall we climb over this thing, or go around it?"

"The underbrush is thick here—and there might be snakes, though we have seen none. I think we had better use your victim as a causeway."

The two men helped Miss Weston up to the gigantic shoulders, and they walked the length of the huge creature, more and more amazed at its bulk. From nose to hind quarters it must have measured a full fifteen feet, and in his heart Jones wished that he might have transported the head to his rooms in New York. How he could have gloated over the surprise of a friend of his who was a big game-hunter and very proud of certain rhino-heads and lion-skins, trophies of African expeditions.

He reloaded his rifle carefully and resumed his position as rear-guard with a new confidence in its powers which took no heed to the fact that only by a lucky accident had his shot struck a vulnerable spot.

Many times as they marched silently ahead, the underbrush by the wayside swayed and bent, crackling, to the
passage of animals of which they caught not even a glimpse.
Once a lynxlike beast as big as a large panther dropped
silently into the middle of the path ahead of them, glared
for a second into the bull's-eye of Sergius, and with another spring was gone before he could fire at it.

This incident, however, encouraged the three, for it
seemed as if most of the jungle inhabitants shunned the
blinding electric lights as they would have shunned a
campfire.

And at length there came to their nostrils a whiff of
noxious odor which told the two men that they had successfully passed the first barriers to their escape. Vile smell
though it was, it came welcome enough just then, for it
was the odor of the fungi that grew about the roots of the
death cabbages.

Jones realized with pleasure that they had passed the
great spider's trap without even being aware of it. He had
subconsciously dreaded more than anything also going
past that dark incline, at the foot of which waited the
thing of long, black, shining legs and protuberant eyes.

But as the full force of the stench enveloped them,
Miss Weston stopped dead, so that Jones almost collided
with her in the narrow path.

"Stop—I can't go on into this—this horrible vapor!"
she called after Sergius. He heard, for he turned back
immediately and returned to where they stood.

"What is the matter?" he asked a trifle impatiently.

"This dreadful smell. I can't—"

"Miss Weston, a smell won't kill anybody. At least, this
one will not. Mr. Jones and myself were in the midst of it
for nearly an hour, and we were not harmed."

"But—"

"Do you wish to be left here, then?"

The question was brutal, but it served its purpose. A moment the girl was silent; then she threw back her shoulders and smiled contemptuously. "I presume you would not hesitate to do that, either. No, I will not oblige you by relieving you of my hampering company. I can certainly face anything that you can."

Sergius looked at her with plain admiration on his face.

"Believe me, Miss Weston, this charnel odor is no worse than that of the battle-fields to which you were going. I have been there, also. Will you take my arm now? For we must walk through a very disagreeable place."

"No, thank you!" she—well, she snapped, although it isn't a nice thing to say of a heroine. "I am sure Mr. Jones will offer all the help I may need."

"Very well." The prince shrugged, and without more ado they passed from the forest of slender palms into the safe way, broken, perhaps, by the very creature which they had encountered and ungratefully slain that night.

CHAPTER XI

As the three staggered out, one after another, from the acid-fumed fungi onto the wiry grass of the central space, their ears were rent by a sound of hideous and continued screaming which drowned out all other noise entirely. Startled and shuddering, both Sergius and Jones directed the rays of their lanterns toward the sound, and a most extraordinary picture leaped into view.

The scene of the tragedy was one of the larger death-cabbages. Its seventy-five-foot leaves were spread almost flat, and all the inner tentacles were writhing and squirming upward, so that at first glance it looked as if this vegetable flesh-eater were all on fire with slim, scarlet flames. Then, as they moved their search-lights upward, they saw what it was that screamed.

Clinging with huge claws to the upper stalk, just below
the tuft, was a dark, winged thing, and all about its body
and head the tentacles were wound and fastened. So wide
were its frantically beating wings that even where they
stood, a hundred yards away, the wind of them struck their
faces in heavy gusts. The stalk swayed and bent under the
strain, but the tentacles had firm hold, and continually
new scarlet cords shot upward to aid in the binding of
the captive, until its body was no more than a bundle of
flaming red.

The screaming grew weaker; the wings fluttered spasmodically for a few moments longer, then drooped down
helpless. The tentacles took hold upon them, also. Into
the field of light a pointed, serrated thing rose slowly,
followed by others upon all sides. The death cabbage was
closing its doors to feast in sacred privacy.

A moment later the vision of trapped prey was shut
from their eyes.

With a long, shuddering sigh, Sergius turned his own
light slowly about the grim ranks encircling the glade.
Everywhere it fell upon spread leaves and living, ready
tentacles Only one or two other of the cabbages were
closed. Doubtless their dinner had come to them earlier
in the evening.

"What are they? What is this place you have brought
me to?"

It was Miss Weston. Both men turned to her with a
guilty start, realizing that in their fascinated absorption
they had for the time forgotten her.

"I am so sorry," apologized Sergius, as if he and Jones
had invented the vegetable horrors, as her tone implied.

"It is like—it is like a circle from Dante's *Inferno!*"
exclaimed Jones, laying his hand pityingly on the girl's arm,
and wishing with all his heart that he had never acceded
to Sergius' wishes; that they had left the girl at the caves,

or stayed there themselves. What might not the effect of having witnessed such a scene be upon the mind of a delicate, high-strung woman?

But she drew slightly away, and spoke again to the Russian. From first to last she gave Mr. Jones no more attention than one grants to a supernumerary—a necessary adjunct to the play, but scarcely of more human interest than the furniture.

"You are sorry!" she repeated scornfully. "Your sorrow is rather late, it appears. Where is the aeroplane?"

The nihilist bowed gallantly to her contemptuous tone.

"As usual, Miss Weston, you speak directly to the point. The aeroplane is—why, where in the name of Heaven is it?"

For his light, flashing up the glade, encountered only empty space. The aeroplane, which they had left not far from where they now stood, had disappeared.

Jones felt his heart begin a slow, systematic descent toward his toes. If the machine were actually gone, what would they do? Then he gave a joyful cry as his own light, dancing spritelike over the grass, flashed upon something broad-winged and motionless over near the wilted death-cabbage which had so nearly made a meal of him and Sergius.

"There it is! It's all right! It's there!"

"Thank God!" breathed Miss Weston, frightened momentarily out of her attitude of disdainful indifference.

"But how did it get there?" frowned Sergius. "Miss Weston, you must not go so near as that to the cabbages. Will you wait here with Mr. Jones, while I go after the plane?"

"I will not," she replied instantly. "We will either all go, or none of us will go, whichever you please. Oh, I'm not troubled for your safety, Prince Sergius. Don't imagine that. But if you should be killed or injured, who is to pilot the plane?

"I am overwhelmed by your solicitude for me," murmured Sergius, bowing again. "If you must go, keep behind us. Here, take this light and one of the rifles. Yes, please, I want my hands free. Come on, then."

He set off at a swinging stride, followed by Jones and Miss Weston, who looked pale by the reflected light of her lantern, but very determined indeed.

The plane, they found, was fairly in the midst of the many-colored fungi. But worse, and more important, it was quite near to a thirty-foot vegetable which they had just had good testimony, would make no more than a good meal on all three of them. In fact, as they approached, it seemed to sense them, and stretched out a dozen hungry tentacles in their direction. Two or three of these, feeling blindly, encountered a rear strut of the aeroplane and curled about it. Then the tentacles contracted suddenly, and the aeroplane rolled backward an inch or so.

"That won't do," cried the nihilist, and seizing a forward strut he braced himself and pulled, but with no apparent effect. More tentacles reached toward him as he stood there, but he was partly shielded from them by the plane itself.

To his credit be it said that Mr. Jones, without an instant's hesitation, dropped his rifle, handed his torch to Miss Weston, and springing to Sergius' side flung his weight also into the tug-of-war. But it was evident that the strength of the vegetable was greater than their combined efforts. The utmost they could, do was to hold the machine where it was.

After several muscle and nerve-straining minutes, the nihilist said to Jones in a low voice, not to be overheard by the girl, "My friend, there is only one thing to be done and that is creep back there, over the tail, and cut some of those tentacles."

"Impossible! Why, the others would get you in a second."

"I don't care if they do. I will cut them also. They are strong, but a knife goes through them easily. Do you not remember yesterday afternoon? Miss Weston, will you keep both lights trained on the rear of the plane for a few moments, please? I am going to try something."

"I won't let you do it—" began Jones, but with a spring Sergius had mounted upon the plane and was working his way toward the rear.

The withdrawal of his strength was accompanied by a surge of the aeroplane backward, and Jones had to use all his muscle and attention to keep it in place. Sergius was now out of his sight, but by a sudden swaying and jolting and a scream from Margaret Weston, he knew that his too-daring companion must have been found by one or more of the questing tentacles.

The machine swayed again violently, then he heard Sergius' voice.

"Hold those lights steady, Miss Weston. Ah! two at once. Roland, we needn't have been so worried—one might as well be afraid of a stick of celery. You devil! Would you?"

There was a strangled, gasping sound, another scream from the girl, then the Russian's voice again, somewhat hoarser but still cheerful. "He almost got me that time— but not twice! That is right. Send me a few more feelers! Pull! Pull, Jones, with all your force!"

Jones obeyed with the strength of desperation, as a sudden lightening in the weight and a renewed swaying told him that Sergius had jumped to the ground. Slowly at first, then with gathering ease and speed the plane moved. In a minute it was out of the fungi and rolling clear upon the turf.

The second that he dared, Jones let go and ran around to the rear. To his great relief there was his nihilist friend, leaning against a strut and wiping his forehead. Miss

Weston joined them with the lights, and they all stared at one another in silence.

Then Sergius dropped his handkerchief, and brought his hand down upon his thigh with a resounding slap.

"What a fool I am!" he exclaimed. "What an utter fool! All I had to do was to climb into the pilot's seat and start the propeller. Even that brute could hardly have outpulled the engine. And my neck would have been saved a very unpleasant experience." He felt of it tenderly, then laughed.

"Well, it is over now. Some inquisitive beast must have come by here and given the plane a push, so that it rolled down that little incline."

He began a careful examination of wires, struts, taut varnished canvas, propeller blades and last, and most important, the engine itself and its tank. In a few minutes now their very lives might depend upon the thoroughness of that examination.

"I can find nothing wrong," he said at last, and his announcement was greeted with an involuntary sigh of relief from both his companions.

"Miss Weston," he continued, "I think you and Mr. Jones can manage to occupy that seat together. At any rate, in a few minutes we will be out of this intolerable odor. Here, Miss Weston, put on my coat, since you will find it cold in the upper air, if you will be so kind as to cover your face with your hands when we get up, you will not need goggles. Are we all ready?"

"I shall certainly not take your coat," said the girl indignantly, waving the garment away. "Not that your comfort is so important, but I know a little about flying, and if you became numbed by the cold, what would happen to us?"

Sergius laughed. "There is no danger of my becoming numbed in the few minutes that we will be in the air. Your dress is a great deal thinner than my tunic. I am sorry, but you will have to take it or we cannot start."

"Let her take mine," interposed Jones. "I have nothing to do but sit still, and it really doesn't matter whether I get numb or not.

"You are very kind, Mr. Jones." Miss Weston smiled sweetly upon him. "Yes, since you insist, I shall be glad to borrow your coat."

And suiting the action to the words she took it from him and slipped into it. Sergius frowned and looked as if he were about to say something, then checked himself and turned away, putting on his own coat without any further protest. But Mr. Jones caught what looked like an expression of amused triumph on Margaret Weston's beautiful face. It was the first time that she had really succeeded in annoying Sergius Petrofsky.

A few minutes later, having pushed the machine to the extreme end of the glade, turned so as to face the open run, they all took their places and strapped themselves in. The rear seat was a tight fit indeed for both Jones and Miss Weston, but it was only to be for a few minutes, and the girl murmured that at least she was glad she did not have to sit so close to Sergius.

Mr. Jones might have felt more flattered if she had not put in the "at least."

The Russian started his engine, the propeller began to revolve, and a second later the plane rolled forward across the uneven grass. They did not gather speed very quickly, however, and it looked as if the machine would refuse to rise in the limited course. Twice Sergius raised the elevator, and twice the plane continued on its rough and bouncing course up the glade, refusing to leave the earth.

They were now perilously close to the further end and the plane was running at a speed of about sixty miles an hour. To stop was impossible, and for a time it seemed as if their career was to end in the maw of a particularly wide-spread and hungry-looking death-cabbage, when just at the last minute he again raised the elevator, the plane tilted slightly and took the air beneath its taut canvas wings.

They barely cleared the crest of the deadly vegetable, and with their hearts still in their throats found themselves shooting onward and upward, away from the valley of death.

Yet even as they drew in their first full breaths of relief and clean, cool air, Death itself, though in another form, rose after them.

The first consciousness that they were the object of attack came as Sergius banked his wings and swung in a wide circle, preparatory to straightening out on the seaward course. As the machine tilted against the light breeze, a large, dark thing shot by its nose, just missing the plane by a foot or so, and causing even the iron-nerved Russian momentarily to lose control.

The plane dipped and shot downward at a dangerous angle. They had risen scarcely four hundred feet, and there was not much room for evolutions. He just saved them from destruction, and rose again, casting anxious glances about in the darkness, for they had extinguished the electric torches before rising.

The girl was not aware that anything had happened, for she had covered her face with her hands to shield it from the sharp wind of their flight. Jones stared about as anxiously as their pilot, but could see nothing. Sergius' eyes must have been, as he had said, of an unusual kind, for presently he shouted and pointed into the darkness.

A second later something huge came up from below, actually grazed the left wing, and was gone again.

Jones knew that the dark thing must be one of the flying monsters, of which this was the third they had encountered, and he earnestly hoped that its interference was purely accidental. He said nothing, fearing to frighten

Miss Weston, but on a sudden impulse he loosened the strap that held both of them, with a vague idea that if they should be flung to the earth they might have some chance of jumping clear.

That Sergius was fully aware of the danger was made evident, for he began to climb in a swift, steep spiral. Birds of the night hardly ever fly high, and if they could reach the upper levels of the air, so easily accessible to them, they would be safe.

But the evil genius of Joker Island had no idea of permitting them to escape so simply. Again, with a wild beating of vast pinions, the winged peril was upon them. This time it struck downward from above and even the skill of the nihilist could not save them.

Of what happened next Mr. Jones was never able to give a coherent account. Probably the weight and impact of the creature partially stunned him. At any rate, his next conscious memory was of finding himself swinging and dangling over empty space, his arms and hands firmly buried in something that felt like warm fur, and that he was being carried along in great swoops and lunges, so that it required his utmost strength to keep from being jerked off.

Chapter XII

Wide, frantic wings were beating on either side of him, and even in that desperate moment he realized that he must have grasped the flying monster at the instant it struck the aeroplane. Doubtless much against its will, it was now carrying him along as an equally unwilling passenger.

As a matter of fact, he was clinging to its fur and the skin of its breast, which was fortunately very loose, affording an excellent handhold. But Mr. Jones was no acrobat, although he was certainly playing the part of one. Already his hands were numb and aching. He wondered if he could manage to climb around and up to the creature's back, but gave it up as a feat too great for his weakening muscles.

Suddenly he found himself laughing wildly. He had remembered the story of Sindbad and the Roc, which had carried him into the Valley of Diamonds. But the Roc bore the sailor in its claws, and this creature was not half so obliging.

Looking downward, Jones was sure that they were far higher than when the beast had struck them. He should, even swinging so dizzily through the air, have caught a glimpse of light where the fire must still be blazing by the cliff, or perhaps, if they were very high, the lights of the other encampment outside the wall. But all beneath was a black void, under what seemed a swirling, dancing firmament of stars.

Then, sick and giddy, the moment came when Jones knew he must shortly let go his grip upon skin and fur and whirl down, breathless, helpless, into the waiting arms of death. Suddenly he began to kick violently, and swing his body from side to side. If he went he was determined that his involuntary captor should go with him.

Came a harsh scream from above, a few mad circles, and then, though the wings still beat, he knew that they were dropping with dangerous speed through the empty blackness of space.

The fall, however, ended a great deal sooner than Jones anticipated, and not upon the earth but in the sea. There was one terrific splash, as beast and man struck the water.

Mr. Jones, being of course underneath, had decidedly the worst of the dive. In the first place he had expected to be hurled into the maw of a death-cabbage, perhaps, or to be dashed to pieces upon the earth, or, if he were lucky, that they might break their fall upon the crest of one of the tall, slender palms. The one thing which he did not anticipate was to be plunged into a cold bath. His mouth

BESTIA SECRETUM

was open, and his lungs nearly empty of air when it happened, and the consequence was that he nearly drowned before recovered sufficient sense to let go of the fur to which he was still clinging with the tenacity of the dying.

Even then it was more by good luck than presence of mind that he reached the surface, for all the water was in a whirl with the flapping struggles of the creature which had brought him there. Fortunately, although evidently it could not swim, its convulsive efforts pushed it along, so that Jones came up at last a few feet clear of the worst of the turmoil.

The sea was running in long, smooth, oily swells, nearly as kind as quiet water to the gasping swimmer. He cleared his lungs, then turned on his back and floated, drawing in the air in huge draughts.

As his blood became reoxygenated, he began to feel a certain curiosity. What had become of the enemy? Turning again he swam slowly and quietly, reserving his strength, and looking anxiously about from the top of each swell as it came under him.

The sea, which was free that night from the phosphorescence that often characterizes those waters, reflected very little light, from the stars. He could see nothing—no land, no monster—nothing but the stars above and beneath—blackness. He felt as if he had been dropped into a sea of India ink, a sea where no man or beast had ever come or sun shone upon.

Then he remembered the possibility of sharks and hoped devoutly that no company of that sort would arrive.

His clothes dragged him down, and he determined to be rid of them, at least. He kicked off his shoes and at last, by working carefully, got rid of his khaki tunic. The puttees were hardest to deal with, but he finally got them off, followed them with his breeches, and even shed the thin, loose-fitting silk underwear, as a last slight impediment to what he intended to be a fight to the finish for life and the chance to get back and finish his voluntary job of helping Sergius, or find and bury his remains. The latter contingency seemed the more likely one.

The water was warm, the slow, even swells friendly, and Mr. Jones felt sure that he could keep afloat till dawn, which could not now be far off. What he would do then depended upon circumstances, but he did not really believe the flying monster could have carried him far out to sea, and he hoped that when day broke he would see Joker Island within easy swimming distance. Until then it would be dangerous to strike out, perhaps in the wrong direction, so he floated a great deal, only swimming enough to keep his blood in circulation.

In one of the periods when he was on his back, his ears in consequence being under water, there reached them a peculiar, vibratory, explosive sound. He had heard it before, while floating in the quiet reaches of Long Island Sound, and with a great rush of hope Jones turned over and trod water raising himself as far as he could above the surface and staring from right to left through the blind veil of night.

Nothing.

He turned himself slowly, waiting for the rise of each successive swell to look long. Then he gave a wild shout and letting himself drop back struck out with frantic strokes.

Very small, very far away, he had seen two lights which were not stars, for one was red and one was green.

Had his mood of exultation lasted long he must have perished even on the threshold of salvation, for such a pace as he had set himself would have exhausted the most expert swimmer. Fortunately common sense returned in time, and he realized that since he saw both the red and the green it must mean but one thing. The vessel, whatever it was, was approaching him, probably at a far greater speed than he could possibly attain even if he could have kept it up.

He "loafed" again, rising on each swell with the deadly fear that this time one of the lights would have disappeared, sinking again into the trough with the blissful assurance that both lights still shone.

There is nothing much harder than to estimate distance at night across water. Knowing this from his own yachting experience, Jones floated several times, listening for the engine beat which the sea carried so much farther than the wind. And each time he fancied that it was louder, more distinct.

At last he raised himself again upon the crest of a swell and sent a long, anxious hail across the waste. To his inexpressible joy it was immediately answered.

Ten minutes later Mr. Roland C. Jones was picked up out of the watery vastness of the Pacific Ocean by his own power cruiser, the *Bandersnatch,* which had for three days been cross-quartering those waters in the vain, despairing hope of picking up some trace of him or his body.

CHAPTER XIII

Although the fact was not included in the extensive notices which later appeared in the New York papers in regard to the loss and rescue of the well-known millionaire yachtsman (his own friends told nothing, but one of the sailors talked), there occurred a peculiar psychological phenomenon as Mr. Jones came over the rail of the *Bandersnatch.*

It was as if a dark veil, which he had scarcely known existed, had been suddenly swept away from his mental vision. It had torn a trifle when he recognized one of the men in the dingey which rescued him as his old friend, Henry Martindale. He had sat in a silent, stupid-seeming daze as they were rowed back to the yacht by the sailor who accompanied Martindale, and listened to his friends' exclamations of joy, amazement and congratulation.

But as he stepped, barefooted and naked, upon the white deck of his own, familiar, beloved *Bandersnatch,* that veil split asunder from top to bottom and vanished forever from his brain.

In plain words, Mr. Jones remembered. He remembered how for two years, since the moment when a small, heavy clock, carelessly placed upon a shelf in his stateroom on the *Lusitania,* had fallen at a lurch of the vessel and struck him upon the temple, he had been the victim of that queer mental disease, amnesia. Cared for by the best doctors in London and New York, they had not been able to restore the delicate equilibrium of his brain.

The loss of his memory had been accompanied by physical deterioration, and this winter the physicians had ordered a long cruise through Southern seas in the hope of improving, if not curing, his condition.

They had, exactly as he had informed Jim Haskins, come around into the Pacific by way of the Panama Canal, and were bound for the Philippines when one night Mr. Jones actually did get up out of bed, dress himself, not in yachting clothes but in a grey morning suit, walk out on deck, straight across it, and over the rail, before the men on watch could stop him. In the sea that was running they had been unable to find him, but, although they had from almost the first, given him up as drowned, still his good friends Martindale and Charles Laroux could not bear to leave the spot of the disaster, but cruised up and down, back and forth, for three whole days and nights, ever on the lookout, ever hoping against hope that they might at least bear his body back to New York for burial.

Upon falling overboard the shock of his sudden immersion in the sea had, by one of those little jokes which

Nature sometimes perpetrates, started his mental machin-
ery going again at exactly the place where, figuratively, it
left the rails. The equal shock of finding his rescuers to be
his friends, and the rescuing vessel the *Bandersnatch,* completed the good work, and that deep abyss of two forgotten years, wherein had been lost the great war and many
other memories less vast, was filled.

Once again he could spread out before him the pages of
his past life and find not one leaf missing.

Curiously enough, his first thought, after the sweeping
realization of it all came over him, was of his cousin, the
Hon. Percy Merridale, whom he had been going to visit on
that unlucky voyage across the Atlantic.

"Poor old Percy," he said, paying no heed to the flood
of questions which were pouring from the lips of both his
friends, "why, he was killed along with half his regiment
at the very beginning of the war. And here I have been
wondering what he would think because I did not arrive
in London on time!"

"You have, eh?" asked Laroux, looking at him keenly.
"Then you remember that you did start for London?"

"Oh, yes. I remember everything now. Lord, what
chums you fellows have been, putting up with the crazy
whims of a man with only half a mind. But by Jove, I'm
cold. If you'll have the steward get me something hot to
drink, and let me get dry and into some clothes, I'll be
glad to tell you all about it."

With bitter self-reproaches at their own neglectful-
ness, Laroux and Martindale fairly hustled him below and
to bed. They would hear nothing of his dressing, but on
one thing he held out. He was perfectly willing to go to
sleep—he had never felt so utterly tired out in his life—
but they must promise to hold the *Bandersnatch* where she
was, or at least near to it, until he awakened.

To this his friends agreed, and Jones slept the sleep of exhausted but perfect health for eleven straight hours.

It was three o'clock in the afternoon when he appeared on deck, and he immediately sought his two friends. They greeted him eagerly, for they were more than anxious to know how he could possibly have kept afloat for nearly three days, and settling comfortably down beneath the awnings on the breezy afterdeck, they all lighted their excellent cigars and the story began.

Before he had progressed very far their interest became other than that of curiosity, and as he went on, two of the three cigars were allowed to languish and die unheeded. From curiosity they passed to amazement, and from amazement to carefully suppressed incredulity.

This, however, caused Jones no uneasiness, for it was about what he had expected. Finishing the incident of the flying monster with the utmost complacence and indifference to their more than dubious glances, he called for Captain Janiver.

"Captain," he said, "I want you to locate for me an island which I know to be in this immediate vicinity, although beyond the horizon in some direction. What land is there hereabouts?"

The captain shook his head. "The only island I know of within a hundred miles is hardly worthy of the name, Mr. Jones. It is nothing but a high, barren chunk of rock sticking up out of the sea. As far as I know it has never even been named."

"Oh, yes, it has," smiled Jones. "That island is Joker Island, and I want you to put the old *Bandersnatch's* nose about and take us there just as fast as she'll slouch through the water."

"Very well, sir, but—"

"Why, Jones, old man, we were at that place ourselves, and there isn't anything there!" This from Laroux.

"You were there?"

"Of course. Janiver remembered the place and we went, on the slim possibility that you might have been washed ashore. We cruised all around it, and even landed wherever there was a beach. We found some footprints and a few old, tin cans, but there was certainly nothing else."

Jones grew suddenly very white. He had a sensation of sickness in the pit of his stomach, and an overwhelming consciousness of some dreadful disaster impending, he himself scarcely knew what.

"Captain Janiver," he said between his teeth, "put this boat about and do as I directed."

The captain touched his cap and obeyed, not without a curious glance over his shoulder. He was familiar with the idiosyncrasies of his owner—all developed, however, within the past twenty-four months, and he sighed as he gave the necessary directions.

"Too bad," he murmured, shaking his gray head sadly, "too bad. Such a good-natured, quiet young fellow as he is, too."

As for Jones himself, he resolutely declined to speak another word on the subject until he had himself visited the scene of his recent adventures. Clinging passionately to the belief that they had actually occurred, he forced his mind to dwell upon the question of what might have happened to Sergius and Miss Weston after he left the aeroplane in such an unexpected manner.

He was possessed by a really loving concern upon this matter, although the love was not for the Boston girl but for Sergius Petrofsky, who had in the short space of three days won a place in his heart never before occupied by any man, even his faithful friends Harry Martindale and Charlie Laroux.

The two latter let him alone, when they perceived that he no longer wished to talk. Like the captain, they were accustomed to some rather strange moods in their friend, although they had hoped for better things with the recovery of his memory.

About five o'clock the rapid little *Bandersnatch* raised a blur upon the southern horizon, which soon developed into a dark blot, then gradually took shape as the familiar black outline of the crater-wall of Joker Island.

With the sight all Jones's courage returned. He could not sit still, but paced back and forth across the deck, and when at last they came to anchor in the very bay where the *Monterey* had lain, he fairly tumbled into the small launch which was lowered to accommodate Jones, his two friends and a couple of sailors.

Of course the *Monterey* was gone, but there was the place where the nihilists had been encamped, though now no tents raised their brown canvas against the cliff, Springing from the launch Jones rushed up the beach and examined the place where they had been. There were, as Laroux had said, a few tin cans scattered about, a good many footprints, and the ashes of a fire, but these might have been there for any length of time.

He ran down the beach, hoping to discover the marks left by the aeroplane's launching, but this had been upon the smooth, hard sand near the water, and the tides had obliterated them, if they had really ever been there. If they had been there! But they had been—it had happened! It was all so indelibly imprinted upon the tablets of his brain that it was clearer than any other event in his whole life.

The caves, then. Beckoning to Laroux and Martindale to follow him, he pressed on to the rocky promontory hiding the cleft, or ravine. Well, that was there anyway. And there were caves, too, hundreds of them. Into which of them had he crawled, following Prince Paul and Miss Weston, followed by Jim Haskins and the two sailors? This one surely, or—no, it might have been this, or any one of a dozen others.

He felt the touch of a hand upon his shoulder.

"Look here, old man," said Martindale with a gentle indulgence which seemed to Jones well-nigh intolerable by reason of its implications, "you must not take this so hard. Now listen. Charlie and I know you are absolutely all right now—absolutely all right. Don't let there be any question in your mind of that. Your memory has returned, and you can go on to the Philippines, or back to New York and take up your life exactly where you were before it—that accident on the liner—happened.

"But just now you are suffering from the memory of a particularly vivid hallucination. If we didn't think you were all O.K. we wouldn't tell you that, you know. We'd humor you, and say we thought it was all real. But you wouldn't want us to do that now, would you? You'll believe, won't you, that while you were here on the beach, thrown-up by the storm you—well, dreamed a whole lot of things that couldn't possibly have happened? Then, still dreaming, you started to swim out to sea again, thinking you were pursued by these impossible monsters, and so we picked you up, by about one chance in a million. The currents are very strong about here, Janiver says, and they carried you a long way—clear out of sight of the island. Can't you believe all this, which is the truth, and let the rest go along with the last two years?"

He spoke earnestly, with a deep and loving tenderness, which made Jones extremely uncomfortable. How could he convince these men that those things had really happened? That there, within the island, was at least one other friend of his, possibly in dire need of help, if he yet lived? Then Holloway, Prince Paul, Haskins, the beautiful, sharp-tongued girl—

Suddenly the mental defenses which he had raised gave way and went down before the flood of damning, almost unendurable conviction.

"Harry," he said hoarsely, staggering a little where he stood, "will you and Laroux get me back to New York? Just put up with me till—till we get back to New York, won't you?"

"Don't be a fool, Rolly," cried Laroux, springing forward and actually shaking him, but with a roughness that was all friendship. "You aren't crazy—you never have been crazy—you've been in a sort of delirium, like you have when you're down with fever. You're right as Harry or me. If you weren't you wouldn't be ready to believe the truth. It was nothing but plain, ordinary delirium, I tell you."

"Well, maybe it was," conceded Jones, with a somewhat sickly smile, "but whatever it was, I know I want to get away from this place and back to New York. I want to see brick buildings, and ride on every-day street-cars, and eat dinner in a Broadway café. You boys have been the best, most patient friends a man ever had. Will you promise me something?"

"Of course," broke in Laroux, "but look here, Rolly, just to satisfy you entirely suppose we stop in at Frisco and find out if such a yacht as the *Monterey* was chartered recently by a bunch of Russians, and—"

Jones held up his hand. "No," he said. "A man who's been off his nut for two years, and knows it, doesn't have to go around hunting up evidence to support the facts. I want to get back to New York just as fast as the old tub will travel. What I want you to promise is this. Don't ever mention any of this—this crazy dream of mine to me again. I know you won't tell it to anybody else. But—I just don't want ever to hear anything about it—again."

CHAPTER XIV

Three months had elapsed, and Mr. Roland C. Jones remained, to all appearances, a well and mentally sound man. Back in New York he quietly resumed the peaceful

pursuits of his easy-going, pleasant, bachelor life. Laroux
and Martindale adhered strictly and honorably to their
promise and never mentioned to any one the singular
delusion which had marked the termination of their
friend's illness. Indeed, they themselves had practically
forgotten it, thinking of it only as the overheard ravings
of a sick man, not to be regarded as indicating mental
unbalance since the man had regained his health.

Mr. Jones's first act on reaching New York had been
to consult an eminent specialist in diseases of the brain,
and have himself examined for insanity. The report was
reassuring. Whatever he might have been in the past, this
worthy physician declared him, to be now free from any
taint of the disorder he so feared.

Jones went to the theater, danced, golfed and made
brief cruises in the early spring, but an invitation to a
flying meet was instantly and firmly declined. He never
wished to see another aeroplane in his life. In fact, he
did all that a man could to banish from his memory that
dream which he had dreamed while cast upon the barren
beach of an unnamed—absolutely an unnamed—rock in
the Pacific.

If in visions of the night man-eating vegetables writhed
their flaming tentacles, or strange yet familiar faces smiled
or frowned upon him, he at least never spoke of the matter
to any one.

So the three months had drifted by, and it was the
latter end of March. One morning Jones slept later than
usual—he never was an early riser—and when he sat up
in bed, yawning, his window was a gray expanse against
which sleet drove with a continual desolate rattling.

"Darn!" exclaimed Mr. Jones, at the end of his stretch.
"Another day of 'indoor sports,' I see. How I hate a sleet
storm! Philip!" he called.

Instantly his English man servant, an elderly but intensely efficient individual, appeared bearing coffee, newspapers, and the mail.

"You can get my bath ready. Now, let's see. Who's going to be married, and who desires the extreme boredom of my company—hello, I wonder what this can be—"

"This" was a small flat package, wrapped in white paper and addressed to himself in a small, perfect hand. Unlike a woman, he did not pause to contemplate its exterior, but untied the string immediately. Within the paper was a white pasteboard box, and inside that another box of Morocco leather, unquestionably a jewel case of some sort. He pressed the catch and it snapped open. What-in-the-world—

The whole room seemed to reel and sway about him dizzily. It vanished, and before him stretched a little glade all dark save where two white beams of light flashed and danced. Sergius—Miss Weston—the aeroplane—the flying monster! Was this some cruel joke that his friends had perpetrated against him.

For within the box, upon a bed of white velvet, rested an exquisite affair of gold, encrusted with blue-white diamonds. It was a tiny aeroplane, and enmeshed with it, its wings and the plane's interlocked, was a golden bat, with two tiny rubies for eyes.

Who had sent him this thing? Who had been so cruel as to taunt him with such a reminder of his time of madness? He raised box and jewel in his hand and was about to hurl it across the room when his eyes fell upon one of the letters scattered before him on the counterpane. The writing upon it was in that same small, yet distinctive hand that had appeared on the box-wrapping.

Dropping the leather case Jones hastily seized the letter and ripped it open. He read:

"My Dear Friend Roland:

"Two weeks ago I read in an old newspaper of
your rescue and of your return to your native
city. Until that moment I—we all—believed
you to have been drowned in the sea, as was
the enormous bat which carried you thither.
We found its body washed up upon the shore,
and believe me, my friend, I wept over it for
sorrow at your loss and for such an end to
such an heroic deed as yours.

"I know, however, that you must have been
far more overcome by your terrible experience
than the newspaper account indicated. You
will not need to explain to me that otherwise you would have taken your yacht back to
Joker Island and, if necessary, risked death in
the cavern labyrinth seeking to return to aid
me, if I needed aid. There are some friend-
ships which spring into being without the
need of years to build them up, and though
few words were spoken, I know that ours was
such a one."

"Well, the old son-of-a-gun," murmured Jones, "and
he means it, too." The eyes he raised to Philip, coming to
announce the readiness of the bath, were perceptibly wet,
to that worthy Briton's great, though unrevealed, astonishment.

"Get out, Philip," was Jones's only reply. "I'll bathe
after a while."

Alone once more he eagerly resumed his reading:

"But enough of that. I am coming to New
York soon—this is written from Tokio, where
I have caused to be made a small remembrance

which I am also mailing you—and then we can talk together.

"After you had so courageously and with incredible presence of mind flung yourself upon the great bat—"

Jones grinned, remembering the actual state of his feelings in that moment.

"—and been snatched away into the air, I managed to right the plane and we went on across the wall. I did not even know that you were gone. Miss Weston tried to tell me, but you know how great is the noise in flight. We came down upon the beach and I was overcome with dismay and self-reproach when I discovered that you were missing. I could perhaps have pursued the bat and rescued you from the sea, but then it was too late.

"Well, the yacht—the *Monterey*—was gone. I afterward learned that the traitorous and rascally Ivanovitch, believing that I had been killed or captured in the valley, and wishing to make off with the yacht which he afterward successfully sold, had deserted me early in the afternoon of the day you and I took flight."

"And, of course, Laroux and Martindale had to wait until the *Monterey* was gone before they looked up the island," muttered Jones.

"There was nothing else to be done, so I took Miss Weston back into the valley. We arrived there a little after sunrise and found things at the cave just as we had left them. I pulled

away the rocks and we applied my restorative
to my brother and the rest. They were consid-
erably annoyed at my little strategy, but Paul
was, I am sorry to say, so rejoiced over the
desertion of my companions that he forgave
me and persuaded the rest to do so.

"After making one flight in vain, I crossed
the course of a tramp steamer and succeeded
in dropping upon her deck a letter wrapped
about a stone. It was fortunate that I succeeded, for there was barely sufficient petrol left
to take me to land. The captain of the tramp,
more I fear for the reward which the letter offered than for humanity, turned his vessel to
the island and took us all off, together with
our possessions.

"I have little more to tell you, save that in
the month we spent in the valley Holloway,
Haskins and I (Paul never cared for hunting)
killed off most of the more dangerous animals. They are a peculiar collection. Over on
the eastern side we discovered a cavern, or
grotto, much bigger than any which Holloway
had before explored. In it—it was, of course,
daytime—we found scores of those enormous
bats hanging, asleep.

"They are nothing but bats, although they
are so big. They are fruit-eaters, subsisting
upon the fruit of the palm-trees, something
similar to a large date. I do not believe that it
is their custom to attack other creatures, but,
that they were simply actuated by curiosity.
Still we thought it best to kill them, and their
skins are really wonderful pieces of fur.

"Two of the best are for you and also the hide and head of the bear-creature you killed. We bagged two more of them, and I think they were the last of their kind.

"After we killed off the bats the death cabbages began to wither and decay, and now they, too, are all dead. It is evident that they lived almost entirely upon the bats, which they attracted by their palmlike crests. I do not think the bats could have had any sense of smell, though, do you?

"And now, I come to my conclusion to a very long letter. Mr. Holloway was mistaken in regard to the quantity of the substance, of which I told you, to be found in Joker Island. We were able to obtain altogether only about a pound of it, enough to make perhaps a million rubles' worth of what I told you it would make.

"This is not sufficient for the purpose of which I spoke, so, as both Paul and myself are fairly wealthy, we agreed to divide it among our companions. The largest share was received, of course, by Holloway. We gave him our portion as a wedding present. Did I tell you that Holloway and Miss Weston were married two weeks ago here in Tokio?"

For the love of Pete! Jones thought. First I thought it was Paul, and then I thought it was Sergius, only she didn't want him to know it, and all the while it was Holloway! I'll bet Miss Weston had Jim Haskins wondering if he wasn't the lucky one, too. Guess I was the only one not in the running. Well—

"They have, of course, my very kindest wishes
for their happiness, but Paul—perhaps you
knew of his hopes—he felt very badly. He
has returned to Russia and is now fighting at
the front, having, I fear purposely, obtained
his transference to a very dangerous position.
And why am I not at his side? Because, although those men with me proved traitors,
such a thing would hardly turn me against the
cause. And it is upon a mission for the cause
that I am now about to engage, after visiting
you in New York."

"Hurray!" ejaculated the reader. "Just wait until I in-
troduce you to Messrs. Cocksure Martindale and Laroux!
Oh, when will I forgive you two for the last three months?"

"It is a mission of some danger, perhaps, but
also I think that it might interest a man of
your adventurous disposition. I will tell you
more of it later. Until that moment, my friend,
believe me ever and always your friend and
comrade of the past, perhaps—who knows?—
of the future."
                         "Sergius Alexius Petrofsky"

It was a long letter, but Mr. Jones read it through twice.
Then he laid it down carefully, picked up the little box
and stared at the golden bat and aeroplane with shining
eyes and exultant face.

The sleet still beat upon the window, but it didn't
bother Mr. Jones, for he was far away, on a little rock-
walled island in the Pacific Ocean, which did have a name
after all, and a most appropriate one—Joker Island!

A New Species
Robert Coutts Armour (1921)

Eternally battered by demoniac seas, ringed by reefs wicked as a shark's teeth, outermost of the Outer Hebrides, the isle of Eiarn is but seldom visited by man. The sea-birds own it. Their ceaseless crying cuts shrilly across the boom of the waves breaking at the foot of basalt cliffs, or thundering into the recesses of caves worn by ages of unremitting hammer strokes. They brought Porter to Eiarn.

He was a little grey man, very lithe and active, brown of face from incessant exposure to all kinds of weather, with a twinkle in his grey eyes and the infernal patience of a cat hidden somewhere behind them.

Indeed, there had been need of that last quality before ever he got to the island, for he had waited nearly two months until the launch which he had chartered dared put out; and even then they had lain for a day and a night in the lee of the place ere the cargo she carried could be landed. Provisions enough for half a year had been hurried ashore, and in hot haste the launch's crew erected the hut Porter intended to make his home for the next three months. It was very small, but strongly made of sections which bolted together, with a roof that offered no hold to the wind and a well-fitted door, calculated to resist the pelt of hurricane driven rain. It was placed in a niche a

little below the flat summit of the island, and well ballast-
ed with heavy stones.

"I reckon ye'll no get blawn awa' there Maister Porter,"
said the skipper, as he finished his labours and drew back
to observe the result. "Man, it's no' me that's envying ye.
This is no' canny place. There's tales, ye ken—"

"Oh, I've heard all the yarns," replies Porter. "The sea
folks come here, don't they—mermaids and mermen and
all sort of thing? Well, I dare say I shall be glad of their
company. I'll ask 'em to tea, eh?"

"Mebbe it's you they'd be wanting for dinner," the skipper chuckled; and then since the sea was rising once again,
hurried his fellows aboard.

Half an hour later the little vessel was out of sight down
to leeward, and Porter was monarch of all he surveyed.

His first feeling, so he says, was one of elation. A keen
ornithologist, he had long dreamed of this expedition.
This solitude peopled by a multitude of birds, was paradise enough for him. He had his cameras, a gun and a little
rifle for collecting specimens, egg blowing apparatus, pre-
servatives for notebooks, a full equipment, and inexhaust-
ible material. He was happy.

The weather held fine for something more than a fort-
night, during which he was busy from sunrise 'til far into
the night, grudging the time, spent over meals because he
knew well that such favourable conditions could not last
long.

"Then there came a gale from the northward,—a regular snorter," he says. "I thought I knew something about
wind, but that was an experience I'd hardly care to live
through again. I dared not venture more than a few steps
from the hut, lest I should be torn off the rock and slung
into the sea. The air was full of spray, so that I could
hardly see my feet, and the row was appalling. The whole
island quivered, and grew nervous lest the rock under

which the hut lay should topple bodily on top of me. I put
in a lot of time piling up big stones around the hut and
on the roof. By the time the gale abated it had the place
nearly buried in stones. At a little distance it looked like
some Palaeolithic dwelling, and nothing short of an earth-
quake could have shifted it."

Calm succeeded the hurricane, comparative calm that
is, with a light south-westerly wind that brought rain, and
only a moderate groundswell. Porter seized the opportunity of neap tide to explore certain low-lying ledges
which he had not ventured to visit before, and wandered
a good way from the strip of beach in the tiny cove, or
recess, that was the landing place, 'til the turn of the tide
warned him it was time to return.

"I was disappointed, for I had hoped to reach the mouth
of a cave which I could see from the cove. There were certainly nests in it, and I wanted to observe the habits of the
troglodytes. But there was no sense in risking a wetting, or
perhaps an uncomfortable night in the open, so I took one
or two photographs and turned about. The ledge was narrow, and I had to go slowly. I came to a corner, and was in
the act of slipping round it, when I had a queer sensation
that something was looking at me.

"Perhaps you know the feeling? I remember a fellow
at the Travellers' telling a yarn of how he was stalked by
a lion on the veldt. He said he would have fallen an easy
prey to the brute if he hadn't suddenly felt its eyes boring
into his back, as it were. Well, this was exactly the same
thing. I felt eyes upon me, and a chilly creeping of the
skin along my spine.

"I turned as sharply as I could. There was nothing on
the ledge, absolutely nothing, nor on the face of the rocks
above. Nothing could have scaled that scarp. Then I saw
a ring of ripples spreading across the face of the smooth
water in the cave-mouth, as though something had just

dived there. I waited a minute, but saw no more, so went on and reached the cove all right.

"There is a steep path up from the beach, and the flat ledge behind it, to the hut. I paused at the foot of it, took a final look round, and started up. Then I had the feeling again! I whisked about, with no better luck, for though I thought I saw something vanish from the midst of the cove, the sea was too lively to show any ripples there.

"I climbed the path, puzzling over the matter. Some of the diving birds have an uncanny way of disappearing when one turns towards them, but I had had them stare at me often enough before without feeling it, and, besides, the bird that could have made such a disturbance as those ripples by the cave must have been a monster such as I had never heard of.

"I concluded that it must have been a seal, and then it occurred to me that I had seen none since my arrival, though the island seemed an ideal spot for the creatures. This was the more curious in that I had not seen many along the coast of Lewis, and on the trip out. But perhaps they had gone northward for the summer, leaving one old, solitary bull, who, grown cautious through years, would take no risks. On the whole, I thought this the most likely notion.

"I spent the rest of the afternoon developing an accumulation of plates, and went early to bed to rise with the sun. That was the finest day of my whole stay. The sky was cloudless and the sea nearly calm, so I ventured to bathe.

"What I had called the beach of the cove was in reality a sloping shelf of rock, with shingle in pockets and crevices. It dipped suddenly, so that after wading three or four steps I was in deep water. I swam out for perhaps a hundred yards, turned over on my back, and floated. Except for the gentle heave of the swell, the sea was perfectly smooth.

"Then suddenly I saw a swirl on the surface close to me, the sort of eddy that is caused by a big fish swimming just below the surface, and a moment later had that same old uncanny feeling that I was being observed from behind.

"I turned over, but once again too late. There was a ring of spreading ripples, but nothing more. I did not wait. I am no great swimmer, but, I fancy I must have covered the hundred yards to shore in something close to record time. I think, though not sure, that the Thing accompanied me on a parallel course, until I stood upright and splashed up the shelf.

"I began to dress in a hurry, blundered into my trousers, and, losing my balance; thrust a foot against a sharp stone, cutting it rather badly. I had splashed the rock freely with my blood before I succeeded in stanching the wound. I sat down on a rock to finish my toilet, cursing the ill-luck that would confine me to the neighbourhood of the hut for several days to come, when, round the buttressed end of the island came a fishing-boat. She was well out, but, on seeing me wave, turned towards the cove, dropping her sail to negotiate the reefs about the entrance.

"There were four men aboard her, and it seemed to me that they were reluctant to come ashore. The two who were rowing hung on their oars, while the man in the bow shouted a string of questions, of which I understood nothing, since he spoke Gaelic. I noticed that the man steering had a gun across the thwart beside him—a somewhat unusual piece of furniture for a fishing craft.

"I beckoned hospitably, and made invitation as I hobbled to the water's edge. Finally, the boat came in, disembarked the bow man, and backed out quickly while he waded ashore in a mighty hurry, bursting into a flood of speech as he reached me.

"I fancy he was urging me to come aboard at once, to which I could only reply by shaking my head and pointing to my hut. When he saw the blood on the rocks and noted my wounded foot, he looked very concerned, much more than the matter warranted, I thought, and when at length I made him understand that I would have him come up and taste my whisky; he insisted on half carrying me over the lower part of the path. So far as I could make out, he thought the bloody trail I left on the stones an uncanny thing.

"When we got to the hut, he examined the door before he went in, nodding approval of its strength. While I poured out whisky he caught sight of my gun, and brightened a little, but on examining some cartridges, shook a desponding head, and by vigorous signs signified that he thought the charge No. 8 was the heaviest shot I had—far too light. As for the little rifle, he snorted contempt over it. Certainly a 22-calibre bullet is no great missile, though I have always found it sufficient for my purposes.

"Over the whisky he waxed eloquent. Indeed, it clarified his language signs so much that I understood clearly he wished me to come away with him at once, though it did not suffice to make me understand the reason why. I replied by showing him, on the calendar, the probable date of my departure, some nine weeks later, at which he threw up his hands in despair.

"Finally, seeing me adamant, he took his leave, but not before he had chopped a lead sinker, from his pocket, into slugs, with which he charged a cartridge in place of the despised small shot.

"From the door of the hut I saw the boat slide in and take him aboard, and at once shove off. In a few minutes they had caught a slant of wind, which took them out of sight in a short while, leaving me in a very low mind. In vain I reminded myself that these simple fishers believed all manner of weird legends that every rock of the thousands along coast was the haunt of some watersprite or mermaiden, that seals were the descendants of folks drowned at sea, and that once a year, on the Eve of St. John, they doffed their skins and danced on the beach in human form from midnight to dawn.

"Very likely Eiarn was haunted by some bogey, some baseless fabrication of the Celtic imagination, I told myself. What is more natural amidst perilous seas, where the red dawn comes up like blood, and all manner of queer sounds echo along precipices wreathed in sea mists?

"Yet even as I laughed half-heartedly, I knew that something more tangible than kelpies or witchwork lay behind the fisherman's evident anxiety. There is something very concrete about lead slugs. A man doesn't bother to hack up a good sinker merely on account of hypothetical merfolks.

"Could it be that the Thing was the cause of his perturbation? Had I had a narrow escape? And, above all, what under heaven could It be?

"I had time enough to ponder over the problem, for there was no going far that day. I redressed my wounded foot by the door of the hut, fed myself, and so sat me down again, staring at the cove, fancying at times that I could see something moving swiftly across it, a little below the surface, reflecting that, after all the dredging and netting that has been going on systematically for well over half a century men knew precious little about the inhabitants of the sea.

"Undoubtedly the ocean holds many species of which we have, so far, neither specimens nor record. The great sea-serpent may yet be proved no myth of bibulous sailor men, and the kraken not altogether a figment of the imagination.

"So went my musings, until a fog crept up I sat just within the doorway, the tiny and blotted the cove, the path, and everything but the ground on which I stood, out of sight. I went into the hut, and got out Campbell's

Myths and Legends of the Western Highlands, which I had
brought for light reading, and was soon deep in tales of
warlocks and witches who could raise storms and go to sea
in eggshells.

"I sat just within the doorway, the tiny window of the
hut being useful only as a ventilator. The fog stood like a
wall beside me; through the obscurity the eternal crying of
the birds came fitfully, a thin wailing as of lost souls, that
made a very fitting accompaniment to my reading. The
light was fading. I was on the point of closing my book
and rising to make tea, when, without a sound, something
loomed up out of the fog within a couple of yards of me—a
wavering indefinite thing that looked near as tall as a man.

"A sickening reek swept to my nostrils. Then I yelled
in sheer panic, and at the sound of my voice the Thing
vanished. I heard a rattle of stones, no more: the fog stood
blank as before the visitation.

"'But there can't be anything!' I found myself shouting
to vacancy. 'There's nothing here which could do that!'

"Which is—or was—perfectly true. Nothing of the
apparent size of my phantom visitor able to climb the steep
path from the sea existed in those waters, so far as natural history books recorded. A seal might have made the
ascent, but, allowing for the magnification of the fog, this
must have been the great father of all the seals, something
of the dimensions of the elephant-seal, whose habitat lies
half a world away from Eiarn.

"Thus, having convinced myself by a few seconds' reasoning that what I had seen couldn't exist, I leapt inside
and slammed the door, shooting the bolt with a pang of
regret that it was so frail a thing, then fortifying it with
the heaviest packing-cases. In short, I was for a while in
the bluest of funks.

"Only because I had seen something inexplicable in
the fog? No. Rather it was the result, the culmination, of

all that had gone before, and, most of all, the fisherman's
anxiety for my safety. This Thing must be deadly, or that
big, red-bearded man would never have made so much fuss.
I shoved the cartridge he had loaded into the breech of my
gun, and prepared several others in like manner using a
leaden paperweight. When I had done this I felt happier.
I was ready to protect myself.

"The evening wore on. Nothing happened. Finally I
put out my lamp and turned in, all standing, dropping off
to sleep almost at once, strange to say. Some hours must
have passed before I was awakened by a noise outside, the
sound of one of the stones I had piled against the walls
falling with a rattle. A moment later another followed.
Assuredly the Thing was trying to climb upon the roof.
I lit the lamp, and as the rays streamed from the window
I saw—or thought I saw—something dark move swiftly
across the illuminated patch of fog outside.

"There was no more noise, but though I lay down I
could not sleep again. When wan daylight came at last I
could stand no more, but opening the door, peered out,
my gun ready. Nothing! Except that some shreds of the
blood-soaked handkerchief I had left lying by the door
when I removed it, were scattered over the rocks.

"I went a little way down the path, and found more
shreds here and there. The Thing had come up and gone
back to the sea that way. I grew foxy. I would at least have
notice of its coming, and be ready for it. So I piled a wall
of small stones across in such a fashion that not even a
rabbit could have passed without bringing them rattling
down. Since there are no rabbits on Eiarn, there was little
chance of a false alarm. Afterwards, I prepared a flare of
straw and packing paper soaked with oil.

"I endeavoured to occupy myself with my notebooks,
with little success, the gun between my knees bringing my
thoughts back continually to what might be lurking in the

fog close at hand. I don't think I ever spent a more uncomfortable day, and I was glad when at long last it began to
grow dark, for I felt certain that my visitor would return.

"Leaving the window open, but shading the lamp so
that only a glow could be visible from without, I settled to
my vigil with ears pricking to every whisper of sound. At
nine I ate my simple supper. At ten I gave up the pretence
of reading. By twelve I had grown sulky, telling myself
that the Thing would not come that night. And, only two
or three minutes later, I heard my alarm-wall fall.

"I had rehearsed exactly what I would do, and did it
without a hitch. I lit my flare, flung it through the window, then opening the door, sprang out and let drive a
barrel down the path.

"There was a commotion of rolling stones, a sort of
coughing bellow, a swirl of the fog, and something dark
and indefinite blundered past up the hollow and so to
the plateau beyond. I fired the second barrel into it as it
passed, eliciting another roar.

"Then followed a great outcry from the birds as they
rose before the disturber of peace, but since there was
nothing more to be done I got me in again, reloading as I
went.

"Slowly the racket among the bird folk died away; there
was silence, save for the usual nigh noises. For the time
the enemy was routed.

"But I did not sleep. The gully running past the hut
was the only way down to the sea, so far as I knew, and the
creature might return at any moment, paying me a visit
in passing. However, I was no longer nervous, but rather
eager to have another shot at the beggar. Chiefly I was
consumed by curiosity, my glimpse of the Thing having in
no way enlightened me. I had seen only a dark bulk which
might have been anything, a blur shapeless as a puff of
smoke.

"I puzzled myself 'til daylight, then, since nothing seemed likely to happen, snoozed for several hours. The mist was gone from the upper part of the island when I awoke, though it still hung thickly above the sea. Determined to follow up my quarry and make an end of the mystery, if I could, I snatched a hasty breakfast and hobbled out.

"There was no difficulty in following the trail. A pool of blood where I had built the little wall, and many splashes all up the gully showed that I had hit hard. On the plateau above the trail was still plain. The creature had ploughed straight over the close lying nests, crushing eggs and fledglings in its passage.

"It seemed to have gone blindly for a little way, then steered towards the edge of the cliff, along which it had gone for a considerable distance, evidently seeking a path down. I walked very warily, expecting to come upon the brute at any moment. Several times I halted before a clump of boulders and threw stones. Nothing showed, however, and the trail ran on until I had come to a place almost immediately above the cave I had mentioned. There it plunged into gully so steep that I hesitated to negotiate it with my lamed foot for handicap.

"But after hesitating a little, I ventured so far as a large rock that jutted from the face of the cliff about thirty feet down. The descent took me some time, but at last I was securely seated in a crevice, and able to scan the remainder of the gully.

"As I had thought, it did not go right down, but ceased at a broad ledge some fifty feet above the sea. The mist still hung about the ledge, while I could only catch an occasional glimpse of the dark water below. The vapour swirled with the light breeze, now blotting out the ledge altogether, now thinning 'til it was only a gauze veil, through which I could see boulders and lichen patches wavering indistinctly.

"Something moved on the ledge, something long and large, so like in colour to the rock it lay upon that only the movement revealed it for a living thing. At which moment the mist thickened again, and I saw no more.

"Waiting was my game. I trained my gun between my knees, and watched the eddying drift of the wreaths for a full half-hour at least before they thinned once more; then, as the grey, humped form loomed out again, let drive both barrels.

"From aloft it looked as though a section of the ledge lifted a little, then rolled over into the sea. I had a clear sight of what seemed a webbed paw flailing out in a vain effort to hold on—then there came a mighty splash, and with it a rush of something which flung the water aside like the bow of a destroyer. The sea foamed, I could see two dark forms battling furiously, see the spray discoloured with blood—and then the mist closed down once more, leaving me as far from a solution as ever.

"For several minutes longer I heard the battle, then quiet fell, and when the mist cleared at last, before a gust, there was nought to see but a patch of stained water, which slowly cleared. Though I waited a long while, I saw nothing more.

"That afternoon my fishermen returned, bringing with them, for interpreter, their minister, a pleasant young fellow who spoke English with the Highland clearness of accent. He came ashore, accompanied by the red-beard who had first visited me, while, as before, the boat shoved off and the man in the stern kept his gun at the ready, precautions that no longer seemed ridiculous.

"The minister opened fire as soon as he was within hailing distance, by explaining who he was and why he came.

"'Angus Macpherson here came to me in great distress because he could not make you understand the grave risks you run by remaining here,' he began. 'So I had to come perforce, as it were. Have you been molested? What is all this?'

"He had halted before the first of the bloodstains, while Angus, in great excitement, poured out a torrent of Gaelic.

"'That is the blood of one of the grave risks,' I replied. 'I can give it no other name, since I have only had the merest glimpse of the creature.'

"'And Angus cannot tell what it is, either,' he said. 'There seem to be several. One of our boats has been missing, and the men declare that it was attacked by these things. Remnants of the craft that have been picked up show the marks of terrible teeth. This isle is supposed to be a haunt of the brutes. You had better leave with us. The opportunity may not occur again for a long while.'"

"Well, I left. Solitude is all very well, and birds are extremely interesting, but they may be studied under less exacting conditions. If I had to be continually on my guard, I should be able to do little more. Therefore, we carried my baggage to the boat and pushed off, not without many a backward glance towards the dark mouth of the cave which, I suspect, held the secret of the island."

Here ends the material portion of Porter's narrative. There has been no further light on the matter, though several mysterious disappearances of fishing craft have been laid to the door of the terrors of Eiarn.

Marine zoologists are puzzled. One suggests a new species of seal, larger, more ferocious than the gentle beasts we know of, carnivorous and bloodthirsty. Another gloats on the prospects of discovering a novel sort of alligator which has taken the sea for its province. A third boldly plumps for something altogether new and strange, an amphibious shark-tiger, product of heaven knows what evolutionary process in the mighty deep.

And, while the expedition that is to solve the riddle is being got ready, Mr. Porter wanders the halls of the United Services Museum and all other places where slaughter weapons are displayed, meditating an armament. He does not propose to return to Eiarn without precaution.

A Horror of Darkness
Claude E. Benson (1925)

"I differ entirely," pronounced the Bug-Hunter. "On the contrary, the entire animal creation, man included, has been, and is, physically deteriorating."

Those who know Sgurrpenfell know that it is one of the few patches of earthly Paradise that remain in this thrice happy realm of ours, that it is advisable to write and book rooms three months in advance so as to make sure of getting an answer, that the telegram announcing your advent generally comes to hand two days after your arrival, that even the hardiest of those H— born (the filling in of the hiatus is optional), pass-storming motorists turn disconsolately away from surface and gradient. You are more alone than on the wide, wide sea, because the wireless knows not the existence of S.P.F., as its admirers call it. You can ramble, scramble, paint, or fish to your heart's content.

It is needless to say that those who frequent this delectable spot are of the elect, men of brains, muscle, and taste. On the occasion under consideration the little hostel was wellnigh full. The congregation consisted of almost a dozen men of brains, muscle, and taste. Opportunity of using the two latter was denied them as the rain was coming down in sheets and the wind howling like the Ride of the Valkyrie on a Salvation Army band. Wherefore they betook themselves to the consumption of tobacco and the discussion of matters they did not understand. This proved their brains, because, as Dennis O'Hara, the poet (the only poet of the S.P.F. community), observed: "The man who talks about things he understands—supposing he does understand anything, which he doesn't—is a wet blanket who ought to be put to instant death by slow torture."

It was the Professor of Comparative Astronomy, or words to that effect, who had teed off with a thesis that man was going on from strength to strength, supporting his argument with Channel swims and records, and it was the Bug-Hunter who took him up. [N.B.—It must be understood that the Bug-Hunter was not a professional shikari of domesticated insects. Nay! He was a practical naturalist, the kind of man who cheerfully mingles with crocodiles and cobras, cannibals and man-eaters, if by good fortune he may hit off the trail of a new beetle the size of a threepenny bit.] The audience listened with a semblance of reverent attention that thinly veiled an eager anticipation of rotting as occasion offered. The Bug-Hunter warmed to his work.

"Now, look here," he argued, "what does it say? There were giants in those days. Quite. Now in the time of Goliath, the typical giant of all time, they were rare. And then he was not so much of a giant after all. David borrowed his sword later on for personal use, so he can't have been so very much smaller. Probably men were bigger all round then. And even to-day! Talk of a man twice my size. Rubbish! That would make him twelve feet high and eighty inches round the chest. Rot!"

He challenged the room with a glance. The room was puzzled. Could it be that in defiance of all the rules of the game the man was talking sense? Before a decision had been reached the Bug-Hunter had got his second wind.

"Then there's the animal kingdom. The mastodon and mammoth were bigger than the elephant. You meet pigmy elephants to-day, but giants never."

"But surely," broke in the Professor, "in your explorations you have met some giants, some abnormally big things."

He spoke seriously, in fact the whole room had become serious. There was something serious in the atmosphere, indefinable but existent, and the men knew it.

"Abnormally big, yes. Little giants, so to speak, but I have never met, say, a tiger six feet high at the shoulder, nor heard of one, or anything of that sort."

"Are you quite sure—sure, I mean, that you have never even heard of a creature more than ordinarily large?"

The audience looked at each other, and then at the speaker. That swift glance was an interchange of tacit recognition that in him, or rather, from him, existed that singular atmosphere. The man himself was one of those hard, fleshless, mahogany individuals you can neither hurt nor tire. There was more than seriousness in his question, there was anxiety.

"Ye-es," came the reply. "I admit I have. I don't mean any of the ordinary bogeys of the were-wolf, bunyip type, but something more or less authentic. It was in the hinterland of French Cochin China. Indeed, so convinced did I become that there was something in it that I went, under French protection, to look into the matter myself."

"Well?"

"The terror was genuine enough, but that was all there was 'to it.' The creature only came out at night: no one had ever seen it; and so forth, and so forth. So I came to the conclusion that it was a bogey after all. All the same—all the same," he ended, "I could not help feeling they were keeping something back, lying, in fact—that there was a real something after all."

"Is that all you know? Have you heard nothing more?"

"Ye-es. Let me see. I did hear of some missionary chap going up that way on some such trail. I should like to know if he found out anything, but I have not heard of him since. By the way, his name was something like yours. Let me see, Cotton, was it?"

"Yes. Cotton it was. He was my brother. The bogey killed him, and I saw it happen." Then, looking rather pitifully round the room. "I'll tell you fellows about it if you don't mind. I have never spoken of it before, and it may be a relief."

The men saw the pain in his eyes and acquiesced. Nevertheless, there was not one who had far rather not hear the story, including the naturalist. Then Cotton commenced.

At first he spoke as one constrained, constrained by torture. In a short time, however, he had his emotion in hand and the story became less painful—less painful in the manner of telling, at least.

"My brother," he began, "was not exactly a missionary. He was a Mission Pioneer, something after the manner of Livingstone, a prospector whose job was to fossick out places where a Mission might be planted with some reasonable chance of development. Physically and intellectually he was splendidly equipped for the work—he was a perfect genius at picking up languages, and what was of most consequence, his whole heart was in the enterprise. Now, as these ventures took him into the wildest of wild parts, and as I am something of an explorer and big-game shot"—the hum of recognition from the room disconcerted him for a moment; he checked, then stumbled on—"well, he had no difficulty in persuading me to accompany him.

"The East was his hunting-ground, especially Malaya. 'Africa,' he would say, 'was well in hand, and China was opening up,' and the upshot was that our last expedition found us poking about along the southern frontier of French Cochin China. There, in an evil hour, we heard of a tribe, or rather community, known as the Well-Meaning Ones."

There was a grunt from the Bug-Hunter.

"Which means Fiends Incarnate," he interjected.

"Exactly. Fools that we were not to have guessed as much from the start. Apart from the extreme unlikelihood of such a name being applicable to the folk thereabout, any schoolboy would have at once suggested the classical parallel, the Eumenides, the Well-Meaning Ones, the propitiatory euphemism for the Furies. Somehow the obvious escaped us, never so much as entered our minds, so much so that my brother joyously made a bee-line for the accursed place. To him its name suggested an ideal vedette for missionary outpost work. Moreover, there was any amount of mixed shooting about. You might put up a tiger one moment and a buffalo the next, and bag one after the other, provided neither got you first. This inducement appealed to both of us.

"The capital of this infernal tribe was a place called Boh San, a hill fortress, admirably fortified, with an abundant water supply, and a steep, natural *giacis* sloping down on three sides to the most pestilence-ridden forest that ever killed off Malay, let alone European. The fourth side, the north, was open and tolerably level, the weak spot in the defences—seemingly.

"Seemingly. It was a rugged plain, covered with great blocks under cover of which skirmishers could advance almost to the walls. Beyond, less than a mile distant, the plain ended in a steep escarpment, all rifted with ravines, and buttressed at the foot by masses of huge boulders, forming a labyrinth of caves—a natural fortress to the military eye more impregnable than Boh San itself. 'A rare place for tiger,' I thought to myself. Only no tigers were there, no human beings either.

"For years the Bohsanese had ruled the countryside by terror, that terror which had earned them the title of the Well-Meaning Ones, coupled by judicious raids on any tribes that showed fight. Punishment always took the form of tribute, and tribute always took the form of human beings. What became of these was never known. It was certain that they were not made slaves. Rumour had it that they were sacrificed with horrid rites to some mysterious monster. Nevertheless, such was the fear inspired by the Bohsanese that envoys would go down, alone, with no escort, and select victims, unmolested.

"At length something happened: an envoy selected the daughter of a chief on her bridal day and met with a pointed refusal from her lover that went through his heart and stuck out under his shoulder-blade, and the Malayan worm turned, and when the Malayan worm turns, treading on the tail of a Burmese cobra is relatively a safe and pleasurable pastime. Every Bohsanese at large was massacred out of hand and a confederacy was formed with the express object of mopping up the remainder.

"An expeditionary force was dispatched against the confederacy, and did not return, except piece-meal, literally piece-meal, and then it began to dawn on the Well-Meaning Bohsanese that the terror of their name was gone, and that their number was up, badly. In this strait the Arch-Fiend, i.e. the Arch-Priest, in Council remembered that they were under French protection, a situation they had not hitherto acknowledged, at any rate, not with enthusiasm. The difficulty was to get into touch with the French. This would seem easy enough as the fort was only invested on three sides, but the open side was the plain to the north, and over that neither the fear of the sword, starvation, nor torture, immediate or prospective, would send any solitary Bohsanese. At length, one misty morning, under cover of a false sortie to the south, twenty men broke away for the nearest French post.

"The nearest French post was regrettably sceptical and communicated with the Commandant who, as good or bad luck would have it, was tolerably near at hand with quite a strong fighting force, the activities of some bandits having demanded drastic attention. He was even more callous. Indeed, he expressed an opinion that it would be no bad thing if all the Bohsanese had their throats cut. Nevertheless, as in duty bound to Friendlies, he sent a *sous-officier* with two files of men back with the embassy—to report.

"Two days later four of the deputation, clothes torn, heads bandaged, covered with blood and dirt, staggered back, bearing with them the corpse of the *sous-officier*, foully mutilated. It is, of course, needless to say what had happened. First of all they had massacred the five Frenchmen and then returned to force the Commandant's hand. Their wounds were quite genuine, too, for the Malayan is nothing if not an artist. Their story was that they had been surprised by the enemy and cut down, and that they four alone had escaped out of the battle. They were nearer the truth than they knew. That was precisely what had happened to the sixteen survivors whilst they were engaged in putting finishing touches to the obsequies of the French soldiers. Few people can have been more gratified than those four Bohsanese when, on being marched back to the scene of the alleged ambush, each with the muzzle of a rifle between his shoulders, they saw their late comrades lying as they had fallen, with the four soldiers in their midst.

"This decided the Commandant. He whipped up every rifle he could muster and, strengthened by a couple of machine-guns, marched hot-foot to Boh San and came on the besiegers in the very act of storming the fortress. There and then he 'larned' them not to molest Well-Meaning natives under French protection, and the Bohsanese took care that the lesson should not be forgotten. Consequently on the occasion of our visit a few months later, no dog dared move his tongue against Boh San. This may seem all more or less irrelevant—"

"Not at all," interposed the Bug-Hunter. "I have been puzzling over two things. One, how the French came to let you go unescorted, as I heard your brother did. Two, how you talked so lightly about shooting. I went under guard of ten rifles and even then I simply dared not venture any distance into the jungle. I understand now."

"Thanks, and you will understand too that you, under French protection in being, were as safe in Boh San as you are here, whereas we, unescorted, were absolutely at the mercy of the tribe. If we disappeared, we disappeared, and there were plenty of opportunities of disappearing without foul play.

"Truth to tell we had a very good time at first. Of course, we had agreed to conduct ourselves as foreigners should, that it was the worst possible form to interfere in any way with the religious or social customs of the land, and so forth. True it is that Kenelm, my brother, had set his mind on the reform of these some day—by other hands perhaps—but not yet, not yet, and to this resolution we honestly intended to adhere.

"Someone some time or other said or wrote somewhere that a strong man should be a master of circumstance. That is a characteristically idiotic remark that issues from the armchair of the pseudo-philosopher who has never been up against it. Leaving myself out, Kenelm was an exceptionally strong man, morally, intellectually, and physically. We got on quite all right with the Bohsanese and, what was remarkable, Kenelm was on excellent terms with the Arch-Priest, and so I am convinced we should have continued—but for circumstance. I must just switch off a bit to explain.

"The town or fortress of Boh San was simply a rough parallelogram with enormously thick walls of mud and rubble and a strong gate at the two narrow ends, the north and the south. There was nothing out of the way about this. Similar primitive fortresses, differing in detail but on the same general principle, are to be found all the world over. The unusual features were the Temple and the defences of the north wall. The Temple was in the exact centre of Boh San, a rough parallelogram of sandstone, some sixty feet by forty, and perhaps twenty feet high. The shape of the town had obviously been modelled on that of this block. The sandstone itself had been excavated and worked out into various chambers accessible to the priests alone. The punishment for intrusion by a layman was death. On its flat top the ceremonials connected with the worship of the local god were celebrated in the presence of the people. The features of these celebrations were incantations, chants, fires, and what not, but not sacrifices. Sacrifices there were, as you shall hear, but they took place elsewhere. This local god was a malignant demon whose abode was reputed to be amongst the fissures and crags beyond the plain to the north. These crags were taboo. The god was taboo. To speak of it was taboo: the punishment was death. The whole subject was taboo of taboo, yet the whole community seemed tolerably acquainted with the existence and attributes of this pernicious deity. As a means of egress and ingress except on certain ceremonial occasions the northern gateway was scarcely used. It was opened every two hours during the night for the purpose of changing guard, the guard consisting of a single sentry. If the deity should happen to be out and about and catch him napping, the strength of the garrison would not be seriously depleted by one man missing, and the Bohsanese

had made other provision against contingencies. All along
the north wall at an elevation of some fifteen feet from
the ground, fixed into the crude masonry, was a screen of
horizontal bamboos. It would appear that the deity, not
content with a stray sentinel or such other provision as the
Bohsanese occasionally made, would now and then essay
a domiciliary visitation. To frustrate such undesirable
manifestations of interest the bamboo screen had been
devised. The god would scale the wall as far as the bamboos, but when it came to swinging its weight on these,
the strong, pliable shafts would give, with the result that it
would slip off and return to the ground with considerable
velocity. One or two experiences of this kind would cause
it to give up its projected visit as a bad job and go home to
its rifts and crags. Furthermore, in the event of an alarm,
the guard of worshippers would turn out and line the wall
with their great pronged spears, a kind of cross between
a butcher's knife and a pitchfork. The whole taboo was a
farce, but there could be no doubt that the god was a very
living and very perilous reality. Oddly enough, on being
repulsed, it never sought ingress by the right or left where
the walls were barren of defence. Once inside there would
have been apparently nothing to check it, for the houses
were merely bamboo huts and the open entrances of the
Temple were guarded by nothing more solid than a barrier
of superstition.

"Now it is, I take it, quite unnecessary to say that a
personal interview with this malign deity was what Kenelm especially desired, and I was not one whit behind.
That it was some ferocious natural freak—probably, judging from its habitat and from the nature of the bamboo
defence, some monstrous baboon, I had no doubt, and in
all my experience I had not, till then, met the animal that
had a dog's chance against my rifle—and Kenelm could
shoot, too. The Arch-Priest, however, would have none of

it. I have said he and Kenelm were on excellent terms, and in some unaccountable phase of something approaching humanity, he strongly objected to sending my brother to his death—and death, he affirmed, was the only possible termination of such a venture. I have an idea, however, that he would not have objected to my going—not a little bit.

"The reason of his dislike for me I could not conjecture at the time. The explanation of the good understanding between him and Kenelm was not far to seek. The Arch-Priest was delighted to meet with a foreigner of the potent white race who could converse with him in his own tongue, and conceived also something akin to a liking for the stranger prince—Kenelm looked every inch a prince—who treated him, not as a dog as did the French, but as, at least, an equal: Kenelm never forgot to indicate his recognition of the Arch-Priest as Chief Magistrate of his brass-farthing state. Moreover the Priest, being an Oriental, simply loved being told stories. They are all that way. Take a group of silent, dignified Bedouin and start pitching yarns, and you will have them all round your knee like children in a nursery.

"Kenelm was an admirable *raconteur* and had at his finger ends that unfailing fund of stories for all ages and all passions, the Old Testament. He fitted his stories to circumstance or circumstance to his stories. A master of circumstance and a master of art, he was trenching his way by the Scriptures to the dethronement and destruction of the demon god. A master of art and circumstance! He was, in fact, drawing up his death-warrant.

"We had been in Boh San a week and were on 'stop as long as you like and come back as soon as you please' terms. Kenelm was by way of becoming a power in the state and I—I had not then fallen under the Arch-Priest's displeasure—not exactly a nonentity, thanks to my ability to shoot straighter than most. 'Gun of Death' they called

me, and ability to take life is a faculty that counts high
with the Bohsanese. Then the sky began to darken. The
first danger-signal was an invitation from the priesthood
to view the Temple.

"Kenelm was delighted. I shied like a horse from a
cobra. I acquit the Arch-Priest of any evil intent, but not
the priesthood. Indeed, on reflection, it is quite certain
the Arch-Priest must have repeated Kenelm's stories to his
colleagues. He himself had listened with the innocent, unreasoning pleasure of a child with its nurse. Not so the
priests. It is not less certain that unless Kenelm's pointed
deductions were altogether missed, these narrations must
have been to the Bohsanese Theological College simply
rank blasphemy. In fact, I am pretty sure the suggestion
did not emanate from the Arch-Priest. He was a masterly
man and consequently unpopular. Kenelm had become his
favourite, indeed the favourite of all Boh San, except the
priesthood. Here, then, we have ready to hand a spring of
envy, hatred and malice. Still, officially, the Arch-Priest
was responsible for our admission, and the pontiff who
introduced a foreign devil into the sanctuary would be no
less guilty of sacrilege than the foreign devil and no less
worthy of death.

"The Temple consisted of an outer corridor, an inner
corridor, and the Shrine, which was, in fact, the centre
of the blook hollowed out. There was but one entrance, a
narrow doorway, closely draped with a thin, evil-smelling
curtain. It was lit by apertures in the roof which appeared
to be covered with fine netting. Before entering we were
bidden robe ourselves in priestly robes not less evil smelling than the door-curtain. We objected, but were assured
they were desirable if not for our safety, for our conve-
nience.

"The Shrine was nauseous. In the centre was a well of
clean water, the only clean thing in the place; all else was

damp and dirt and crawling life, which we could sense without at first seeing. As our eyes grew more accustomed to the light we made them out to be spiders, thousands of them.

"I know this and that about entomology, but such spiders I had never seen before nor since. They were about the size of tarantulas, the spread of their legs would about touch the circumference of a saucer, but they were not tarantulas, nor like them. They more resembled overgrown specimens of the big, black, bloated farmhouse spider. It was to keep off these we had put on robes dressed with some mixture these loathsome insects abhorred. They were highly poisonous, the Arch-Priest told us, but their bite was not necessarily deadly.

"All round the walls were hideous representations of these creatures, enlarged in scale and rendered more repulsive by huge blobs of red eyes and faces of Malayan gods, grinning bestiality and cruelty. Kenelm touched my arm.

"'There is danger,' he whispered. 'Let us be going.'

"There was that in his voice that came near to shaking my nerve, not fear, no, nor alarm, but something akin to awe with a shadow of horror behind. It made me glad to go. At the doorway occurred a trivial happening. My foot slipped slightly on the slimy floor and I put my hand to the wall to steady myself. Something got on to my hand and seemed to cling to it. I took it to be one of the musty bits of spiders' web with which the walls were plastered, but on getting past the curtain into daylight, I saw it was one of those loathsome spiders, and sprawling on the back of my bare hand. Of course I did what anyone else would have done—jerked it off and set my foot on the beastly thing. Kenelm did not notice the incident. He was not noticing.

"He was not noticing. He was like a man partly dazed; I remember he was on the point of walking out of the Temple without doffing his malodorous protective garment, and that, on being checked by the Arch-Priest, his laugh, as he stammered out an apology of sorts, had nothing of laughter in it. I remember that the Arch-Priest regarded him curiously—with solicitude, and I have not forgotten the glance with which that unamiable Bohsanese favoured me. It was malevolence concentrated.

"I had other things to think about, however, than hostile priests. I was concerned for Kenelm. I had never seen him like that before, and wanted to get him alone. There was no difficulty about that. The Arch-Priest was no less anxious to be quit of us than we of him. As soon as we were by ourselves Kenelm looked at me questioningly.

"'Did you not feel it?' he asked, after a long pause, and again there was that tinge of horror in his voice. Just for a moment an idea shaped itself that he might have seen the spider, but that I dismissed as trivial, and I had noted that strangeness of tone in the Shrine itself. Nevertheless, all the time he was speaking that wretched insect kept crawling about, as it were, in my brain; yet his words were arresting enough.

"'Did you not feel it?' he repeated. 'The Presence. It was almost tangible. Yes, and the danger is real, real and physical, but the source, the source is spiritual. I have known for years that in the dark places of the earth they worship devils, but never have I set foot before in a home of Satan.'

"I said nothing: there was nothing to say; moreover I had experienced none of the sensations that had so perturbed Kenelm. As for him, he did not seem to expect an answer. He just sat brooding, brooding, brooding, with his chin in his hand. Then he spoke again, very slowly.

"'Yes. The danger is very near and I am the quarry. The evil is directed against me alone. Yes, in very truth, Boh San is a seat of Satan, a seat of Satan.'

"'Very well, then,' I interposed, 'if that's so, let's get out of it and quick, especially if there's danger about.'

"Dear old Kenelm's face cleared on the words and he laughed genuinely.

"'I can see you doing it, old boy. You're exactly the man to rat from duty because it chances to be dangerous, and exactly the sort to appreciate the man who would. Why, I believe you would disown me as a brother if I thought of such a thing. No,' he became serious again, 'face it out I will, and if I perish, I perish.'

"'No, you don't,' thought I, 'not if I can help it anyway. It's all very true about sticking things out to the death if you can do any good thereby—horrid, unpleasant, but it has to be done, but where there's no possible chance of doing any good it is sheer, rank folly.' Those, gentle-men"—here Cotton looked round the silent room—"were my reflections, and I may say at once I have made few more foolish."

There was no reply. Someone struck a match—he had been waiting to do so for fear of interrupting. Then Cotton resumed.

"Of course, I did not say anything of the kind to Kenelm. I just reminded him that Esther, the heroine of his words, did not perish but succeeded beyond expectation, and generally bucked him up. Finally I persuaded him to come for a moonlight stalk with me. I know of nothing better calculated to distract attention from everything but the matter in hand than a moonlight stalk in a leopard country. There was no need for that, however; Kenelm did not so much as open his lips again on the subject that had so distressed him, and long before we started was his old cheery self again.

"We were back with the dawning and by that time, so far as I could judge, any unpleasantness that might have resulted from our visit to the Temple had cleared away. Certainly I concluded that, if looks count for anything, the Arch-Priest assuredly did not love me. On the other hand I was pretty sure my stock had gone up in Boh San generally. My venturing out on a moonlight stalk seemed to indicate that I was something of a superman. I learned from Kenelm, who was a good deal amused, that he found he had got none of the credit, as he was assumed to be insured against accident by the Gun of Death. As a matter of fact it was a perfectly mad thing to do, especially as the moon had barely passed her half, and no credit attached to either of us. I wish now, however, with all my heart— though, perhaps, I am wrong to do so—that if we were out for anything foolhardy, we had gone to see what was to be found on the north of the town.

"All went on much the same as before—much the same, not quite. For instance, I noticed that the Arch-Priest ceased to indulge in long *tête-à-têtes* with Kenelm. He was not less friendly, nor apparently less interested, but he always had another priest with him, and never the same two days running. This annoyed Kenelm a good deal. The object of the Arch-Priest was—to me quite evidently—not to bring new pupils to the feet of Gamaliel but to safeguard himself against any charge of heresy, and before long Kenelm, very unwillingly, began to come round to my way of thinking. Nevertheless, though disheartened, he did not despair. In any case he resolved to hang on until after the full moon which; he had gathered, was to be the occasion of some big religious festival, something especially holy. This annoyed me more than a good deal. I was convinced that the place was getting less and less healthy for us every day.

"'Something particularly holy,' I remember saying with considerable bitterness, 'means something extra-specially damnable. All right. I'll stay on condition that you undertake not to do any Telemachus stunt and barge in to interfere with the racial customs.'

"'All right,' replied Kenelm, with a quiet smile. 'If you don't, I won't.'

"It was the day before the ceremony. I had just finished getting all my traps together, for I was determined to upstick and away at the earliest possible moment, even if it meant a moonlight flitting. There was a sinister atmosphere about Boh San that was telling on my nerves, and even Kenelm was beginning to feel a bit 'edgy.' By way of a little recreation we went off for a shoot. I had an ugly sensation that we were being watched, at any rate at the start. I am afraid that if I had spotted one of these watchers, I should have mistaken him for a wild beast and apologised to the authorities afterwards.

"We did not expect to get much. It was broad day and the country just at that particular part was fairly open. I had taken my stand on one side of a clump of trees and undergrowth and Kenelm was making a tour round it in the hope of putting up something. It was as still—as still as a sub-tropical noon can be, and you cannot have anything stiller.

"All at once I heard a scuffle, a woman's shriek, and Kenelm's voice calling me. I was off at speed. On the way a Bohsanese came staggering past. The blood was pouring down his face and one eye was nearly closed. Had I been anything but a fool, he would have got no further. Then I came on Kenelm.

"He was looking flushed and excited. At his feet, on her knees, was a Malay girl, fondling his right hand and holding it to her lips. He was contemplating the knuckles of his left fist which were badly cut.

"I did not stop to talk. I immediately connected up those damaged knuckles with the Bohsanese's damaged face and was off after him. Curiously enough I remember that something from Macaulay came into my head, something about Strafford, that the execution of an individual was justified if the safely of the State demanded it. Just then Kenelm and I constituted the State.

"Unfortunately, in my haste, I made a noise like a charge of cavalry, and the Bohsanese heard me and, at the first glimpse, bolted to covert. I had a snap at him but he got away. That shot did me a deal of harm—not that it would have made much odds in the long run, I fancy. Up till then it was supposed that it was impossible for me, the 'Gun of Death,' to miss, and I had missed, or rather—worse luck—I had not. The bullet had cut in through the flesh under the left armpit.

"I need not tell you what had happened. The girl, of course, was tribute, brought in by a Bohsanese, her hands tied behind her back, and her back stimulated with a ratan cane: it was all over weals. Kenelm had come across the convoy and had intervened. The Bohsanese had drawn a knife and had run up against Kenelm's left.

"When I got back—I had spent some little time trying to get on the spoor of my quarry and failing—Kenelm was alone. He had got rid of the girl somehow. I did not bother about enquiring. We had quite enough on hand as it was.

"'Safety first!' quoth I, as soon as Kenelm had finished. 'How many clips have you in your cartridge-belt?'

"'Three. Same as you. Why?'

"'Why? We're going to give Boh San and its festival a miss, that's all. It is not more than three days' march to the nearest French station, and two old stagers like ourselves can make that all right. Then we will come back under escort, good and strong, and recover our goods and chattels.'

"'And never shave again,' interposed Kenelm. Then, in reply to my unspoken question: 'I, for one, could never look myself in the face after bolting from a crowd of half-baked Shanskallywags. Besides, I seem to remember when, a good many years ago, two men were examined for a good deed done to an impotent man, they did not shirk the issue.'

"That was just like Kenelm. He put it up to you and there you were—up against it, hard.

"'All the same,' he continued reflectively, 'there is no reason why—in fact, it would be far better, if you—'

"'Oh, shut up,' I said.

"Still I could not but regret having fired that shot, and still more that I had not got my man in the neck. Human life is sacred, squeaks the anaemic pacifist. So it is, I entirely agree, especially mine. At the same time it was borne in on me that the Arch-Priest might take my view, if this matter came before Boh San in Council—my view, with this difference, that human life was sacred, especially his.

"We did not get much sport that day. 'Gun of Death' missed two sitters, one after another, which is a sufficient indication of the state of my nerves. We were not sorry to get back, and we were not sorry to find, that for all the special notice taken of us, we might never have been out of Boh San. At least Kenelm was not. I did not like the sign a little bit.

"I am not going to bother you with a description of the festival. All Boh San that drew sword turned out at moonrise and lined up outside the northern wall, armed to the teeth. In the centre were the priests with a strong bodyguard in front and on either side, especially in front. Every tenth man carried a totally unnecessary torch—the plain, in the light of a full tropical moon, was bright as day. In the rear came some stalwarts from among the women and children. Kenelm and I were in the place of honour, on either side of the Arch-Priest. Then we marched northwards towards those rifted crags.

"It was a question of, as at most religious festivals, favouring with one's tongue, which is classical for keeping silence. Not that that made much difference, for in the clangor and clatter of drums, cymbals, and all kinds of

BESTIA SECRETUM

music one would have had to shout to make oneself heard. Kenelm took advantage of an unexpected lull in the shindy to observe that these fellows had the wind up about something. My reply was:

"'Quite. Have you your Browning handy?' when the Arch-Priest intervened with a quiet gesture of his arms across both our faces. We took the hint, but I noted with satisfaction that Kenelm had cleared his front pocket for action. We were both heeled in the matter of rifles, but it is easy to snatch a rifle, in which circumstances a Browning may come in, unexpected and useful.

"Scarcely had this reflection formulated itself when a cord was dropped over my head, my arms were pinioned, my wrists held, and my rifle snatched. Kenelm was secured at the same moment and in the same way. So swiftly and silently was this accomplished that I doubt if the man in front or three files on either side were aware of it. Kenelm and I behaved exactly in the same way. Kenelm was smoking at the time and the loop missed his pipe. He kept on smoking.

"About the length of a cricket-pitch from the base of the crags we halted, and the Arch-Priest, mounting on a large, flat-topped boulder—evidently a ceremonial rostrum, carved as it was with quaint scrolls—addressed all Boh San. Even at that moment I could not help but notice the ludicrous condition of funk the man was in; one eye was over his shoulder towards the rocks at least as often as on the crowd, and his limbs were, well, like a sprinter's at scratch, ready to get off at once and make the maximum distance in the minimum time. I did not notice these things for long. It became painfully clear that I was the centre of interest and he the counsel for the prosecution.

"The counts against me were that I had forced him, the Arch-Priest, at the muzzle of the 'gun of death,' to take me into the sanctuary; that I had slain one of the sacred creatures, the children of the god, when there; that I had interfered with a Bohsan envoy on his lawful occasions, brutally maltreated him, and finally endeavoured to shoot him, but the god had turned the 'gun of death' aside. The penalty was—he raised his hands and waited, and from the whole assembly rolled back the word 'Death.'

"Even at that moment I could not help appreciating the old villain's anxiety that Kenelm should escape scot-free. Kenelm was less appreciative. He shouted that the man lied, that it was he who had laid violent hands on the envoy and that it was at the Arch-Priest's express invitation that I, very unwillingly, had entered the Temple.

"This last was awkward. The pontiff was an autocrat, a master of men, and as little loved of his colleagues as I of him. Yet he was a master of circumstance, too. Instead of rebutting the charge he pointed to the moon.

"'The time of sacrifice is at hand,' he cried. 'If it pass, the wrath of the god will be upon us. If this man come back unscathed, then we shall know they are both of the gods. If not, this man,' pointing to Kenelm, 'shall be reserved for the next festival.'

"That was a month distant, the artful, kindly old devil. I recognised that at once. So, too, did others.

"'Ay, to-morrow night. The Queen of Heaven' (a very strange phrase that) 'will still be in her glory,' came the reply, and the Arch-Priest could only bow his head.

"Four men led me to the crags. I did not struggle. There was no use, and I might want all my energy when the need came. A fifth carried my 'gun of death' and cartridge-belt before me, abusing and insulting them as if they were living things. Up the crags they took me by steps cut in the live rock, and stopped at the edge of a deep fissure, slanting inwards at an angle of about forty-five degrees. My gun and cartridge-belt were left at the foot of the staircase, and Number Five led the way, with his great pronged spear at the charge. It was shaking like a reed in the wind. To say I was the coolest of the six may, perhaps, not be saying much, but I was. My guards had but one thought—obsession, rather, and that was to be off. Down that fissure I had to go and smart, or be pitchforked down.

"I did find time to wave my hand to Kenelm. I could see him smile a farewell in the moonlight, and then—then he suddenly collapsed. It was just a glimpse. A sharp prod from the butt of a spear admonished me that the blade would come next.

"Some fifty feet down, the cleft ended in a kind of corridor. It was perhaps sixty feet long by about the same height, but the containing walls were not more than twenty feet apart at most. There were fissures on either side, of course, and at least one practicable chimney. The floor was covered with great shattered fragments, some obviously from a recent rock-fall. Along the western edge I could see against the sky the silhouettes of crags that maintained a precarious balance on the very verge.

"All these details were distinct: the rift faced due south and the full moon was at her zenith. At the end of the corridor was an ebony archway, and beyond that, blackness.

"I scrambled towards it. I did not intend to explore it. My plan was to remain a certain time in the corridor, concealed as well as possible, in case some lurking danger should come my way, and then slip out in the darkness by the way I had entered. Still, it was possible that danger might lurk beyond the archway.

"As I got close, I could make out it was the entrance to a tunnel tilting down into the bowels of the mountain. It was pitch dark beyond and nothing was to be gained by going further—when I thought I heard something stirring. I turned and peered into the blackness.

"At first I thought it was a ray of moonlight falling on some dull crystals. Then I saw that they were eyes,

eyes grouped together, eight of them, dull, expressionless, hateful, and behind, a dim, shapeless bulk. It was coming towards me and I knew it was Death.

"I slipped back into the corridor and cast about for a means of escape, and all the time knew it to be vain. Long before I could have struggled out of reach up the chimney the creature would be on me. Long before I could have reached the rocks I had descended I should be overtaken, and, in any case, beyond these were the Bohsanese.

"Upon the realisation an extraordinary clamor broke out and quick on it the spit, spit, spit of Kenelm's automatic. I can only conjecture that his faint was a ruse: I shall never know, here, anyway. Next minute his figure sprang into view against the sky at the top of the fissure. Almost simultaneously a backward glance showed that great menacing form issuing from the archway (even at that moment I noted that those evil eyes had disappeared). Kenelm saw it too.

"'Lie down, old man,' he shouted, and a bullet whistled down the corridor, and then. . . . Then I was brushed aside like a pebble as the monster sprang past me.

"I think Kenelm had time to fire again—in any case he might as well have used a squirt, poor fellow, and it was all over. I should like to think," he looked round the room piteously, "he did not suffer. It was so quick."

There was a sympathetic silence. No one had anything to say and did the right thing. After a pause Cotton resumed:

"What actually occurred I cannot tell. I was dashed aside, flung down, and half stunned, and, before I could get a grip of things, the monster was back, searching for me. I had been flung into the base of the chimney, on my back, face uppermost, that is, but I had sense enough to lie still. Then something light fell on my cheek, then more. I just unclosed my lids and could see above me the shapeless bulk of the creature reared up against the wall, searching and scraping at the sides of the chimney with a limb that looked something like a jointed Turk's head broom. Then it dropped down again and commenced raking about the floor of the corridor.

"It never touched me, though it missed me once and again by inches. Then it swung itself up to the skyline and I could see what it was. It was a spider, like those in the Temple, only quite ten times as large."

"I beg your pardon," began the Bug-Hunter. "Forgive me for interrupting—"

The entire room turned on him in horror. Was the man going to have the unutterably execrable taste to insist on his no-giant argument at such a time? The Bug-Hunter continued, quite unmoved.

"Could you tell me approximately about the size?"

"Yes." Cotton's voice showed neither hesitation nor resentment. "The body was about the size of one of those beer-casks you see on drays. The spread of the legs was perhaps twelve feet."

"Thanks. Then I think I may assure you that your brother did not suffer at all. The ordinary spider is quite poisonous enough, but its mandibles are almost microscopic. That monster's must have been the size of a tiger's holders and surcharged with venom equal to that of a hundred cobras. A touch would have been instant death. Instant and painless." Then, reflectively, "It must have had your unfort—your noble brother in full sight whilst you, so long as you remained prone, were invisible."

"Why?" asked someone.

"A spider's eyes are on the top of its head, to watch out against its winged enemies. Any object on a level with or below its head is quite out of sight."

"And didn't the brute know it?" exclaimed Cotton. He spoke almost with the lightness of a man from whom some heavy burden has been lifted. "It is my conviction, and I think you will all agree with me by and by, that the creature was actually devil-possessed. It was perfectly conscious of its disability. No sooner had it escaladed the containing wall than it swung itself head downwards and searched, literally searched the corridor with those dreadful, unchanging eyes of it; yet instantly on recognition of the nature of the monster I had slipped under cover of a shattered boulder and lay invisible. Why? I cannot explain. Instinct, perhaps. I certainly never anticipated such a move on the part of the spider.

"Its next actions puzzled me completely. It dropped down to the upper exit of the corridor and for a moment I feared it was going to recommence its hunt. But no! It started fussing up and down and to and fro across the rocks and then scurried across the top and went through similar antics at the chasm end. The moon was still shining almost directly into the fissure, which may give some idea of the swiftness of these happenings, and it seemed to me the light was a little duller than before, just a little, screened as it were. I did not dare to go and examine, at any rate not for a time. After a while the monster ceased its gymnastics and took post above me on the edge of the ravine, its ugly head clearly defined against the dark sky. Then, knowing that I could not be seen from above, I crawled towards the opening.

"The infernal brute—I have said it was devil-possessed—had webbed me in. Knowing I was still in the corridor, it had spun a web over both exits so that I could not attempt to escape without giving it instant notice, and that, too, of the exact spot at which the attempt was being made. Now that, I submit, was beyond the intelligence of any spider.

"To say I was not frightened would be to lie. I was sick with fear, but I did not despair. For a moment I was

chilled, chilled to shivering. Then a thought sent my blood
to fever heat. Outside, in the fissure, my dearest brother
was lying dead and, besides, I had a little score of my own
to settle with the Bohsanese. Escape I must.

"How? The solution lay literally to my hand. The floor
of the corridor was littered not only with boulders but
with chips of stone of all sizes. I picked up a pebble and
threw it at the moonlit web.

"The result was what I anticipated. The spider was
there in a flash. There was something hideously alert in its
action and poise. I did not stop to reflect on that. I picked
up another stone and threw it at the other web.

"Back went the spider faster even than it had come. We
are strangely constructed creatures. Within half an hour I
had steeled my courage to face some unknown ordeal, been
heart-broken with grief, overwhelmed with fear, and now
I found myself actually: chuckling at the thought of the
exercise I was giving that brute.

"It would not do to keep up the game too long. It might
try some other device and out-general me at the last. I felt
out a flat fragment of rock, thin as a bit of slate and sharp
almost as a knife, and laid it ready; then, picking up the
biggest stone I could handle, I hurled it through the lower
web and through the archway leading to the creature's lair.

"I do not know whether spiders have any sense of hearing, but I do know that that spider was off and out of
sight down that archway like a flash of black lightning,
and I know, too, that with a bound and two slashes I was
through the web, up the fissure, down the steps, and flat
amongst the blackest of black shadows of the boulders on
the plain in almost as little time as it takes to tell of it,
and not a moment too soon.

"Now I have said that all these happenings took place
within half an hour. All Boh San had come out in proces-
sion to see the sacrifice, not headed by the priests, and

all Boh San had, in due course, returned to the fortress headed by the priests. Nevertheless not one single item of the assembly had lingered on the return journey.

"Still processions at best are slow, clumsy things. At the expiration of half an hour the priests had reached the Temple and had lit the five ceremonial fires, one at each corner of the roof and the other in the centre. Not all Boh San by any means, however, was within the walls. The gate, the northern gate, was still open for the passage of the leisurely votaries. It was just about at that time that the deity of Boh San left its shrine amongst the rocks, the gate, the northern gate, was still wide open.

"It did not pause to look for me. I suppose it caught sight of the fires and they attracted it, or it scented prey. Anyhow, it was away across the plain in gigantic, ungainly bounds at a speed that would have left a gazelle standing still.

"Then across the moonlit stillness came a shriek such as I have never heard before and hope never to hear again, and then a most dreadful wail of despair. At that short distance, less than a mile in a direct line, lit up as they were by the red glare of the fires, I could see much of the details, the frantic, surging mob, jammed and crushed in the open gateway, the white-clothed priests, looking black against the flames, rigid one moment, then scattering, some desperately hurling brands from the fires at something that immediately afterwards loomed huge on the Temple roof. Then from below a tongue of flame shot up, then another. I did not require to look again to realise what had happened. Some of those flaming brands had fallen among the bamboo houses. Boh San was on fire.

"Within was a raging furnace with a raging devil. Without were the night and the jungle, and thither all who could fled for safety (it is remarkable that even at that crisis not one ventured on to the northern plain). Safety!

The jungle tribes had seen the conflagration and had gathered like vultures round a stricken quarry. I think the Bohsanese who perished in the burning fortress were the fortunate.

"I did not linger. I had a duty to perform. I picked up my rifle and cartridge-belt and went to look for Kenelm. He was lying peacefully, his face serene as a saint's, and quite undisfigured. Yes, I am sure his death was instantaneous and painless. I laid him in a cleft in the rock and covered him with stones till I could come and find him more fitting sepulchre. Yet all the time I kept an eye in the direction of Boh San. Before I had finished I could descry a dark, bloated form coming slowly across the plain.

"I had laid my plans for such an event. I slipped away up the hill-side and took post behind those toppling crags at the edge of the corridor. There at least was safe concealment, though that was not the first thought in my mind.

"I found myself panting. I must have hastened, but there had been no need. The monster was closer by then— not much, but close enough to see that it was moving not only slowly but painfully. I make no doubt it had been badly scorched in the burning town. It would have been right fitting had it been consumed there amongst its own accursed altars.

"I had not intended to use my rifle. It was an Express, not a poor, spitfire Browning, all that Kenelm had had, but now the temptation to lay out that foul demon plain for all men to see was strong. I rested my rifle on a rock and fired. The bullet went a fraction too high and struck the body. Probably it went straight through, causing no more pain than a pinch. The second got the monster fairly in the head. It staggered, then came on at increased speed. On reflection my belief is that it was so sorely hurt by fire and bullet that its one aim was to escape to its own horrid abode. I did not think so then. A creature of such vitality I might not be able to stop at all. I fired no more.

"I could hear it dragging itself up the rocks, and as it topped the edge of the fissure I caught sight of its eyes. They were dull. All the baleful light had gone out of them. I heard it, I even dared to watch it, as it scrambled down.

"One of those great balanced boulders I had noted before. So precariously was it poised that it had moved when the spider had brushed against it in one of its rushes to and fro from web to web, and I had shrunk into a fissure in the wall lest haply it should crash down. By this I waited till the monster was beneath me, then pushed with all my might.

"There was a scrunch below and I knew I had not missed. I knew, too, there was no more to be done, yet I sent down boulder on boulder till the perspiration poured from me. Then, bone weary, I struck out for the nearest French post."

There was a long silence when Cotton concluded. Men would have wished to have asked a score of questions, but all felt that such would have been unseemly. At length the Professor spoke:

"It is, at least, a consolation for you to think that your brother, if he has any knowledge of what happens here, must be satisfied."

"Yes," replied Cotton. "I think he is satisfied. At Boh San, the Seat of Satan, now stands a Medical Mission. At the Cotton Memorial Hospital, so far as human skill may, the sick are healed, the lame walk, the blind receive their sight, and, what is nearest to dear old Kenelm's soul, the Gospel is preached. Yes, I think he is satisfied."

The Ocean Leech

Frank Belknap Long, Jr. (1925)

I heard Boucke beating with his bare fists upon the cabin door and the wind whistling under the cracks. I objected to both and I opened the door wide. Boucke came in then, with a fierce rush of wind. He was a curious little man, with the sea and sky in his eyes, and he spoke in pantomime. He pointed towards the door and ran his fingers savagely through his reddish hair, and I knew that something had nearly finished him—I mean finished him spiritually, damaged his soul, his outlook.

I didn't know whether to be pleased or horrified. Boucke seemed more human with his queer, vivid gestures and flaming eyes, but I couldn't imagine what he had seen up on deck. Of course I found out soon enough.

The men were sitting about in idiotic groups of twos and threes and no one saluted me when I stepped out from the shadows of twisted cordage into a luminous stripe of moonlight.

"Where's the boatswain?" I asked.

Several of the men heard my question, and they turned and stared at me, and deliberately tittered.

"It took the boatswain!" said Oscar.

Oscar seldom spoke to anyone. He was tall and lean and his jaundiced scalp was fringed by yellow hair. I distinctly recall his dark, hungry eyes and his fringe of hair glistening in the moonlight. But the rest of Oscar I can no longer visualize. He has faded into an indefinite ghost of memory. It is curious, though, how clearly I remember every other shape and incident of that amazing night

Oscar was standing by my elbow, and I turned suddenly and gripped his arm. It reassured me to grip his strong, muscular arm. But I knew that I had hurt him, for his shoulder jerked and he looked at me reproachfully. I presume Oscar wanted me to stand upon my own feet. But he made a sweeping motion with his arm to assure me that it didn't matter. The wind whistled about our ears and the tattered sails flatted and wheezed. Sails can speak, you know. I have heard sails protest in chorus, each sail with a slightly different accent. You get to understand their conversation in time. On still mornings it is wonderful to come up on deck and hear the sails whispering among themselves. They make gestures, too, and when they are tired they sway pathetically against the sky.

I took a turn about the deck and bawled out the men and told them to go to the devil. Then I got my pipe out and blew grotesque yellow effigies into the cold air. They danced in the moonlight and made the situation irredeemable. I came back to Oscar eventually and asked him pointblank what he meant by "it." But Oscar didn't answer me. He simply turned, and pointed.

Something white and gelatinous oozed over the rail and ran or slid for several feet along the deck. Then a larger bulk seethed out of the darkness and stood poised above the black stern-post. A second object descended upon the deck, coming down with a thud and running at a tangent with the first over the smooth, polished boards. I saw two of the men get quickly to their feet, with wildish, jerky motions, and I heard Oscar shout out a curt command.

The thing upon the deck spread out and became broader at its base. It reared into the air a livid appendage encircled with monstrous pink suckers. We could see the suckers loathsomely at work in the moonlight, opening and closing and opening again. We were affected by a queer aromatic stench and we felt an overpowering sense of physical nausea. I saw one of the men reel backward and collapse upon the boards. Then a second idiot keeled over, and a third—a third actually advanced toward the loathsome object on his hands and knees, as if fascinated.

At that moment the moon seemed to draw nearer, to actually careen down the sky and hang above the cordage. Then suddenly the amorphous tentacles shot forward, like released hawsers, and struck against the nearest mast, and I heard a splintering, and a noise like thunder. The arms quivered and seemed to fly in all directions. Then they flopped back over the side.

I fastened my eyes upon our black topsail mastheads, and questioned Oscar in a very low voice. "Did that take the boatswain?"

Oscar nodded and shuffled his feet. The men on the deck whispered among themselves, and I knew intuitively that a spirit of rebellion was rife among them. And yet even Oscar exonerated me!

"Where would we have been if you hadn't brought us in here? A-drifting, probably—rudderless and sailless. Our sails may look like the skin on a water-logged corpse, but we can use 'em—when we can get the masts into shape. The lagoon looked innocent enough, and most of us were for coming in here. But now they whine like yellow puppies—and blame it on you. The idiots! If you just say the word—"

I stopped him. for I didn't want the men to take his proposal seriously, and he spoke loud enough for them to hear. The men, I felt, were scarcely to blame—under the circumstances!

"How many times has the *thing* crawled over the sides?" I asked.

"Eight times!" said Oscar, "it took the boatswain on the third trip. He shrieked and threw up his arms, and turned yellow! It twined itself about his leg, and set its great pink suckers to work on him; and the rest of us could do nothing—nothing! We tried to get him away, but you cannot imagine the sheer pull of that white arm. It oozed slime all over him, and all over the deck. Then it flopped back into the water, and carried him with it!

"After that we were more careful. I told the men to go below, but they only glowered at me. The thing fascinates them. They sit there and deliberately wait for it to return. You saw what happened just now. The thing can strike like a cobra, and it sticks closer than a lamprey; but the idiots won't be warned. And when I think of those quivering pink suckers I feel sorry for them—and for myself! He didn't utter a sound, you understand, but he turned livid under the gills and his tongue stuck out horribly, and just before he disappeared over the side I noticed that his lips were all black and swollen. But as I told you, he was immersed in yellowish slime, in ooze, and the life must have gone out of him almost at once. I'm sure that he didn't really suffer. With God's help, it's we who have to suffer!"

"Oscar," I said, "I want you to be quite frank, and if necessary, even brutal. Do you think that you can explain that thing? I don't want any wretched theories, Oscar. I want you to fashion a prop for me, Oscar, something for me to lean upon. I'm so very tired, and I haven't much authority here. Oh, yes, I'm supposed to be in command, but when there is nothing to go upon, Oscar, what can I say to them? How can I get them down into the cabin? I pity them so. What do you think it is, my friend?"

"The thing is obviously a cephalopod," said Oscar, quite simply, but there was a look of shame and horror in his eyes, which I didn't like.

"An octopus, Oscar?"

"Perhaps. Or a monstrous squid! Or some hideous un-classified species!"

A fabric of greenish cloud covered the face of the moon, and I saw one of the men crawling on his hands and knees along the deck. Then he gave a sudden, defiant scream, ran to the rail and held out his arms. A white exudation ran the entire length of the rail. It rose up and quivered amidst illimitable shadows, and then it poured in an abominable stream over the scuppers and enveloped the hectic form of the wretch, and it made no sound. The poor fool tried to get away. He screamed, made shocking grimaces, fell down upon the deck and tried to draw himself along by his hands. He pawed at the smooth slippery surface, but the thing had wound its tenebrous tentacles about his leg, and it pulled him. It pulled him slowly and hideously.

His head struck against the scuppers, and a crimson stream, no wider than a hawser rope, ran down the deck and formed a miniature pool at Oscar's feet. A sucker fastened upon his right temple, and another got in under his shirt and set to work upon his bare chest. I tried to get to him, but Oscar held fast to my arm, and would not tell me why. The body became white, slimy, changed before our eyes. And not one man stepped forward to prevent it. Suddenly, while we watched, the dead man, whose eyes had already glazed, was jerked forcefully toward the scupper's, again and again.

But he wouldn't go through. His head was soon pounded into an unimaginable resemblance of something we didn't care to think about, and we became deadly sick. But we watched, strangely fascinated, even perhaps more than a little resentful. We were watching something brutal and incredibly alive, and we beheld it in an unrestrained exercise of all its faculties. There, under a shrouded moon, in the phosphorescent wilderness of exotic waters, we saw the law of man outraged by something mute, misshapen, blasphemous, and we saw industrious retching matter, brainless and self-sufficient, obeying a law older than man. older than morality, older than sin. Here was life absorbing another life, and doing it forcefully, and without conscience, and becoming stronger and more exultant through the doing of it.

But it couldn't get the body through the scuppers. It pulled and pulled, and finally let go. The wind had gone down, and oddly enough, as it let go and fell back into the dead calm of water, we heard an ominous splash. We rushed forward, and surrounded the body. It seemed to swim in a river of white jelly. Oscar called for something which had become necessary, and we wrapped it up decently and threw it overboard. But Oscar repeated a few words mechanically out of the little black prayer-book, which he imagined were appropriate. I stood and stared at the dark opening in the forecastle.

I don't know to this day how I got the men through that dark opening. But I did it—with Oscar's aid. I can see Oscar standing with his glistening, head against a voiceless wilderness of stars, I can see him shaking his fists at the slinking cowards on the deck and shrieking out commands. Or were they insults? I know that I stepped forward and helped him, and I think I must have used my fists, for later on I discovered that my knuckles were bruised and discolored, and Oscar had to bandage them. It is queer, how Oscar has faded in my memory, for I thought a great deal of him, in spite of his queer ways, and his large hungry eyes, and his fringe of yellow hair. He helped me get the men into the forecastle, and so did Boucke. Boucke, with perfectly horrified face, and with lips quivering and struggling with a vicious inarticulateness!

We drove them in like sheep, but sheep often rebel and are troublesome. But we got them in. and then we turned and looked back at the gaunt masts, swaying soullessly against the lifeless, somber regularity of calm sea and sky, at the hanging ropes and frizzled sails, and at the long, moon-washed rails, and the encrimsoned scuppers. We heard Boucke inside, blubbering idiotically to the men. Then something made a dreadful guggling sound in the water, and we heard a loud splash.

"It's risen again," said Oscar, in a tone of despair.

I sat in my cabin, reading a book. Oscar had bandaged up my hands, and left, and he had promised not to disturb me

I endeavored to follow the little printed signs on the white page before me, but they called up no images, stimulated me to no response. The words did not take shape in my mind, and I did not know whether the stupid phrases that I sought to understand formed part of an essay or a short-story. The title of the book itself I cannot now recall, although I think that it had something to do with ships and the sea, and derelicts, and the pitfalls of over-imaginative skippers. I fancied that I could hear the water lapping against the side of the ship, and now and then a great splash.

But I knew that a portion of my brain hotly repudiated both the lapping and the splash, and I assumed myself that the nervous excitement under which I labored was but physical and momentary, and in no sense psychic or due to outside causes. My senses had been appalled, and I now suffered a natural reaction from the shock; but no new danger threatened me.

Something pounded upon the door. I got quickly to my feet, and it did not occur to me at that moment that Oscar had promised that no one should disturb me.

"What is it you want?" I asked.

There was no direct or satisfactory answer, but a queer guggling noise came to me through the door, and I fancied that I could hear a quick intake of breath. A horrible, intense fear took grim possession of me.

I looked at the door in white horror. It shook like broadyards in a gale. It bent inward under a terrific impact.

Thud followed thud, as if some monstrous body had hurled itself forward only to withdraw and to come back with additional momentum. I quelled an impulse to cry out, and I opened my mouth and shut it, and opened it again. I ran forward to assure myself that I had really bolted the door. I fingered the bolt caressingly, and then I retreated until my back was against an opposite beam.

The door bulged inward hideously, and immediately afterwards there followed a great crash, and a splintering and a sundering of wood and a retching of hinges. The door gave, fell inward and was lifted up on the back of something white and unspeakable. Then the panel was hurled violently against the wall, and the thing under it rolled forward, with terrible and increasing velocity. It was a long, gelatinous arm, an amorphous tentacle with pink suckers that slid or oozed towards me across the smooth floor.

I stood with my back pressed against the beam, with only my harsh, stertorous breathing to keep it at bay. I could see that it did not fear me, that arm, and I could do nothing. It was long and white and it *slid* towards me. Can I make you understand? And Oscar had bandaged my hands, and they were but feeble, fumbling instruments. And that thing was utterly intent upon its purpose, and it did not need eyes to guide it across the floor.

An ungodly, aromatic odor had entered the cabin with the thing, and it overpowered me almost before the tentacles seized upon me. I endeavored to slough off the great, loathsome folds with my bandaged hands, but my crippled fingers sank into the jellylike tissue as in soft mud. It was palpitating, living tissue, but it seemed to lack substantial body, and it gave horribly. It *gave!* My hands went right through it, and yet when it gripped me it was elastic and it could tighten its grip. It strangled me. I felt that I could not breathe. I bent and twisted but it had wound itself about me, and it held me, and I could do nothing.

I remember that I called for Oscar. I shouted myself hoarse, and then I think I was dragged ruthlessly across the floor, through the smashed-in door, and up the stairs. I remember now how my head pounded upon the stairs as we ascended, I and the thing, and I think that my scalp bled, and I know that I lost three teeth. I received dreadful blows, cuffs, from the corners of stairs, from the edges of doors, and from the smooth, hard boards of the deck itself.

The thing dragged me out across the deck, and I remember that I saw the moon through folds upon folds of obscenely bloating jelly. I was buried deep down within fatty, obscene folds that shivered and shook and palpitated in the moonlight!

I no longer felt any desire to protest or to cry out, and the thought of Oscar and a possible rescue did not fill me with elation. I began to experience sensations of pleasure. How am I to describe them? A peculiar warmth pulsed through me; my limbs quivered with a weird expectancy. I saw through the folds of animate jelly a great reddish sucker, or disk, lined with silver teeth. I saw it descend rapidly through the folds. It fastened upon my chest, and a momentary revulsion made me claw ludicrously at the nauseous tissue surrounding me. There was a kind of cruelty in the refusal of the flimsy stuff to offer any resistance. One could go on that way forever, clawing and tearing at the fatty folds, and feeling them give, and yet knowing that nothing could possibly come of it. For one thing, it was utterly impossible to get a hold on the stuff, to get it between your hands and squeeze it. It simply flipped away from you and then it rushed back and solidified. It could condense and dilate at will.

My feeling of horror and antipathy disappeared, and a new tide of exaltation, of warmth, of vigor surged over me. I could have wept or screamed with pleasure and genuine ecstasy.

I knew that the monster was actually drawing up my blood through its fumbling, convulsive suckers. I knew that in a moment I should be drained as dry as a grilled carbonado, but I actually welcomed my inevitable dissolution. I made no effort to conceal my glee. I was frankly hilarious, although it seemed unjust to me that Oscar should have to explain to the men. Poor Oscar! He tied up the loosened ends of things, smoothed over vulgar and disagreeable realities, made the raw, ungarnished facts almost acceptable, almost romantic. He was a precious stoic, and gloriously self-reliant. That I knew, and I pitied him. I distinctly recall my last conversation with him. He was slouching along the docks, with his hands in his pockets, and a cigarette between his teeth. "Oscar," I said, "I didn't really suffer when that thing fastened upon me! I didn't, really. I enjoyed it!" He scowled, and scratched his ridiculous fringe of hair. "Then I saved you from yourself!" he cried. His eyes blazed, and I saw that he wanted to knock me down. That was the last I saw of Oscar. He faded into the shadows after that, but had I kept him with me I might have been wiser.

The jelly about me seemed to increase in volume. It must have been three feet thick about my head, and I am sure that I saw the moon and the swaying mast-heads through a prism of varying colors. Waves of blue and scarlet and purple would pass before my eyes, and a taste of salt came into my mouth. For a moment I thought, not without a certain resentment and hurt pride, that the thing had really absorbed me, that I was a portion and parcel of that quivering, gelatinous mass—and then I saw Oscar!

I saw him looming above my obscene prison-house with a lighted torch in his hand. The torch, viewed through the magnifying folds of jelly, was a thing of flawless beauty. The flames shot out and appeared to cover the entire deck, and to go flying up against the darkness. The cordage and the luminous rails seemed afire, and a red and ravening serpent lengthened parallel with the scuppers. I saw Oscar clearly, and I saw the great spiral of smoke that streamed from the tails of flame, and I saw the swaying, encrimsoned masts, and the black sinister opening in the forecastle. The darkness seemed to part to let Oscar through with his torch and his stoicism. He swayed in the darkness above me, that silent, quixotic man, and I knew that Oscar could be trusted to put an end to things. I had no clear idea of what Oscar would do, but I knew that he would make some sort of brilliant and satisfying end.

I was not disappointed, and when I saw Oscar bend and touch the folds of jelly with his great, flaming torch I wanted to sing or shout. The folds quivered, and changed color, A maddening kaleidoscope of color passed before my eyes—flaming scarlet and yellow and silver and green and gold. The sucker released its hold upon my chest and shot upward through the voluminous folds. A terrific stench assailed my nostrils. The odor was unbearable: I threw out my arms and fought savagely to break through to reach the air and light and Oscar.

Then I felt the heat of Oscar's torch upon my cheek, and I knew that the tissue about me was falling away and burning to shreds. I saw that it was dissolving also, turning into oil, into grease, and I felt it hotly trickling down my knees and arms and thighs. I closed my lips tight to keep from swallowing large quantities of the nauseous fluid, and I turned my face to the deck to protect my eyes from the falling fragments of sizzling tissue. The creature was literally being burnt alive, and in my heart of hearts I pitied it!

When Oscar at length helped me to my feet I saw the last of the thing disappear over the side. Its arms were horribly charred and the suckers were gone, and I caught a momentary glimpse of dangling, frayed ends and reddish knobs and bulging protuberances. Then we heard a splash and a queer guggling sound. We looked at the deck, and saw that it was covered with greenish oil, and here and there great solid chunks of burnt tissue swam in the hideous porridge. Oscar bent and picked up one of the fragments. He turned it right side up in his hand, so that the moonlight fell upon it. It contained in its five-inch expanse a four-inch sucker. And the sucker opened and closed while Oscar held the thing in his hand. It fell from Oscar's hand like a leaden weight and bounded into the air. Oscar kicked it overboard and looked at me. I looked away towards the black topsail masthead.

The Abu Laheeb

Lord Dunsany (1926)

When I met my friend Murcote in London he talked much of his club. I had seldom heard of it, and the name of the street in which Murcote told me it stood was quite unknown to me, though I think I had driven through it in a taxi, and remembered the houses as being mean and small. And Murcote admitted that it was not very large, and had no billiard-table and very few rooms; and yet there seemed something about the place that entirely filled his mind and made that trivial street for him the centre of London. And when he wanted me to come and see it, I suggested the following day; but he put me off, and again when I suggested the next one. There was evidently nothing much to see, no pictures, no particular wines, nothing that other clubs boast of; but one heard tales there, he said— very odd ones sometimes; and if I cared to come and see the club, it would be a good thing to come some evening when old Jorkens was there. I asked who Jorkens was; and he said he had seen a lot of the world. And then we parted, and I forgot about Jorkens, and saw nothing more of Murcote for some days. And then one day Murcote rang me up, and asked me if I'd come to the club that evening.

I had agreed to come; but before I left my house Murcote surprised me by coming round to see me. There was something he wanted to tell me about Jorkens. He sat and

talked to me for some time about Jorkens before we started, though all he said of him might be expressed by the
one word 'liar.' Jorkens was a good-hearted fellow, he said,
and would always tell a story in the evening to anyone who
offered him a small drink;—whiskey and soda was what he
preferred;—and he really had seen a good deal of the world,
and the club relied on stories in the evening;—they were
quite a feature of it;—and the club wouldn't be the club
without them, and it helped the evening to pass, anyway;
but one thing he must warn me, and that was never to believe a word Jorkens said. It wasn't Jorkens' fault; he didn't
mean to be inaccurate; he merely wished to interest his
fellow members and to make the evening pass pleasantly. He
had nothing to gain by any inaccuracies, and had no intention to deceive; he just did his best to entertain the club,
and all the members were grateful to him. But once more
Murcote warned me never to believe one of his tales, or any
part of them, not even the smallest detail of local color.

"I see," I said, "a bit of a liar."

"Oh, poor old Jorkens," said Murcote, "that's rather
hard. But still, I've warned you, haven't I?"

And, with that quite clearly understood, we went down
and hailed a taxi.

It was after dinner that we arrived at the club; and we
went straight up into a small room, in which a group of
members was sitting about near the fire, and I was introduced to Jorkens, who was sitting gazing into the glow,
with a small table at his right hand. And then he turned to
Murcote to pour out what he had probably already said to
all the other members.

"A most unpleasant episode occurred here last evening,"
he said, "a thing I have never known before, and shouldn't
have thought possible in any decent club—shouldn't have
thought possible."

"Oh, really," said Murcote. "What happened?"

"A young fellow came in yesterday," said Jorkens. "They tell me he's called Carter. He came in here after dinner, and I happened to be speaking about a curious experience I had once had in Africa, over the watershed of the Congo, somewhere about latitude six, a long time ago. Well, never mind the experience, but I had no sooner finished speaking about it when the young fellow—Carter or whatever he is—said simply he didn't believe me, simply and unmistakably that he disbelieved my story; claimed to know something of geography or zoology which did not tally in his impudent mind with the actual experience that I had had on the Congo side of the watershed. Now, what are you to do when a young fellow has the effrontery, the brazen-faced audacity—"

"Oh, but we must have him turned out," said Murcote. "A case like that should come before the Committee at once. Don't you think so?"

And his eye turned to the other members, roving till it fell on a weary and weak individual who was evidently one of the Committee.

"Oh—er—yes," said he unconvincingly.

"Well, Mr. Jorkens," said Murcote, "we'll get that done at once."

And one or two more members muttered "Yes," and Jorkens' indignation sank now to minor mutterings, and to occasional ejaculations that shot out petulantly, but in an undertone. The waters of his imagination were troubled still, though the storm was partly abated.

"It seems to me outrageous," I said, but hardly liked to say any more, being a guest in the club.

"Outrageous!" the old man replied, and we seemed no nearer to getting any story.

"I wonder if I might ask for a whiskey and soda?" I said to Murcote, for a silence had fallen; and at the same time

I nodded sideways towards Jorkens to suggest the destina-
tion of the whiskey. I had waited for Murcote to do this
without being asked, and now he ordered three whiskies
and sodas listlessly, as though he thought there weren't
much good in it. And when the whiskey drew near the
lonely table that waited desolate at Jorkens' right hand,
Jorkens said, "Not for me."

I thought I saw surprise for a moment pass like a ghost
through that room, although no one said anything.

"No," said old Jorkens, "I never drink whiskey. Now
and then I use it in order to stimulate my memory. It has
a wonderful effect on the memory. But as a drink I never
touch it. I dislike the taste of it."

So his whiskey went away. We seemed no nearer that
story.

I took my glass with very little soda, sitting in a chair
near Jorkens. I had nowhere to put it down.

"Might I put my glass on your table?" I said to Jorkens.

"Certainly," he said, with the utmost indifference in
his voice, but not entirely in his eye, which caught the
deep yellow flavor as I put it close to his elbow.

We sat for a long time in silence; everyone wanted to
hear him talk. And at last his right hand opened wide
enough to take a glass, and then closed again. And a while
later it opened once more, and moved a little along the
table and then drew back, as though for a moment he
had thought the drink was his and then had realized his
mistake. It was a mere movement of the hand, and yet it
showed that here was a man who would not consciously
take another man's drink. And, that being clearly estab-
lished, a dreamy look came over his face as though he
thought of far-off things, and his hand moved very absent-
ly. It reached the glass unguided by his eye and brought it
to his lips, and he drained it, thinking of far other things.

"Dear me," he said suddenly, "I hope I haven't drunk your whiskey."

"Not at all," I said.

"I was thinking of a very curious thing," he said, "and hardly noticed what I was doing."

"Might I ask what it was you were thinking of?" I said.

"I really hardly like to tell you," he said, "to tell anyone, after the most unpleasant incident that occurred yesterday."

As I looked at Murcote he seemed to divine my thoughts, and ordered three more whiskies.

It was wonderful how the whiskey did brighten old Jorkens' memory, for he spoke with a vividness of little details that could only have been memory; imagination could not have done it. I leave out the details and give the main points of his story for its zoological interest; for it touches upon a gap in zoology which I believe is probably there, and if the story is true it bridges it.

Here then is the story: "One that you won't often hear in London," said Jorkens, "but in towns at the Empire's edge it's told of often. There's probably not a mess out there in which it's not been discussed, scarcely a bungalow where it's not been talked of, and always with derision. In places like Malakal there's not a white man that hasn't heard of it, and not one that believes it. But the last white man that you meet on lonely journeys, the last white man that there is before the swamps begin and you see nothing for weeks but papyrus—he believes in it.

"I have noticed that more than once. Where a lot of men get together, all knowing equally little, and this subject comes up, one will laugh, and they will all laugh at it, and none will trust his imagination to study the rumor, and it remains a rumor, no more. But when a man gets all alone by himself, somewhere on the fringe of that country out of which the rumor arises, and there's no silly laughter to scare his imagination—why, then he can study the thing and develop it, and get much nearer to facts than mere incredulity will ever get him. I find a touch of fever helps in working out problems like that.

"Well, the problem is a very simple one; it is simply the question whether man with his wisdom and curiosity has discovered all the animals that there are in the world, or whether there's one, and a very curious one too, hidden amongst the papyrus, that white men have never seen. And that's not quite what I mean, for there are white men that have seen things that not every young whipper-snapper will believe. I should rather have said an animal that our civilization has not yet taken cognizance of. At Kosti, more than twenty years ago, I first heard two men definitely speak of it,—the *abu laheeb* they called it,—and I think they both believed in it too; but Khartoum was only a hundred and fifty miles off, and they had evening clothes with them, and used to wear them at dinner, and they had china plates and silver forks, and ornaments on their mantelpiece, and one thing and another; and all these things seemed to appall their imagination, and they wouldn't honestly let themselves believe it. 'Had three or four fires round his tent,' said one of them, telling of someone, 'and says that the abu laheeb came down about two a.m., and he saw it clear in the firelight.' 'Did it get what it wanted?' said the other. 'Yes—went away hugging it.'

"And one of them said in a rather wandering tone: 'The only animal that uses—' He was lowering his voice, and looking round, and he saw me, and said no more. They turned it all away at once with a laugh or two, as Columbus might have turned away from the long low line of land and refused to believe a new continent. I questioned them, but got no information that could be of any use;

they seemed to like laughter more than imagination, so I got jokes instead of truth.

"It was weeks later and far southwards that I found a man who was ready to approach this most interesting point of zoology in the proper spirit of a scientist, a white man all alone in a hut that he had near the mouth of the Bahr-el-Zeraf. There are things in Africa that you couldn't believe, and the Bahr-el-Zeraf is one of them. It rises out of the marshes of the White Nile, and flows forty or fifty miles, and into the White Nile again. And one can't easily believe in a white man living all alone in such a place as that, but somebody has to be the last white man you see as you go through the final fringes of civilization, and it was him. He had had full opportunities of studying the whole question of the abu laheeb, he had had years of leisure to compare all the stories the natives brought him, which they shyly told when he had won their confidence, though what he won it with he never told. He had sifted the evidence and knew all that was told about it; and in long malarial nights, with no one and nothing to care for him but quinine, he had pictured the beast so clearly that he could make me a very good drawing of it. I have that drawing to this very day—a beast on his hind legs something like a South American sloth that I once saw, stuffed, in a museum; built rather on the lines of a kangaroo, but much stouter and bigger, and with nothing pointed about his face; it was square and blunt, with great teeth. He had hand-like paws on shortish arms or forelegs.

"I must tell you that I was in a small dahabeeyah, going up those great rivers, any great rivers I might meet, leaving civilization because I was tired of it, and looking for wonders in Africa. And I came to this lonely man.— Lindon his name was,—full of curiosity aroused by those words that I had heard in Malakal. And talking to Lindon like two old friends that have spent all their schooldays

together, as white men will who meet in that part of
Africa, I soon came to the abu laheeb, thinking he would
know more of it than they knew in Malakal. And I found
a man grown sensitive, as you only can grow in loneliness:
he feared I would disbelieve him, and would scarcely say
a word. Yes, the natives believed in some such animal, but
his own opinion he would not expose to the possibility
of my ridicule. The more questions I asked, the shorter
the answers became. And then I drew him by saying,
'Well, there's one thing he uses that no other animal ever
did,' the one mysterious thing about this beast that had
haunted my mind for weeks, though I did not know what
on earth the mystery was. And that got him talking. He
saw that I was committed to belief in the beast, and was
no longer shy of his own.

"He told me that the upper reaches of the Bahr-el-Zeraf
were a god-forsaken place: 'And if God forsook the Zeraf,'
he said, 'He certainly didn't go to the Jebel,' for the Bahr-
el-Jebel was worse. And somewhere between those two
rivers in the desolation of papyrus the abu laheeb certainly lived. He very reasonably said that there were beasts in
the plains, beasts in the forests, and beasts in the sea; why
not in the huge area of the papyrus into which no man
had ever penetrated? If I chose to go to these god-forsaken
places I could see the abu laheeb, he said. 'But, of course,'
he added, 'you must never go up wind on him.' 'Down
wind?' I said. 'No, nor down wind either,' he answered.
'He can smell as well as a rhino. That's the difficulty; you
have to go just between up wind and down wind; and you
always find the north wind blowing there.'

"It was some while before I discovered why one can't go
up wind on him. I didn't like to over-question Lindon, for
questions are akin to criticism, and you cannot apply criticism and cross-examination to the patient work of imagination upon rumor; it is liable to destroy the whole fabric,

and one loses valuable scientific data. Nor was Lindon in
the mood for the superior disbelief of a traveler only just
come from civilization; he had had malaria too recently to
put up with that sort of thing. It was as he was giving me
various clear proofs of the existence of some such animal
that I suddenly realized what it all meant. He was telling
me how more than once he had seen fires in the reeds, not
only earlier in the year than the Dinkas light their fires,
but in marshes where no Dinka would ever come, nor a
Shilluk either, or any kind of man—marshes utterly desolate and for ever shut to humanity. It was then that the
truth flashed on me—truth, sir, that I have since verified
with my own eyes: that the abu laheeb plays with fire.

"Well, I needn't tell you how the idea flared up in my
mind to be the first white man that had ever seen the abu
laheeb, and to shoot him and bring his huge skin home,
and have something to show for all that lonely wandering.
It was a fascinating idea. I asked Lindon if he thought my
rifle was big enough,—I only had a .350,—and whether
to use soft-nosed or solid bullets. 'Soft,' he said. I sat up
late and asked him many questions. And he warned me
about those marshes. I needn't tell you of all the things he
warned me against, because you see me alive before you;
but they were there all right, they were there. And I went
down the little path he'd made from his house to the bank
of the river, and went on board my sailing boat under huge
white bands of stars, and lay down on board and looked up
at them from under my blankets until I fell asleep, while
the Arabs cast off and the north wind held good. And
when the sun blazed on me at dawn I woke to the Bahr-el-
Zeraf. Scarlet trees with green foliage at first; we were not
yet come to those marshes.

"Well, for days we went up the Zeraf, past the white
fish-eagles, haughty and silent and watchful on queer
trees, with birds sailing over us that I daren't describe to

you for fear you should think I exaggerate the brilliancy of their colors. And so we came to those marshes where anything might hide, and be utterly hidden by those miles of rushes, and be well enough protected from explorers by a region of monotony more dismal than any other desolate land I've seen. And all the while the sailors were talking a language I did not know, till my imagination, brooding in that monotony, seemed to hear clear English phrases now and then starting suddenly out of their talk, commonest phrases of our daily affairs, on the other side of the earth. I would swear that I heard one of them say one evening, 'Stop the bus a moment.' But it couldn't have been, for they were talking Dinka talk, and not one of them knew a single word of English; I used to talk Arabic of a sort to the reis.

"Well, at last we came on fires in the reeds, burning at different points. Who lit them I couldn't say; there were no men there, black, white, or grey (the Dinkas are grey, you know). But I wanted absolute proof; and then one day I found his tracks in the rushes. He bounds through the rushes, you know, often breaking several of them where he takes off, and sometimes scattering mud on the tips of them as he springs through; then alighting and taking off again, leaving another huge mark.

"I examined the rushes carefully, till I was sure that I had his tracks. And then I followed them, always watching the wind. It was a dreadful walk. I went alone so as to make less noise. I wanted to get quite close and make sure of my shot. I had a haversack tied close round my neck, and my cartridges were in that. Even then it got wet sometimes. The water was always up to my waist, and often it came higher. I had to hold up my rifle in one hand all the time. The reeds were far over my head.

"Sometimes one came to open spaces of water, with huge blue water-lilies floating on them. And it was always deeper there. Sometimes one walked upon the roots of the rushes, and all the rushes trembled round one for yards, and sometimes one found a bottom of good hard clay and knew one could sink no further. And all the while I was tracking the abu laheeb.

"The north wind blew as usual. I was too old a shikari to be walking down wind, but I was not always able to act strictly on Lindon's advice about never going up wind on the abu laheeb, because his tracks sometimes led that way. At any rate, that was better than the other direction, for he would have been off at once. You wouldn't believe how tired one can be of blue water-lilies. At any rate the water was not cold, but the weariness of lifting each foot was terrible. Each foot, as one lifted it for every step, one would rather have left just where it was for ever. I don't know how many hours I tracked that beast, I don't know what time was doing while I walked in those marshes. But in all that weariness of spirit and utter fatigue of limb I suddenly saw a scrap of quite fresh mud on the tip of one of the reeds, and knew that I was getting near him at last. I put the safety catch of my rifle over, and suddenly saw in my mind what I was so nearly doing for Science. Of all the steps Science had taken from out of the early darkness toward that distant point of which we cannot guess, which shall be full of revelations to man, one of her footsteps would be due to me. I could, as it were, write my name on that one footprint, and no one would question my right to.

"I got nearer and nearer. I was no longer weary now; and suddenly, closer than I had dared to hope, was a little puff of smoke above the rushes. I stopped for one moment to steady my breath, and got my rifle ready. In that moment I named him—yes, I called him *Prometheus Jorkensi*. There was a patch of dry land ahead, and the rushes still protected me. I moved with ten-inch paces so as to make no ripple, but I couldn't keep the rushes quiet; perhaps the north wind blew stronger than I thought, for he never seemed to hear me. And then, oh so close that it couldn't have been ten yards, I saw the little fire on a patch of earth; and the rushes still hid me completely. I saw a patch of brown fur and a huge body crouching. I could only guess what part of the body I saw, but a vital part I thought, and I raised my rifle. Still it had no idea I was anywhere near it. And then I saw its hands stretched out to the fire, warming themselves by the edge of those bleak marshes. I don't cut much ice, you know; I didn't then; no one had ever heard my name, or, if they had, it meant nothing; and here was I on the verge of this discovery, with the proof of it ten yards away just waiting for a rifle bullet. I'd shoot a monkey, I'd shoot an ape, I'd shoot a poor old hippo; I wouldn't mind shooting a horse if it had to be killed, though lots of men can't bear that; but those black hands stretched out over the fire were the one thing I couldn't destroy.

"The idea that flashed on me standing amongst those reeds I have been turning over in my mind for years, and it always seemed sound to me, and it does even now. You see, of all the links in the world that there are between us, and of all the barriers against those that are not as us, it seems to me that there is one link, one barrier, more outstanding than any other you could possibly name. We talk of our human reason, that may or may not be superior to the dream of the dog or the elephant: we say it is—that is all. We say that we alone have belief in an after-life, and that the lion has not: we say so—that's all. Some of them are stronger, some live longer than us, many may be more cunning. But there is one thing, gentlemen, one thing they haven't got, and that is the knowledge of fire. That seems to me the great link, the great bond between all who have it and the barrier against all who have not.

Look what we've done with it: look at those fire-irons,
that fender, the bricks of which this house is made, and
the steel structure of it; look at this whole city. That's our
one great possession—knowledge of fire. And, when I saw
those dark hands stretched out to that fire on the edge of
the marshes, that is what I thought of all at once, not at
such length as I have told you of course,—it flashed all
through my mind in a moment,—but during that moment
I hesitated, and the abu laheeb saw the sun on the tip
of my rifle or heard me breathing there, for he suddenly
craned his great neck over the rushes, then stooped again
and scattered the fire with his forepaws with one swift jerk
into the reeds all round me. They were alight at once, and
through the flame and smoke I only dimly caught sight of
him leaping away, but, above the crackle of the burning
reeds and the thump of his hind legs leaping, I heard him
uttering gusts of human-like laughter."

He paused a moment. We were all quite silent, thinking
what he had lost. He had lost a famous name. He shook
his head, and seemed full of the same thoughts as the rest
of us.

"I never went after him again," he said. "I had seen
him, but who'll believe that? I have never quite been able
to bring myself any more to try to shoot a creature that
shared that great secret with us."

There was silence again; we were wondering, I think,
whether his scruples should have prevented him from doing so much for Science. I suppose that the too-sensitive
and over-scrupulous seldom make famous names. A man
leaning forward, and smoking a pipe, took his pipe out of
his mouth and broke the silence at last.

"Mightn't you have photographed him?" he said.

"Photographed him!" said Mr. Jorkens, straightening
himself up in his chair. "Photographed him! Aren't half

the photographs fakes? Here, look at the *Evening Picture*. Look at that, now. There's a child handing a bouquet to someone with its left hand, so that both of them may expose as much of their surface as possible to the camera. And here's a man welcoming his brother from abroad. Welcoming indeed! They are both of them being photographed, and that's obviously all that they're doing."

We looked at the paper and it was so; they were almost turning their backs on one another in order to be photographed.

"No," he said, and he looked me straight in the eyes, and flashed that glance of his from face to face. "If Truth cannot stand alone, she scorns the cheap aid of photography."

So dominant was his voice as he said these words, so flashed his eyes in the dim light of the room, that none of us spoke any more. I think we felt that our voices would shock the silence. And we all went quietly away.

The Whistling Monsters
B. Wallis (1926)

Deegan groaned. He lay tightly trussed on the narrow strip of shingle beach that stretched from the placid, somber pool to the great cliff here thrusting its vast bulk across the chasm, which hereafter continued simply as a gloomy, narrow cleft riven possibly by some Cyclopean convulsion of bygone eons.

The man by his side made no response and continued to stare at the opposite wall with increasing intensity, as though oblivious to the tight-drawn rawhide thongs which bound them both. With a scowl of irritation, Deegan painfully twitched his grizzled head to one side and succeeded in catching a fleeting glimpse of Vance, his partner.

"Well, what are you so quiet about?" he snarled. "What are you thinking about, anyway? When these blasted thongs dry out you'll make enough noise, I'll gamble!" he sneered, alluding to the fact that the Indians with customary cruelty had soaked the lashings, previous to the trussing, so that their captives might taste the tortures of hell for many fearful hours before death released them. Indeed, now and again a slight twist of lip or quiver of muscle already indicated that the thongs were contracting, and no more than an hour had passed since the two men had been brutally flung on the sharp-edged rubble.

"Thinking about? Well, what would I be thinking about—grand opera or Einstein?" replied Vance with no effort to conceal the contempt which for some while had been simmering within him; in so many ways had his partner fallen short of the clean-cut standard the college-bred man held as the unquestionable creed of good fellowship.

"Reckoned you was sayin' your prayers, or maybe worryin' over having no pajamas," sneered Deegan with ponderous sarcasm, inwardly assured that the young fellow was flushing with resentment.

Curiously these two had come together and joined fortunes in this wild crude country. Barely a month before, a few drinks in a garish saloon had afforded the only introduction the etiquette of the Guianas demanded. For six months Dick Vance had manfully wrestled with the appalling accounts of a certain branch bank to which the influence and indifference of a wealthy uncle had banished him when the crash following upon his father's sudden demise exposed the flimsy structure upon which the departed parent had built his reputation for probity and solidity. Straight from Harvard to this dreary slavery could have but one ending for such a spirited, athletic young fellow, and the inevitable happened. Moreover, Deegan required the five hundred which constituted Vance's sole legacy from a father who had often thrown away more than this upon a single night's entertainment. Had it not been Deegan, then certainly some other and possibly more unsavory adventurer would have pulled the trigger which shot Vance from his desk into the savage wilds of the interior.

From the first day's strenuous upstream paddling the partnership had proved far from amicable, close association discovering a diversity of habit and temperament neither could bridge. The college man of cleanly habits and sensitive breeding held no point of kindred amity with the grizzled illiterate partner who had doggedly held his own since early boyhood in bitter warfare with the roughest of his kind and the rawest of implacable nature.

In a hundred trifling daily details each jarred on the other and aroused his enmity, and indeed, had it not been that mutual welfare demanded the protection and aid of each other, their partnership would have been brief. However, this was impossible; possessed of strong wills, neither had the slightest intention of abandoning the search for the gold, of whose presence in the distant range Deegan affirmed he had reliable testimony. And it was this range for which they were heading when disaster overtook them. Therefore, though entirely against their liking, they held together.

To such a length had this intolerance of each other carried them that on every occasion when divergence of opinion was possible a set course was adopted only after a prolonged wrangle; and twenty-four hours back, on arriving at an outlying spur of their objective, they had decided to encamp and reconnoiter for a day or so. Even on such slight provocation they came into conflict, Vance preferring a space of almost clear and level ground backed by a bluff and affording unbroken observation on all other sides, a practical and commonsense suggestion Deegan would naturally have adopted had Vance not unfortunately voiced his approval. Immediately Deegan had proffered bitter opposition, and in such matters the weight of years and experience prevailed against youth and inexperience. And it came about that their camp lay close to a strip of dense jungle sweeping from the level ground far up a steep slope between two out-flung ridges. As dawn broke the disaster occurred; rushed by the wild Amaripas—a little-known and implacable savage people of the upper Guiana—the two men were quickly overpowered before they had time to snap a trigger.

Expecting at the best an instant and bloody ending, the captives were surprised to find themselves picked up

quietly and borne shoulder-high by some half a dozen stal-
wart savages. An hour or so later they had been silently
flung on the shingle beach, and after a hasty but very
efficient tightening of the bonds their captors had departed with barely a dozen words spoken. And in truth Vance
had noted that they appeared ill at ease and eyed the spot
with alert glances of apprehension.

From where Vance lay, he failed to note any reason for the
Indians' apparent dread of the place. True, it was wild and
forbidding like all canyons, though lower down he had noticed many sections where the walls on each side receded
and gave place to steep slopes of broken hillside running to
the base of distant bluffs. But here at the journey's end the
walls drew in and towered aloft in vast frowning heights,
and the canyon terminated, or at any rate continued only
at a higher level, for the shallow creek through which the
two men had often splashed now fell from a great height
into the wide black pool they lay beside. Certainly it was a
wild, cheerless spot, and the walls were grimly black, and
stained by weather and age, and dank with a pervading
seepage from the surrounding hills; only coarse ferns and
pendulous giant mosses clinging to clefts and niches to
hint that life could still survive even in this grim sterility.
Yet beyond the inborn antipathy of the human species to
gloom and solitude Vance failed to note any reason for
their marked distaste of the spot.

"Deegan, you're a blithering fool, and a blind one, too,"
asserted Vance dispassionately, and the deliberate insult of
his tone pierced the tough armor of its target.

"You—you blasted pup!" was all the enraged Deegan
could retort.

"Suppose we cut out this stuff," suggested Vance in a
bored and weary tone. "I merely intended to draw your
attention to the fact that the rubble across this pool is, I

presume, a fair sample of the beach under us, and if you note closer to the wall the fragments are larger and, being higher up, not waterworn. Now it seems to me that possibly by a distressing effort we might reach this jagged stuff, and—well, perseverance and friction have been known to have a deteriorating effect on many substances," he added meditatively.

"Curse your highbrow junk! What in thunder are you—?" And then abruptly Deegan's wrathful growl subsided and a sudden surprise and fierce hope swept into his eyes.

"Huh! That's so—well, what of it! We ain't there," he said grudgingly, yet commencing to strain and contract his muscles in an effort to roll on his side and verify Vance's surmise.

About the same second both succeeded in facing the bluff. Hardly a dozen feet distant it towered upward for at least two hundred feet, and for the first fifty feet it presented a face almost as smooth as a vast sheet of plate glass, black, vitreous and sheer. Plainly an intrusive stratum of igneous origin, for across the pool also lay this forbidding face; while above and to each side of its thirty-foot width the enclosing bluff was badly shattered, a jumbled mass of deep fissures, broad ledges, and receding terraces where grew a matted miniature jungle of stunted shrubs, rank creepers and giant mosses fed by the seepage from many a mile of surrounding range and here coalescing into tiny rivulets that ceaselessly dripped as a transparent veil down the bare lowermost wall. Age, extreme age, was indelibly stamped on this somber chasm, and the grim walls were touched by vanished eons when the new-born world scarce had been released from the labors of its birth.

But for the two fettered men there lay but one absorbing problem—the dozen feet of sloping rubble which stood between them and the more recent droppings of larger sharp-edged fragments which lined the base of the bluff.

How could that space be traversed? For only by the most strenuous effort and a more than Spartan stoicism had the little matter of a mere turning where they lay been effected, already their drying rawhide fetters had drawn so taut.

Deegan was the first to break the silence. "I dunno," he said thoughtfully. "But I'll try." And for the first time in many days his voice had lost the jeering, overbearing note which had so angered his partner. "Say, Vance, are you game to help? It'll be hell, but we got to win, and I ain't sure I can stay with it alone." And as if the acknowledgment exposed a flaw in his manhood, his voice betrayed a shy hesitancy almost ludicrous in one of his self-reliant, assertive nature.

"Go ahead, Deegan, I'll do my best," said Vance simply. As before he had been the nearer to the pool, so now he was the farther from their goal, though barely by a pace.

"Well, it's this way. I got it doped out I'm going to roll up this blasted slope, but if I ain't got a stopper behind I'll roll back sure. If you could hitch around to grab my pants in your teeth I reckon between us we might make shift to wedge you T-shape agin' my middle and you'd act as a stopper for my next turn uphill. It'll hurt like hell, partner," Deegan added gravely and apologetically.

"What if it does? If you can stick it, that goes with me," Vance replied stubbornly, though not ill-naturedly.

And without further parley they commenced as frightful and grueling a contest as ever was waged; for from the first moment it required indomitable will to endure the excruciating agony which racked every inch of their swollen, tortured flesh—a trial of endurance and fortitude in which neither of the contestants would admit a better man than himself, and each would rather have died of agony and exhaustion than suffer defeat.

Inch by inch they wormed their way across the sloping rubble, and with every inch some stiffening thong cut even more deeply in the sunken furrows where the flesh had burst and the thong vanished. Sweat and blood bathed them in mingled streams, clotted and dried as it welled through their garments, so that soon they caked and rasped the flesh beneath, wearing it into broad raw weals where the exposed nerves ceaselessly writhed in torment.

Life had resolved into a mere sensation—a frightful nightmare of pain—and an obsession which dominated it: the obsession that no torture hell could conjure would compel either to slacken for a single second and acknowledge himself the lesser man. Alone, or with a kindred spirit, then the thing would have been impossible—simple flesh and blood could never have endured it, and life itself would have been gladly surrendered to sink into the Nirvana of surcease.

How long the passage of that dozen feet encompassed they never knew. Time had ceased, swallowed up in the greater dimension of sensation, and alone was marked by the inches of the gory trail they had come. And at last they scaled that slope.

"Done, by heaven!" croaked Deegan raucously.

And Vance simply laughed a harsh, choking cachinnation more animal than human; then for a little both lay still and silent

"Got to get moving—scrapes stiffen soon," muttered Deegan, and the thick utterance issued from his cracked lips as though dragged forth by rack or fire.

"I know—keep moving," mumbled Vance in response to some hazy train of reasoning. And at once his muscles responded to the suggestion and commenced to work and strain against the hellish bite of his fetters.

A little fumbling and squirming and Deegan found a sharp-edged fragment firmly lodged, and successfully wedging himself in a position which brought his bound wrists in contact with it he commenced a ceaseless sawing movement that only his iron muscles and indomitable will could have sustained. Between his fettered wrists, where he essayed by this primitive tool to fray the thongs, the space would scarce have housed a knife-blade, and quickly the jagged stone had rasped the flesh from his wrists and hands as each slight motion backed by the weight of his bulk drove the rough edge deeper between them. But moment after moment, without pause, the clocklike pulsing of muscle held on, and ever his upturned rugged face was set as grim and passionless as the rock beneath him. Then suddenly Deegan rolled on his side and a deep groan broke from his blood-stained lips, and in the same breath there followed a whispered curse.

"Hell's curses on the scum!" he said with intense bitterness.

"You're free!" exclaimed Vance harshly.

"I got the use of my arms—but the blasted things seem made of red-hot stone," growled Deegan as he strove to recover their mobility. And in a little his arms, moving in curious mechanical jerks, obeyed his will. "I'm boss of you, anyway!" he muttered, savagely eyeing with morose vindictiveness the offending members. Then picking up a sharp-edged splinter of the black rock, he turned his efforts upon his legs, and shortly the last thong had been severed.

"Blast you!" he cried, and picking up a handful of the crimson-painted lengths he cast them savagely into the pool below; and scarcely had they alighted with a loud swish and a flutter of spray when a deep-noted, resonant whistle rang out, echoed from wall to wall and died away in a trembling whisper.

The slightest movement now was for Vance unspeakable torture, yet with a single convulsive heave he turned on the instant to face the apparent source of that astounding sound, some twenty feet up the opposite dank bluff where at the lower end of the pool the black ledge gave place to the fissured, friable country rock. Deegan had jerked unsteadily to his feet and stood staring blankly across the pool.

"What in thunder was that!" he cried in a hushed voice as the echoes ceased.

"How should I know?" replied Vance in a hoarse whisper. "A whistle! But who would whistle here! And where is he!"

"But it *was* a whistle!" asserted Deegan irritably. "And it came from up there," he added, pointing to the spot both had instantly identified as its source. Yet it was plain that there no human being could have escaped immediate detection; for though the rock was badly fractured and fissured, and rank growths of giant mosses and broad-leaved creepers lay in dense covering, it was obvious that no cover existed for anything approaching the bulk of the human species.

As their gaze swept searchingly the grim and aged wall, that clear, shrill, single note was again repeated, but now in a higher key and rising to a penetrating clarity of volume at its abrupt cessation; and now it seemed located at the extreme limit of the canyon where a transverse rent gaped mistily through the veil of spray into which the little creek in its final leap had dissolved before reuniting in the somber pool.

"But what is it!" exclaimed the elder man in a hushed tone of great bewilderment as he leaned forward and peered frowning at the partly opaque veil of saturated vapor through which loomed but mistily the fissure, thereafter passing behind an outflung buttress which seemed to conceal some slight recession of the wall at that spot.

"Say, Deegan, it might be as well to cut me loose," said Vance impatiently; for unable to view this fresh location his pangs with avid savagery renewed their torture.

"Sure! Anyway, the quicker we beat it the better. There's something mighty queer around here," replied Deegan as he straightway dropped to his knees and, selecting a sharp-edged splinter of rock, rolled his partner quickly, though not ungently, face downward and commenced to saw vigorously at the thongs about his wrists. For all his thick fingers and stiffened muscles he wrought so skilfully that he barely grazed the swollen flesh that almost hid the taut lashings. And as he worked, the astounding whistle several times burst out afresh in new and widely separated locations, yet never for a second did he relax his toil until the numbed arms fell apart and the agony of liquid fire coursed through Vance's quickened veins.

"Keep your arms moving, no matter how it hurts," counseled Deegan tersely as he turned to the other fetters, apparently oblivious of the increasing numbers and volume of the vibrant metallic chirpings, each succeeding its predecessor so rapidly that it seemed as though some signal was being transmitted from one to another of their unguessable sources.

Then the last thong had been severed and Vance was free; and though for the succeeding few moments his release afforded him no greater freedom of movement and his sufferings were no less, yet the clamor had abruptly increased so obviously that his gaze flitted in startled surprise from point to point, seeking some tangible source of the momentarily increasing din.

"Look there! I saw the brush move up there!" exclaimed Vance as he extended jerkily a stiff and swollen arm, pointing to a spot within the narrowed radius of vision from his prone position; here a wide V-shaped crack came to an apex almost at the canyon floor a little below the lower end of the pool, and so densely massed were the dwarfed rank growths therein that the least move amid it could not help but sway a wide area above.

"Yes, I get it! There's more above—must be a crowd, whatever it is," asserted the older man, staring intently at the spot which from his erect position he could discern much more extensively and distinctly. And the movement swaying the vegetation was at once perceptible to him.

Then Vance, who had not ceased his efforts to regain control of his limbs, succeeded in struggling to a sitting posture. Now another angle of the canyon was thrust upon him, and his field of view embraced their own side of the water. High up the towering wall where the grim igneous strata dipping at a sharp angle sank below the enclosing broken bluffs, a bold boss of weathered surface exposed its smooth nudity. Here a something, neither shrub nor creeper, had caught his eye.

"Deegan, what's that?" he cried in an urgent whisper, and his partner, wheeling sharply, glimpsed for a second the moving thing before it vanished with a soundless flowing swiftness.

"Like a snake," declared Deegan, pondering. "But it wasn't a snake," he added with conviction. And then just beside them a little fragment of stone hit with a harsh clatter and bounced to the rubble slope below, in a fraction of a second spanning the space they had blazed with their blood and an hour of frightful agony.

"What the devil now!" exclaimed Deegan as he jerked back his thick muscular neck and stared up at the black height above them.

At the same second they both saw it.

"Hullo!" cried Vance.

"Hell!" growled Deegan.

For a moment they gazed in wonder at the clear-cut crest, fully fifty feet above where the crumbling, riven rock had sloughed away and left a broad, sharp-edged shelf.

"Say, this gets on my nerves! We'd better get a move on; can you make it?" cried Deegan with anxious solicitude.

"In a fashion—once I get moving I guess I'll be all right," replied Vance doubtfully. And as they spoke both men remained staring intently at the queer, dull yellow blotch that lay balanced and motionless in unnatural poise partly overhanging the edge of the shelf.

This thing was unlike anything they had ever seen, or dreamt of. It seemed such an indescribable, structureless mass for a living creature to possess; yet no doubt of its living nature had lain upon them from the first glimpse. But what was it?

Unconsciously groping for some base of familiar similarity by which to mend their abruptly shattered certitude, they utterly failed to grasp a single point of resemblance to any form of terrestrial life within their knowledge. In some dim fashion there lay a suggestion of remote kinship to those lingerers of a long bygone age, the marine octopi, this thing having an indefinite number of long tapering tentacles and an oval central mass maintaining an erect posture, gourdlike in shape, and a sickly yellow hue which tinged every inch of its many folds and ridges. But here resemblance ceased, for the snaky limbs arose from a wide, thick membrane fully three feet in diameter, which radiated from the central protuberance, of which it was plainly an extension that dwindled to a mere parchment webbing between the repulsive tentacles at their base. Two smooth grisly lengths were drooping down the wall and obviously gripping tightly to some slight prominence, for their great sinews rose like steel cables far into the flaccid membrane. It was the nameless thing of a nightmare; so bizarre and inexplicable that for a moment the two men stared in blank amazement—stared until an undulating movement swayed the thick membrane and another tentacle came rapidly writhing down the smooth black rock, swinging gently from side to side, touching lightly and searchingly here and there until some feet below it had reached its full extension and there it remained tapping softly at the glassy surface as if seeking to discern a second point of hold. Then from the motionless mass above broke a deep, clear, metallic whistle; and as if the note conveyed some intelligible message the neighbor chorus that had somewhat diminished now burst out afresh from a score of varied points.

"There must be dozens of these uglies!" exclaimed Deegan in surprise. "Here, Vance, I don't cotton to these freaks—what in tarnation they are beats me! Let's clear out of this—can you make it?" he queried uneasily as he stared frowning about the canyon.

"I'll do it somehow—this din seems to be getting closer. Give me a hand," said Vance in a low voice as he stiffly stretched out a swollen arm.

As Vance arose to unsteady balance by the aid of his partner's arm, a dark shadow swept above them across the rubble slope and drove with a loud splash into the pool and vanished amid the flying foam.

"What's that?" exclaimed the two startled men as with one voice, whipping around to eye the agitated waters where rings of speeding ripples sped to the shore; yet nothing but these broke the somber expanse of water. Whatever had dropped had vanished. With unity of thought they wheeled around to stare again at the queer thing perched above—it too had vanished!

"Why, it must have been that brute leaping!" cried Vance.

"Beats me—never saw the mate of it!" asserted the older man as both once more turned to gaze at the still heaving waters. But the pool was no longer untenanted, for gently rising and falling with the slight ripples there floated the bulbous dome and yellow drapery of the queer thing they had wondered at. Now they could discern the monster in

more detail, and it was quite clear that this bizarre structure was as interested in them as they were in it. The two
large circular spots they had glimpsed were undeniable
eyes which with an winking stare observed their least move
intently. Coal-black, glassy, oval, lidless, they yet contained that indefinable something that the intelligent eye
alone has command of. And the seamed and wrinkled dome
in which they were set vastly emphasized the impression
that a cold, calculating entity was coolly scheming some
malignant move. Too, they perceived that this creature was
provided with formidable mandibles, dull white hornlike
prongs which rested crossed just beneath the implacable
eyes; sharp, curved and tapering, they looked capable of
inflicting a terrible wound, though the puffed and pucker-
ing surface behind them appeared repulsively flaccid. All
around this queer nodding dome floated the thick membrane from which long tentacles, half-submerged, sprang
at close intervals. For a moment the men regarded this
inexplicable thing in blank amazement.

"I don't like the cut of that thing—it ain't noway
scared," said Deegan in a low voice. "It's giving us the
once-over before starting something."

"Looks like it—by George, yes! It's on the move!" cried
Vance, eyeing it uneasily. And with reason, for of a sudden
the heavy, wide membrane had moved, contracted rearward,
and apparently impelled by the rapid thrust the creature
shot forward with the undulating ease and celerity of a fish.
Again the movement was repeated, bringing it closer to the
bank on which they stood, and it was coming with deadly earnestness straight for them. Yet the whole extraordinary creature was so obviously of such a flaccid, unstable
texture that one could not view its approach with serious
concern—and yet the brute was heading straight for them!

"Sheer off, you blasted abortion!" exclaimed Deegan
somewhat contemptuously as he snatched up a couple of

small rocks and sent them whizzing viciously at the near-
ing thing. Thud! the first stone had struck it between the
great saucer eyes, appeared to sink deep into the conical
creased surface, then fell aside with a distinct rebound
as though impelled by something akin to the elasticity
of rubber. The second missile flew skidding across the
streaming membrane. Instantly its progress was arrested,
and long, thin, snaky tentacles arose from the water and
lashed with savage whippings, churning the vicinity into a
miniature vortex of swirling foam.

Something in the sight seemed to quicken a dormant
ferocity within them, and in a flash the two men were
snatching at the rubble and raining stone after stone upon
the wounded brute, insensate rage warming and limbering
their powerful muscles. Though Vance was yet unsteady
on his feet, at such short range the fusillade would have
felled a steer; in a moment the flailing arms lashed but
feebly, then subsided to a mere convulsive twitching on
the surface, though in such confusion of half-submerged
tangled loops and knots that it was impossible to descry
any particular effect of the bombardment. It had drifted
close to the beach, yet neither man seemed eager to view
more closely the mangled mass.

They stared for a little in silence, then Vance said slowly, "What's happened to its mates?" And for the first time
it came to them that the weird whistling had ceased and
not a whisper of sound echoed from the grim walls. Yet the
silence was as the soundless vibrations of alert watching
things saturating the air with the intensity of their desire.

"Hanged if I know," said Deegan; then with sudden
decisions "I ain't stuck on this layout—let's beat it. Can
you make it?" he queried. "Come on, I'll give you a hand
till you limber up," he added impatiently as he caught the
younger man by the elbow and pulled him, not ungently,
in the direction they had come.

"One second—there's something I want," said Vance quietly as he freed himself and in a couple of rapid, unsteady strides reached the dripping black face of the forbidding ledge. Quickly snatching up a large jagged fragment he struck a few heavy blows where a wandering vein of rougher surface, though of similar hue, ran diagonally upward.

Looking closely, one might note that numerous similar thin streaks meandered across the wall. Something, two small fragments no larger than a pigeon's egg and curiously oval in their cleavage, dropped into his waiting hand. These he dipped into a hip pocket as he swung around and regained his open-eyed partner.

"What're you doing? I'll gamble there ain't a grain of yellow in the whole caboodle," cried Deegan, contemptuously impatient.

"Likely—but it's interesting," said Vance shortly; and Deegan, flicking upon the black wall a shrewd glance of disapproval that but confirmed the indifference with which he had from the first viewed its somber nakedness, again caught his partner by the arm, and straightway they hurried toward the neck-shaped outlet of the canyon.

They had gone but a few steps when the whistling broke out anew, with a clamor far exceeding its former volume. Every crack, fissure and niche appeared to add its vociferous quota to the harshly vibrant chorus. And each note was now louder, shriller, and more vehement, as if expelled by the stress of maddened craving and diabolic rage at the retreat of the two men. It needed no fine sensitiveness to grasp that these invisible things were utterly inimical and malignant.

"By God!" exclaimed Deegan, startled; "these things are watching us—they mean to rush us!" And in his tone lay no trace of its former contempt.

"Looks that way," assented Vance. "Hullo!" he cried, and the two men suddenly halted as first one, then quickly following it a second dark mass shot from the opposite cliff out of the broken face above the alien ledge. Broad blotches of shadow flung across the speckless fading blue roof of sky as they came with the planing swoop of a waterfowl clear over the pool and alighted with soft thuds on the beach at the water's edge—alighted on a fringe of drooping tentacles which for a foot from the outspread membrane were so rigidly tensed that they acted as a cushion for the landing.

Before the staring men could move a hand the strange things were on the move and coming straight for them with a rapid gliding motion, their tentacles in swift ever-changing movement darting ahead in apparent confusion, while other writhing lengths in the rear with lightning change of rigidity held the bulk of the things above the ground. Each movement was so rapidly executed that no pause or hesitation could be discerned, and the result was an odious, undulating progress. Abruptly a sense of impending awful peril came upon the watching men, and snatching at the sole weapons remaining to them they shot a hail of jagged rubble crashing into the repulsive brutes. At such short range, no more than half a dozen paces, every shot struck with terrific force, and in an instant the loathsome things were halted and beaten to the ground, where with wildly lashing tentacles they savagely strove to combat the hail of biting missiles which were tearing and gashing deep pits and long ragged furrows, wounds exuding ghastly entrails and revolting yellow-tinted slime in abominable squirming tangles and hideous gushings.

Eviscerated, almost cut to ribbons, their tenacity of life was amazing, the great mutilated membranes throbbing and heaving incessantly while even the severed tentacles writhed and lashed out viciously. Yet it had been a simple matter to overcome these extraordinary brutes.

"Settled their hash quick enough, anyway!" cried Deegan exultantly. "But what are they?" he added, viewing the horrible welter with a puzzled scowl.

"I never even dreamt such things existed," said Vance; and the two men stepped forward a pace from their line of march alongside the face of the bluff, to view the remains more closely.

In that second it happened! Neither actually saw, though likely each sensed, the noiseless dropping of the deadly thing. Something clammy and soft, yet weighty, fell full upon Vance, covering his head and shoulders with a slimy, clinging darkness. No mere inert blotting out of vision, but a living, strangling horror constricting upon his throat, face and chest with an unrelenting pressure that every moment grew more deadly and agonizing. Around his arms and chest gripped seeming steel cables beyond his desperate strength to burst, holding him helpless while he suffocated in the black unknown.

For the first second or so he heard a faint shouting as if coming from an immense distance; then it ceased as the buzzing in his head grew to a roaring that engulfed every other sound. Only he knew that something caught him up and leapt far in one swift motion. Then he was prone on the rubble and jarred by a rain of racking blows. But ever that frightful embrace of death was closing in tighter and tighter upon him, invading ears, eyes, mouth, nostrils. His head was bursting with the clamor of blood-engorged veins, and stabs of awful pain swept flames of crimson through black nothingness.

Then suddenly the terrible pressure ceased and the horrible mask was torn away; blurred daylight drenched his eyes and his heaving lungs were rapturously gulping honest air, though through a viscous, filthy-tasting slime that lay around his lips and in his eyes. His face was being rubbed roughly, and in a moment he saw again the glorious sky and rocks and the rugged, anxious face of Deegan peering close to his and calling over and over, "Don't move, Vance! Don't move!"

Though still dazed, he recognized that he lay stretched close alongside the grim black bluff where a concave face almost roofed them. A pace or so away throbbed and writhed a fearful mangled thing of squirming tentacles and a great, flat mass with revolting, dragging entrails crawling from a gaping ragged wound that had slit the thing from rim to center.

At the sight a violent nausea came upon him.

"That's it, get rid of the poison! I had to cut the damned thing in two before it would loosen up," said Deegan with apologetic approval.

"It leapt on me?" queried Vance with a shiver as the sickness passed and his strength returned.

"Sure! And if another had jumped me we'd both be dead meat by now. Though they ain't too tough to carve," asserted his partner grimly. "But this ain't only the start, there's hell a-coming—half a dozen flopped into the pool while I was busy. They ain't doing nothing yet, just watching—going to rush us for sure," he growled, angrily nodding toward the water.

"Half a dozen!" exclaimed Vance hoarsely, as he leaned forward, and at the sight of the strange floating masses he involuntarily shrank back against the wall. There was no gainsaying his partner's estimate, for a space many yards in diameter was covered with the repulsive yellow membranes, each surmounted by the globular headlike excrescence, their great flat eyes turned intently upon the men. Silent and motionless they stared as if but awaiting some decisive second, though as Vance moved a slight stir pulsed through the entire mass.

"Yes, and by their music I reckon there's six hundred more to come. They're killers—a couple could strangle a buffalo," he added, eyeing the floating things appraisingly. "I tell you these ain't no garden bugs, and we got to get. Hullo! here's another bunch of the joy-birds," he cried in grim irony as fully a dozen of the brutes shot from the opposite cliff and in a planing dive dropped beside their fellows, where after the momentary commotion of their arrival they rested quietly.

"I don't figure what they're aiming at," said Deegan in a low voice. "But there's no mistaking they've got us in a tight corner—if we quit this for the open they'll jump us from above. Yet if they come for us we can't hold them off—not a bunch like that. Say, Vance, take a squint up the way, maybe there's a chance of pulling out that way. I'll watch—by God! Quick! They're on the move!" he cried excitedly, with a sudden tense note.

As Vance, with nausea vanished and pain-stiffened muscles abruptly supple, wheeled to scan the cliff, in that fraction of a second he glimpsed the ghastly welter of weird things awake to vigorous movement and come in a solid mass through a swath of foam straight for the beach at their feet. Noiseless, swift, and direct, there could be no doubt of their deadly intention.

Then came the whirr and hiss of heavy missiles as Deegan desperately sought to stay their advance for but a few fateful seconds. With eager searching eye Vance scanned the naked wall in which the canyon ended. In an instant he grasped the fact that the heights here were not entirely hopeless, for everywhere lay great seams, gaping cavities and projecting ledges, where the dying throes of some titanic convulsion had plucked asunder this vast chasm. Behind the veil of falling spray loomed the dark blur of a huge rent that swept upward from the quiet pool until a sharp turn of the canyon—obviously some shallow off-shoot and cul-de-sac—hid its higher flight. Steep it certainly was, but not impassable; and so deep and high-roofed a fissure that one within need hardly stoop as he clambered. Still higher the bluffs were badly shattered and the whole cliff-face fell back in a series of vast irregular steps whose every rung would likely harbor a miniature plateau where a man could rest in perfect safety. Yet it was entirely a gamble; ascent might become impossible at a score of points: but they were desperate men and instantly his mind was made up.

"Listen, Deegan!" he cried quickly. "It's just a bare chance—there's a crack behind the fall, big enough to stand in—goes away up, lots of foothold above—looks as if we might make it. What do you say? It's a chance!"

"Sure!" like a whip-crack came the voice of Deegan. "Quick! sling the dope—these blasted things are landing!" he gasped between the delivery of a storm of missiles.

"Hug the bluff to the end, then jump for the pool, clear through the fall—lower end of the crack this side. Say when!" cried Vance.

"All set! Go ahead!" And as he shouted he whirled around, and brushing the cliff-face, tore madly to the canyon end. And in that second the hidden swarming life of that dreadful place forsook concealment and came hurtling, from a score of gaping fissures and deep shelves, through the heavy stagnant air. Dark masses of inconceivable frightfulness of outline passed above the racing men and landed splashing in the pool, at its brink, or thudded horribly on the rubble-beach. In a moment both the pool and the beach behind them were seething with a solid mass of hideous, writhing life; yet as if their trussed helpless prey had earlier drawn the things to an invisible migration, but an odd one or two dropped abreast of them, and the bulk were concentrated many paces in the rear, a

mischance that they instantly sought to remedy. On they
came in a crested rushing wave of lashing and fighting
tentacles, striving to clamber and expedite advance upon
one another's bodies. But now the two men were abreast
the fall, and without a second's hesitation had wildly leapt
across the rubble and hurled themselves clear through
the liquid veil. Emerging from the green depths they had
but to stretch forth a hand to grip the upward sloping
shelf. A scramble, and both stood safe upon it, in the twilight of the space held void and dry by the roof above. To
their relief the shelf proved wide and none too steep for
ascent, though greasy with slime and oily weed. The
thought of that frightful onrushing wave of malignant
monsters spurred their muscles to the utmost limit.

"Watch yourself!" cried Deegan as he took the rise with
an agility amazing in one of his years and bulk.

In a moment they had passed from the sheltering curtain and were clambering ever steeper heights. The rent
narrowed as it swept upward and followed the turn of the
shallow offshoot, and now they had to grip with hand and
foot most precariously. Then some twenty feet above the
summit of the odd intrusive stratum the passage dwindled
to a mere thread utterly untenable. But luck was now as
friendly an ally as before it had been obdurate, and not
ten feet below lay a little plateau; a few feet of flat smooth
rock, the first of the innumerable rungs in semblance of
giant steps which reached to the distant summit.

Lithe and silent at once both men dropped, and breathing
hard they stood side by side with fierce eyes minutely scan-
ning the neighboring fantastic crags. In a hundred spots
amid this chaos of riven, seamed, cluttered rock hideous
death might lurk unseen and almost brushing them. That
these horrible things could scale such heights was indis-
putable, and that very second they might be noiselessly
clambering to them amid the jagged surrounding crags.

Motionless and tense the two men listened, but never a whisper broke the deathly silence; even the melancholy note of the fall was here by some acoustic freak unheard, and the now invisible pit from which they had ascended might well never have existed for all the proof that came to them of its loathsome occupants. Those few tense moments of escape had seemingly obliterated the horror that preceded them. Yet in the suspense of dread waiting they experienced even more fully the peril of their position.

"Vance," said Deegan in a gruff whisper, "this cursed place has got my goat! We've got to get a move on or dark will be on us—and night here—"

"Dark! Night!" echoed Vance with a shiver of horror. "Not here—anything but that! You lead, you're a better man than I am here," he added simply.

"Come on!" said Deegan, swinging round and making inward, where a steep slide of huge fragments debouched to the little plateau.

As he moved, a dark, ragged mass hurtled above Vance, passed indeed so close that the wind of its descent stirred his wide-brimmed headgear, and struck something with a sickening squelch, and there was Deegan staggering and fighting desperately, tearing at long, sinuous tentacles that implacably gripped at the flailing arms and in a second had bound them with a score of grisly twining coils; while the thick raging voice was abruptly quenched and usurped by abominable inarticulate mumblings and inhuman whisperings. Vance gazed with benumbed horror at a headless trunk which swayed with grotesque stumbling and pointless motions. From feet to start of the massive chest it was Deegan; above, coil upon coil of rigid tentacle hid and held his arms immovable, and a great formless sprawling mass—yellow, oily, wrinkled—completely covered every inch above like a ghastly hood—a hood that with loathsome contractions and undulations was fitting

itself as a mask into every contour of shoulders, throat
and head.

Vance was no weakling, and never a drop of craven
blood coursed through his veins, yet only the stimulus of
desperation nerved his muscles to the deed as he hurled
himself upon the frightful thing and with bare hands tore
frantically at the tough, viscous cables. Not by a fraction
of an inch could his fiercest efforts loose their steel embrace, but from the smooth and oily lengths his fingers
slid impotently away. Indeed, so tremendous was their
contractile strength that the coils were almost buried in
the victim's body, and in many places the sole evidence
of their existence were the swollen ridges on each side.
Instantly Vance realized that the ghastly pressure of those
frightful coils must have expelled the breath from Deegan's lungs even as the impervious hood was closing her-
metically upon him. Assuredly this creature was the most
horrible engine of death the world had yet engendered, it
was appalling beyond imagination! And the horror of the
thing reached its culmination in the utter soundlessness
of the killing; coldly, implacably, noiselessly the brute was
strangling its victim, and never a whisper of his death
agony now pierced the deadly hood, only the jarring clash
of rock and Deegan's iron-shod boots broke the shroud of
silence which encompassed them.

There was no time to search for a weapon such as Deegan found to hand on the rubble below, around lay naught
but clean-swept, unbroken surfaces; farther on, a rock
slide debouched upon the little plateau where doubtless
search would discover some crude weapon, but meanwhile
the precious seconds spilled the sands of ebbing life.

Madness, a vast overwhelming volcanic rage swept upon
him; with a hoarse scream of insane wrath and hate he
leapt straight at his partner and bore him cradling to the
smooth floor, and without a second's pause thrust his face

savagely into the heavy viscous folds where the hood had
contracted in the depression below its victim's jaw. The
lance-pointed, horny mandibles opened wide and snapped
fiercely with a click as the brute writhed violently to meet
this unexpected attack, but the strong jaws and teeth of
the attacker were buried deep in the glutinous thing and
held with bulldog grip; yet never a tentacle released its
frightful grasp.

Worrying the thing like a starving wolf, by main force
he tore loose a strip of the foul stuff, a strip which came
away in long, clinging, ragged strands which stretched
with rubberlike elasticity and parted recoiling to his face
in sticky tenacity. In a flash his teeth had closed again
deep in the gaping wound. For the moment he is an ele-
mental caveman, born of ancestors barely emerged from
inarticulate bestiality, who craved to tear his foe to shreds
with the only weapons nature had given him. Now whipping tentacles assaulted him, strove with vicious might to
enwrap him in their grasp, but the greater number still
gripped tight their prey, and every second the strong white
teeth were tearing, burrowing, rending silently deeper and
deeper into the clammy slime and glutinous stringiness.
Foul clots of greasy filth and gushes of heavy, stinking
liquid filled his nostrils, eyes, and mouth. Yet the brain
of the caveman was wide-awake, and a savage triumph
pulsed through it as with terrific force he hurled, assailant
and victim crashing against the wall from which they had
dropped, at the same second by a mighty heave twirling
the living missile so that the full force of the impact was
taken by the central globular mass. With a vile squelch
the thing burst asunder into a dozen ragged segments,
and a shower of warm greasy slime spattered his face and
hung in clots and a drapery of adhesive, sluggish, dripping
entrails. At once the binding tentacles lost their rigidity.
In a flash he was tearing them apart, heedless of their

savage death throes; one supreme effort and he had wrenched the thing from its anchorage, swung it on high and whirled it crashing many feet away, where with convulsive flailing it lay an indescribably hideous sight.

In terror he gazed at the silent figure of Deegan. The thought that after all death might be the victor and he be left solitary in that frightful wilderness was a thought too appalling to endure. It came to him that the rough, unlettered Deegan was indeed a tower of strength and security; and in that moment the scales of prejudice and petty class distinction dropped forever from his inner vision.

But as he bent to listen for the beat of that staunch heart Deegan's eyelids trembled, then slowly opened. In a flash Vance had loosed his partner's throat-band, and using his hat he fanned gusts of reviving air upon him. As the massive chest drank ever deeper of the craved elixir, soon life flamed up again unimpaired. Weakly he raised his head, and at once his gaze was rooted in horror on the mangled, palpitating thing that had so nearly wrought his destruction.

"That thing! It fell on me!" he muttered hoarsely. "That thing!" he repeated dully as though stupefied by horror. "It strangled me—and I was helpless in that awful choking darkness. Oh my God!"

"I know—a nightmare of hell!" said Vance, and his voice shook. "But Deegan, we've got to get through right away—dark will be on us soon. That crowd down there will scent us for sure if we stay here—I reckon this brute was just an odd loafer hanging around. Anyway we can't stop here," he urged impatiently, for Deegan, though evidently greatly recovered, still remained motionless, staring like one hypnotized by the squirming of the loathsome thing. Then suddenly he became aware that Vance was watching him.

"All right—give a man a chance to get his wind back," he growled sullenly. "But you're right—it is near sundown," he added, rising quickly to his feet with such obvious agitation that it was plain the mere thought of approaching night had aroused in him an almost frenzied terror.

"All right, this looks as good a chance as any other," said Vance shortly, and now his voice was cool and firm as he swung into the lead, while Deegan, closely following, did not notice the order of their going.

Deegan sat on the park bench stolidly smoking, just as he had sat for nearly two hours, and just as Vance had left him. That very morning, penniless and woefully dilapidated, they had landed in exotic Georgetown, and dumped two very efficient though unlovely rifles alongside their meager baggage in the stuffy compartment assigned them by the half-caste proprietor, who with a single shrewd glance apportioned to a day the tenure justified by such slender assets. Thereafter, unable to endure the fusty poverty of their apartment, they had gravitated to the trimly beautiful Botanical Gardens—at this hour virtually deserted—and here had entered into a desultory discussion of the ways and means of alleviating their indigency. Deegan, save for the labor of his hands, had no solution to offer; and Vance shortly sinking into an apathetic self-commune and betraying but the most ephemeral interest in the subject, naturally the discussion languished.

Abruptly Vance had risen and casually observed, "Say, Deegan, there's a man I know hangs out in this burg—I'm going to look him up. He may know of something—wait here for me." And then immediately he made off at a brisk pace, leaving his partner open-mouthed but uncomplaining to his solitary vigil.

That was nearly two hours back: and the great-thewed, rough-hewn Deegan, whose daily life for forgotten years had been an almost monotonous repetition of desperate risks lightly accepted and miraculously survived, became at once a hesitating, even timorous, intruder amid such alien environment. Visions of unguessable accidents, or fateful, youth-enticing allurements, assaulted his imagination more and more persistently as the moments sped.

Yet never a twinge of doubt had sobered him when with Vance, in the gray of dawn, like a living tornado the two men had burst upon the slumbering savages, yelling roaring curses as they laid about them with rough-fashioned clubs; in a twinkling they had swept their despoilers into a panic-stricken rout, never doubting but their assailants were the loosed diabolical spirits of defunct men thirsting to wreak vengeance upon the guilty; a rout that lost nothing of its frenzied haste when the crashing reports of two retrieved rifles added to the din and left the demoniac visitants with undisputed leisure to the salvaging of their pilfered packs. Then came toil-filled weeks of unavailing search for the yellow lucre, defeat, and the wearisome return.

"Hullo, Deegan! Longer than I reckoned," hailed a cheerful voice, and Deegan awoke from his gloomy revery. "About time we had some eats," added Vance with decision.

"Eat? Yes, we got to eat—I reckon there's nothing for it but to slough the guns; lucky if we raise ten bucks apiece—and I hate like hell to do it," was the grudging assent of the seated man.

"Guns? Not this trip. See here!" And pausing, Vance lugged from his hip pocket a little wad of bills, and peeling off several, thrust them into his partner's thick fingers, saying: "A hundred apiece—that should keep us going till we pull out."

"Pull out! What you talking about!" said Deegan blankly as he stared in wonder at the notes.

"Well, here's the short of it—just a hunch, fool luck, you can't beat it! Likely you remember I pocketed some bits of rock from that queer ledge, also maybe you noticed now and again a chunk you fired into that awful bunch was heavy as lead!" queried Vance tersely.

"That's so, even then the heft of some of it worried me," said Deegan thoughtfully. "But just junk—not a color to a ton, I'll take my oath," he added with conviction.

"Right, there wasn't; but it lay in veins all over and black as the ledge itself—lying trussed, I was closer than you and couldn't help marking them, then somehow it got rubbed into me that some of the rubble had an odd shape— all curves and round lumps like small plums sticking out. Just now I've come from a man who used to do business with the bank I was in, got to be quite friendly with me. Likely you've heard of him, Cameron, mining expert and manager of the Arequipa mines. Took a chance on his being straight or throwing me out; well, he's a white man— 'nough said. Just took a squint at the chips I dumped on the table, promptly shut the door and said: 'Young man, spit it out!'

"When I'd got it off he studied a while then observed quietly, 'I don't know if you two went crazy or had a nightmare, but I'm going to chance it. I'll stake you both, though I want you to get a hustle on, beat it back to that crazy canyon and stake the whole country. Your partner is wise to the outfit necessary—go to Ramon's, tell him to bill me. Leave those stones with me, too risky toting them around; and mind, not a drop of booze until the stakes are in. By the way, we go fifty-fifty—that suit you?'

"I nodded.

"'All right, see me before you leave,' he said. 'Good day.'

"'But what is it!' I asked, staggered by all this.

"'What is it! My suffering aunt! He asks what is it!' said he, glaring at me. 'Well, you young lucky ass, it's about the richest samples of pitchblende, the radium ore, I ever clapped eyes on; worth heaven only knows how much.

Which reminds me likely you haven't got any too much now—here, I'll 'phone the bank to cash this.' And he was scrawling a check as he spoke.

"Before I knew what had happened he'd shooed me out. That's all there was to it. Now let's eat; we can chew the rag over a decent meal."

"Well, I reckon luck's your middle name, and even chances he's white—but you're the whitest guy I ever struck, which is aces high with me," said Deegan slowly. "Yes, we'll eat—and after that we'll raise the dust on the trail back to blow that nest of devil-spewings to the hell they came from," he added in fierce triumph, as, rising, the two adventurers swung off to town and hard-earned success.

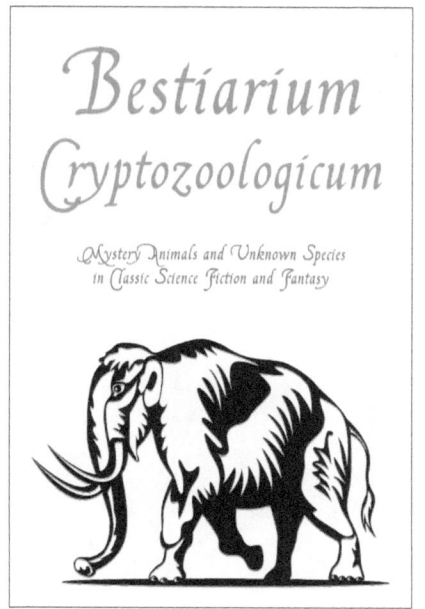

Bestiarium Cryptozoologicum

Mystery Animals and Unknown Species
in Classic Science Fiction and Fantasy

zoologica fantastica

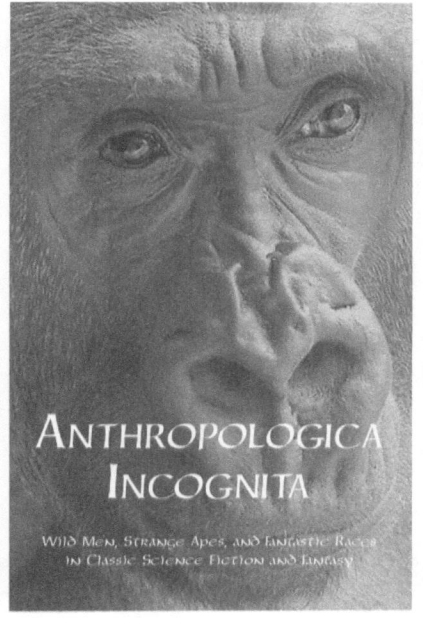

ANTHROPOLOGICA INCOGNITA

Wild Men, Strange Apes, and Fantastic Races
in Classic Science Fiction and Fantasy

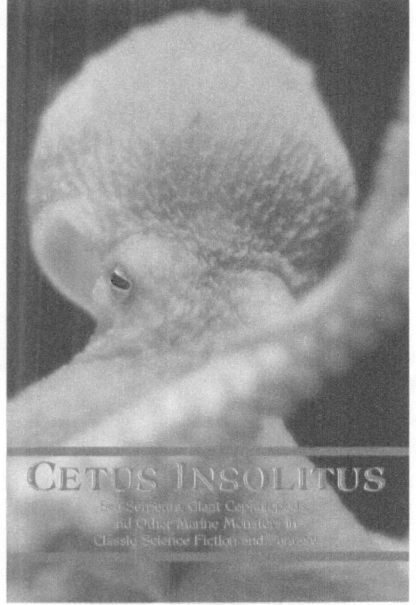

CETUS INSOLITUS

Sea Serpents, Giant Cephalopods,
and Other Marine Monsters in
Classic Science Fiction and Fantasy

Coachwhip Publications

CoachwhipBooks.com

Sauria Monstra

Dinosaurs, Pterosaurs, and Other
Fossil Saurians in Classic
Science Fiction and Fantasy

Invertebrata Enigmatica

Giant Spiders, Dangerous Insects, and other Strange Invertebrates
in Classic Science Fiction and Fantasy

Flora Curiosa

Cryptobotany, Mysterious Fungi,
Sentient Trees, and Deadly Plants in
Classic Science Fiction and Fantasy

Arboris Mysterius

Stories of the Uncanny and Undescribed
from the Botanical Kingdom

Coachwhip Publications
CoachwhipBooks.com

BOTANICA DELIRA

MORE STORIES OF STRANGE,
UNDISCOVERED, AND MURDEROUS
VEGETATION

HORTUS
DIABOLICUS

*Further Twisting Tales of
Menacing Flora and
Malignant Fungi*

Edited by Chad Arment

WULF

TALES OF WOLVES
AND WEREWOLVES

EDITED BY
CHAD ARMENT

CATS OF SHADOW,
CLAWS OF DARKNESS

Stories of Were-Cats, Ghost Cats,
and Other Supernatural Felines

Coachwhip Publications

CoachwhipBooks.com

A HAUNTING NOTE

Music of the Uncanny and Inexplicable in Classic Speculative Fiction

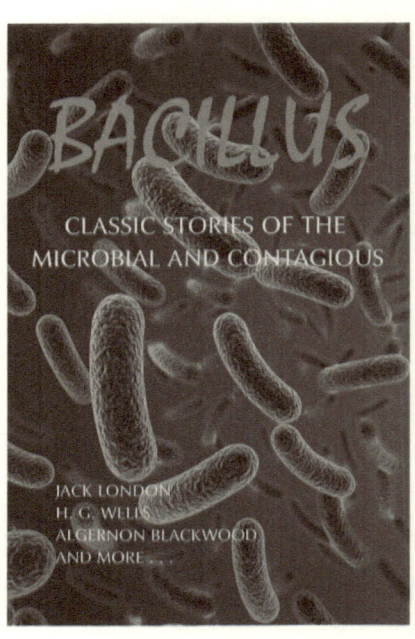

BACILLUS

CLASSIC STORIES OF THE MICROBIAL AND CONTAGIOUS

JACK LONDON
H. G. WELLS
ALGERNON BLACKWOOD
AND MORE . . .

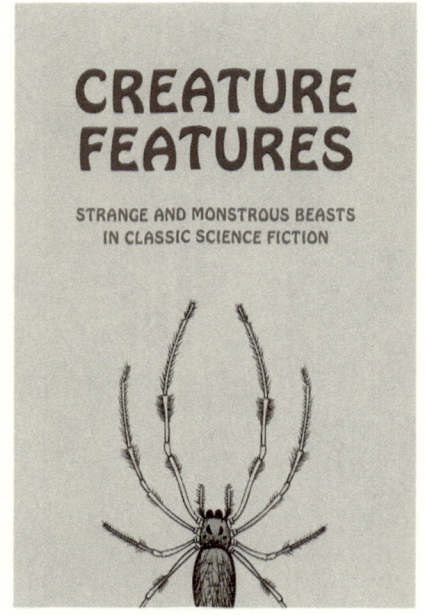

CREATURE FEATURES

STRANGE AND MONSTROUS BEASTS IN CLASSIC SCIENCE FICTION

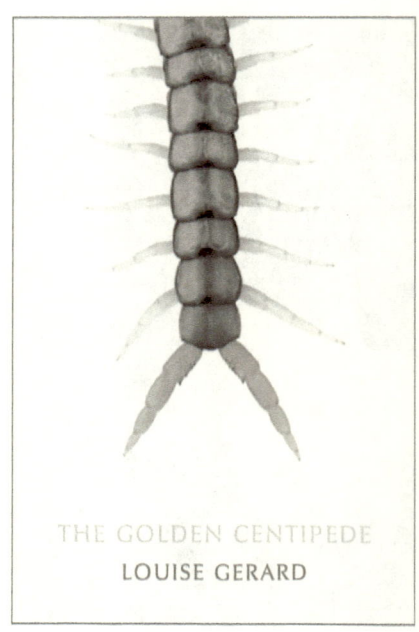

THE GOLDEN CENTIPEDE
LOUISE GERARD

Coachwhip Publications

CoachwhipBooks.com

Coachwhip Publications

CoachwhipBooks.com

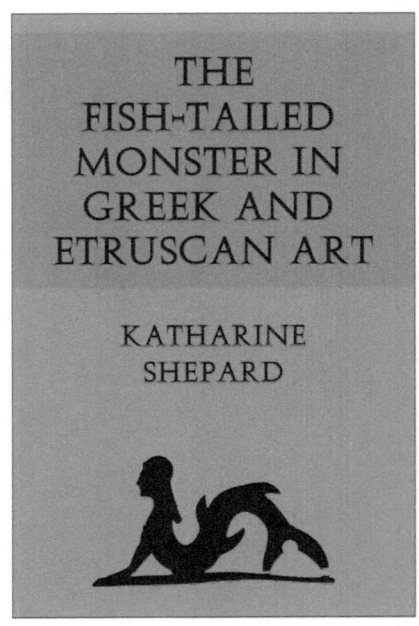

Coachwhip Publications

CoachwhipBooks.com

Coachwhip Publications

CoachwhipBooks.com

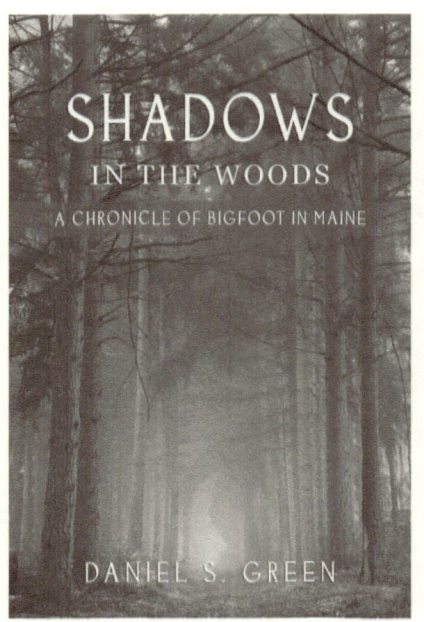

SHADOWS
IN THE WOODS
A CHRONICLE OF BIGFOOT IN MAINE

DANIEL S. GREEN

BLUE TIGER

Harry R. Caldwell

Introduction by
Roy Chapman Andrews

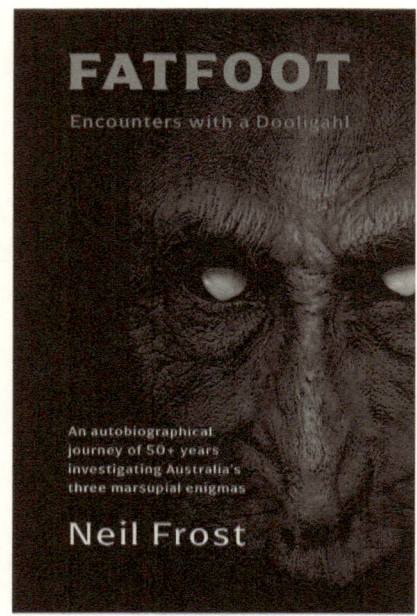

FATFOOT
Encounters with a Dooligahl

An autobiographical
journey of 50+ years
investigating Australia's
three marsupial enigmas

Neil Frost

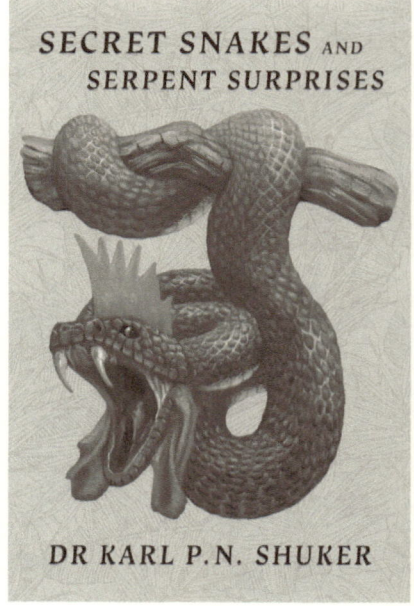

SECRET SNAKES AND
SERPENT SURPRISES

DR KARL P. N. SHUKER

Coachwhip Publications
CoachwhipBooks.com

KATHARINE LUOMALA
THE MENEHUNE
OF POLYNESIA
AND OTHER MYTHICAL LITTLE PEOPLE OF OCEANIA

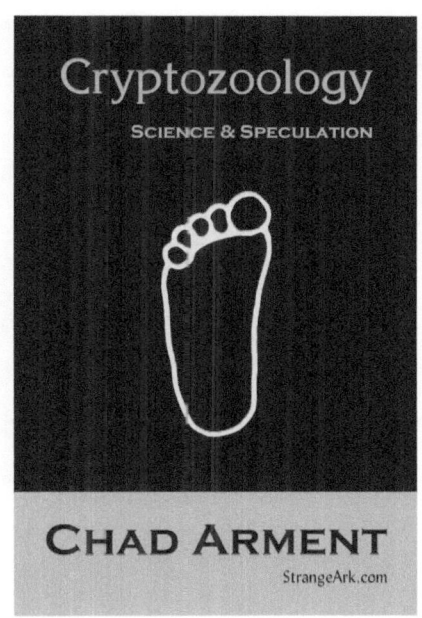

Cryptozoology
SCIENCE & SPECULATION

CHAD ARMENT
StrangeArk.com

FAR-OUT, SHAGGY,
FUNKY MONSTERS

A What-it-is
History of
Bigfoot in
the 1970s

DANIEL S. GREEN

'WILD GORILLA' IS SEEN IN COUNTY
The Wild Man
THE
HISTORICAL DEAD GIANT
BIGFOOT aming
SECOND EDITION r Carni
A MONSTER APE ROAMS
WOODS, SCARES SCORES
GORILLA (?) ROAMS Monster Monkey,
Roaming Woods,
SNYDER COUNTY Alarms County
MIFFLIN COUNTY ON
HUNT FOR 'MYSTERY
ANIMAL' IN WOODS
CHAD ARMENT
AN IDAHO MONSTER AT LARGE.
A MONSTER IN THE MOUNTAIN.

Coachwhip Publications

CoachwhipBooks.com